THE GRISSOM CONTENTION

COLONIAL EXPLORER CORPS BOOK 2

JULIA HUNI

IPH MEDIA

The Grissom Contention Copyright © 2021
by Julia Huni. All Rights Reserved.

All rights reserved. No part of this book may be reproduced in any form or by any electronic or mechanical means including information storage and retrieval systems, without permission in writing from the author. The only exception is by a reviewer, who may quote short excerpts in a review.

Editing by Paula Lester of
Polaris Writing and Editing

Cover Design © J. L. Wilson Designs
https://jlwilsondesigns.com

This book is a work of fiction. Names, characters, places, and incidents either are products of the author's imagination or are used fictitiously. Any resemblance to actual persons, living or dead, events, or locales is entirely coincidental.

Julia Huni
Visit my website at http://www.juliahuni.com
Printed in the United States of America
First Printing: Jan 2021
ISBN: 9798716953352
IPH Media

BOOKS BY JULIA HUNI

Colonial Explorer Corps Series:
The Earth Concurrence
The Grissom Contention
The Saha Declination

Recycled World Series:
Recycled World
Reduced World

Space Janitor Series:
The Vacuum of Space
The Dust of Kaku
The Trouble with Tinsel
Orbital Operations
Glitter in the Stars
Sweeping S'Ride
Triana Moore, Space Janitor (the complete series)

Tales of a Former Space Janitor
The Rings of Grissom

Krimson Empire (with Craig Martelle):
Krimson Run
Krimson Spark
Krimson Surge
Krimson Flare

If you enjoy this story, sign up for my newsletter, at juliahuni.com and you'll get free prequels and short stories, plus get notifications when the next book is ready.

*For Lance Honda
faithful reader and friend*

CHAPTER ONE

THE SHUTTLE SHOOK. A lot.

"Is this normal for an atmo trip?" the thin girl beside me asked. Her fingers bit into the armrests.

"Sometimes. There can be a fair bit of turbulence over the ocean." I peered out the window. Far below, the blue of the ocean had transitioned to the gray-green of the northern continent of Grissom. "And over the land, I guess."

Her pale eyebrows drew together, her eyes scrunched closed. "I've never left the main continent."

I gaped at her. "What made you decide to join the Explorer Corps, if you've never left your home continent?"

Her eyes peeled open a fraction, and a glimmer of a grin flickered across her lips. "I wanted to see the galaxy?"

"I hope we make it that far."

She gulped. "Really?" Her voice squeaked. "Are we going to crash?"

I patted her hand. "No, of course not. CEC pilots are the best in the galaxy." Besides, this shuttle was probably automated, which, statistically speaking, made it safer.

Static blasted from the speakers and through our audio implants.

Everyone winced. A deep voice said, "This is the captain. Prepare for a rough landing. Seatbacks up. Assume the crash position."

Several screams echoed throughout the shuttle. I locked my seat into the launch-and-land position and helped the girl next to me do the same. "Put your head on your knees." I demonstrated. "Wrap your arms around your legs."

"Should I close my eyes?"

"I'm not sure it matters. If you believe in God, you might want to pray." I squeezed my eyes shut and took deep breaths. *I'm not going to make a deal, but I'd appreciate it if we land safely. I'll try to be a better person. And I wish Liam was here.* Stroking the sair-glider's soft fur always calmed me.

The captain's voice cut through the rumble of half hysterical conversation. "Silence. Now!" The voices stilled, the whimpers did not. After a few seconds, the ride smoothed out. The voice returned. "You can sit up now. We're through. We'll be landing at the Academy in five minutes."

"What happened?" the boy across the aisle from me yelled. "I want to know what happened!" Several other voices took up the shout.

A new voice came over the intercom. "Enough. You will be briefed when we land. Maintain silence for the duration of the flight."

I peeked at the girl beside me. Her face was pale, but she gave me a little bit of a smile, her lips pressed tightly together, as if she were physically stopping herself from speaking. I grinned.

The shuttle touched down and rumbled across the tarmac to park. As soon as the craft stopped, the boy who'd yelled unlatched his restraints and surged to his feet. "What the hell was that?"

The door to the cockpit opened with a bang. A tall, thin woman stepped out. She wore the black Colonial Explorer Corps uniform with a single star on each shoulder. "That was your first test. *You* didn't pass."

We all stared at her for a fraction of a second, then the boy attacked. "A test?" His voice cracked. "How dare you treat us this way! Do you know who I am?"

Do people really say that?

"Do *you* know who *I* am?" the woman replied.

"Admiral Zimas," I whispered. Dad had sent me her biography—she'd been assigned to command the academy a few months ago. Several other cadets gave the same answer.

"Correct." She pointed at the standing boy. "My office. Now." She turned and marched out of the shuttle.

The boy stared defiantly around the shuttle. "She'll be sorry. My dad will take care of her." He yanked his bag from the netting under his seat and stumbled out the door.

"I wouldn't be in his shoes for all the credits in the galaxy." The ship's pilot stood in the doorway to the cockpit. He nodded to the rest of us. "Unbuckle your restraints, grab your stuff, and form up."

We grabbed our gear and filed off the ship. At the base of the steps, a cadet wearing a single stripe on his collar directed us to places on the tarmac.

"What's your name?" my seatmate asked.

"I'm Siti Kassis. You?"

"Aneh Jones." Her eyes narrowed. "Did you say Kassis?" At my nod, she continued, "As in daughter of Nate Kassis? Legacy cadet?"

I raised my eyebrows as I took my spot in the formation. "Legacy?"

Aneh gave me a hard look, then turned to face front. A uniformed woman wearing captain's insignia strolled along the rows of cadets. "Welcome to the Academy. I'm Captain Fortescue—I'm the plebe advisor. I work with the cadet leadership team who will be conducting your training. You are the plebes—in case that wasn't clear. New cadets in their introductory training. If you survive the summer, you'll become first years."

She cleared her throat. "You will be trained and tested every day. Take a lesson from our friend." She turned her head, and we all followed her gaze. The young man from across the aisle followed Admiral Zimas away from the group. "You won't see him again." She looked at each of us. How she managed that with over a hundred of us staring back, I don't know, but I wanted to learn. "Some officers would give you a long speech about the honor of being selected or your duty to the colonial union. I figure you know that, or you wouldn't be here. Cadet officers, take your squadrons. Best of luck."

I made a face at Aneh, trying not to turn my head. A soft giggle reached my ears.

"I am Cadet Wronglen." A broad man with familiar features stood before our group. He wore a cadet uniform with three slashes on the collar. "If you hear my voice through your audio implant, follow me. Stay in your lines." He turned and marched away. Along the formation, other senior cadets were leading groups away.

"I guess that's me." I picked up my bag.

"Me, too," Aneh whispered as we followed the crowd.

Wronglen. That couldn't be a coincidence. There had been a Lieutenant Wronglen on our mission to Earth. She and I hadn't gotten along. I gritted my teeth. Just my luck to get a relative. But maybe he was only taking us to our next location?

Wronglen's voice came through the audio. "Welcome to Charlie Squadron. I'm your cadet commander."

Drat.

The sun glowed through the clouds high overhead. It was mid-morning and overcast. The heavy, damp air wrapped around us like a warm blanket of overripe fruit and flowers. The northern continent featured the infamous Swamps of Grissom. While the academy wasn't technically in the swamps, we could still smell them.

At the end of the runway, our three straggly lines turned left onto a road toward a large stadium. We marched down a wide ramp, under the seating, and out to the field. As we left the shadows of the building, the noise of hundreds of people talking reached us. The stands at the far end of the field were full of brightly garbed people. Our leaders took us to the sidelines, half of the new plebes on each side of the wide field. It was covered in odd, green foliage. I squinted at the thick, wide leaves—almost like a succulent. They bounced back up as we walked, leaving no footprints.

We stopped in rough ranks near the full stands. "Don't we get chairs?" someone muttered behind me.

Wronglen spoke again. "This is graduation. New cadets always arrive in time to see the ceremony. After the new officers are sworn in, they will go on leave and then report to their duty assignments. *You* will spend most of the summer here, with a few cadet officers such as myself guiding you. Pay attention to the ceremony. This is why you're here."

It had taken a long time for me to get here. I'd spent the last few months—and twenty years in deep sleep—on a CEC mission with my father. When we started, I wasn't sure what I wanted to do with my life. But at some point during the trip, I'd decided I wanted what my father had—a chosen family of strong, smart, loyal teammates. And the Corps was the place to find that.

A stage had been erected on the lawn, leaving a green strip between the stands and the stage. Rows of white chairs stood there. Horns blared through the loudspeakers and our audio implants. A martial brass fanfare played, and the people in the stands went silent.

As the music faded, a line of white-uniformed officers walked out of the stands and took the stage. After another blare of trumpets, ranks of cadets, also dressed in white, marched onto the grass. They lined up in front of the chairs.

Admiral Zimas stepped forward. A huge hologram of her head and shoulders appeared behind her. After welcoming the families of the graduates, she talked about duty and honor and all those things senior officers always blather on about at ceremonies. I tuned her out, wondering how she got from the far side of the airfield, changed into her white uniform, and made it up there so quickly. And what happened to the mouthy kid who had gone with her?

I tuned in again when the grav belt team took the skies. I'd used a grav belt on Earth, and even done a few tricks while being towed behind a grav bike, but these cadets were phenomenal. The synchronized loops, spins, and proximity maneuvers made my stomach drop. Around me, my classmates gasped and cheered.

"I want to do that," Aneh whispered.

Me, too.

The team flew across the arena, low over the heads of the spectators, dropping a brightly colored trail that fluttered to the ground. Spectators jumped and grabbed. Thunderous applause erupted as the fliers zoomed away.

The admiral stood. "And now, cadets of class fourteen–six, it's time to take your oath." Her head tilted up, making it obvious she was now addressing the families. "Here in the Colonial Explorer Corps, we don't commission individuals. One of our prime values is teamwork. Explorers don't survive when they go solo. And so, even at commissioning, we do things as a team." As she spoke, the graduates filed out of their rows and formed up into four squadrons.

Her gaze dropped to the cadets. "Alpha squadron, step forward!" A block of cadets took two steps forward and stopped. A rank of officers marched to the front of the stage, facing the cadets.

As one, they raised their right hands and repeated the words of the Explorer Corps oath. "I pledge to explore the galaxy, protecting and defending my Explorer team, and finding new worlds for humanity. I owe my allegiance to the colonial government and the officers appointed over me. I will strive to bring no harm to the planets we explore." Two more squadrons of cadets repeated the oath, each with a different rank of officers leading them.

When the last group returned to their seats, the admiral moved forward. "Congratulations, class fourteen–six," the admiral said. "You are now ensigns in the Colonial Explorer Corps. Go forth and find!" The admiral's party marched off the stage. A voice echoed through the speakers: "Families, you may come down and pin your new ensigns." The music returned, louder and brassier.

Wronglen spoke through our audio again, the music muted to a bare murmur. "Charlie Squadron, follow me to the dorms." He walked along the sideline in front of us, waving an arm over his head in a circle. Then his arm dropped to point toward the entrance we'd used earlier.

CHAPTER TWO

We followed Wronglen along the sideline of the field.

"You'll be with me for the next year. If you have problems, or questions, you'll talk to your flight commander first. If they can't resolve it, you'll come to me." He turned, walking backward as he spoke. "I shouldn't have to see you very often." He grinned, but it didn't look like a friendly smile. "We'll do a personnel review every quarter, and I will be teaching some of your classes." He turned again, walking faster. "Get to know the other people in your flight. They will be your family and your support system for the next three years."

As he spoke, we exited the stadium and turned away from the flightline. We continued between two buildings, through a narrow alley. On the far side, a green quad stretched out. Tall buildings surrounded the broad lawn. They had wide arching windows and tall columns holding up narrow balconies. Each building rose three or four stories, and they were all made of the same smooth, pink-toned stone.

On the far side of the quad, Wronglen entered one of the matching buildings. We followed him inside, into a wide, empty lobby. A broad flight of stone steps led up to a dark balcony. Wronglen stepped onto the bottom stair and turned to face us. "This is your new home. Senior cadets, like me, have quarters on the second floor. Mid-year cadets are on the third floor. You—plebes—are on the top floor. And yes, you have to take the stairs. It's good for you. But not these stairs. These are for the upper classes. Your stairs are at the end of the hall." He gestured to a dark corridor leading away from the lobby. "Your names are on your doors. Find your rack, put on your uniforms, and put away your gear. I'll send for you in thirty minutes."

We shuffled along the hallway and into a utilitarian stairwell. At the top of the three flights, a heavy door opened onto a narrow corridor. I found my room about halfway down and threw my bag on the top bunk. A few seconds later, a blonde girl followed me into the room.

"I'm Felicity Myers." She held out a fist to bump. "You're Siti Kassis."

I raised my eyebrows. "Did you read that on the door?"

She shook her head. "I knew we'd be roommates. I have my sources."

"That doesn't sound ominous at all," I said. "Do you care which bunk you get?"

"Not as long as it's the bottom one." She smirked and put her bag on the bunk. "They had to put us in the same room. Legacies stick together."

"Legacy?" I unzipped my bag and began putting my clothing into the drawers. Eight sets of underwear, all white, and eight pairs of socks. Folded and rolled according to regulations.

Felicity moved to the other dresser. She pulled stacks of lacy lingerie from her bag and laid it lovingly in place. "Children of Corps officers. My mother is Admiral Tarabel Myers."

"I didn't know that was a thing. Aren't they going to confiscate all those pretty undies?"

She laughed. "Not if they know what's good for them."

Had she not seen what happened on the shuttle? It wouldn't surprise me if that kid disappeared. The admiral had been angry.

"Mom and Zimas go way back." Felicity shoved a stack of brightly colored shirts into the next drawer. She chattered about her mother's high-ranking friends as we finished unpacking.

I opened the tiny closet next to my dresser. A dark uniform hung on the single hangar. "I guess this is what we're supposed to wear."

Felicity sneered at the jacket and pants. "Field uniforms are so unflattering. I got mine tailored." She pulled a jacket and pants from her bag and threw them on the bed. They looked just like mine.

When we were dressed, I could see the difference. Her pants clung to her rear end, and her jacket accentuated her waist. Mine fit like a bag.

"Come on." Felicity opened the door.

"Where are you going? Didn't that squadron commander say to wait until he contacted us?"

Felicity glanced at her holo-ring chronograph. "He'll be calling in a few minutes to tell us to meet in the ready room. If we go now, we can get the best seats." She headed down the hallway.

After double-checking that our room was in order, I followed her. She seemed to have excellent intel. We clattered down the stairs and out on the first floor. Doors lined the hallway, with silver plates designating their use. Most were classrooms, but one had Wronglen's name. It must be his office. At the far end of the hall, a door labeled "ready room" stood open.

Felicity threw herself down on one of the functional couches near the windows. "Ugh. As uncomfortable as they look."

I sat next to her. The fabric was smooth and slick, but the cushion had some bounce. "How did you know where to go?"

"Didn't you take the tour?" She raised an eyebrow at me. "Oh, I forgot, you were *busy*." She smirked.

"Did you take a tour?" I asked. She didn't seem like the tour type.

She laughed. "I had a personal tour, of course. I've been here many times. I told you, my mom and Zimas are friends."

"How many legacies are there?" I asked, as other students began filtering in.

"There are lots of them," she said. "But only a few who are important. You, me, Mira Trabiano in Bravo squadron, and Derek Lee in Delta. You recognize those names?"

I nodded. Trabiano and Lee were admirals in the Explorer Corps. "I'm surprised you count me."

"Your dad's only a commander," she said, her tone condescending. "But no one's going to ignore the *Hero of Darenti Four*."

Aneh hurried into the room, darting between other cadets. She plopped down beside me on the couch. Felicity raised an eyebrow at her and looked away. Great, this would be fun.

"Felicity, this is Aneh," I said.

"Hi, Felicity," Aneh said.

Felicity nodded but said nothing. I grimaced at Aneh. She grinned back, bouncing a little in her seat. The other cadets found places, chattering as they did so.

"Attention!" Half the students in the room jumped to their feet. The rest of us followed a fraction of a second later. Two older cadets marched in and stood at the front.

Wronglen strolled into the room. "When a senior cadet enters, the first to see them should call attention." He pointed at a boy by the door. "That should have been you."

"That's why I sat over here," Felicity whispered.

Wronglen's eyes narrowed as he reached the front of the room. He glared at Felicity but said nothing. "Take your seats."

"Welcome to Charlie Squadron. As I said on the way over here, I'm your cadet squadron commander. Smith and Lawrence," he gestured to the two cadets standing behind him, "are your flight commanders. Each flight has a mid-year cadet acting as flight sergeant. You'll meet them in a few minutes. They should be your first stop if you have problems."

Wronglen strutted across the room as he spoke. "There are currently seventy-two cadets in this squadron, thirty-six in each flight. Those of you who are good at math will think this means twenty-four cadets per class." He smirked at us. "You'd be wrong. The plebe class is larger."

This guy was a piece of work. There were thirty of us in the room, so obviously the plebe class was larger.

"We expect to lose at least ten of you before the end of the year. Most of those will disappear this summer." He laughed. "Some of you will decide to leave on your own. Others will be...encouraged to go."

He swung around. "Smith, Lawrence, you're up. I'm outta here."

As he strode out the door, Smith called, "Attention."

We all jumped to our feet again.

"Is that going to happen all the time?" Aneh asked.

I nodded. "Get used to it."

A woman's voice came through my implant. "If you hear me, follow me." The female cadet at the front of the room raised her hand. "Let's go." She pushed through the cadets and out the door. Aneh and I followed her.

I glanced over my shoulder. Felicity stood in place, fluttering her eyelashes at the male cadet. He leaned forward and said something. She smiled, fluttered her eyelashes again, then turned to follow us. Maybe she was right about the staff putting the legacies together.

Lawrence led us into another room. This one looked identical to the first, with the same uncomfortable couches and chairs. "Shut the door," the woman said.

I checked the hallway for stragglers then closed to the door.

"I'm Cadet Lawrence," she said. "Each squadron has two flights. We are Blue flight. We'll be referred to as Charlie Blue. The rest of our squadron is Orange flight. You'll report to me for the summer. Flight commanders swap out a few times a year." She glared at each of us in turn. "I expect all of you to do your best. We seniors get graded on how our flight performs, and I expect nothing but the best."

Did she know any other words besides "best?"

"Sit down. Let's get to know each other." We sat. She pointed at me. "Introduce yourself."

I stood. "I'm Serenity Kassis. You can call me Siti."

"We'll call you Kassis," Lawrence said. "You don't have to stand up unless the squadron commander is here. I'd expect a legacy to know that."

"I didn't even know what a legacy was before today." I sat. "I wasn't really planning on coming to the Academy."

Felicity rolled her eyes but didn't say anything.

"Must be nice," a boy said.

"Who are you?" Lawrence demanded.

"I'm Toby."

Lawrence's nostrils flared. "Is that your last name? We don't do first names here."

The boy coughed. "Abdul. I'm Toby Abdul."

"Tell the class what a legacy is, Abdul," Lawrence said. "In case there's anyone else who doesn't know." Her eyes flicked to Felicity and away.

"A legacy is someone whose parents were in the Corps," Abdul said.

"Not just in the Corps but high-ranking officers," a girl said. "I'm Wendinelle Terrine. My mom was a maintenance sergeant. Technically, I'm a legacy, but no one would call me that."

"Correct." Lawrence pointed at me. "You're a legacy, with a capital L. The only kind that counts."

"Counts how?" I asked. "I wasn't expecting any special treatment, good or bad."

Lawrence chuckled sourly. "You may not be expecting it, but you'll get it. Both."

Fantastic. I waved both hands. "I don't know much about the Academy, so all this legacy crap isn't going to do anyone any good. I'd rather be treated like everyone else."

"You heard the *unlegacy*," Lawrence said. "No special treatment. Next." She pointed at Felicity.

"I'm Felicity Myers, and I'm a legacy—a real legacy." She smirked at me. "I know what it means. And I expect the rest of you to remember, too. My mother—Admiral Myers—is very interested in my progress."

Lawrence's nostrils flared again. Felicity's eyes narrowed, and the older cadet gave a tiny nod. Apparently, Admiral Myers was a force to be reckoned with.

"Next." Lawrence pointed at Aneh.

The skinny blonde stood. Then she sat down again. "Oops, sorry. I'm Aneh Jones. I'm nobody."

We went around the room meeting our new flight mates. Seven of us were children of explorers or ship crew. The other eight were civilians.

"Here's how it works. We'll have classes in the morning and practical exercises in the afternoon." Lawrence leaned back in her chair and put her feet up on the desk. "There's lots of PT—physical training. Running or weightlifting in the mornings. Sports in the late afternoons. There will be inspections. But this isn't a military academy, so there's no marching."

"But we have uniforms," a civilian named Feodor Franklin said. "And there's a salute, right?"

"We have uniforms because what we do can get dangerous and messy. The uniforms are made to protect you. The Corps provides equipment, including clothing. We also have rank, so we can tell who's in charge.

There is a salute, but it's mainly for formal occasions. You won't see people doing that in the field."

"I'm sure I saw saluting on Earth," I said without thinking.

Lawrence's feet dropped off the table with a thud as she sat upright. "The unlegacy says there was saluting on Earth. I must be mistaken. If it happened on Earth, it must be right."

I held up both hands. "Look. I'm not trying to cause trouble. I'm just saying I saw some people salute when we were...out there. Maybe they screwed up. Or were schmoozing my dad. People do that."

"Are you suggesting I should schmooze you because of your father?" Lawrence surged out of the chair. She might be ready to knuckle under to Felicity's mom but not to my dad. Commander wasn't high enough rank? Or something else?

"No! I'm not suggesting anything. I told you, I don't want any special treatment." I mimed locking my lips and throwing away the key.

Lawrence came around the desk, glaring at me. "That's a good idea, unlegacy." She turned back to the group. "As I was saying, we'll have field training in the afternoons. Part of that will be learning how things really work in the Corps, when we're on assignment. But that's later. For the first few weeks, we'll learn practical survival skills. Then you'll have your plebe campout: Exercise Trial by Fire." She smirked.

"I've heard about that," Terrine said. "They dump us out in the training field, and we have to survive for a week on our own."

"Not quite," Lawrence said. "It's usually a week, but you're not completely on your own. And it isn't only about surviving. You'll be tasked with a mission to complete. If you complete the mission early, you get to come back early. So, you'd better pay attention in these first weeks of classes—you'll need those skills to excel. Which is what I expect my flight to do!" She glared at us again.

The door opened, and a short boy walked in. He raised his hand in the salute I'd learned as a kid. Lawrence saluted back.

"I thought you said no one does that?" Abdul said.

I shook my head. Abdul was going to need to learn to keep his mouth shut.

"Puh-lease," Lawrence said. "We salute all the time. You people are so gullible. This is Cadet Mason. He's our flight sergeant. That's his job description, not his rank. We're all officer candidates here, but mid-years fill the sergeant's role. You'll call him Cadet Mason." She stood and headed for the door. "They're all yours."

"Thanks, sir." Mason waited until the door shut behind Lawrence and turned to face us. "Did she tell you about the assignment board?"

"No, sir," Felicity said.

"Didn't think so. They like to let us mid-years do all the work. I'll show you how to log into the system and check the schedules. We'll do that after lunch. For now, are there any questions before we hit the chow hall?"

Aneh's hand rose. "Do we have to march? To lunch, I mean?"

"We don't march here," Mason said. "Didn't she tell you anything?"

"Yeah, but she lied about the saluting," Aneh muttered.

"That's 'yes, sir,' not 'yeah.' I outrank you."

"Yes, sir," Aneh repeated. "Was she lying about anything else, sir?"

"How's he going to know?" Abdul asked. "He wasn't here."

Mason glared.

"Sir," Abdul added.

Mason rolled his eyes. "There's no marching. There is saluting. Anything else?"

We shook our heads.

"Fine. I'll give you a run-down on everything on our way to the chow hall. Stay together and keep your audio implants set to my channel. Anyone want to chicken out?"

"Hell, no!" Felicity yelled.

We stared at her.

"It's a Corps ritual." Mason raised his eyebrows at me. "A legacy should know that."

I shrugged. "I heard it once." I glanced at Felicity. "On Earth. No one explained."

"Well, now you know. Anyone want to chicken out?" He yelled it louder.

"Hell, no!" we chorused.

"Better not." He led us out the door.

CHAPTER THREE

LUNCH WAS QUIET. Plebes weren't allowed to talk at meals for the first week. Apparently, it was meant to instill discipline and respect. Or maybe it was to make sure we ate everything on our plates. The food was terrible, so we needed an incentive to shovel it in.

Mason kept up a running commentary, telling us about customs in the CEC and pointing out important people as they arrived and departed. He showed us how to use the academy directory to tag people. We could review the listing in the evenings, complete with photos, so we could remember them the next day.

"We'll spend the rest of the afternoon getting acclimatized." Mason picked up his tray, and we followed suit. "I'll take you on a tour of the campus, show you where classes will be held. We'll have PT—physical training—at three. At four, you'll get scanned for uniforms, then you'll have half an hour to clean up. Dinner at five. After dinner, you'll get your dorms shaped up. Any questions?" He waited until we all shook our heads. "Good. You've got a short break to do whatever you need to do. WCs are out the door and to the right. I'll meet you in front of the building in five minutes. Go!"

THAT AFTERNOON, we returned to our dorms, sweaty and tired. We'd walked the entire campus, then run around the flight-line. Twice. I'd tried to stay in decent shape since we left Earth, but I had not been very successful. I collapsed onto my desk chair.

Felicity flounced in and shoved the door shut. Her face glowed, and she patted her hairline with a towel. "That was invigorating."

"Sure, that's what I'd call it." I closed my eyes and groaned. "Invigorating."

"You really should have prepared for this, Siti," she said. "Your father must have told you what to expect."

I opened my eyes. "We didn't talk much about the Academy while we were on Earth."

She grimaced. She seemed to take my references to Earth as a personal slam—as if I were shaming her by bragging about my real-world mission.

"I only decided to come here a few weeks ago."

"That's why the civilians hate us," she said. "We have experiences and advantages they don't. None of them could have come here with only a few weeks' notice. It takes months to get accepted if you're not a legacy."

I shrugged. "I was accepted through the regular application process—twenty years ago. Then Dad got the assignment to Earth, and we went into deep sleep. I was kind of surprised they'd kept my slot available."

She smirked. "They wouldn't do that for a civilian. You're a legacy, whether you like it or not. You've already taken advantage of that. Own up to it and use it." She grabbed a pink bag from her drawer. "I'm getting a shower before dinner. I hope they didn't use up all the good sonic waves."

I chuckled at the lame joke because she obviously expected it. "I'm right behind you." I was pretty sure they had real showers—water wasn't an issue here like it was in arid Virgilton on the main continent. But if she preferred a sonic shower, that meant more hot water for me.

AFTER DINNER, we returned to our rooms. Our remaining uniforms—printed to our scanned measurements—had been delivered, so we spent some time putting things away. Felicity's additional luggage had been delivered as well. Her overflowing closet included several evening gowns as well as street clothes.

"You have plenty of space in your closet." She held up a handful of heavily-laden hangars. "I'm going to stick these in there." She shoved my uniforms against the wall and hung her gowns in the space. Then she grabbed an outfit and shoved the closet closed. "I'm going out. You want to come?"

I raise my eyebrows in surprise. "I thought we were supposed to organize our dorm rooms."

"I'm as organized as I'm going to get. Derek and some friends are taking me downtown. You should come with us." She pulled on a flowered tank top and tight jeans. A small purse appeared from another drawer, and she slung it over her shoulder.

"Are you sure we should do that?"

"What are you worried about? No one is going to mess with us." She smiled a nasty smirk. "The advantage of being a legacy."

"I don't have anything else to wear." I glanced down. I'd worn my uniform from Earth on the trip here and hadn't brought any civilian clothes.

Her lips curled. "I suppose you'll have to do." She waved the door open. "Come on."

My side of the room was inspection ready. Although I hadn't learned any secrets from my father, I'd been smart enough to read the cadet manual before arriving. My bed was made, my drawers were properly organized, and my few personal belongings were locked away. I followed her into the hall.

As we passed the next room, Aneh waved through the open door. "What are we supposed to do now?"

Her roommate, Terrine, looked up from an e-book. "I'm going to study."

Felicity laughed. "Study what? They haven't given us any work yet."

"We have our books," Terrine said. "I like to get ahead."

"Whatever." Felicity grabbed my arm and pulled me away from the door.

Aneh followed us into the hallway. "Where are you going?"

"Downtown. You want to come?" I didn't look at Felicity as I asked.

Felicity swung around, hands on hips. "This was supposed to be a private party."

"The more the merrier, right?" I challenged her.

"You really don't understand how this works." Felicity pointed at Aneh. "You stay here." She turned away and headed toward the stairs. "Siti can come if she wants. If she's smart."

"You should go," Aneh whispered. "She's used to getting her way."

I looked from Aneh to Felicity. I didn't like my roommate's high-handed attitude. "I'm going to pass for tonight," I said. "I had a long day."

"Whatever." Felicity pushed open the stairway door and disappeared.

"I don't think you should piss her off," Aneh said. "She seems like the type who will get even."

"I think my legacy status protects me a little," I said. "Do you need help with your room? Got your shirts folded and socks rolled?"

"We're good," Terrine said, finally looking up from her book. "Aneh is right though. Felicity is the vengeful type."

"Then I have to watch my back," I said. "What's that book you're reading?"

WE SPENT the evening studying the survival manual Terrine had downloaded. The lights flickered at 10 PM, and a recording came through our audio implants. "Lights out in thirty minutes."

"I'm going to head back to my room," I said. "Thanks for letting me hang with you."

"Anytime," Aneh said. "I'm going to get some air before bed. Want to walk with me?"

"No, thanks." I groaned and stretched. "I've had enough walking for one day."

I returned to my room and got ready for bed. My Academy logo'd sweats and a tank top would work for sleeping. I grabbed my toothbrush and headed down the hall.

"You seen Aneh?" Terrine asked as I passed her door.

I checked the time on my holo-ring. "No. She'd better hurry."

The door at the top of the stairs slammed, and Felicity strolled down the hall, a satisfied smile on her face. When she spotted me, she stopped. "I thought you were outside talking to Micah."

"Micah who?" I paused by the bathroom door.

"Micah LeBlanc." Her eyes went kind of distant and dreamy. "He's a friend of Derek's. Smart. Good looking. Rich. I'd swear it was you he was talking to."

"No." I turned. Something was off. "Was it Aneh?"

Her eyes flickered. "Maybe." She gave an elaborate shrug then flounced past me. "I'm going to bed."

I tapped my toothbrush against my palm. Follow the rules and mind my own business or risk missing curfew to check on Aneh?

Who was I kidding? I didn't play it safe. I hurried down the steps and out the door at the bottom of the stairs.

"You're going to miss curfew," a high voice said. Aneh. "You'll get a ton of demerits."

Where was she? I strode across the path and pushed aside the branches of a hedge.

A tall boy with shoulder-length strawberry blond curls stood beside Aneh, holding her wrist. "I don't have to worry about stuff like that. My dad is friends with the commandant."

Aneh yanked, but his fingers tightened around her wrist. "Maybe you don't, but I do. Let me go."

"Give me a kiss, and I'll let you go." He smiled, his perfect teeth flashing in the overhead lights.

"No. Let me go." Aneh pulled harder.

"Let her go." I stepped through the hedge. "And maybe she won't press charges."

The boy released her hand like a hot coal. "There's nothing to press charges for. I haven't hurt her."

"Maybe we should let the JAG decide that," I said. "It sounded like sexual harassment to me."

Aneh shrank back, edging away from the boy.

He laughed. "The JAG won't touch me. I'm untouchable."

My eyes narrowed, and I crossed my arms. "Really? Do you want to put that to the test?"

"It's fine," Aneh said as she crept behind me. "Let's go inside, Siti. We don't want to be late."

"Siti?" The boy's grin widened. "Felicity told me about you. I think you and I can be a strong team."

"No, thanks," I said. "I don't partner with harassers."

"It was nothing. Just a misunderstanding." His eyes moved from my face to Aneh's. "Right?"

"Right," she said, her voice low and strained. "Just a misunderstanding. Siti, let's go. Lights out in five."

I pointed two fingers at my eyes, then rotated them to point at him. "I'm watching you."

He winked at me. "I'm mighty fine to look at."

"Ugh." I spun and pulled Aneh through the hedge. "Who's the jerk?"

Aneh sprinted up the stairs behind me. "Micah LeBlanc. His dad is some big money financier. And he's friends with the legacies. We need to watch each other's backs. I don't think he likes being beat."

"Let's get back to our rooms. Do you want to report this?"

"To who?" She hiccupped. "We're supposed to report stuff to Wronglen. He's a legacy, too."

"He is?" I thought for a moment. She was probably right. Petra Wronglen, whom I'd known on the *Return in Glory,* had referenced her illustrious past more than once. I snickered. She'd probably been frustrated by my lack of awe. "We could go to the commandant. She didn't let that kid on the shuttle get away with anything. What happened to him, anyway?"

"She sent him home. I heard Lawrence mention him to Smith when they split up the squadron."

"If Admiral Zimas was willing to kick him out for being snarky and entitled, surely she'd do the same for that brat LeBlanc."

Aneh shook her head sadly. "LeBlanc said his dad is friends with Zimas. And Felicity's mom. You've heard what Felicity says—they aren't going to believe me over him. They might even kick me out for accusing him."

"She wouldn't kick you out—you're the victim here. No one's going to expel you for standing up to a bully." As I said the words, I realized I had no idea if they were actually true. My father wouldn't have stood for that, but he wasn't the commandant of the academy. Who knows what might have changed in the last twenty years while we'd been in deep sleep?

"No. I just want to forget about this. I'll make sure I'm with someone when he's around." She pushed open the door to the hallway. "You'll help me, right?"

"Of course. But I still think—"

"No! I worked my tail off to get this appointment. I'm not going to let a bunch of entitled legacies and their friends get me thrown out." She slanted a look at me. "No offense."

I grinned. "None taken. They aren't my people."

CHAPTER FOUR

OVER THE NEXT TWO WEEKS, we got used to the schedule. We woke every morning at five-thirty then had physical training. We got twenty minutes to shower, get our rooms into inspection order, and report to the lobby of the building. Then we walked—not marched—to the chow hall.

After breakfast, we had classes in the history of the Corps, case studies of planets they had explored, and basic principles of exploration. After lunch, we had practical studies where we learned basic survival skills. Lawrence and Mason taught us to build shelters, set snares, and dress game.

"This is why we do the basic survival test." Lawrence tapped on the map displayed on the screen behind her. "When you're exploring a new planet, anything can go wrong. You need to be prepared to survive. And you need to know that there may be no rescue coming. Your life is in the hands of your team."

I looked around at my squadron mates. Did I trust them to keep me alive? Some of them were undoubtedly asking the same thing about me.

Aneh raised her hand, the morning sun slanting in onto her pale hair. "You said we'll do our first practical field experience next week. I don't think we're ready for that." She looked at the rest of us. "Abdul still couldn't get a fire started. My snares didn't catch anything. And Felicity refused to skin that critter she caught."

Felicity glared at Aneh.

Lawrence laughed. "Consider it an opportunity to succeed. Exercise Trial by Fire, also known as TbF. We'll monitor you around the clock, so no one dies." She headed for the door. Halfway out, she stopped and looked back. "And you'll have some supplies of course. We wouldn't drop you naked and alone. That's ridiculous." She disappeared down the hall.

We all laughed nervously. "I've seen vids where they do exactly that," I muttered to Aneh.

"Drop you naked and alone?" Her voice cracked.

"They call them reality shows, but there's nothing real about them." At least I didn't think there was.

Felicity stood and glared at Aneh. "Thanks for throwing me under the shuttle, Jones. You'll get yours. Come on, Siti."

"She's not wrong." I crossed my arms and stayed in my seat. Over the last few days, I'd had enough of Felicity's superiority. "You did refuse to skin that critter. We'd all be hungry if you were in charge of dinner."

"I don't intend to be the cook," Felicity said. "One of these grunts can do that. I'm a leader."

"Grunts?" Terrine stood and loomed over Felicity, her fists clenched. "Just because your mom is an admiral doesn't mean you can look down on the rest of us."

Felicity snorted. "You obviously don't understand how the Corps works. Come on, Siti. Last chance."

I glanced around at the rest of the class. Three kids had already washed out, so there were only twelve of us left. Felicity had made so many enemies over the last two weeks. Why was she was still trying to reel me into her clique? "I'm going to stay here and study."

Felicity's eyes narrowed. "Are you sure? Micah and Derek are meeting me for lunch."

"Have a lovely time." I flashed a phony smile. "I guess I'll see you back in the dorm."

Felicity stormed out, the door slamming behind her.

The rest of the squadron turned to me. "That was probably a very bad move," Aneh said.

"You've made an enemy." Terrine moved to the chair behind Aneh.

"That Micah LeBlanc creeps me out. And I'm sick of her legacy this and legacy that. Having a parent who's an admiral doesn't make her better than anyone else. It certainly doesn't make her better at survival. I think we have a better chance if we work together. And without her."

"We definitely have a better chance." Terrine tapped her fingers on the desk. After a second, she looked up. "You're the only one who's done this in real life. You'll have to tell us what to do."

I laughed. "I didn't have to do any surviving. I helped set up a camp and looked around a planet that was already occupied." My lips clamped shut, and a chill went down my spine. Was I supposed to talk about Earth?

Ten pairs of eyes snapped to me. "Already occupied?" Abdul asked.

Oh, crap. I'd stepped in it.

"Yeah, didn't you hear about that?" Yvonne asked. Her last name—Agarwal—was too hard to say so we used her first. "It was on all the vid feeds. Galactic news ran a special report. The Gagarians had already landed when our team arrived."

"No. That's not right," a pudgy boy named Chymm Leonardi di Zorytevsky said. "Those people came from Lewei."

"That's not what I heard," said McDowell Rendi. "I heard they were cannibals who had survived since we left. Five hundred years on a polluted rock turns you into a monster."

I shook my head. "None of that's right."

"Well, what happened then?" Aneh asked. "You were there. Tell us."

"Let's study this survival stuff," I said. "When we're ready to take a break for lunch, I'll tell you the story."

AFTER LUNCH, we met in the field. It wasn't really a field; it was a clearing in the forest behind the Academy buildings. Each flight had a separate location with a supply shed and benches around the edge of a clearing. We practiced putting up living modules and tents, activating the force shield, and learned our basic hunting and foraging skills. That afternoon, Lawrence and Mason were waiting when we arrived. Felicity was nowhere to be found.

"There's been a slight change of plans," Lawrence said. A deep groove had appeared between her eyebrows which we had learned meant she was either angry or thinking hard. My credits were on angry. "Cadet Myers has been reassigned."

That seemed like cause for celebration, not anger. "What do you mean, reassigned?" I asked.

Lawrence's lips thinned. "What I said. She's been moved to Delta squadron. Orders came down twenty minutes ago."

"You all know who her mother is," Mason said.

"No speculation," Lawrence snapped. "We'll be getting a new cadet from Delta. Two, actually. Apparently, Terrine is being reassigned, too."

Terrine yelped. "No. I want to stay here."

"That's not your decision." Lawrence made a slashing motion. "We follow orders."

Terrine glared at Lawrence, her eyes turning glassy. "But I want to stay with Charlie Blue. Why would she do this to me? She doesn't even like me."

"You're the smartest one here," I said. "You've read all the manuals and case studies. You're an asset, and she won't hesitate to make use of you."

Terrine gritted her teeth and growled. "No one makes use of me."

"Enough." Lawrence flicked her holo-ring and pulled up a file. "We have our orders."

Terrine crossed her arms in defiance. "I won't go."

"Yes, you will." Lawrence's voice softened. "You don't have a choice. Remember, your loyalty is to the Corps, not your flight. You're here to become an explorer. You'll be a good one. Don't let her ruin that for you." She grimaced, as if realizing she'd just laid the blame on Felicity. "I mean don't let the *circumstances* spoil that for you."

Terrine blinked again and sniffed. "I was finally getting to feel like we were a team."

"Your new flight will be your team," Lawrence said. "Mason, escort

Terrine to Delta squadron. And bring back our new cadets. Make us proud, Terrine."

Terrine slowly climbed to her feet. She snapped out a salute and followed Mason out of the clearing.

Lawrence watched them leave then turned back to us. "While we wait for our new cadets, let's talk about bug-out bags. You know what they are?" Several heads nodded. Her eyes narrowed, and the crease deepened. "If you'd done the reading, you would know. Basic needs, in an easy-to-carry backpack. We've got lightweight bags here in the storeroom. There's a list of practical ideas on your assignment board." She cleared her throat. "Due tomorrow: each of you will refine the list and stock a bug-out bag. For now, practice setting snares." Lawrence placed her hand on the access panel of the supply shed, and the door popped open. "You should know what to get by now."

We filed in to retrieve the fine cable and knives then spread out around the circle. I searched the edge of the woods for a good branch.

Aneh pushed ahead, deeper into the trees. "Siti, over here."

I pushed through the underbrush to her.

"See that trail? Those critters run along here."

Yvonne had trapped one of the large rodents yesterday. They were the size of an Earth rabbit, but with short, pointed ears and long, wide tails. Lawrence had assured us they were good to eat. Thanks to Felicity, we hadn't had to test that. Yet.

Aneh worked quickly, pounding a stake into the ground and hooking up the wire. "Will you help me with my bug-out bag?"

"Sure. How'd you do that so fast?" I picked up a branch, but it broke when I flexed it.

"I've done this before." She arranged her snare across a narrow game trail. I wouldn't have noticed it if she hadn't pointed it out to me. "We live on the fringe. My cousins hunt for food."

"You weren't doing this well yesterday." I narrowed my eyes.

"Because Felicity was watching me. She kept asking questions and making me nervous. Now that she's gone, I can do my work."

"Sorry. I'll stop asking—"

"No, you're fine. I like you." She grinned at me then returned to her work. "She was nasty. She wanted me to tie her snares for her."

"Did you talk to Lawrence?" I found another stick and used the handle of the knife to pound it into the dirt. The knife hilt hit my thumb. "Ow!" I shook my hand, but that made the throbbing worse. "*Ow!*"

Aneh bit her lip, but the corners of her mouth twitched.

"Go ahead and laugh. I know you want to."

Aneh snickered. "You have to sharpen it." She grabbed my stick and showed me how to whittle the point.

"Charlie Blue!" Lawrence's voice came over the comm. "Assemble!"

We picked up our tools, leaving Aneh's snare in place. Back in the clearing, two male cadets waited beside Lawrence. One was tall and muscular, with dark skin and tightly curled hair. The other was a bit shorter, with a slender build and almond shaped eyes.

"Peter! Joss!" I ran across the clearing and threw my arms around the two boys. "What are you doing here?"

Peter smiled and gave me a quick squeeze.

Joss pounded my back, grinning. "We couldn't let you have all the fun."

Lawrence cleared her throat. I stepped away from the boys but couldn't wipe the smile off my face. Joss winked, and my smile widened.

"Cadet Kassis seems to already know our newbies." Lawrence raised her eyebrow at me. "Care to do the introductions?"

"Sure. This is Joss Torres and Peter Russell." I pointed to each boy in turn. "They're from Earth."

CHAPTER FIVE

THE REST of the afternoon went by in a blur. Peter and Joss were both skilled in setting snares, and they helped the rest of us. At three, Lawrence called us together. "Russell, Torres, Jones—you're excused from PT. Jones, you'll move in with Kassis. Russell and Torres will take your old room."

Aneh squealed, clapping her hands.

Lawrence rolled her eyes. "Enough. Each of you grab a backpack for the bug-out assignment then back to the dorms to put on your PT gear. The rest of you will meet me in front of the building in fifteen. Rev-ball against Charlie Orange."

After dinner, the flight met in the ready room to brainstorm supplies for our bug-out bags.

"Siti!" Joss trotted into the room and grabbed me in a bear hug, lifting me off my feet. "Can you believe we are all here together?"

"No, I can't." I pushed away and pointed at each of them. "You need to tell me how this happened. It takes months or even years to get accepted to the Academy." Unless you're a legacy, the little voice in my head reminded me. "How did you get here?"

"Your dad had something to do with that," Peter said. "It was part of the deal he cut with your government. Kind of an exchange program. A few weeks ago, he told Zane and Mara that the Academy would accept two candidates from Earth."

"And they picked the two best, of course." Joss flashed his cocky grin.

Peter smacked his friend on the shoulder. "Mara sent word out through her networks, but no one else volunteered. They don't want to leave Earth. But I've always wanted to come out here. When we ended up in the Dome, I was so pissed that I hadn't gotten to see a new planet. This really is—"

"—a dream come true." Joss finished the sentence with a high falsetto. He fluttered his eyelashes.

Peter smacked his shoulder again. "And why are you here? Go ahead, tell the lady."

"I'm here to meet hot alien chicks," Joss said in a deadpan tone.

"None of us are aliens," Aneh said from the doorway. "I'm Aneh, but I'm from Grissom. I guess you're supposed to call me Jones."

Peter stood up and offered his chair. "You've got some great survival skills, Aneh-call-me-Jones. Real pro-level stuff."

"You're not so bad yourself," Aneh said.

Were they flirting?

"I'm still a newbie at this stuff," Peter said with a headshake. "We've only been learning woodcraft since we came out of the Dome. Everest has taught us a lot, but you tie a snare like you've done it your whole life."

"Yeah, you're as good as Everest," Joss said.

Aneh's brow wrinkled. "Who's Everest?"

While Joss told her about their life on Earth, I moved closer to Peter. "What about Jake?"

Peter looked confused. "What about him?"

"Did he come with you?"

"No." Peter looked away. "Jake has no interest in leaving Earth. Or Lena."

"It always seemed like you two were inseparable." I fiddled with my holo-ring.

Peter shook his head. "We're close, but he has Lena, and Mom, and Mara. And part of the deal is we can call home once a quarter."

My eyes widened. "Real-time? Interstellar calls are expensive."

Peter grinned. "Yep. It's part of the treaty. Being friends with the leaders of a whole planet that someone else wants can be lucrative."

I laughed. "I'm glad Zane and Mara were able to negotiate good terms. How's Liam?"

"He seemed kind of sad last time I saw him. I think he misses you."

Warmth sparked in my chest. I wasn't sure the blue and white sair-glider would miss me. He'd been in very good health when I found him, which made me think he'd had another owner. But he'd never tried to find that person. Sair-gliders were usually one-master animals, but Liam seemed to be the exception. "I can't wait until fall when I'm allowed to have him here. But I figured he'd be fine without me."

He shook his head. "No, he was definitely pining for you. I guess your dad is a poor substitute. Probably doesn't feed him enough Chewy Nuggets."

Cadet Mason knocked on the door frame to get our attention. "You've got twenty minutes in supply to outfit your bug-out bags. You ready?" We grabbed our lists and followed the flight sergeant out of the room.

AN ALERT KLAXON BLARED, jerking me out of a sound sleep. I rolled out of the bunk as the lights flashed on. "What's going on?"

Aneh sat up, rubbing her eyes. "I don't know." Her voice was tight. "It doesn't sound good though."

Wronglen's voice came through our audio implant. "Charlie Squadron! Assemble on the quad."

We scrambled into our utility uniforms. As we headed out the door, I grabbed our bug-out bags.

"Do you think we'll need those?" Aneh asked as we ran down the hall.

"The timing of whatever this is seems pretty coincidental, since we put these together two days ago." I handed hers over as we ran. "I'd rather carry it than be without."

Peter and Joss saw me coming. I slapped my bug-out bag as I ran. Peter nodded and darted back into the room. By the time I reached their door, he had returned with their backpacks. He thrust one at Joss. "Carry your own crap."

We hurried down the hall, shouting to our squadron mates to grab their gear. "Is this a legacy secret?" Abdul asked.

I shook my head as I ran past. "Nope, just a hunch." We straggled out the door and formed up in the quad. The other squadrons assembled in front of their dorms.

Cadet Wronglen paced in front of us. "Where the hell are the rest of your people, Smith?" He looked at the clock on his holo-ring. "Why is Charlie Orange the last to get out here? You people are an embarrassment! Give 'em twenty!"

Cadet Smith pointed at the dorm. "Last two coming now." He jogged toward the latecomers. "Charlie Orange, you're late! Who told you to go back for your bags? Move! Move! Move! Drop your gear and give me twenty!"

I waited for them to throw me under the shuttle, but they dropped their bags and pumped out twenty push-ups.

Wronglen's voice came through our implants. "Welcome to Exercise TbF: Trial by Fire." We could hear the capitalization of the title in his voice. "Each flight will be dropped in a different sector of the playing field. Your goal will be to find the other half of your squadron. If you were smart enough to grab your bug-out bag, kudos." He glared at us. "But next time, don't let it slow you down! Each flight will be given a command key. It's a box about this big." He raised his hand as if he were holding something in his palm. "When you find the other half of the squadron, you'll connect the two command keys and receive the mission brief."

He turned to Lawrence and Smith. "Flight commanders, take your teams to the transport. Plebes, you will be watched and graded during this entire exercise." He stressed the word entire. "You are always under surveillance. Remember that. Work together. The flight that completes the mission first wins a week of inspection-free time. Plus, of course, bragging rights."

We all cheered.

"Anyone want to chicken out?" The squadron commanders hollered it together.

Every cadet on the quad bellowed, "Hell, no!"

Wronglen waved his arm in a large circle. Smith and Lawrence headed in opposite directions.

"Follow me," Lawrence said through the comm.

"What's inspection-free time?" Aneh asked.

"It means they won't be checking our dorms for a week." Joss hiked his bag up onto his shoulders as we jogged behind Lawrence. "No need to make your bed, or roll your socks, or dust the top of the doorframe."

"That doesn't seem like much of a reward," Aneh said.

"Are you kidding me?" Yvonne said as she moved closer. "No inspections means more free time. It's the one commodity you can't get around here. Most cadets would kill for that. But the bragging rights are the real prize."

We climbed into a large transport. We were down to ten cadets in our flight by this time, so even with Mason and Lawrence, the vehicle was not full.

"Do you know where we're going?" Yvonne asked Lawrence as we fastened our restraints.

Lawrence smirked. "If I did, I wouldn't tell you. Where's the fun in that?"

"How long will we be out?" Marise asked. She was a quiet girl, but we all listened when she spoke because she usually knew her stuff. She was almost as well-versed in Explorer Corps lore as Terrine had been. If she didn't know how long we'd be out, then no one did.

"You heard Wronglen," Lawrence said. "TbF is up to a week long. Sometimes it's much shorter. It all depends on how quickly you can find your teammates and how fast you achieve the objective."

"What was the objective when you were a plebe?" Marise asked.

"Everyone strapped in?" The male voice came over our implants. He didn't wait for us to confirm. "Lift off in three. Two. One. Mark."

The vehicle rose smoothly from the ground. Through the small windows, we could see the lights of the Academy as they dwindled beneath us. We quickly reached a cruising altitude, and the ship shot away into the darkness.

"It's usually a capture the flag kind of game," Lawrence said. "We had to find a transmitter that was hidden in the field. But that was two years ago, under a different commandant. Things change."

"You're allowed to tell us?" I asked.

Lawrence smirked. "I'm allowed to answer *almost* any question from now until we land."

The other cadets began firing questions at her so fast she couldn't answer any of them. Peter stuck his fingers in his mouth and whistled. Heads snapped in our direction.

When Peter didn't speak, I did. "One at a time. Give her a chance to answer. Marise, you first."

"Are there any tools hidden in the course?" Marise asked.

Lawrence's eyes went wide in admiration. "Good question. No. You'll be given some supplies, but there's nothing hidden."

"Yvonne." I pointed at the girl.

"How far away and in what direction will the other flight be?" Yvonne asked.

"Flights are dropped within a day's walk of each other. I don't know what direction. You'll need to figure that out."

"That's easy." Rendi flicked his holo–ring. "We've got all kinds of positioning tools. Or we can just call and ask them."

Lawrence's eyelids dropped. She knew something about the holo-rings.

"Will our holo-rings work?" I asked.

"Good catch." She nodded. "There is no holo-ring coverage in the course."

"You can't drop us without our holo-rings! That's crazy!" Rendi cried. "I've never been without mine since the day I turned seven!"

"What if there's an emergency?" Aneh blurted.

"They're watching us," Peter said. "They'll know."

"Hey, Wronglen said we have to find the other flight then get the objective." Joss drummed his fingers on his armrest. "But he also said the *flight* that wins, gets the prize. Are we working *with* Charlie Orange or competing against them?"

"Both." Lawrence grinned again at our expressions. "You can't complete the mission without the other flight. But only one flight wins."

We nodded. Although we had shared a dorm with Charlie Orange for the last few weeks, we barely knew those cadets. Every class and exercise had been done with only our flight-mates. Charlie Blue was our team. We didn't feel any allegiance to Orange.

The transport began to drop. We peered out the windows, but I couldn't see anything. No lights. No buildings. No roads. As the craft settled to the ground, I thought of one last question. "Can you tell us anything else to help us?"

Lawrence gave me another grudging nod. "I can. You'll be given a float plate with supplies for a week. Everything on that float was chosen for a reason. A reason specific to this exercise." She made eye contact with each of us, as if trying to impress that fact on us.

"Right," I said. "Everything is valuable."

"Not just valuable," Lawrence said. "Integral."

The transport settled to the ground, and the troop door opened, forming a ramp to the ground. "Everyone out!" Lawrence stood and waved her arm in a large circle like Wronglen had done earlier. Her arm dropped and she pointed out the door. "Good luck."

We trooped out. The transport had settled in a small clearing, and its lights illuminated a thick forest surrounding us. A heavy mist enveloped us—not quite enough to be classified as rain but just as annoying. A tinge of sulphur and rotting wood wrapped around us. As we got our bearings, Mason emerged from the transport, guiding a float plate. It held a pile of smooth sided boxes. He lowered it to the ground. "Unload this."

"We don't get to keep the float panel?" Peter asked as we scrambled to unload the thing.

Mason laughed and waved a tablet. "What do you think this is, vacation? You can keep the float panel, but I have the controls."

"Are you staying with us?" Aneh asked.

"I'll be watching from mission control back at the base," Mason said. "But I can't help unless there's an emergency. And you'll have to forfeit to receive help. If there's a serious emergency, we'll forfeit on your behalf."

As he spoke, the transport started to lift, blowing mud and dirt at us. Mason jumped onto the slowly rising ramp and waved before walking into the transport. It folded shut and flew away.

I blinked the dirt out of my eyes and flicked on the light attached to my bug-out bag. The others followed suit. Only Franklin and Rendi hadn't brought their bags.

"Come on, Charlie Blue, let's get to work!" Joss pointed at the float panel.

Peter flashed a thumbs-up and grabbed a crate.

"Why does he do that?" Aneh asked.

"Do what?" I took another box and set it on the pile.

Aneh set her crate down and held up her fist, thumb sticking up. "Is it a secret signal?"

I laughed. "It's an ancient Earth gesture. It means everything's good. Or 'yeah, I got it.' Or, if you're the sarcastic type, 'shut up.' It's pretty similar to this." I performed the well-known three finger salute.

"Huh." She looked at her thumb. "I like it."

We unloaded the smaller boxes, stacking them on one side of the clearing. The larger one, I recognized. "That's a living mod." I got behind the large crate and laid my hands against it. "This thing has its own grav lifter," I told the rest of them. "It's strong, but the mod cube is heavy. It will only rise a few inches from the ground. But it's enough for us to push it. Give me a hand."

"Marise, help me inventory the rest of this stuff," Peter said as the team gathered around us.

Rendi, Franklin, and Joss joined me beside the mod cube. I opened the panel on the side and pressed a button. The cube rose a few centimeters from the ground. "Now push! Let's put it over there." I pointed at a spot a few meters away.

A bright streak of red blasted out of the forest beyond our clearing, exploding in a bright star above the trees. We all turned to stare.

"What the hell was that?" Rendi asked.

"Flare." Marise held up a gun-shaped item. "We have one too, but ours is blue."

"Blue? Why blue? The other one was red."

We all turned stares of disbelief on Joss. Then Yvonne laughed. "I forgot, you two are still kinda new. Blue is our color. Red is Alpha Squadron. And green," she added as a green flare burned into our eyes.

"Is that how we're supposed to find the others?" someone asked.

Marise's eyes snapped to mine. "Yes!" we said together.

"Someone track where those flares are coming up," Marise called out.

"On it," Aneh said. She pulled out her knife and started gathering straight sticks. As each flare went up, she cut some kind of marking into one and pointed it toward the flare, creating a compass in the center of the clearing.

"Clever. Did you get the first two?" I asked.

"Pretty close."

"We probably don't want to be last," Marise said.

"Good point." I pointed at her. "Do you know how to shoot that thing?"

She shook her head.

"I do." Franklin stepped forward. We all stared at him. "What? I come from the islands of Sally Ride. We use flare guns all the time."

Peter held out his fist with the thumb extended upwards. "Go for it."

Franklin gave him a weird look. "Sure." He pointed the gun straight up and pulled the trigger.

We all ducked as the thing fired, the flare streaming upward with a trail of blue.

"There's a white one." Aneh pointed with a stick then added it to her collection.

"What color will the Delta Black flare be?" Joss asked. "Can't see black in the dark."

Another white flare went up, this one with dark sparkles in it. "I guess that answers that question." Marise put the flare gun back into the crate she'd been inventorying. "That's Felicity's flight."

"Derek Lee is there, too," Peter said. His jaw tightened. "And LeBlanc."

"How d'you know that?" I asked.

Peter's eyebrows drew down. "That's the flight we got transferred out of, remember? We know all those guys. They're kind of cutthroat."

"Black is definitely an appropriate color for them." Joss nodded.

"This isn't good." Aneh stood in the center of her compass sticks.

"We'll have to outsmart them." I waved off her concerns.

"Then we'd better move." Aneh pointed at the sticks by her feet then raised her hand to point through the trees. "Charlie Orange is that way." She turned ninety degrees. "Delta White is that way." Then she spun to the opposite direction. "Delta Black is that way. We're directly between White and Black. We don't want our camp right between them, do we?"

"No!' half the flight yelled.

"How are we going to move all this stuff without a working float panel?" Franklin asked.

A grin spread over my face. "We don't need the panel. The living mod has its own lifters, remember? We might even be able to load some of that stuff on top. Let's see how much it will hold. Start loading."

I looked around the little group, zeroing in on Chymm. "You're our tech expert. Do you have a way to translate Aneh's stick compass to something more mobile? We don't want to lose track of where the others might be."

"I have a real compass." He shrugged off his backpack and started rifling through it. "I built it yesterday in the electronics lab. Thought it might be handy. It has a simple analog device and a more sophisticated electronic one. Not sure if it will work out here..." He grunted in satisfaction as he pulled a small box from the bag.

"Why wouldn't it work?" I asked.

He shrugged. "If they've blocked holo-rings, they might have a way to block positioning satellites too." He fiddled with the box, and it lit up. Teeth flashed in his dark face as he grinned. "Seems I over-estimated them."

"Fantastic!" I followed him to the sticks laying in the center of the clearing. "Hey—we know White and Black are about a day's walk apart. That's what? Twenty clicks?"

"Thirty," Marise said. "According to the manual. But I'm not sure we'd make that kind of time." Terrine wasn't the only one who had studied hard.

"If we know distance and direction, can we pinpoint their current location?" I asked.

"Not really," Chymm said. "We don't know where we are between them. For example, if White is only two clicks from us, then Black could be almost twenty-eight klicks away. But maybe White is ten klicks away.

Black would be twenty. Or closer—they said 'up to' a day's walk. Based on where those flares appeared to be coming up, I'd say they're maybe ten or twelve klicks from us."

"Do what you can." I clapped him on the shoulder. "The more information we have about their whereabouts, the better." I turned back to the supply crates.

"We can get about 80% of it onto the crate, then it starts to drop. Quickly." Joss tapped the crate with his hand.

"All right. Let's take a few minutes to go through our bug-out bags and see how much of the small stuff we can add to our packs. We don't want anybody overburdened, so don't take more than is realistic for you." I shrugged off my backpack as I spoke.

"Who put you in charge?" Yvonne commanded.

I looked up. "No one. But someone has to be. Do you want to do it?"

Yvonne flung up her hands. "No."

"I vote we make Siti the boss," Joss said.

"I second," Aneh sang out.

"Hang on." I stood. "The Corps isn't a democracy."

"No," Marise said. "But you stepped up. In my mind, that proves you're a leader. I can't imagine anyone else here taking charge."

My face heated. A couple of the others made noises, but no one stepped forward to take charge.

"It's decided then," Marise said, her voice belligerent. She was the most skilled member of our team, and if she thought I should be in charge, the others were bound to agree with her. She gave me an ironic glare. "You want to chicken out?"

"Hell, no?" I replied uncertainly.

She smiled and gave an awkward thumbs-up.

CHAPTER SIX

CHYMM JUMPED UP, waving his device. "Got it!"

"Great." I hurried to him. "Can you set a heading on that? Who am I kidding? Of course you can. Set a heading for the orange flare." I gripped his shoulder and swung him toward the rest of the group. "Let's get loaded up and moving."

We distributed smaller items among us. In addition to the command key, there was rope, wire, some magnets, the flare gun, a week's supply of meal pacs, and water purification bottles.

"What do we do with the empty crates?" Marise asked. "Lawrence said everything had a purpose. Do you think we'll need them?"

Joss picked one up, the light material flexing in his hands. He flipped it over and set it on his head. "Makes a great rain hat."

We laughed. The heavy mist had drenched our hair. Even a crate-shaped hat might be desirable if we were out in this much longer. Fortunately, our uniforms kept us dry.

"There weren't any backpacks or bags. If we hadn't brought our bug-out bags, we could have used them to carry the supplies," Yvonne suggested.

I nodded. "Are they light enough to carry on the mod cube?"

Joss flipped the crate off his head and onto the floating mod. The pile bobbed but held. "One works. How many we got?"

"Load up whatever you can. Franklin and Rendi can carry some since they don't have backpacks." I raised my eyebrows at them. "Right?"

"You got it, boss." Franklin grabbed two crates and tried to nest them inside of each other. "Poor engineering. I'd have made them stackable."

"Are you an engineer?" Rendi asked as he picked up two more crates.

"I've taken a few classes." Franklin yawned. "Didn't finish my degree. Came here instead. What was I thinking?"

"Joss, you take point," I said. "You have the most real-world experience."

Joss saluted. "Yes, ma'am." He strapped a long knife to his belt.

"We say 'sir' in the Corps," Yvonne reminded him.

"Where'd you get that?" Rendi pointed at Joss's knife.

"It was in the crates." Joss raised an eyebrow.

"Why do *you* get it?" Rendi asked.

"Because I know how to use it. And my hands aren't full of crates."

"Any other dangerous tools in there?" I asked.

Marise shook her head. "There were two knives. I gave the other one to Aneh."

"Remember, this is a training exercise." I narrowed my eyes at them. "We shouldn't be planning on hurting anyone. Or anything, unless we need to eat it. I can't imagine the commandant would send us here if there were dangerous animals."

"Man is the most dangerous," Peter said.

"It's only cadets here." I glared. "We'll be in deep trouble if we injure someone. Keep the knives in their sheaths unless we need to cut a branch or skin our dinner." I watched them until they all nodded. "Great. Move out. I want to get as far from here as we can before daylight."

Joss let us along a rough game trail that headed in the general direction of Charlie Orange. Yvonne and Peter pushed the floating crates, maneuvering them between the trees. A couple of times, we had to go off the path to push the crates through.

"Hey, Siti," Peter called. "Can we pull this with the rope? Like we did—"

"—with Tiah!" I finished the sentence with him. "I can't believe I didn't think of that before. Who has the rope?"

We tied the rope to a ring embedded in the front of the living mod. Peter tied the other end around his waist, dragging the pile of crates behind him. With the grav-lifters on, it would be no more effort than pulling a balloon. Yvonne trailed behind, nudging the stack back on track when they swung off the trail. We picked up the pace.

As we moved closer to the infamous swamps of Grissom, our feet sank into the marshy ground. Although it was nighttime, the temperature was still warm. In minutes, we were all sweating. Lack of sleep and the sludgy terrain slowed us down. After about an hour of walking, we arrived at a small clearing beside a stream.

"Let's stop for rest," I said. "Is it dry enough to sit down?"

"There are some logs over here," Marise said. "I'm not sure we should set the crates down, though. They might sink in. Ugh, the mud stinks."

I opened the panel on the side of the cube to check the charge. "At the rate we're going, this is only going to last another klick or two. We need to find a place to set up camp."

"We should send out some scouts," Joss suggested.

"Good idea." I pointed as I spoke. "Joss, take Yvonne and go that way. Twenty minutes. If you don't find anything, come back. We don't want to lose anyone. Rendi and Marise, head that way. Peter, you take Abdul and go that way."

They headed into the trees, leaving the rest of us by the crates. "Let's fill up the water bottles. Purifiers should make this stream water drinkable."

Franklin pulled a bottle out of his pack and wandered down to the stream. As he got closer, his feet started sinking into the soft ground. "Hey! This stuff is sucking me in."

"It's a swamp," Aneh said. "The ground gets softer close to the water."

"Get me out!" Franklin cried. "I don't need a lecture, I need help."

"Calm down," I said. "We don't need two people stuck in the mud. Chymm, grab the rope from the crates and throw the end to Franklin."

It took Chymm three tries to get the rope to Franklin, but he finally succeeded. Franklin grabbed it and started pulling. The pile of crates drifted toward the stream.

"Stop pulling!" I commanded. "You're taking our supplies with you. We need to tie that rope to something more stable."

Aneh and Chymm untied the rope then wrapped it around the thickest tree near the stream. "We can use it as a pulley to pull Franklin out of the mud," Chymm said.

"Fill the bottle before you come back," Aneh said.

"Good call." I pulled out my bottle and edged closer to Franklin. "Hang on." I hurried back to the pile of crates and grabbed one of the empties. Loading as many water bottles as I could find, I carried it toward the stream. When the ground started getting soft, I set the crate on the ground and pushed it toward him. "Fill those up, too."

Franklin grumbled but did as I told him. When he finished, I leaned out to grab the crate and drag it away from the mucky ground. The crate dug into the mud, sending a waft of sulfurous gas into the air. I coughed.

Chymm and Aneh pulled the rope around Franklin's waist. He cried out. "It stinks!"

"Pull harder," Aneh said.

Franklin's feet popped out of the mud. A stench enveloped us as Franklin rolled to safety. "Arg! My ankle!" He curled into himself, holding his left leg.

I grabbed the end of the rope, and the three of us hauled him to safety.

"I think it got caught on a root or something." Franklin moaned. "I'm sure it's broken."

"It's probably not broken," I said. "Let me take a look."

"Are you a medic?" he snapped, rolling away from me.

"No, but I've sprained an ankle before. Let's get your boot off."

Franklin moaned and cried as we untied the wet, muddy boot. The knots were slippery and tight, but eventually we got them untangled. I wiped my fingers on some grass as Chymm eased the boot off his foot and unpeeled the sopping sock.

His foot looked normal.

"Does this hurt?" Aneh asked as she flexed his foot.

Franklin yelped.

"We should probably wrap it, just to be safe." Aneh patted his shoulder. "Where's your first aid kit?"

"He doesn't have one," I reminded her. "No bug-out bag."

"Right. I've got some things." She opened her bag and pulled out a small packet. "This is a compression cuff. It will help prevent swelling and immobilize the leg." She unwrapped the small, flexible package and wrapped the material around his leg. She pressed a button on the side, and the material went rigid. "It's made of the same stuff they use for the living mods. Flexible when deactivated. Rigid when you need it. Chymm, can you help him put the boot back on?"

We shifted Franklin to the fallen log. He winced with each step. "Lesson learned," Franklin said. "Water is bad."

"A better lesson would be 'check the ground before you walk on it'," Aneh said.

"Help me run the filters on these bottles." I set the crate near Franklin and sat down. "Chymm, tie our supplies to the tree. We don't want to lose them."

As we activated the filters on the bottles, my headlamp dimmed. "We need to set up camp quickly. My battery is dying."

"Mine too," Aneh said. "But I have another one in my bag. There were four with the supplies."

"Excellent. It's a good thing we brought our bags." I pulled a meal pac out of my bag and ripped it open. These things had enough calories for combat operations, so having a snack now wouldn't short me later. "If you eat one, I recommend the green." I pulled out a smaller green packet and returned the larger one to my bag. The others followed my example.

"I see how it is," Joss said. "You send us out scouting and eat all the good snacks."

I grinned. "That's exactly how it is. Pull up a log and tell us what you found."

He shook his head as he sat. "You gave us the short straw. Nothing but swamp that way."

Yvonne nodded as she shrugged off her backpack. "It starts smelling real nasty not far from here."

Abdul stumbled into the clearing a few minutes later. "We found a spot."

"It's not perfect," Peter said. "But it's better than here."

I stood and pointed to the log. "Take a load off. We'll wait till Rendi and Marise get back, let them rest a few minutes, and then head out. Oh, and turn off your light while you're here. We'll need them for setting up camp."

Rendi and Marise straggled into camp just as I was starting to get worried. Rendi's pants and boots were soaked through. "He found the swamp," Marise said.

Aneh giggled and pointed at Franklin's boots. They were covered in mud from his trip to the stream. "So did he."

After they had rested, we followed Peter and Abdul into the underbrush. "Try not to break any branches," Peter said. "If anyone comes this way, we don't want to lead them to our camp. There's a tiny trail here—stay on it until we're out of sight of the clearing."

"I'll try to clear up any telltale signs," Joss said. "Like those boot prints." He pointed to the mess by the stream.

Yvonne shook her head. "Don't worry about them. They'll fill in soon. By morning, none of them will be visible. But we need to brush away any marks left on the trail. Grab a fallen branch and we'll sweep."

We headed into the woods again. Chymm helped Franklin limp along. About fifty meters off the main trail, Peter pushed into the deep underbrush.

"Grab these brambles," Abdul said. "They'll spring back in your face if you don't catch them." He handed them off to Marise. She held them back as Yvonne and I wrangled the crates through the bush.

Joss and Aneh caught up and took the bramble vines from Marise. "These are perfect for hiding our trail," Aneh said. "If we brush out the footprints leading to this bramble, it will spring back into place and cover the path. We should be home free." She rubbed the branch she held against the dirt, obscuring our tracks.

"How do you know so much about this stuff?" Joss asked. "I didn't think any of the colonies were wild enough to learn woodcraft."

She smiled. "I grew up in the fringe—out in the wild lands of the southern continent. We used to camp in an area a lot like this—not as wet, but wild. My dad is a big 'leave no trace' guy."

Marise nodded. "She's right. I have a cousin who went through the Academy a few years ago. When he heard I was coming here, he loaded me up on this stuff. Told me all about this area."

"So, legacies really do know all the secrets?" Joss asked.

"Don't call me that. My dad works for a living." She laughed. "He's enlisted. He was a phase 2 guy before he came to the Academy. You know, the team that goes in after the jump beacons have been set and does the detailed planetary analysis."

"What about that cousin, though?" Joss pushed another bramble aside. "He must have told you stuff. I can't believe you've been holding out on us!"

"He wouldn't give me any details of the exercises," she said. "He told me about the area, but he wouldn't say a word about the actual missions."

"Would you two stop yacking so we can catch up with the rest?" I asked.

Joss winked and nodded to Marise. "We're coming. But you want us to do a good job, right?"

Aneh let the vines snap into place behind us and a few meters later, tossed her branch aside. "If anyone gets this far, they'll see our tracks, so the dead branches won't give us away."

"You didn't cut those branches from anywhere they'll notice, did you?" I asked.

Joss gave me a disgusted look. "We know what we're doing."

"You put me in charge," I said. "It's not that I don't trust you—"

"But you don't trust me," he finished.

It was my turn to wink. "You got it."

CHAPTER SEVEN

WE CAUGHT up with the others and followed them to a small clearing. A stony bulge prevented the trees from growing. "This is one of the weird features of this area," Marise said. "I remember my cousin Jamal talking about it. There are these upthrusts of bedrock—like mountains growing up through the swamp. Probably some ancient volcanic thing. They're solid ground in the middle of the swampy areas. Perfect for camps."

"Let's get the shelter set up right there," I said. "Then we'll set a guard, and the rest of us can get some sleep. Joss, set up the rotation. The rest of you unload the cube. Stack the stuff right there." I pointed.

"Why there?" Yvonne asked, her voice a little belligerent.

"The wind is blowing from that direction." I pointed. "If we set the mod here, we can put the entrance on the lee side, which will help us keep the temperature even. If we have to live here for a week, I'd prefer to do it in as much comfort as possible."

"Fair enough."

We spent the next few minutes unfolding our new dorm. This was a minimum comfort living mod—no showers, no hammocks, no AutoKitch'n. It had a composting toilet, for which I was grateful. I hated squatting in the woods.

"It will provide shelter," I said. "And we can set the access panel to our handprints, which means we have secure storage. If this is a competition, I expect the other squadrons to cause some mayhem."

"You think they would steal our stuff?" Aneh's eyes were wide.

Yvonne laughed. "How naïve can you be? Yes, they'll steal our stuff. They want to win, just like us. And some of them won't know how to do this stuff, like find a rocky clearing or set up the mod."

"I can't believe they never showed us how to do this. How were we supposed to know if we didn't have Siti?" Abdul complained.

"Did you read any of the assigned reading?" Marise asked. "It was all in there."

Abdul looked away. "I figured they'd show us the important stuff during our field exercises."

"It's all important stuff," Peter said. "What's next, Siti?"

"Let's finish setting up." I looked at Marise. "What's the purpose of those crates? Lawrence said everything we received was important."

Marise held out her hand. It had been drizzling since we landed. Our uniforms shed the water effectively, but some of it still managed to run down our necks. My feet were cold and damp, and my hair was soaked. I wanted nothing more than to take off my wet clothing and sleep, but there was work to be done.

"We can use them to collect water." Marise tipped her hand and watched the water drip off it. "Then we won't have to go back to the stream to refill our water bottles."

"Sounds smart. Although it might've been smarter to put them on top before we finished unfolding." I tipped my head back and aimed my light at the roof. "How are we going to get them up there?"

"Aneh is tiny." Joss laced his fingers together and held them out to form a step. "It'll hold her weight, right? I'll boost her up."

Aneh turned to look at us, the whites of her eyes shining in the lamplight.

Marise nodded. "It's built to hold these crates full of water. They mass way more than she does."

Aneh nodded. "Let's do this." She stepped into his hand, balancing against the side of the cube.

"Three. Two. One. Go." Joss heaved.

Aneh flew upward, throwing the top half of her body onto the flat roof of the mod. She rolled and pushed, disappearing from view. "I'm up!"

We passed the crates up to her. "There are little grooves in the roof. These crates snap right into them. Ingenious." She finished installing the crates then shimmied over the side. Joss caught her and lowered her to the ground.

"I wonder if there's some way to pipe the water down?" Franklin tilted his head. "That's what I would do."

"We'll only be here a week, tops," I said. "If we have time tomorrow, we can work on upgrades to the camp. For now, let's get that guard rotation set and get some sleep."

"Got it," Joss said. "It's 2 AM. Marise and I will take the first shift. We'll wake Rendi and Yvonne at four."

"Sunrise is at six, so we'll all want to be up by then." I held my fist out to Joss. "Nice work. Everyone else, hit the rack."

It took a few minutes of squabbling to get everyone settled. I had to separate Abdul and Franklin, like a couple of children. "If I hear another peep out of anyone, you'll sleep outside," I said finally.

The others cheered. Within minutes, I heard snores.

I woke briefly when the guard changed. "Anything?" I whispered.

"Nothing," Marise said. "Go back to sleep."

POUNDING ECHOED THROUGH THE ROOM. "Wake up, sleepyheads!" a voice called out. It took me a second to remember where we were.

"I'm going to kill him," Marise muttered.

I flicked my holo-ring to check the time. "Crap." No holo-rings. "Let's get moving, everyone. We need to find Charlie Orange today."

I stumbled out of the living mod, rubbing my eyes. They felt like someone had dumped sand in them. Dim light filtered into the clearing. The sun must be rising, but it wasn't visible through the trees. Someone had pulled out a tiny stove and was heating some water.

"Where did that come from?" I asked. It hadn't been in the crates.

Peter held up his hand. "One of my flight-mates helped me make it. I thought it might come in handy."

"One of your flight-mates?" Marise asked sharply. "Delta Black? Maybe it's a trick. Could they be using it to track us?"

"With what?" Peter asked. "Besides, I was part of Delta Black when I made it. They'd have no reason to sabotage me. Then."

Marise didn't relax. "I wouldn't put it past those legacies to sabotage a teammate."

"Chymm, can you take a look at it?" I asked. "Is there any way it could be damaging us?"

Chymm circled around the small stove. He took the bottle of water off and set it aside. After turning off the flame, he lifted it carefully and examined it from all sides. Then he set it down and gestured for Peter to relight it. "No electronics in there. I don't see how they could be tracking it unless they have some kind of heat sensor. And even then, they'd have to be close enough to distinguish it from a person or an animal."

"Awesome." I gestured. "Those red stew pacs taste a lot better when they're hot."

While we ate breakfast, we discussed our options.

"I think we should leave someone here to stand guard," Marise suggested.

"I thought you hid our tracks?" Rendi asked.

"We did." Joss sat up straight and narrowed his eyes at Rendi. "You saying we did shoddy work?"

Rendi held up his hands. "No. I'm just wondering why we need a guard if no one can find us."

"Because nothing is for sure." Joss relaxed and took another bite of his stew. "I agree with Marise."

I nodded. "We'll leave two people here. But we should take some of this stuff with us. Lawrence said every item was vital to the mission. I think we should have it with us when we find out what that mission is."

"Maybe we should figure out what you can do with this stuff," Franklin suggested. "I mean, we know what to do with the crates. And the lights and the water bottles were obvious. What's the rope and the wire and the magnets for?"

"And don't forget the flare gun and the knives." Joss tapped the weapon strapped to his belt.

"If Chymm hadn't had a compass, could we have made one with any of that stuff?" Yvonne asked.

Chymm nodded. He swallowed and choked on the stew. Abdul leaned over to pound him on the back. When he could speak again, Chymm said, "Yes. Super easy with the wire and magnet. Plus a bowl—or crate—of water."

"Then we don't need to take any of this stuff." Franklin shoveled more Chewy Nuggets into his mouth.

"It's not heavy, and it could be useful. I say we take the wire and rope." I pointed at Franklin. "How's your leg?"

Franklin started then reached down and rubbed at his boot. "It's still sore."

"Then you can stay here. Who wants to stay with him?" No one responded. I chuckled. "Don't all volunteer at once!"

When we finished eating, we reloaded our bags. Peter lifted the camp stove. "It's not heavy, but I don't know if there's any point in carrying it. If we can secure the mod, I'll leave it here."

"Good call," I said. "Let's leave half the meal pacs, too. Anyone else have nonessentials they brought with them?" I watched in surprise as Marise, Yvonne, and Aneh rose and deposited items inside the living module.

"Who's staying with Franklin?" Yvonne asked.

Abdul held up a hand.

I shook my head. "After the way you two squabbled last night? I think we need to leave an adult here. Any other volunteers?"

Aneh raised her hand slowly. "Only because I'm probably the least useful."

"I wouldn't say that," Joss said. "You've been useful several times." He made a lifting motion.

Aneh laughed.

"Perfect. Aneh and Franklin will stay here. We'll leave the flare gun with you. Fire it if you have any problems." I motioned for Marise to hand it over.

"Do you think we'll have problems?" Aneh asked.

"Better safe than sorry," Marise said. "Would you feel better if you had a knife?"

Aneh shook her head violently and held up empty hands. "No!"

"Point us in the right direction, Chymm." I made the circling motion Lawrence and Mason had used.

We returned to the trail we'd been following. It was wider here and well packed. We followed the path for a ways, then turned off onto a narrower track. Yesterday's rain had stopped, but it was still damp and warm. Before long, we had removed our jackets, tucking them into packs or tying them around our waists.

We stopped every hour for a short rest. We didn't have a clock, but Joss estimated the time based on the location of the sun. It wasn't very accurate, since the cloud cover hadn't burned off. After about three hours, Joss flung up a hand. We stopped.

"Someone's coming. Should we hide?" Joss asked.

"Why?" I'd been thinking about this as we walked. We were assuming the other flights were enemies. And I guess, in a way, they were since we were competing. But Lawrence hadn't told us to avoid them. We'd made that decision based on our feelings about Felicity and Delta Black.

Whoever was coming couldn't be Delta Black. They were coming from the wrong direction. "What are they going to do to us? We're explorers, not soldiers dropped behind enemy lines. Besides, they're watching us from mission control. No one is going to do anything dangerous."

"What if the mission is to capture another flight?" Rendi asked. "And whoever this is has already got their mission briefing?"

"Why would our mission be to capture people?" I pointed at the patch on my shoulder. "Explorer Corps. Our mission will be to find something. Or watch something. Let's see who it is."

We strung out along the trail. I slid past Rendi and Yvonne and grabbed Chymm's arm. "You should put that away, though. We don't want to risk losing it." I pointed at his compass.

Chymm nodded and shoved the box into his pocket.

"Who's there?" I called out. "This is Charlie Blue."

"Hey, we've been looking for you." A pair of cadets with Charlie

Orange patches on their shoulders stepped out from behind a huge, moss covered tree.

"To ambush us?" Rendi asked.

The two looked at each other and laughed nervously. "Not you," the taller one said. "But anyone else... yeah, maybe."

"Have you seen any others?" I asked. "Did anyone try anything?"

"Not yet. You're the first we've run into. But you know the other squadrons wouldn't hesitate to take us out," the shorter one said. "I'm Zhou. That's Mel."

"Take you out how?" When they didn't answer, I went on. "Where's the rest of your flight?"

"We split up," Mel said. "We figured we'd find you faster that way."

"Yeah, we've been looking all night." Zhou covered a yawn.

"You didn't set up a camp?" Peter asked.

"We left our stuff where they dropped us. With a guard of course." Mel jerked her head in the direction from which they'd come. "Do you have your command key with you?"

We all nodded.

"Perfect," Mel said. "Let's get back to the base, so we can find out what the mission is."

We followed Mel and Zhou into the forest. They'd used a knife to hack a trail through the brambles and underbrush.

"Why didn't you follow a game trail?" Peter asked.

"We decided a straight line would be better. That way, we'd be able to find our way back."

"You can't have traveled very far doing that," Marise said.

"Far enough to find you," Mel replied.

"I guess so," I said. It was a good thing each flight was to be judged individually. These guys didn't seem too bright.

It took another hour to get back to their drop point. Their white living mod sat in the center of a small, stony clearing, still folded for shipment. Three cadets sat atop it, but they jumped down when they saw us approach.

One of them pointed the flare gun at us.

"Hey, we're friends." Joss tapped his shoulder patch.

Zhou and Mel nodded. "They're Charlie Blue. They have the mission brief."

"Awesome!" the smallest cadet crowed. He opened one of the crates beside the mod and pulled out a command key with an orange stripe along the side. "Give me yours."

I stepped forward, clutching ours. "We need to touch them to activate."

The little guy made a gimme motion again.

I narrowed my eyes at him. "I'm not giving this to you. Hold it out, and we can touch them."

He gave me a sulky glare and held out his box. I touched our blue one against it, and they clicked together. The screen on the side lit up, half blue and half orange. Words scrolled across it.

"Congratulations. You have achieved the first part of your mission. To complete this exercise, you must set up a camp that meets the following specifications." The message continued to scroll, telling us to set up our living module in a safe location with a clean water supply, schedule a guard rotation, and conceal the path to the drop zone.

"That's all?" Marise asked in surprise. "But we've done all that. Lawrence said it was a capture the flag game."

I shrugged. "She also said it might be different."

My holo-ring vibrated, so I flicked it. Lawrence's voice came through my audio implant. "Mission complete. Good job. Pack up your supplies and return to your drop location. Leave no trace. Lawrence out." My implant went dead.

Mel looked at us in shock. "Why did your ring activate? This is a no holo-ring zone! Are you cheating?"

I glanced at my team. "We've been recalled. We need to go." I pulled on my command key, and it snapped away from their device.

"You've been recalled?" Zhou repeated. Then he laughed. "You have to forfeit! Get lost, losers. Come on, Big Orange! Let's get to work."

"We need to hurry," Yvonne whispered. "It will take us a while to get back to the drop zone. They could get their camp set up and be done before we get there. And they're already at their drop spot."

I made "let's go" motions, urging the team back the way we'd come. We walked quickly, checking over our shoulders to make sure we weren't being followed. But why would they follow us? They knew the mission and that we would be of no use to them.

Once we were out of sight, we broke into a jog. "Good thing Franklin stayed back at the camp," Abdul said. "He would really slow us down."

"I don't think it matters." I slowed to a walk, and the others matched my pace. "Lawrence said 'mission complete.' We're done. This mission was supposed to take up to a week, so I don't think we're in any hurry to get back."

"Then why were we running?" Yvonne asked.

"Good question," Peter said. "I guess we all bought into the idea that this was some kind of cutthroat competition. Like Siti said, we forgot what the Corps' mission is. We're explorers, not combatants. This was never meant to be a duel to the death."

"Stop where you are!" a male voice cried out.

Four cadets armed with long, sharpened spears jumped out of the trees ahead of us. Four more closed in behind.

I looked at Peter. "You were saying?"

CHAPTER EIGHT

MIKE LEBLANC SWAGGERED FORWARD. "You were so easy to follow. Hand it over."

"That was Orange, not us." I stepped forward. "Hand what over?"

"The mission. We know you met up with your sister flight, so you have the mission. We need it."

I shrugged. "It won't do you any good. You can't read the message without the orange command key." I slowly pulled the blue-striped box from my pocket. "See? I only have our half."

He growled in frustration. "What did it say?"

I snorted. "You wouldn't believe me if I told you."

Felicity poked her pointed stake in my direction. "Tell us what it said."

"Or what?" Marise stepped forward. "You'll poke us with your pointy stick?"

"I might." Felicity waved the stake and pouted.

"That's a terrible idea." Peter turned to look at the cadets behind us. "Fendel. Riviera. Do you really think threatening us is a good plan?"

"Shut up." LeBlanc now stood beside Felicity, holding a pair of knives. Lee joined them, also wielding one. "If we wanted the help of a Neanderthal, we would've asked."

"Where'd you get that?" I pointed at LeBlanc's knife. "There were only two in the supplies. Why do you have three?"

"We have four." Lee jerked his chin, his eyes focused behind me.

I looked over my shoulder. One of the cadets behind us also carried a knife. "Who did you take those from?"

"I told you she wasn't too stupid." Felicity nudged LeBlanc. "We relieved Bravo Purple of their supplies. Now we're taking yours."

"That's not what this is about." I shook my head. "Stealing supplies from other teams isn't how you win."

"Says you." LeBlanc waved his knife at us. "Hand over your stuff."

Would they do anything? Lee and LeBlanc looked like they might try. The other five seemed nervous, as if they'd been swept up in something that had gotten out of hand. I turned to them. "You don't have to go along with this."

Bam!

Pain exploded in the back of my head. I staggered, grabbing Marise to keep from hitting the ground. LeBlanc switched his knife to his left hand and shook his right. "Shut up and give us your stuff, or I'll do it again."

Static filled my head, but anger warmed my chest. Who the heck did these black holes think they were? "What the hell? Are you idiots? You won't get away with attacking another cadet."

LeBlanc laughed. "You think not? It's your word against ours."

I stared at him. "They said we're being watched. There must be drones all over these woods." I could probably hear them if my head wasn't buzzing.

Lee and Felicity looked around wildly, their eyes wide. "I don't want to hurt anyone," Lee muttered.

LeBlanc glared at him.

I leaned forward. "If you think you'll get away with this, you're as crazy as you look!"

LeBlanc lunged. Joss flew in front of me, blocking LeBlanc's swing with his own knife. The two of them grappled, the knife blades clanging. Someone screamed.

"Stop!" Peter surged forward and grabbed Joss by the shoulders. Rendi came with him, shoving LeBlanc away. "Give them what they want. It won't make a difference."

"He's right," Marise whispered as she tried to pull the backpack from my shoulders. "We've already won, remember? This won't help them at all."

"But what if it's a trick?" I hissed back at her. "I wouldn't put it past them. Tell us we finished when there's more to do. This was supposed to take a week. How do you know we won't get back to camp and find out we have to wait out the week?"

"We left supplies in camp." Marise kept her voice low as she shrugged off her own pack. "Aneh and Joss can trap game. We have the water collection system. We have what we need to survive a week." She tossed the bag to the ground.

"Fine." Anger seethed through my veins, but she was right. We didn't want anyone to get hurt. I rubbed my throbbing head. Anyone *else*. I slid my backpack off my shoulders without turning to look at the others. "Give them your bags. How are you going to carry all that stuff?"

"Riviera. Juarez," LeBlanc barked. "Go through their stuff. Take anything that's useful."

Two of the cadets moved forward and started digging through our bags. They took our meal pacs, the rope and wire, and the knives. One of the boys held up our command key. "What about this?"

"Siti was right. That's useless to us. Unless you want to go after Orange, and even then, who knows if it would work again?" LeBlanc lounged against a tree, swinging his knife back and forth. It swished through the air, the sound chilling. "Get that stuff loaded in your bags so we can go. We still need to find White."

The two boys shoved the meal pacs into their own bags. "I can't carry anymore," the shorter one said. "My bag is full."

"What about your pockets?" LeBlanc snapped.

The short boy waved at his bulging jacket. "I'm fully loaded. Look at me."

"Fine." LeBlanc stomped forward. "Give me those. Felicity. Lee. Take some of these."

"I have all I can carry," Felicity said. She leaned down and lifted the small pink purse by her feet.

"That's a pretty little bag, Felicity," I said.

She glared at me. "It cost more credits than your entire wardrobe. Fendel, take Siti's backpack. You can wear it on the front to carry more food."

I kicked it down the path. "Be my guest. It's worthless to me since it's empty."

"Let's get this done. We still have to complete the mission." LeBlanc picked up my backpack and threw it at the boy holding the meal pacs. He turned and glared at me. "Get out of here. Before I change my mind about using this knife."

I made eye contact with Marise and Joss. "Let's go, Charlie Blue." I pushed past Felicity, knocking into her shoulder. Hard.

"Watch it, unlegacy," she growled. She grabbed my forearm and pulled me close to whisper in my ear, "Micah and Derek are dangerous. You don't want to mess with them." She squeezed, hard.

I yanked my arm away and nudged Rendi. "Get moving. Back to camp. I'm right behind you." I waited until the rest of the flight filed past. Joss and Marise closed in around me, and the three of us backed out of the clearing. "Good luck!" I called over my shoulder as we ducked into the woods.

When we were out of sight, I stopped. "Joss, watch our six. Make sure they aren't following us. If we have to stay the rest of the week, we want a secure base."

"You got it, boss."

I turned to Marise. "Stay with him. Nobody travels alone until we're away from here."

"We might not want to travel alone after that, either," Joss said.

"What d'you mean?" I asked.

"Those three are not used to being crossed. Leblanc is vindictive to boot. We need to watch our backs when we return to campus."

"This should get them expelled," I said.

The other two snorted.

"You don't know how this works, do you?" Marise said. "They're legacies. Untouchable."

"They assaulted another cadet." I rubbed the back of my head. "They stole from us. Are you telling me the administration will look the other way?"

Joss and Marise exchanged a look. "I guess we'll find out when we get back," the girl said.

"So, let's get back, then. The sooner the better." I bumped fists with the other two. "Watch out for them. I'll see you at the camp."

"Pack it all up!" I yelled as soon as we reached the camp.

Aneh jumped to her feet in alarm. "What's going on?"

"Didn't you get the message? We're done. Let's get packed up. Where's Franklin?" I shrugged off Aneh's hand and hurried toward the mod.

"He's inside. He was falling asleep, so I told him to take a nap."

I banged on the outside of the cube. "Get up! Time to go." I slipped my hand on the access panel, and the door unlocked. "This thing is coming down in five seconds."

Franklin sat up, rubbing his eyes. I strode across the tiny room and grabbed his arm. "Let's go. We need to get out of here as fast as we can." I gathered up things we'd stored inside and carried them out. Aneh was already on top of the mod, pulling down the water crates. She filled the empty water bottles with the rainwater collected in the first crate, then tossed the rest to the ground.

We folded up the cube and activated the grav lifters. Chymm opened the panel to check the charge. "I hope this is enough to get us back to the drop zone. We only had a few hours of sunlight to recharge."

"We'll take it as far as we can." I grimaced. "They took the rope, so we'll have to push it by hand."

"I made some more." Aneh held up a circle of something.

"You *made* rope?" Rendi asked. "How do you make rope?"

"This is a swamp." Aneh unrolled the rough material. It was only about three meters, but it would be enough to tie the cube to someone's belt. "I cut some grass and twisted it into rope while I was waiting for you."

"Where'd you learn to do that?" Yvonne asked. "Will you teach the rest of us? It seems like a valuable skill."

Aneh blushed. "My rural upbringing comes in handy."

We met Joss and Marise on the trail. "They didn't follow us," Joss said. "If they had, I'm sure they would've tried something by now. But they want to find the other half of their squadron, so they need to move."

I shook my head then winced when pain stabbed through my brain. "What a waste of time for everyone."

CHAPTER NINE

THE TRANSPORT DESCENDED to the drop zone. "Good job, Charlie Blue," Mason said as he rode the ramp to the ground. "Where's your living module?"

I jerked my head. "It's about half a click that way. We left Franklin, Abdul, and Joss to guard. It ran out of juice."

"You aren't going to make us carry it here, are you?" Yvonne asked.

"Why would we do that?" Mason asked. "You completed the mission. It's our responsibility to pick you up."

"But Wronglen said leave no trace," I said. "Leaving the mod would be a trace."

Mason cracked a smile. "It would be, but there are extenuating circumstances." His smile faded as he handed me a grav lifter. "You know how to use this?"

I nodded and hurried into the woods. When I reached the three boys, they had wrestled the cube a little closer to the drop zone. "This will make it easier. I thought you were going to wait there."

"We got bored," Joss said. He'd probably done most of the lifting, since Franklin still had a bum leg, and Abdul was wiry rather than muscular.

I connected the grav lifter to the mod, plugging it into the panel on the side. "These are set up to daisy chain." I flipped the switch, and the cube lifted off the ground. "Let's get it back to the transport."

We pulled the mod back to the clearing, Franklin limping in our wake. When we reached the transport, the boys pushed it up the ramp and latched it into place. Then we all climbed in and sagged into our seats.

The transport landed in the quad. Mason led us to the medical clinic to get checked out. "When they release you, you can head to the chow hall. Then return to your quarters. We'll have a hot wash tomorrow at nine. Don't talk to anyone outside the flight until then." He nodded, making eye contact with each of us. "Good job."

After he left, Aneh raised a hand. "What's a hot wash?"

"It's when we talk about what happened and what we should have done better." Yvonne rubbed her eyes. "I know you guys are tired, but it would be a good idea to record your thoughts before bed. You don't want to forget anything important tomorrow."

The medical team split us up, putting us through the med pods in shifts. "Even if you feel fine, we need to check you out," a medic told us. "Consider it part of the exercise." Nobody argued.

I SAT in the chow hall, poking at my food. We'd had plenty to eat during the exercise, so I wasn't really hungry.

Joss and Peter sat down across the table from me.

"Do you guys do everything together?" I asked sourly.

"No," Peter said.

"Yes," Joss said at the same time with a laugh.

I smiled weakly. "I'm so tired, I can't eat. Which is stupid—that wasn't a very long mission."

"You took a pretty good blow to the head," Peter said.

"The med pod fixed that," I said. "Why can't they fix tired, too?"

"I don't think that's how they work." Joss shoveled some food into his mouth and spoke around it. "Even if they fix your body, it still needs rest. And fuel."

Peter scowled at Joss. "I know your mother taught you not to talk with your mouth full."

"She's not here."

Peter rolled his eyes then turned back to me. "That was a pretty stressful twenty hours. And we barely slept. We should be tired."

"What are we going to tell them about Delta Black?" Aneh asked as she put her tray on the table beside me and sat.

"We'll tell them the truth," I said. "They said they were watching us. If that's true, they saw everything that happened."

"Do you think they were watching everything?" Aneh asked. "How would they do that?"

"Siti's dad's team had some pretty amazing drones," Joss said. "They were tiny and almost silent. Those woods could be full of them."

"I think it depends on who's on the briefing team," Peter said slowly. "If Felicity is to be believed, her mom and the commandant are very close. Is telling her staff that Felicity is a psychopath a good choice?"

"LeBlanc is the real psychopath," Joss said. "I can't believe he made it through the psych eval."

"Maybe he didn't have to take one," I said. "I didn't."

All three heads snapped in my direction. "You didn't?" Aneh asked. "It was a big deal when I applied. Three days of evaluations."

The boys nodded in agreement.

"Really?" They did treat the legacies differently. They ate in silence while I pushed the food around my plate. "I still think we tell the truth. That way, we don't have to come up with a story. You know Rendi or Abdul would just get it wrong." I snickered.

The others joined in.

When Joss had finally finished the mountainous pile of food on his tray, I pushed back my chair. "Are we agreed then? We'll tell them the truth."

"Deal." Peter raised his water glass. We all clinked our glasses.

The hot wash took hours. We met Wronglen, Lawrence, and Mason in the squadron ready room.

"The Academy leadership will review my report." Wronglen took a seat and leaned back, putting his feet on the table. "They'll look at this recording, if they feel it's warranted."

I summarized the events of the exercise for Wronglen, Lawrence, and Mason. The others in the flight chimed in when necessary. I tried to keep my narrative factual, but my voice cracked with anger as I got to the point where Delta Black attacked us. "I thought LeBlanc might hurt someone with that knife. The others seem to be using them as props, but he looked dangerous." I rubbed the back of my head where he had hit me.

"Were you watching?" Aneh asked.

The three older cadets exchanged a look but said nothing.

"Were you?" Yvonne pinned Mason with a stare. "You said you'd be watching."

Mason gave a short, jerky nod. "I saw part of the altercation. The vid was fuzzy. And from what I could tell, Joss also had a knife."

"Wait a minute!" I jumped to my feet. "LeBlanc struck me with his knife hilt. And then he came at me. Joss protected me. You can't blame him for that."

Wronglen held up a hand. "I didn't see what happened, but your version of the events will be recorded in my report."

"You didn't see what happened?" I growled through clenched teeth. "Mason—"

"Cadet Mason," Wronglen snapped.

My nostrils flared. "Cadet Mason," I repeated, enunciating each syllable carefully, "saw what happened. Why didn't you?"

"If Cadet Mason saw it," Peter said, "it must've been recorded."

Every head in the room swung toward him. "That's right!" Marise, Yvonne, and Chymm said together.

The senior cadets exchanged another look.

"What?" I snapped.

"I told you, the vid was fuzzy. And the recordings—*some* of the recordings—were damaged." Mason looked at a spot behind me as he spoke.

"Really? Damaged, you say." I crossed my arms and leaned back in my seat.

Mason nodded, still not looking at me.

"I assume the part that was damaged included the altercation between us and Delta Black?" I raised my eyebrows.

Mason nodded again.

"It wasn't our fault," Wronglen said. "I mean, I wasn't there when it happened, but I'm sure it wasn't Lawrence's or Mason's fault. Some kind of equipment malfunction."

"Where were *you*?" I asked, pausing before adding, "Sir?"

"That's none of your business, cadet." Wronglen's feet flew off the desk as he sat up. "I have better things to do than watch you all the time."

"No, you don't." I surged to my feet. "Your job during this exercise was to watch us. Sir."

"You have no idea what my responsibilities are." Wronglen jumped up. "You've just come off a successful mission and were injured, so I will ignore your insubordination. I've heard enough."

"We haven't finished telling you—" I started, but he cut me off.

"I've heard enough to write my report." He stopped at the door. "If you have more to say, tell it to Lawrence. She can put it in hers."

Lawrence waited until the door shut, then she turned to me. "You won't get anywhere with him. He's a legacy, too, but no one in his family ranks high enough for that to mean much. He's fanatically loyal to the Corps and has transferred some of that loyalty to the idea of legacies."

"It's like a cult," I said.

"Sometimes," Lawrence agreed. "I will include what little Mason and I saw—and your report. I can't guarantee that will get past him, though."

"Isn't there any external oversight?" Peter asked. "Someone who can investigate this kind of thing? Not only the attack but why the vid was damaged?"

Lawrence shook her head. "You could try internal affairs, but I'm not sure you'd get very far."

Yvonne put a hand on my arm. When I looked in her direction, she shook her head slightly.

"Can we finish this hot wash? I'm getting tired." I rubbed my head again.

Lawrence nodded, and I finished giving my report.

Lawrence and Mason asked questions—a lot of questions. "We'd like each of you to record an individual statement, too," she said. "I don't know if anyone will ever see it, but in case we need it."

WHEN WE FINALLY FINISHED, we went to lunch. Two other teams had returned, but they were in medical, so we had the chow hall to ourselves. We grabbed our food and sat at a table near the wall.

"What are we going to do?" Joss asked.

I shrugged. "What can we do?"

"What about this internal affairs thing?" Franklin suggested.

Yvonne shook her head. "No. They're supposed to be independent and impartial, but the chief of the academy's internal affairs—Commander Hughes—is the commandant's best friend. They've known each other since they were cadets and spend a lot of time off-duty together."

"I thought Felicity's mom was the commandant's best friend," I said.

"Actually, the three of them were very close in their cadet days." Yvonne looked nervously around the room then shoved a cookie in her mouth.

"How do you know?" Marise asked.

Yvonne swallowed and looked around again. She leaned forward and lowered her voice. "My dad warned me before I came. He said if you can't run a problem up the chain, internal affairs is *not* a good choice."

"Are you saying he anticipated you would have a problem?" I asked.

"No. Maybe. I think he wanted me to be prepared for anything."

"Maybe we should talk to whoever runs the surveillance equipment," Peter suggested. "Joss and I used to do a bit of that back in the Dome. I'm not saying we could *do* anything, but we should be able to understand what they're talking about."

I looked around the table. They were all focused on me, waiting to hear what I wanted them to do. I swallowed the butterflies in my throat, and they made a home in my stomach. I wasn't used to being in charge or responsible, and the idea that I might make the wrong decision and get us all in trouble terrified me. I took a deep breath.

I tapped my fork on the plate, trying to order my thoughts. Peter reached over and grabbed my hand, stopping the clinking. My lips twisted. "Let's not do anything that could get us expelled. Peter and Joss, why don't you see if you can find out who runs that equipment? If you do, talk to them. Don't *do* anything, just ask questions."

I turned to Yvonne. "Can you contact your dad? We're allowed local calls this weekend. Ask him for any suggestions."

She nodded.

I looked at the rest of them. "Any other thoughts on what to do?"

"Maybe you should talk to *your* dad, Siti," Marise suggested. "He's the most likely to be able to help us."

"I don't know if I can reach him," I said. "I'll try, but he's not local."

"If he's still on Earth, I can have my dad talk to him," Joss said. "He might be able to arrange a call for you."

"I guess we need to decide if this is what we want to spend our 'get out of jail free card' on." I winked at Peter. This was a phrase he had used in the past. It referenced an old game they used to play on Earth. "Not that he wouldn't help me more than once but getting Zane to set up a call should be a last resort. Is this urgent enough to warrant an interstellar conversation? Joss and Peter only get one per quarter. Maybe I should send a regular message to Dad."

"There's something you haven't considered." Chymm fiddled with his napkin. "If someone was able to get an exercise recording deleted or damaged, don't you think they'll have hooks into the comm system?"

We all stared at him.

Chymm squirmed. "It's what I would do. But maybe they haven't."

"No, you're probably right," Peter said. "We need to think this through. Is talking to our parents a bigger risk than saying nothing?" He made eye contact with Joss for a second. "We have a little experience with this level of control, and fighting it requires a lot of care."

Joss nodded. "Pete's right." He looked around the room. "We should also operate under the assumption that we're always being monitored."

"We are screwed, then," Marise said. She picked up her sandwich. "May as well finish our last meal."

CHAPTER TEN

As we exited the chow hall, Cadet Wronglen met us. "You have fifteen minutes to get cleaned up and report to the commandant's office. Dress uniforms." The grim look on his face made the butterflies in my stomach go into nuclear mode.

Ten minutes later, we met in the hall, dressed in our formal white uniforms. "Is everyone here?" I asked as I counted noses. If we had time, we'd check each other over to make sure everyone was squared away, but it would take five minutes to get across campus. "Let's go."

We hurried down the stairs and across the quad. On the far side, we entered the administration building and took the steps to the second floor. This building was built in the same architectural style as the rest of the Academy—tall ceilings, wide doorways with arches, highly polished stone floors. Our shoes clattered on the shiny tiles as we hurried into the commandant's lobby.

A thin man with gray hair sat at a desk on the far side of the wide room. He looked up as we entered but didn't acknowledge us.

Franklin threw himself down in a chair.

"Get up," Marise growled at him. "Cadets don't sit down."

Franklin huffed but stood.

We waited what felt like hours. The old-fashioned clock on the mantelpiece above the equally old-fashioned fireplace ticked loudly. The thin man's fingers swiped through screens on his holo. I turned my eyes away, not wanting him to think I was snooping. We stood in a loose formation, trying not to squirm.

I checked over everyone's uniform without being obvious. Chymm's insignia was crooked, and Joss had a scuff on his shoe. If we weren't in the commandant's waiting room, I'd fix both, but the old man made me nervous. I tried to get both boys' attention, but they didn't look my way.

Finally, the thin man looked up. "You can go in now."

The inner office was as large as the lobby. A comfortable-looking seating area filled one end, with a wide, empty space between that and the huge desk at the far side. Two walls with high arched windows looked out onto the quad. The windows must have had some kind of coating because the sunlight did not come in, but we were able to see out clearly. We took up positions in the empty middle, standing at attention.

Admiral Zimas stood behind her desk, smiling. That was unexpected.

I stepped forward and saluted the admiral. "Charlie Blue, reporting as ordered, sir."

"At ease," she said. "I want to congratulate you on your victory. You completed that exercise faster than any team in the history of the Academy. It's unfortunate we had a data error—I would have liked to have reviewed the vids."

I bit my lip, unsure what to say.

Franklin had no such doubts. "We can tell you what happened. The legacies in Delta Black attacked us." Marise kicked his leg, and he added, "Sir."

Zimas strolled up to Franklin, standing nose-to-nose with him. She looked him up and down then adjusted the rank pin on his collar. "Do you have any evidence to support this outrageous accusation, cadet?"

Franklin gulped and said nothing. Unfortunately, Rendi decided to help out. "If the vids hadn't crapped out, we would." His voice cracked.

"Making unsupported accusations is a bad idea." Zimas's calm voice sent shivers down my spine. "It's not a habit we like to see cadets develop." She took a step back and surveyed us all. "Attention!"

We snapped to attention. She walked between us, examining each cadet in detail. As she went, she muttered notes under her breath—probably reporting demerits to the tracking system. When she finished, she returned to her desk and sat. "There will be no further discussion of this topic. You are dismissed."

"But we won!" Rendi protested.

Joss grabbed his arm and dragged him out the door, the rest of us in their wake. The thin man watched us leave but didn't speak. We continued out the door and down the stairs. As I started across the quad, Franklin called out, "Sorry."

Ignoring him, I kept going. When we reached the white tiles in front of our dorm, I stopped and turned. "Remember what we said about being careful?"

Franklin hung his head. "I know, but it seemed like a golden opportunity."

"Well, at least we know where she stands." Peter clapped Franklin on the shoulder. "I hope it didn't cost more than it was worth."

"What do you mean?" Rendi asked.

"You know we just racked up a pile of new demerits," Joss said. "So much for our inspection-free week."

"They can't take that away!" Rendi said.

The rest of us laughed bitterly.

"They can do whatever they want," Peter said. "It's their game. Their rules." He scratched his head and looked at Joss. "I can't believe we signed up for this."

Joss raised an eyebrow. "Idealistic idiots, aren't we? If I'd known it was going to go down this way..."

"You aren't thinking of leaving, are you?" I asked, alarmed. Peter and Joss were my closest friends here. Aside from Aneh, of course. But I'd known the boys longer.

"It will take more than that to chase me away," Peter said. "I told you, this is the dream."

"Let's get out of these straitjackets," Chymm said. "Then I suggest we play a game of ultimate rev-ball."

"I'm not in the mood," Yvonne said.

Chymm gave me a meaningful look. If pudgy, lazy tech-head Chymm wanted to play rev-ball, there was a reason.

"Excellent suggestion," I said. "We'll play rev-ball. Get our feelings out on the field. All of us." I didn't wait for discussion but headed into the dorm.

Aneh followed me into our room. "I don't feel like playing, either."

I pulled off my jacket and hung it on a hanger. As I turned away from the closet, I caught Aneh's eye and tapped my ear. I slid my fingers into my hair and pulled off my ponytail holder, hoping anyone watching hadn't seen the tap.

Aneh's eyes went wide, and she nodded. "I guess it would be better than moping here, though."

We pulled on our sports gear and met the others in the hall.

"Everyone ready?" Joss tossed a rev-ball from hand to hand.

"Franklin and Rendi aren't here." Aneh pounded on their door. "You guys coming?"

The door opened, and Rendi peered out, his eyes wide.

"Are you coming?" Aneh asked again.

Rendi shook his head. He mumbled something.

"What?" Aneh asked.

Rendi cleared his throat. "We're being sent home."

CHAPTER ELEVEN

FRANKLIN STOOD in the doorway behind Rendi. "You'd better go before you get in trouble too. Our orders say we're not to talk to you."

Aneh threw her arms around Rendi. "It's not fair."

Chymm put a hand on her shoulder. "We should go. They aren't supposed to talk to us." His words were hard and clipped, and his face was white.

"Chymm's right," I said. "We should go. I'm sorry, Franklin. Rendi. I wish there was something we could do."

Franklin shook his head. "It's not your fault. Good luck."

I bumped knuckles with each of them and walked away, blinking back tears of rage. How could they expel a cadet simply for telling the truth? And there was nothing I could do about it! A call to my dad would be monitored. Then I'd be out the door, just like Franklin and Rendi.

On the other hand, I was a legacy, too. Surely, they couldn't kick me out as easily? My dad would demand to know why. Maybe I could use that to help the others.

When we reached the athletic fields, Chymm kept walking. Usually, we used the closest available field, but he took us to the far side, where the last field butted up against the fence surrounding the campus. When we arrived, he shrugged off the jacket he'd thrown over his T-shirt and pulled something out of the pocket.

As he hunched over whatever it was, I called the group closer. "Everyone in!"

"Why are we huddling?" Abdul asked. "There isn't another team."

I shrugged and pushed out a fake laugh. "I'm chilly and I didn't bring a jacket. You all can keep me warm."

Joss's eyes narrowed.

Marise blinked, then her face went blank. "It *is* a bit cooler than usual." She rubbed her arms.

"It's like room temperature out here," Abdul said.

Marise stomped on his toes. His mouth opened, and she stomped again. His teeth clacked together.

We stood in an awkward huddle for a few moments, then Chymm said, "Done."

"What did you do?" Peter asked.

"It's a scrambler." He held out the device he'd pulled from his pocket. "It should scramble the audio and vid from this corner of the field. If we're being monitored, it will look like another 'outage.' I hope."

"What do you mean, you hope?" I asked.

"I haven't tested this device against the Academy's systems." He set the box on a bench. "How could I? I don't have access to their surveillance. But this design has worked on every system I *have* tested."

"How did you get this into the Academy?" Joss asked. "They searched all our belongings."

"They searched mine, too." Chymm grinned and tapped his temple. "I have the plan up here. I built this in the electronics lab."

"Monkey Man!" Joss held up a hand, as if he were waving.

Chymm knocked his knuckles against it uncertainly. "Monkey Man?"

"Yeah. Chymm sounds kinda like 'chimp' but you're da man. So 'Monkey Man.' It's a term of respect."

We all shook our heads.

"Uh, no thanks," Chymm said.

Marise leaned down to peer at the box. "How did you know we'd need it?"

Chymm pulled her away and draped his jacket over it. "I didn't, but I like to be prepared. I come from an unusual family. My parents are kind of paranoid about government oversight."

"And the CEC let you join?" Peter asked.

Chymm shrugged. "I didn't advertise my parents' hobbies. But I didn't forget everything I've learned, either. As soon as I saw how impervious the legacies seemed to be, I figured I should start building up an inventory of useful devices."

"What else do you have?" I asked.

"We should play." Chymm made a gimme motion at Joss. "Toss me the ball. Someone will probably come out here to see why the system isn't working properly."

Chymm and Joss picked teams, and we started a lackluster game of rev-ball. Before long, our competitive spirits had kicked in, and we played in earnest. After Joss's team made a second goal, I called a time out.

"I need some water." I headed for the benches. The others followed, and we sprawled on the grass near the sideline. "Has anyone checked on us?"

"Someone came to the first field a few minutes ago then left," Aneh said between gasping breaths.

Chymm checked his device. "They sent a drone out, too."

"You can monitor as well as jam?" I asked.

"It's not actually jamming, more like introducing some static. Enough to scramble conversations and vid. They could probably still identify us." He threw the jacket over the device again and scooped up his water bottle.

"What's the difference?" Peter asked.

Chymm began explaining, but I tuned him out. I didn't need to know the details—the basics were enough. "We can't use this too often," I told the others.

"It might be best to leave it out here," Chymm broke off his explanation to suggest. "That way, the issue is limited to this field, and they might not connect it to us."

"Where are you going to hide it?" Joss waved at the field. "That thing is pretty big."

"It's actually two pieces," Chymm said. "I connected them to a single power supply, to save space. The scrambler and its battery are the smaller part. I might be able to stick it under a bench."

"How about putting it outside the fence?" I suggested. "That way, if they find it, it could be someone other than a cadet. Maybe a Gagarian spy." I widened my eyes. Peter and Joss snickered.

Chymm looked at the fence and nodded thoughtfully. "Might be a good plan. Let's play another round. I'm going to wander over that way during the game. Your movements should cover for me."

The game started again, and soon we were playing all out. Running, jumping, and throwing helped me burn out my anger. At some point, Chymm must have hidden the device, but I didn't even notice.

"Time out!" Marise called. "I've had enough."

Others chimed in. I recognized Chymm's voice from behind me, so I agreed. "Fair enough. Let's hit the showers."

WE MET up again in the shower room. Chymm looked at the small box in his hands and tapped his eye then shook his head. He tapped his ear and nodded. No cameras, but audio surveillance was on.

I opened a cubicle and dropped my clean clothes onto the bench. Then I turned on the shower, angling the water away from me. Still fully clothed, I stepped back into the main bathing room. One by one, the others followed my example.

"It looks like five showers is enough to cover our voices." Chymm stared at the small box in his hand. "Six to be safe, and we'll need to talk quietly. We can't do this often unless it's a normal time for all of us to be in here."

"First thing in the morning and after sports it is," Joss whispered. "That should be enough time to plan whatever we need."

"Combined with breaks from rev-ball," Peter reminded him. "As long as they don't discover the box. Will you know if they do?"

Chymm's head waggled side to side. "I'll know when we go out there, but not before. I don't have any remote monitoring. They'd see that signal."

"Let's make this quick. What are we going to do?" Peter asked.

"I can't believe they're already gone," Aneh whispered.

Franklin and Rendi's room had been open and empty when we'd returned from the athletic fields.

"I found this in our room." Abdul held up a scrap of paper. "They must have slid it under the door."

"What does it say?" we asked.

"Charlie Blue. We hate to go. We'll try to push for an investigation from the outside. Best of luck to you."

"I'm not sure that's in our best interests," Peter said. "If they've got someone nosing around, Zimas is likely to double down. More surveillance. More demerits."

We'd each discovered twenty demerits for "uniform violations" awaiting us when we returned from the sports field. Mine included dings for crooked insignia—it wasn't—and unpolished shoes—not a smudge on them. Usually a uniform violation netted one or two demerits at most. Zimas was sending a message.

"Maybe our best plan would be for me to push the envelope," I said. "I'm a legacy. They can't toss me out without good reason. If I ask questions, they can't silence me like they did Franklin and Rendi. My dad's the freaking Hero of Darenti Four—I need to use that."

"No," Aneh cried. "We can't lose you, too." Marise and Chymm nodded.

"That's what I'm saying. They can't toss me out."

"Us, too." Peter swiveled a thumb between himself and Joss. "We're here as part of the treaty. Kind of untouchable, I think."

"Do you?" Joss's brows lowered. "I never got that impression from Lee and LeBlanc. They called me the Neanderthal."

"Yeah, they were jerks. But they're just cadets." Peter pointed at each of us. "Like us. They have no idea what our real status is. It would be a treaty violation to kick us out without egregious evidence."

"Ooh, big words, Professor." Joss laughed.

"Just because you prefer books with pictures..." Peter rubbed the back of his neck. "I read the treaty. I say Siti's right. The three of us should push for answers."

"Right now," Marise said, "we need to finish this conversation. For one thing, we're going to run out of hot water. But also, it would look suspicious if we are in here too long."

"You're right." I pushed open my cubicle door. "So, that's the plan. Joss, Peter, and I will see what we can find out. The rest of you, stay under the radar. Don't say or do *anything* to bring attention to yourselves." I looked at the others. Chymm and Aneh looked scared. Yvonne and Marise seemed resigned. Abdul appeared confused. I jerked my head at Peter and pointed my eyes at Abdul. Peter nodded. He'd talk to Abdul.

CHAPTER TWELVE

THE NEXT MORNING, I went in search of Cadet Wronglen. The cadet leadership office on the first floor of our building was empty. Charlie Orange was still in the field. How could they possibly take this long to set up camp? If I were Wronglen, I'd either switch some of the cadets between Blue and Orange—which I hoped he didn't think of—or do some remedial training with the entire squadron. It appeared we could teach them a few things.

I headed across the quad to the mission control center, located in the basement of the building next to the administration. No one had said it was off limits, and Wronglen hadn't sent us a schedule for the day, so I felt justified in going.

A small sign on the wall next to the main stairs listed the various organizations inside the building. Mission control was on floor -1. I followed the small arrow to a nondescript door under the wide stone steps. There was an access panel next to the door. The door didn't slide open at my approach, so I laid a hand on the panel.

The panel lit up. "Identification," a calm voice said.

"Kassis, Serenity." I rattled off my ID number. "Requesting a meeting with Cadet Wronglen." I crossed my fingers, hoping that wouldn't get me sent away.

"Please wait." The panel went dark.

I took a quick turn around the entry hall, trying to burn off some nervous energy. Despite my bravado in the shower room yesterday, I wasn't sure this would work. Admiral Zimas outranked my father. I was counting on his celebrity status to keep me safe, and I wasn't sure it was enough. He'd been out of the limelight for twenty years while we traveled to Earth. His current status as ambassador to Earth *should* protect me, but I hadn't studied local politics since I returned. Maybe ambassadors weren't important enough. Maybe Earth wasn't considered as big of a prize as it had been before we left. Maybe finding people there had diminished its value.

The door slid open, and Wronglen strode out. "What do you want?"

"Sir." I tried to keep my voice respectful and even. "I'd like to discuss the exercise with you again."

Wronglen crossed his arms and stared down at me.

"I've got to ask, sir, are you related to Petra Wronglen?" This was probably the wrong time to ask this question, but the resemblance was so strong. He wore the exact same disgusted expression she had often directed at me.

His eyes narrowed. "She's my aunt. I don't know her, though. She left when I was a baby. Why do you ask?"

"There's a strong family resemblance." My face heated. "I'm not saying you look like a woman, but you have the same eyes, and…"

His lips twisted in the familiar sneer. "I knew she was on the mission to Earth. I wasn't sure you had met her."

"She did quite well." It was the truth, and maybe praising his relative would put me in his good graces. I certainly wasn't going to tell him she didn't like me. "She was the captain's executive officer by the time we got there. The ship's representative at all of the discussions with the Exodus survivors."

The corners of his lips quirked. "I'd heard she was involved with discussions with the locals, but that was all I knew. What did you want to talk to me about? I'm sure it wasn't my family."

I looked around the empty lobby. "Can we go for a walk?"

"I need to monitor Orange." He jerked his head toward the basement door. "Have you been in the mission control center?"

Where was he going with this? "Yes. Kinda. The only time I've been down there was for the hot wash. We didn't get a tour."

"Come on. I'll show you around." He slapped his hand on the access panel, and the door whooshed open.

I followed him down the steps, my brain spinning in overtime. What was going on? He seemed almost friendly. Completely unlike the cadet commander we'd barely gotten to know over the last couple of weeks.

He led the way in silence. We reached the bottom of the stairs, and he put his hand against another access panel. The door slid open, and I followed him into a hallway.

"That's mission control." He pointed through an open door. Inside the dimly lit room, a group of senior and midyear cadets sat at workstations watching banks of holograms. Wronglen pointed at an empty station, and I moved toward it.

He stepped up behind me and pointed over my shoulder. "This is Charlie Orange's drop zone. They completed their mission, and they're packing up. Normally, their flight commander and sergeant would be monitoring from this workstation, but they're in the transport."

He swiped that screen to the side and flicked some controls. Another hologram appeared.

"Hey, that's us," I said. The view pixilated and resolved as I watched.

"That's the recording. Everything with Charlie Blue is kind of glitchy."

"Everything?" I stared at the screen. "And only Charlie Blue?"

His head shook. "No. Delta Black was also glitchy."

"Can you show me our camp? But in the middle timeframe—while most of us were on our way to Charlie Orange."

"Sure." He slipped past me and sat down. His fingers flicked through a few more control screens. "There you go."

This vid was grainy and fuzzy like the rest. It glitched in and out several times. Was this the same tech Chymm had installed on the rev-ball field? But this seemed to be centered on us, not a location. "What about when we met Delta Black?"

He turned to look at me. "There's nothing to see. But I'll show you." He scrolled through the timeline and pulled up the vid. He was right. Whatever was interfering with the cameras seem to have doubled in intensity with both flights together. The vid was mostly gray static, with an occasional clear shot. Like when Joss lunged to intercept LeBlanc's knife attack.

"Can we have a copy of this?" I asked. "Chymm is pretty handy with technology—he might be able to get some clear frames."

Wronglen looked around the room. Although several of the senior cadets had turned to look when we came in, they didn't seem to be paying us any attention now. He gave me a tiny nod. "Let's go. I'll show you the rest of the facility."

I followed him to the hallway. "This is the break room." He pushed open another door so I could see. There were tables, chairs, and couches. An AutoKitch'n stood on a counter in the corner. "We take meals here during an exercise, so we don't have to leave the facility." He closed the door and continued on. "There are bunks down here, shower rooms, everything you need for a week of surveillance."

He opened the last door and beckoned for me to follow him. The room was dark. He flicked the control and lights came on. Eight bunks lined the walls, stacked four high on each side. Some of them had belongings scattered on top.

"We can talk here." Wronglen sat on the lowest bunk and patted the mattress beside him. "There's no surveillance. I want you to know that I agree with you about the legacies. These specific legacies."

I crossed my arms and leaned my shoulders against the opposite bunk. "You do?" I wasn't going to give him any information in case this was a trick.

"Absolutely. My family has served the Explorer Corps since its beginning." He rubbed his hands on his thighs. "I've always believed that CEC officers were above reproach. I ignored the complaints of my civilian flight mates when I was a plebe and a midyear. But I saw your medical report. You had a serious concussion, and the report said it was caused by blunt force trauma. I suppose you could have slipped and hit your head on a rock or a tree, but the report says the injuries were consistent with being struck with a hard object."

"Why are you telling me this?"

"Will you please sit down?" He patted the mattress again. "There's no surveillance in here, but there's no guarantee someone isn't listening outside the door. This room is not soundproof."

I dropped down beside him.

"Look. I know I've been a jerk. But something strange is going on, something I can't explain away. Last year, I would've kept my mouth shut and let this happen. But I heard the audio."

My heart pounded in my ears. "What audio?" My voice cracked.

"The day LeBlanc threatened Aneh. I heard the three of you. This whole campus is under constant surveillance."

A wash of anger made my voice louder. "Why didn't you do anything?"

He shook his head and put a finger to his lips. "I didn't hear it until this morning. Lawrence sent it to me. I don't know where or when she got it. I started looking for other incidents. There have been several in the Delta Black dorm."

"Why don't you report it?" I had to ask, but I already knew the answer.

His lips tightened. "Because no one will listen. And I'll get expelled. I only have a year to go. Maybe I can fight this when I get out into the real Corps, but I'm not willing to give up my career over it. But you can do something. You're one of them. You are untouchable."

"What can I do?" I wailed. "I want to stop it, but I don't know what to do."

"I would tell you to talk to your father, but I'm sure the calls are monitored."

"Does that matter? They know I'm not happy with the status quo. If I'm untouchable, then hearing what I say to him shouldn't matter. I mean, if I call him and say, 'Hey, Dad, things are going great except legacies are beating people up,' what are they going to do to me?"

"Unless you can afford a direct call to Earth, any message you send will be a recording." Wronglen shook his head. "Do you really think that message would get out?"

"Good point. I guess I need to get Peter and Joss on this."

"The Earth boys? What can they do?"

"Didn't you know?" I smiled. "They get a free call home. It's part of the treaty. And so are they. They're more untouchable than I am."

Wronglen looked skeptical. "The Neanderthals are untouchable?"

"Don't call them that." I jumped up and my hair snagged on the bunk above. "Ow."

"Let me help you." Wronglen stood and leaned over to look at my hair.

"I don't need your help." I yanked hard, leaving a few strands of hair wrapped around a screw. I took a deep breath. Wronglen was risking a lot by talking to me, and I shouldn't throw that away. "Don't call them Neanderthals. They are human beings—just like you and me."

"I'm not sure why they got that nickname," Wronglen said with a self-conscious laugh. "I won't use it again."

"No, just don't use it around me. You don't want anyone to think you're changing sides." I took a few steps away, but the room was tiny. I turned back. "They're called Neanderthals because they were born hundreds of years ago. I'm not sure that's common knowledge, but it's true."

He stared at me, his mouth open.

I giggled. "I probably looked the same when they told me. Peter—Cadet Russell—was in deep sleep for five hundred years. Joss only did two hundred or so." I snickered again. "Only."

"But that's not possible. Human beings can't survive deep sleep for that long."

"That's what Dad said. He was wrong." I watched him silently for a moment. "I probably wasn't supposed to talk about that. I had an out-brief before I left Earth, and they gave me a list of things that were classified information. That wasn't one of them, but I got the impression it wasn't meant to be common knowledge."

"It seems like someone else must have known that," Wronglen said. "Otherwise, where did the nickname come from?"

I moved toward the door. "Good point." I turned back before the door opened. "If we need to talk again, how can I—"

He rubbed his hands against his thighs for the second time in the short conversation. "I guess we should have some kind of code word."

"Are you going to keep being a jerk?" I asked. I smiled so he'd know I wasn't blaming him. "You don't want anyone to think you're siding with the losers."

He chuckled. "I guess I'd better. I can probably help you more if I'm not under suspicion. If you need to talk to me, tell Lawrence. Don't give her a reason. I'll clue her in."

He stepped up next to me. He was tall, which surprised me for some reason. I guess I'd been thinking of him as a male version of Lieutenant Wronglen, and I towered over her. "Let me check the hallway. I don't want anyone to know we've been in here together."

My face went hot. Spending time alone in the bunk room with a senior cadet was probably a good way to get a reputation. But better they think we were up to something innocuous, I supposed.

The door slid open. Wronglen poked his head out then motioned for me to follow him. He took me upstairs and opened the door at the top. "You're lucky Charlie Orange is on their way home," he said. "If they were still in the field, I wouldn't have had time to talk to you. Get back to your dorm. I'll post the schedule for the rest of the day."

I saluted and hurried out of the building.

CHAPTER THIRTEEN

WHEN THE REST of the flights returned, they posted the results of the exercise on the virtual board. Charlie Blue ranked number one. I was a little surprised because I thought they might have figured out a way to drop our score. Delta Black came in third, even though they were second to last to return to base. The scoring rubric wasn't posted, so we had no way of knowing what anyone earned points for.

The entire class gathered in the auditorium for the exercise review. Captain Fortescue, our advisor, made a rare appearance.

"We've gone through the vids." The captain flung up her arm. A printed list appeared behind her and on each of our holo-rings. "Some of the flights did quite well. Obviously, we need to have a discussion about following instructions."

She strode across the front of the stage, glaring down at us. "This is the Explorer Corps. We are not pirates. We don't attack other teams, we don't steal equipment, and we certainly don't injure anyone. The objective of this exercise was simply to find the other half of your team and set up a camp. Each flight had sufficient equipment to accomplish that task without taking from anyone else. And yet, when we picked you up, many of you were missing items you should have had. Either you're very poor at keeping track of CEC equipment, or there was some pilfering."

She moved back to the center of the stage. "Unfortunately, due to some technical issues, we are unable to corroborate any testimonies. And since none of the missing equipment came back to the Academy, we don't know where it went. We're at a dead end. We will sweep the exercise arena to find the missing items. And if we find evidence pointing toward who took them, there will be repercussions."

She flung her arm at the screen again. "These are the things we will be concentrating on over the next few weeks. You will have another field exercise at the end of the summer, and we want to make sure you're ready for it. Item number one: living mods."

We spent the rest of the morning on a review of how to set up an Explorer camp.

"This is all in the manuals," Marise whispered. "If they just read—"

I smirked. "That's why we won. We had you, and you know how to read."

AFTER LUNCH, we headed to the sports fields. We were scheduled to play Bravo Yellow on the far field. Yellow had returned from the exercise late last night, so it wouldn't be much of a game. They were likely to be exhausted. We hurried out so we could talk before they arrived.

Chymm strolled to the fence. He leaned down to tie his shoe, and when he stood, he gave us a thumbs-up. "Still running."

"Could it be a decoy?" Abdul asked. "Like they left it turned on, but it's not doing anything?"

"I suppose they could try to spoof it," Chymm said. "But I checked. It's actually working."

I had told them about my conversation with Wronglen. His attitude toward us had not changed since that meeting. "I'm not sure if that means he was playing me, or he really is on our side. Either way, he's a good actor." I turned to Peter. "What's the story on your call home?"

Joss and Peter exchanged a narrow-eyed look. "We are authorized one call per quarter," Peter said. "I've been trying to figure out how to set that up. I finally got ahold of that little skinny guy who works in the admiral's office. Apparently, he controls cadet communications with the outside world. And he told me that we have to wait until the end of the summer term to call. No cadets are allowed to speak to anyone outside the school until after Prime Survival Week. School policy."

Joss crossed his arms. "Which sucks because the whole point of the call was for us to be able to report back if there were problems. Dad was nervous about sending us here and wanted to make sure we had a way to talk to him. They're bending the rules but not breaking them."

"I guess we have to keep pushing from here." I pulled off my jacket and flung it onto the bench.

"Are you sure that's a good idea?" Marise asked. "Maybe we should keep our heads down until Peter can call."

"Maybe we should talk to Captain Fortescue," Aneh said. "She said there'd be repercussions."

Yvonne laughed. "She said what she needed to say to keep us complacent. Promise the idiots that you'll take care of the problem, without offering any concrete solutions. They couldn't find any evidence, she said. Ha!"

"I'm with Yvonne on this." Chymm took the rev-ball from Joss and tossed it high overhead. He caught it with a thud. A look of mild surprise crossed his face. "She didn't say they'd punish Delta Black. She said there'd be repercussions. The way things work around here, we'd be the ones to experience the repercussions."

"So, what now?" I asked.

"Now we play rev-ball. Here comes Yellow." Chymm flung the ball at the rest of us.

Joss snatched the ball out of the air and grinned. "You gotta be faster than that to catch me off-balance."

The next few weeks went by in a blur. Our class load increased, our homework volume doubled, and the sports competitions ramped up. Several times, we played matches *with* Charlie Orange against the other squadrons. We rarely interacted with Orange off the sports field, though.

Our classes focused on the proper way to set up a camp, setting guard rotations, and what to do when things went wrong. In addition to setting snares and cleaning game, we learned to start a fire, both with a starter and using sticks and rocks. They taught us to test and purify water without the handy filter bottles, to build shelters, and bare-bones first aid. And they added "specialized activities" to our schedule.

"I'm trying out for the grav belt drill team," Aneh told me one morning.

I stared at her in disbelief. "You?"

She nodded. "Why not? I'm not scared of heights, and I love carnival rides. It looks like so much fun. Come with me?"

I shrugged. "I dunno. That seems like a lot of extra work. Did you see the practice schedule? All your free time would be gone." We didn't get much.

She shook her head. "Not really. There's team times built into the schedule starting this week." She pulled up a file on her holo-ring. "See—an hour every day for 'specialized activities.' We're all expected to have one."

Lawrence had mentioned that the previous week. "I was thinking about swimming," I said.

"You can swim anywhere." Aneh grabbed my arm. "Who gets to fly?"

"We had synchronized grav belt drills in prep school. It wasn't all that."

Aneh's eyes widened. "You got to fly in prep school? I thought that was discontinued decades ago."

"I'm old, remember? I went to prep school twenty years ago." I smirked. "I wasn't on the team, but I got the same basic training everyone got. Why did they discontinue grav drill?"

Her shoulders hunched. "Some kid committed suicide during a competition. He went way up, then turned off his belt."

"Ugh. That's horrible."

"Yeah." Her lips twisted. "They got rid of the school grav drill teams. But it's safe now. They recalled all the belts and added safety protocols. Join the team with me!"

I bit my lip. "Okay."

Aneh squealed and threw her arms around me. "Tryouts are this afternoon."

TRYOUTS WERE NOT DIFFICULT. In fact, no one was cut. "The bigger the team, the better," Cadet Pietro said. Then he grinned, a nasty, snide expression. "We'll make the cuts after the rest of the cadets come back to the academy. This is just practice. Open auditions will be held the first week of fall term."

"I don't care," Aneh whispered. "I still want to try it. If I don't make the real team, at least I'll have had this chance."

I patted her arm. "You'll make the team. I've never met anyone as dedicated as you. You'll practice your butt off and show up the rest of us."

She grinned. "You bet your grav belt I will."

The first week, we learned simple maneuvers, most of which I remembered from my prep school days. Aneh checked a belt out from supply and spent every free second training. She got up half an hour early so she could run through the routine before breakfast.

"You're going to kill yourself with all this extra work," I moaned one morning when she bounced out of bed at five. "Then they'll shut down grav drill again due to your untimely death."

She laughed. "Flying a grav belt is better than anything. I'd rather fly than sleep!"

"Get out of here so I can get my last thirty minutes of beauty rest." I threw a pillow at her.

She laughed, threw the pillow back, and headed out the door.

THAT AFTERNOON, we met in the ready room as usual. Lawrence joined us to give us the rundown on the next week's activities. "When classes start in the fall, you'll learn more about Explorer Corps history and the laws applying to our missions. I hope you've been paying attention to the practical stuff we've been pushing since TbF. You'll need all of those skills for Prime Survival Week."

Abdul raised his hand. "What's Prime Survival Week?"

We all stared at him.

"Haven't you read anything?" Yvonne demanded.

"We're not all book nerds like you," Abdul snapped back.

"They talk about PSW in the recruiting literature," Aneh said. "Even *I* knew about it before I got here."

Abdul glared at Aneh.

Lawrence waved to get Abdul's attention. "PSW is the end-of-summer trial. We drop your flight in an undisclosed location. You have to set up camp and begin exploring."

"How is that any different from the last exercise?" Abdul grumped.

"First of all, it's just you." Lawrence leaned back in her chair. "You don't work with Charlie Orange on this one."

Joss barked a laugh. "We didn't work with them last time."

Lawrence waved that away. "I know. Once you're in the field, some challenges will be thrown at you. That's the difference."

"Oh, you mean challenges like being attacked by another flight?" Abdul asked.

We all glared at him.

"I'm sick of not talking about this," Abdul muttered. Joss punched his arm. The smaller boy glared but shut up.

"No, no one will attack you." Lawrence flicked her holo-ring and pulled up some vid. "This is last year's exercise. If you pay close attention, you'll see Cadet Mason."

Mason groaned. "That's not the vid where I fall in the lake, is it?"

"Of course it is." Lawrence snickered and flung a holo-vid onto the table. "What else would I show?"

In the vid, a flight of cadets, led by Mason, walk along the edge of a low cliff. Below, brilliant blue water sparkles in the sunshine. A noise that sounds like a wooden horn played by a piece of machinery echoes through the room. A herd of large, horned animals stampedes toward us. The three-legged beasts have shaggy fur and wide faces. Their eyes roll, and they snort. Most of the cadets shoot up from the ground, their grav belts whining with exertion. Mason stumbles and does a double-take. Then he races away, toward the cliff edge. Realizing he's trapped, he turns to run parallel to the water. But the beasts surge around him, and he falls off the cliff. The beasts thunder on.

Lawrence laughed.

"That was smart," Chymm said. "The herbivores of Sarvo Six won't eat you, but they can trample you. They won't jump off a cliff, though."

"He didn't know that." Lawrence snickered. "Don't make him out to be smarter than he is."

"Thank you, sir, may I have another?" Mason said in a wooden tone, his face brilliant red.

"When does this happen?" Peter broke in to ask. "The exercise. Will we get some warning, or will we be woken up in the middle of the night again?"

Lawrence shook her head. "They only do that the first time. It's meant to throw you off-balance."

"Mission accomplished," Chymm said.

Lawrence nodded. "This time, you'll be involved in the planning phases. In fact, that starts next week. Each flight will decide what to bring with them, based on a mission brief and environmental description. It's meant to simulate a phase 2 arrival."

Abdul opened his mouth, but I held up my hand. "Read the book, Abdul. A phase 2 mission is the one that goes in after the jump gates have been set up."

Peter rubbed his hands together. "That's my kind of mission. Since I can't do the deep sleep thing. Not that I want to." He slanted a look at Joss.

His friend nodded. "I'm not going in a freezer again unless my life depends on it."

Yvonne tilted her head. "Really? Most cadets are here because they want the glory of first contact. That means being on the phase 1 team."

Joss snickered. "Been there, done that."

Yvonne's eyebrows drew down. "The only first contact mission in history was Darenti Four, and that was before we were born."

"Before *you* were born," Peter corrected. "I was born five centuries ago, remember? But Joss was referring to when we met Siti."

I rolled my eyes. "Not first contact. More like recontact."

"I feel like I've known you guys forever," Yvonne said. "I forget you three have this whole other history."

"That's what plebe summer does to you." Lawrence stood. "That's part of why we do it the way we do. We're trying to build a team, and that team building is accelerated under pressure. TbF will either cement a flight or tear them apart. Look at Delta White."

Seven members of Delta White had resigned from the Academy when they returned from the field exercise. Probably because they were victimized by Delta Black, but no one had asked for my opinion. The story was they had "failed to gel" as a team.

"You get the weekend off." At the door, Lawrence turned. "That doesn't mean you can leave campus. But you have free time. I suggest you use it to study the mission materials I've sent to your files." She stared hard at Abdul. "The Academy doesn't give you free time to have fun. Consider it an opportunity to succeed."

As she left, Chymm sighed. "It's the Corps way."

I flicked my ring. "Hey, here's a question. Why do phase 1 teams go into deep sleep?"

Yvonne's lip curled. "Because it takes fifteen to thirty years to get to an unexplored planet? You should know that—you did it."

"I did it, but I didn't have a lot of choice. Dad said, 'Let's go,' and I went." I scowled in thought. "I guess I could have said no—I had already been accepted here, but I didn't know if I really wanted to do it. But my question is why does the phase 1 team—the landing team—go with the first ship? Why not wait until the CEC ship launches the jump beacons then jump in and land? It seems like valuable personnel are tied up for decades at a time for no reason."

"That's an interesting question," Chymm said. "We were talking about it in my electronics club." Chymm had been putting his tech skills to the test while Aneh and I learned grav belt routines. "They've actually perfected an AI-driven ship that can reach a planet much faster—no need for life support or artificial gravity or supplies, so they're wicked fast. They travel at speeds humans can't survive. When they reach the system, they install the jump gates, and the phase 1 team can jump in. The first ships were launched almost fifteen years ago, but that's been classified until recently. The first one successfully installed jump gates earlier this month. They launched a phase 1 team a few weeks ago."

"That's so cool!" CEC capped explorers at eighty years of deep sleep.

My trip to Earth had burned twenty, limiting my usefulness to the Corps. AI jump gate installation would be a game changer.

Peter and Joss exchanged a look. "Maybe we can be phase 1 explorers after all," Peter said. The boys slapped their hands together.

"That still doesn't answer why they haven't always done it that way!" I spoke over the comments. "The ship's crew would have been gone for decades, but there's no reason the explorers had to go with them."

Marise shrugged. "You'll have to ask your dad. I'm sure he knows why." I nodded absently.

"Hey, any of you guys know Tovar from Alpha Green?" Aneh asked.

"That dweeby kid on the drill team?" I squinted at her. "Why?"

She blushed. "No reason."

Joss shook his finger at her. "Nope, nope, nope. No dating the enemy."

"He's not the enemy!" Aneh's face went redder.

"If he's not with us, he's against us," Marise said. "Stick with your own flight."

Aneh sighed. "It's not like we have time to date, anyway."

"Even if you did—" Joss flexed his pectorals. "You've got prime beef here. Why would you want that stringy, green chicken?"

CHAPTER FOURTEEN

SATURDAY MORNING, we slept in. I made it all the way to seven-thirty before I couldn't stay in bed any longer. I grabbed my workout clothes and snuck out of the room without waking Aneh. After dressing in the shower room, I left my sleeping gear hanging on a peg behind the door. When I came out, Peter, Joss, and Marise were waiting for me.

"Time for breakfast?" Peter asked.

I nodded and yawned.

After we ate, Joss grabbed a rev-ball, and we wandered out to our favorite field.

"Do you think it's—" Marise broke off, jerking her head toward the fence.

I shook my head. "I think it's too cold to stand around. Let's play."

We played a hard and fast game. Joss and I had scored two goals against Marise and Peter when Chymm and Yvonne wandered up. I was breathing heavily and called a timeout. "Where's Aneh and Abdul?"

Chymm held up a finger and looked down at a device strapped to his wrist. Then he nodded. "We're good."

"Did you invent a new toy?" Yvonne asked. "Don't let Marise near it."

Marise narrowed her eyes. "I don't break electronics."

"I did!" He fished in his pocket. "The electronics club has been awesome. Tovar from Green showed me—"

"You mean Aneh's crush?" Joss asked.

They laughed.

"He's on drill team *and* electronics club?" Peter asked.

I grabbed Chymm's arm. "You haven't told them about this, have you?"

"No, of course not." Chymm glared. "But they all know about the 'glitch' out here. Why do you think this field is in use so much of the time? They don't know it's me, though."

"Good. Tell us about the thing on your wrist."

"Oh, I was being stupid before." Chymm slapped his forehead. "All I needed was a communications device. I checked out a vid drone. I said I wanted to vid our game so we can improve our playing. It's not working, so I know my jammer is." He showed us the fuzzy screen.

"I'm not sure that was a great idea," Marise said, apologetically. "Now we have to move because your drone isn't working."

Chymm stared at her, his face blank.

"You came out to vid, and it doesn't work." Marise raised her eyebrows. "We need to move over there so you can record us."

Everyone groaned. Chymm slapped his forehead again, harder.

"Dude. Stop that." Joss pulled Chymm's hand away. "It's no big deal. We'll sit here for a while, resting. When we get ready to play again, you can discover the problem, and we'll move."

"Yeah. We only have one more day before we start the PSW anyway." Yvonne patted Chymm's other shoulder. "We aren't going to have time to come out here for secret chats."

"And this is our free time," Marise said. "We can hang out here talking for as long as we want today."

"Too bad it's not warm enough to sunbathe." Yvonne pulled her jacket more tightly around her.

"Then let's get down to business." I stood and turned to face them. "Wronglen still hasn't sent me the vid. And we've been completely unsuccessful—"

"Is that Aneh?" Yvonne pointed.

Aneh ran across the field toward us. As she got closer, the expression on her face turned my stomach to ice. "What's wrong?" I called.

"Abdul—" She choked on the end of his name.

"Please don't tell us he's gone," Yvonne said.

Aneh nodded, tears spilling down her face. She and Abdul had bonded over their common lack of information about the Corps. While Abdul was content to be ignorant, Aneh often researched things she didn't understand or asked us to explain and then shared with Abdul.

"Obviously, someone was listening to our flight meeting yesterday." I rubbed my temple. "Or maybe Lawrence reported him. We need to be super careful for the next few days. Once we're on the exercise, I doubt they'll eliminate us—at least not until we return."

Everyone nodded.

"Let's go back to the dorm and plan our strategy for this exercise." I made eye contact with each of them. "For real. Playtime is over."

We spent the weekend developing our plans. The mission brief said we would be dropped on a planet that sounded very similar to the area near the Dome. Coniferous forests, comfortable temperatures, rocky ground. We were assigned a base camp on a high plateau that was not easily accessed. Grav belts would allow us to get up and down, and a force shield would keep us safe from any land-based animals.

"Is this on a different planet?" Aneh asked.

"It's probably a different location in the exercise field." Marise said. "It wouldn't be cost effective to send us to another planet when they have all this land."

"Didn't Lawrence say they do these on Sarvo Six?" Yvonne put in.

"I said it was Sarvo Six," Chymm said. "I recognized those herbivores in the vid."

"Sarvo Six is in the fringe," I protested. "It would take months to get there."

The others laughed.

"They got upgraded jump beacons about three years ago." Marise patted my arm. "It used to take months, but now you can get there in days. Like S'Ride or Kaku."

We estimated the supplies we would require for the two-week trip and added an additional fifty percent to be safe.

"Are they going to let us take that much extra?" Yvonne asked as she recalculated the number of meal pacs we need.

I shrugged. "We can ask. If they say no, then they say no. We should plan for both."

We'd taken over one of the classrooms on the first floor. Virtual boards on the walls were covered in Peter's tidy printing. Yvonne and Marise shuffled stacks of paper, and Chymm built up a small pile of electronic equipment he had devised.

Joss waved a sheet of recycled paper.

I took it. "Tell me what I'm looking at. I can't read your chicken scratch."

He ignored my wisecrack and pointed at the paper. "I'm requesting stunners for all of us."

"Why did you write it on the paper?" I asked.

He shrugged. "Everyone else's writing stuff down. I was feeling left out."

I rolled my eyes, and he laughed.

Marise had found a stack of case studies, so we had some historical data to base our plans on. It was her idea to request extra supplies. "The flights that win always had extra stuff."

Lawrence strode into the room. "Pack up. It's time to go."

"You said we were going to leave tomorrow," I said.

Lawrence's face darkened. "That was the plan. I don't know why they've pushed your departure forward. It's not normal. Do you have your supplies?"

"No," we all said at once.

"We were supposed to submit our requests by noon today." Marise flicked her holo-ring and popped open a countdown timer. "We've still got two hours."

"Please tell me you've requested some of your supplies." Lawrence looked from face to face.

I nodded. "We put in preliminary requests yesterday. We were planning to update them once we finished this last review."

Lawrence dropped into a chair, sagging with relief. "Thank the stars!"

"Are we *all* leaving early?" I asked.

Lawrence shook her head. "I don't know. They only told me our flight had been pushed up. I guess we'll see when we get out to the quad. Let's go over to supply and collect your gear. You have your bug-out bags, right?"

I nodded. We'd started carrying them with us after the first exercise. None of us wanted to be without the essential gear.

"Do we have time to go to our rooms and get the rest of our stuff?" Aneh asked.

"No." Lawrence herded us out of the room. "You don't take personal items on a mission."

"What about our clothes?" Aneh asked.

"Everything is provided." Lawrence pushed through our small group and headed out the door.

"They print new uniforms for you," I told Aneh as we followed the senior cadet across the quad. "Everything including underwear. It's all packed together to save space."

"No personal items at all?" Peter grinned. "Not even a sair-glider?"

"On a real mission, you take some personal things." I stopped beside Lawrence at the door to the supply building. "Pictures are on your holo-ring, of course. Reading material, also on the ring. Some people bring along small trinkets or personal keepsakes. But you don't take anything you can't afford to lose."

"You won't have time for reading or looking at pictures." Lawrence waved her hand at the access panel, and the supply building's door opened. "And your holo-rings have been scrubbed to academy basic."

"What?" Marise flicked her ring. "I had some important data on mine!"

"It's temporary—for the exercise. You can download all the school manuals and any reference files you saved to your class drive," Lawrence said. "I'd do it right now."

Marise's nostrils flared. "Is that to put us on an 'even footing?' I had extra research saved locally."

"Sorry." Lawrence shrugged. "They don't tell me their whys. I was kind of surprised they scrubbed 'em. They didn't do it when I was a plebe. But a lot of things are different this year."

We shuffled inside. Although it looked like all the other buildings on campus—fancy arches, wide windows, and high ceilings—the supply center was a huge, multi-level warehouse. We took the float tube down one level and stepped out into an echoing chamber. A tall desk stood to one side, with three people behind it. The short female was the supply sergeant we'd met earlier in our training. The others wore officers' uniforms. My stomach sank as Admiral Zimas turned to look at us. Then I recognized the last person.

"Dad!" I lunged forward then stopped myself. Explorer Corps cadets didn't hug officers.

My dad had no such qualms. He hurried around the desk and wrapped his arms around me. "Good to see you, Siti. It's been a long summer."

I squeezed him tight. "You have no idea. I have so much to tell you."

"We don't have time right now." He released me and stepped back.

"Dad, it's important. Possibly dangerous."

"Nate." The admiral strode closer, giving Dad the stink eye.

"You have an exercise, and I have meetings." He glanced at Zimas. "I was lucky to catch you. I'll see you when you get back."

"Best of luck, Charlie Blue," Zimas said, her expression bland. "Sergeant Cole has your supplies ready. Safe journeys." Her eyes narrowed as she looked at me, but she turned away. My father squeezed me one more time, then followed her to the float tube.

"Perks of the rank," Cole muttered, glaring at me. "I didn't get to see my kid off." She raised her voice. "This way." She headed across the warehouse. "I'm sending the manifest to your holo-rings. Check against the inventory lists on the pallets. You'll take these with you to the flight pad."

My ring buzzed. I flicked it and pulled up a list of equipment.

"You were right, Siti." Marise grimaced at me. "They cut our request by a third. Good thing we asked for extra."

Sergeant Cole's head snapped around. "Don't say that out loud," she whispered. "Did your flight commander put you up to that? They aren't supposed to help you that much."

"It was her idea." I pointed at Marise. "She's a smart cookie."

"You requested a class C living mod," Cole said. "That's unusual."

"We thought we might want to establish a forward base," Yvonne said.

"Still, don't tell anyone you over-planned." Cole slapped her hand down on a shrink-wrapped pallet. "They'll take away any extra."

"There isn't any extra." Marise consulted the listing on the side of the pallet. "We'll have just enough to get through the two weeks."

Yvonne read off the list on the side of the pallet while Marise checked items off on her manifest. "It's all here," Marise said at last.

"Perfect. I need a print—" She held out her tablet. Joss pushed his thumb against the device, and it bleeped. "Take it away."

"Is there a tablet to control the lifting panel?" I asked.

"Did you request one?" Cole asked.

My eyes widened, and she barked out a laugh. "I'm kidding. It comes with the panel. Here." She handed me a tablet and checked me out on the basic operations. Then she pointed toward a large door at the far end of the room. "Out that way and straight to the flight pad. Good luck, cadets."

I flicked the lift button, and Joss pushed our pallet of supplies out the door.

CHAPTER FIFTEEN

A RAMP SLOPED UP to the wide pad behind the supply building where a transport waited. It was smaller than the one we'd taken to the first exercise and painted a green camouflage pattern. Huge rubber tires raised it off the ground, and a ramp folded down to access the cargo area. We loaded the pallet, and the pilot locked it down. He showed us how to fold down the jump seats and strap ourselves in.

"I've never ridden in one of these before," I told Aneh.

"You think I have?" She dropped into the seat beside me.

"Not really. Has anyone heard where we're going?" I raised my voice as the engines fired on the transport.

Heads shook.

"This model of transport has a short range," Chymm said. "And it's a road vehicle. Doesn't fly."

"How do you know?" Aneh asked.

Chymm raised his eyebrows. "Did you see the tires?" He tapped the seatbelt. "This is the standard road-model restraint. All of the Corps' flying craft have five-point straps."

The vehicle vibrated and headed across the pad toward the front gate of the campus. We roared along the highway, the tires loud. The vehicle seemed old—it rattled and knocked. Conversation was impossible.

An hour later, we finally stopped. The driver opened the back door. "Everyone out. Your flight leaves in half an hour."

"Flight?" I asked. "Where are we going?"

He shook his head. "No idea. I was told to get you here." He pointed at the ground.

We climbed out onto the tarmac. A long runway stretched into the distance. The ugly, squat buildings behind the transport gave no clue to our location.

"I know where we are," Marise said. "This is Grissom North Field. It's a military shuttle field. The original landing place of the colony ships."

"That explains why those buildings look so old," Yvonne said.

"The Academy is right over there." Marise pointed across the tarmac at some trees.

"Why did it take an hour to get here?" Joss asked.

"You have to go all the way around," Marise said. "Around the Academy and the rest of Grissom North base. There is no direct access."

"I wonder why they didn't fly us out of the academy field?" Aneh asked. "We landed there when we arrived."

"Your pallet's unlatched," the driver said. "Take her out."

I flicked the tablet and tapped the lift button. The pallet rose about ten centimeters, and Chymm and Yvonne pushed it down the ramp to the ground.

"Hurry up!" a voice called. A man wearing a gray coverall stood on the tarmac beside a battered-looking shuttle. "Get yourself loaded. We've got a launch window in twenty minutes."

The man helped us lock our pallet to the floor of the cargo hold and showed us how to strap into the jump seats mounted to the sides of the cargo area. These dusty seats had the five-point restraint Chymm had mentioned.

"Where are we going?" I asked the man. I was beginning to feel like a recording on repeat.

The crease between his eyebrows deepened. "Don't you know?"

I shook my head.

"We're dropping you on Sarvo Six." He checked my restraints.

"How long will that take?" Chymm smirked at me.

I rolled my eyes.

"Four days, tops." He checked the other cadets' harnesses. "Stay put. We're launching soon." He opened the door to the cockpit and disappeared.

"Sarvo Six?" Chymm said again. "I still don't understand why they do this off-world. The Academy has a huge exercise field. Why would they have a cadet exercise—a plebe exercise—off world? That's crazy!"

We were slammed sideways in our seats as the shuttle launched. My teeth—and everything in the vehicle—rattled as we surged down the runway. Then nothing. The rattling and the noise stopped. We'd lifted off.

"This is your pilot," a voice said. It sounded like the same guy who helped us load. "You can call me Bob. We're en route to the *Traveling Salesman*. Transit time will be twenty minutes."

"The *Traveling Salesman*?" Chymm asked. "That sounds like a civilian ship."

"You think?" Yvonne rolled her eyes. "Everyone, try your holo-rings again."

No one got a signal. "Do you think he's blocking us?" Peter jerked his head toward the cockpit.

"These older shuttles have ferian-laced tiles outside. It blocks most internal signals," Chymm said. "The integrated comm gear has to link through the tile to an external array. The pilot can call out."

"So could we, if we could use that." I pointed to a comm station at the rear of the cargo hold. "Do you think you could make it work, Chymm? When we leave atmo?"

"Sure." Chymm pulled his backpack out of the netting under the seat and started sorting through it. "Who you gonna call?"

"Ghostbusters!" Peter and Joss yelled.

"What?" Chymm asked.

We bounced through some turbulence, then the flight smoothed as we left the planet's atmosphere. The pressure of the harnesses relaxed, and my body rose away from the seat.

Chymm unbuckled his restraints and pushed across the cabin. He grabbed a handle and smoothly rotated himself into alignment with the wall. He pressed a button, and the screen lit up. "This thing is ancient! I've never used a system this old."

"How old?" I started unfastening my belts.

"Twenty, maybe thirty years." Chymm tapped the screen, shaking his head.

I laughed. "I can help." I flung the straps aside and straightened. The movement pushed me away from the chair and toward the overhead.

Aneh grabbed my ankle and hauled me back to the deck. "Why do you want to call someone?"

"This is a civilian craft," I said. "Now is the perfect time to record a message to my dad. The Academy won't be monitoring these comms."

"Clever!" Marise said.

"Thanks." I pushed off at an angle and flew toward the comm station. "Too fast!" I flung out my hands then yanked them back to my body. I didn't need broken wrists. I curled into a ball and bounced my shoulder off the wall. Chymm grabbed my arm and twisted me around.

"Hook your feet under that." He pointed at a bar protruding from the deck. His shoes were curled beneath it, keeping him down.

Behind me, someone retched.

"Haven't you been in freefall before?" Yvonne asked.

I glanced over my shoulder. Joss, his dark face unnaturally pale and slightly green, shook his head a fraction.

"Our flights to Grissom all had artificial gravity." Peter didn't look too good, either. "Have you?"

Yvonne's lips quirked. "My uncle is a trader. He flies a shuttle a lot like this one. I've been up and down to his ship a gazillion times. I love it."

I turned back to the task at hand. "Here's the problem. You have to connect your ring to the interface." I showed Chymm how to select the network and enter the codes.

"Why do you know how to do this?" he asked. "You aren't a techy."

"No, but I'm old, remember?" I grinned and patted the console. "I spent twenty years in deep sleep. I learned to use these as a kid."

I flicked a few icons and swiped through the screens. "There's something wrong with this thing." I slapped the console harder this time. "It's not connecting."

The door to the cockpit slid open, and Bob floated in the opening. "It's not working because it's broken."

"What if something had gone wrong back here?" Aneh asked.

"On a routine launch?" The man laughed. "Do you know how many of these operations I've flown? Nothing's going to go wrong. Besides, I can't afford to fix it. You kids shouldn't be out of your seats. We'll be docking in ten minutes. I suggest you strap in." He grinned. "It might get a bit rough."

I pushed back to my seat and latched my restraints. "Chymm, what are you doing? The man said buckle up."

"Just a second." Chymm had popped open the front panel. He fiddled with the modules inside. "Got it."

"It's working?" Marise asked. "Send a message."

The ship jolted. Chymm flew across the compartment.

"Do you think he's making it rough on purpose?" Yvonne gulped. "Like the pilot on the shuttle to Academy?"

I blinked. "Do you think that was on purpose?" We passed Chymm hand over hand to his seat. The ship jerked again. Chymm pulled the straps over his shoulders, his eyes still on the comm console.

Yvonne snorted. "That was a total set-up. That kid is an actor. I saw him in a vid."

"Maybe he was an actor *before* he joined the Academy?" Aneh suggested.

"Before and after." Yvonne shook her head. "Once I saw him in the vid, I did a bit of research. He was hired to scare us."

"What is going on?" Peter asked. "Is this how the Academy is normally run?"

We all shrugged. "None of us have been to the Academy before, so how are we supposed to know?" I asked.

Something thunked, and the ship shuddered. I dropped into my seat as the larger ship's artificial gravity grabbed our shuttle.

"Welcome to the *Traveling Salesman*," our pilot said. "I'll be back in a second to unlatch your pallet. You'll need to help me move it to the main cargo bay." The connection went dead.

We released our safety harnesses and retrieved our bug-out bags. Chymm pulled his backpack open and wandered to the comm system while the rest of us converged on the pallet. The back of the shuttle folded down, creating a ramp into a large cargo bay. Two other shuttles sat to our right, and a huge pile of crates filled the left wall. A number of people dressed in coveralls similar to Bob's maneuvered equipment, lifting and shuffling the crates.

Bob pushed between us and showed us how to unlatch our pallet from the floor of the shuttle. "Take it over there." He waved his arm toward the inner bulkhead. Two other pallets with academy-branded shrink wrap sat there. "Tie it down using the straps." He indicated the webbing still draped across our pallet.

"Are there other cadets on this ship?" I asked.

Bob nodded. "Two other teams so far."

I grabbed his arm as he started away. "Do you know which teams? What are their names?"

"I didn't have time for a chat." He pulled away from me. "You can talk to them later."

As we followed the rest of our team across the cargo hold, Peter nudged me with an elbow. "Why do you want to talk to them?"

"More information is good. Maybe they'll have learned something we didn't." I bit my lip as Marise and Chymm latched the straps to the deck. Yvonne tightened the webbing.

"But what if it's Delta Black?" Peter asked. "They could cause us all kinds of trouble before we even get to the planet."

"True enough." The rest of Charlie Blue gathered around me when they'd finished securing our cargo. "Listen up, folks. There are other flights on the ship. If we run into Black, we need to be very careful. I don't think anyone else will try anything—they should have learned from the last exercise that this isn't about eliminating the competition."

Bob strode up and examined our work. "You done? I'll show you where you'll be staying." He turned and headed toward the door.

The ship was as old and dingy looking as the shuttle. A faint whiff of dirty oil tainted the sanitized air. Peeling paint covered the walls. We followed Bob along a scuffed corridor, carefully stepping over loose deck tiles. He took us up several flights of open steps and stopped at a door.

"This is your bunk. There's a sanitation module inside and space for your hammocks. Food will be delivered to you. You are not to leave this compartment unless you are summoned by one of the crew." He slapped his hand on the access panel, and the door slid open.

"We have to stay in this tiny room for four days?" Joss blocked the doorway.

"That's the rules. Our contract with the Academy is to deliver you to Sarvo Six. We're not required to provide any kind of entertainment." He leveled a challenging look at Joss. "And we don't need you wandering the passageways, causing trouble."

"We didn't expect entertainment." Joss moved into the room. "And *we* don't cause trouble."

"You said we could talk to the other teams," I said. "They aren't assigned to this compartment, too, are they?"

"No, they have their own. You can use the intercom." He made a pushing motion. "In you go. I don't got all day. I got another run to make."

"More cadets to pick up?" I tried to stall.

He grabbed my shoulder and turned me toward the compartment. "None of your business. Get in there." One more gentle shove, and the door shut behind me.

CHAPTER SIXTEEN

I TURNED. The rest of the flight stood there, staring at me.

I stared back.

"That was unexpected," Yvonne said.

"Which part?" Peter asked.

"All of it."

I shoved my hands in my jacket pockets. Soft fur brushed against my hand. I glanced down, and caught a glimpse of blue and white and bright little eyes. "Liam!"

The little sair-glider scrambled up my arm and rubbed his body against my cheek.

"How did you get here?"

"Is that a sair-glider?" Aneh hurried closer. "He's so cute."

"He must have come with your dad," Peter said.

"Dad wouldn't have brought Liam on purpose," I said. "That's definitely against the rules for a plebe."

"That little guy is pretty smart," Peter said. "Remember how he helped us find you in the caves? He probably hitched a ride in your dad's pocket."

"And climbed into mine when we hugged." I snuggled Liam to my neck. "You are definitely the smartest glider I've ever heard of."

"From what I've read," Marise said, "they're very good at survival skills.

A lot of explorers have them. But I didn't know they were that intelligent. And I thought the Corps only had females. Where did you get him?"

"Can I pet him?" Aneh asked.

"I found him on the *Return in Glory,* and no one claimed him." I put my hand by my shoulder, and Liam jumped to it. Then I held him out to Aneh. "He's very smart for a glider. He seemed so much more aware than the other gliders in the camp. But I've never had one before, so maybe I'm biased."

The door slid open. As I swung around, Liam leapt off my hand.

"So, this is where they keep the riff raff," Felicity said. Behind her, Lee and LeBlanc smirked.

"What are you doing here?" I ground my teeth. "You're supposed to stay in your own compartment."

Felicity sauntered in, circling around us. I trusted the others to keep an eye on her because I didn't want to turn my back on the other two. She came back to my side and paused, one hand on her hip. "Lovely place you have here."

"Thanks. I'd invite you for tea, but I don't have any, and more importantly, I don't want to." I shot her a glare.

"As if I'd accept." Her lip curled, and she shuddered dramatically. "You should've stuck with us, Kassis. Delta Black's quarters are much nicer." She pushed past me, ramming into my shoulder. "And we're going to kick your butts on this exercise."

The three Deltas laughed and strolled down the corridor. The door slid shut.

"Didn't Bob say cadets had to stay in their quarters?" Yvonne asked.

"When have *they* ever done what they were told?" Aneh replied.

"This isn't an Academy ship," Peter said. "If they can wander around without getting in trouble, so can we." He strode up to the door and put his hand against the access panel.

Nothing happened.

"Try it again," Josh said.

Peter did. Again, nothing happened. Each of us took a turn.

"We're locked in." Marise crossed her arms. "I guess the crew was given different instructions for them."

"Or someone in their flight figured out how to get it open."

Chymm snorted. "No one in Delta Black is that smart. I could probably open this door, but it would damage the mechanism. I'm not going to do that."

"Good choice. Let's try to make this place as comfortable as possible," I suggested. "Bob said something about hammocks."

"They're over here." Yvonne pointed to a pile in the corner.

Liam lounged atop the pile.

"At least they didn't see him." I hurried across the room. As soon as he saw me coming, he launched himself into the air and straight to my hand. "I'm sure they would've caused all kinds of trouble over him."

The pile contained ten hammocks and a crate of meal pacs. We strung up the hammocks and decided who would sleep where. Marise inventoried the crate. "There's enough food for ten cadets—which means we have twelve extra meal pacs—that's one and a half for each of us." She started tossing the packages at us. "I think we should stow them in our bug-out bags now—with the way things have been going, we won't get a lot of notice when we have to leave."

"What about the hammocks?" Yvonne asked. "Should we take the extras?"

Chymm held one up. "This says property of the CEC Academy. I think we'd be foolish to leave them behind."

We loaded our backpacks with food, and Joss and Marise each took an extra hammock.

"That was fun." Joss slid down the wall to sit on the deck. "Now what?"

"Bob said we could use the intercom," Chymm said. "Let's see who else is on the ship." He tapped the screen below the access panel. It lit up, and he scrolled through some information.

"You need my help?" I asked.

"No," Chymm said. "These haven't changed much in the last thirty years. They've got us listed by flights—all eight. Shall I call someone?"

"Let's check in with Orange," Aneh suggested. "We might have to work with them anyway."

"Good plan," Yvonne said.

Chymm tapped the interface. After a few seconds, he shook his head. "No one is answering."

"Try one of the others," I said. "There were only two other pallets in the cargo bay. I think Bob was going back to get another group."

"I wonder why they didn't bring us all up together?" Marise asked. "They easily could have fit Orange in the shuttle with us."

Yvonne's eyes narrowed. "They're stacking the deck. Treating us differently."

A voice came out of the intercom. "Blue, is that you? This is Terrine."

"Terrine!" Aneh cried. "How are you? Are they being nice to you?"

"Aneh?" Terrine asked. "Who else is there?"

Aneh listed us off. "Are the legacies with you?"

Terrine laughed bitterly. "They're out exploring the ship. They told the rest of us to stay here, and we've learned to do what we're told."

"Can you get out?" Chymm asked. "We're locked in our compartment."

A whoosh emanated from the intercom. "The door opens," Terrine said. "But like I said, we've learned to do what we're told."

"I wish you were still with us," Aneh said.

"Me too." Terrine was silent for a moment. Then the door whooshed again. "I gotta go." The signal cut.

"I bet the legacies just came home." Aneh slid down the wall. "I hope they aren't too mean to her."

"I'll bet she's useful to them," I said. "They're not dumb enough to bite the hand that feeds them. At least I don't think so."

"Hey, look!" Chymm said. "Bob said they weren't here to provide us with entertainment, but they did." He had found another access panel and figured out how to activate a holo-vid.

"What's on that?" Yvonne asked. "Anything to do with our exercise?"

Chymm shook his head. "It's all old entertainment vids. Nothing useful, but it will keep us from getting too bored over the next few days."

By the end of the third day, we'd proven Chymm wrong. We had watched every vid we could stand—most of them were terrible. Or disgusting.

Marise had produced a pack of playing cards, and we took turns teaching each other games. Late the third night, Liam woke me by chittering in my ear.

"What is it?" I whispered.

The door opened.

Liam rumbled, an almost inaudibly low vibration. Was he growling?

"Go away," Joss barked. The rest of us tumbled out of our hammocks.

The legacies stood in the doorway.

"What do you want?" I demanded.

Felicity's jaw tightened. "Nothing." She turned away, and the door slid shut.

"Good thing we posted a guard," Joss said.

"When did we do that?" Yvonne asked.

Joss's lips twitched. "We didn't. But I've been expecting something like this. So, I've been sleeping down here." He patted a pile of blankets on the deck.

"You don't need to do it alone," I said. "Liam woke me before the door opened. And we can take turns."

Joss shrugged. "I don't mind. I don't like those things anyway." He pointed at the hammocks.

"Obviously, *they* can open *our* door," Yvonne said. "What do you think they were planning?"

"I don't know," Chymm said, "but I'm worried about our cargo."

We all stared at him.

"Do you think they'll take our stuff?" Marise asked.

"I think they'll take anything they can get away with," Yvonne said. "And damage anything they can't."

"At least we have our bug-out bags. I wonder if the other flights brought theirs." I stroked Liam's soft fur.

"Charlie Orange started carrying theirs after the first exercise," Peter said. "I think some of the others did, too."

"Hopefully they're smart enough to keep them under guard," Joss said.

WE SPENT the rest of the trip the same way—playing cards, watching vids, and spoiling Liam. Joss set up a guard rotation, so we had someone awake at all times, watching the door. The legacies dropped by two more times but left when they saw eight pairs of eyes staring back at them.

Finally, the captain made an announcement. "The *Traveling Salesman* has achieved orbit around Sarvo Six. We'll begin dropping you to the surface in the next twenty minutes. Be ready to go."

"Roll up your hammock and stuff it in your bag." Yvonne unsnapped hers from the wall hooks. "Everyone got enough room?"

"Whose meal pac is that?" Marise asked.

Peter leaned down and grabbed it. "Empty." He flattened it and slid it into his bag then looked up to see us watching. "What? It's a waterproof pouch, and it masses almost nothing. It might be useful."

"We've been throwing them away!" Aneh wailed.

"It's okay," I said. "We still have the full ones. If we need a pouch, we can empty those. How many do you have, Peter?"

Peter finished closing his bag. "Only the one. I actually stuck it in because it seemed easier than taking it to the trash." He pointed at the waste slot near the sanitation mod.

"Speaking of waste, I'm going to use the loo while I've got the chance." Marise handed her bag to Joss. "Don't leave without me."

"Wouldn't dream of it." Joss set her bag at his feet while he shrugged into his own.

About an hour later, the door opened. Bob stood before us, his face unreadable. "Ready?"

"As we'll ever be," I said. In my pocket, Liam growled. I glanced down in surprise. He'd only done that when the legacies showed up. I stroked his head. Maybe all visitors made him nervous in these surroundings.

We filed out into the corridor. Bob poked his head through the door to give the room a once over. Then he gave me a speculative look. "You took everything?"

"We did." I said it as matter-of-factly as possible, as if it were our right.

He nodded. "Good plan. I hate to see you at such a disadvantage. You seem like nice kids."

We hurried after him as he strode down the corridor. "What kind of disadvantage?" Peter asked.

We reached a cross corridor, and Bob stopped to look around. He turned to face us. "That one group. Delta Black. They got a lot more stuff than you do."

"More stuff?" I stepped closer. "What you mean? What kind of stuff?"

He shook his head. "I'm not supposed to tell you anything. But they got electronic gear. And some weapons."

"Weapons?" Aneh's voice squeaked.

"For protection, maybe. Or hunting." Bob shook his head again. "I dunno. I saw—" He broke off and hurried on. We chased after him.

The cargo bay door opened. Only Bob's shuttle occupied the wide bay. The other supply pallets were gone, and shredded shrink wrap fabric lay scattered near ours. Someone had cut through the wrap and pulled out the smaller crates. Anger burned in my chest. "What happened to our supplies?"

"I told you," Bob said. "You're at a disadvantage."

Our living mod sat by itself in the remains of the shrink wrap. I fingered the blue material. Even the wraps had been part of our plan, and now this one was useless. The crates that had been on top lay scattered around the cargo area. At least I assumed they were our crates. "Did Delta Black do this?"

Bob spread his hands. "I didn't see nothing. I'll give you a few minutes to pick up whatever you can find."

My eyes stung. Tears of anger and frustration threatened to spill out, but I blinked them back. "Spread out, everyone. Find whatever is left."

As we moved through the cargo bay, Bob loaded our living mod onto his shuttle. I brought an empty crate to the back of the craft. "Has everyone else already gone dirtside?"

Bob nodded. "The black team went with Erdos. Felina took the yellow and I took the green ones down. Then we came back for the rest of you. Blue team was slated to drop last. I'm sorry this happened."

I picked up one of the flexible crates and set it beside the shuttle. "Can you get surveillance vid of this area?"

He stared at me.

"Please, Bob. This is important. Delta Black is dangerous, and the Academy doesn't care because—well, it doesn't matter why. But if you can get a copy of that surveillance vid and send it to this address," I swept my father's contact to him, "it could save our lives."

"Save your lives? Do you really think you're in danger?"

"Would you want to be dropped on Sarvo Six with only this?" I gestured to the mod cube and my backpack.

Bob's face paled. "That's a wild place down there. I'll send the vid if I can get it. Do you want me to send a message if I can't?"

"Yes. Do you have a recorder? My dad can help us, but only if you get word to him."

"Maybe you shouldn't go." Bob scratched his head. "I could drop you in the town. Or—"

"No. If we go AWOL, none of us will ever be able to come back to the Explorer Corps. We can do this. With your help." I grabbed the crates the other cadets had stacked beside the shuttle and moved them inside.

Chymm joined me in the shuttle, the others following. "We found a few things. I think we'll be okay."

I nodded to Bob. "You heard the man. Take us dirtside."

CHAPTER SEVENTEEN

"You can use the comm system back here," Bob said as strapped into our seats.

I shook my head. "It doesn't work, remember?"

"Your buddy fixed it." Bob tilted his head toward Chymm.

"He did?"

Chymm nodded. "Didn't get a chance to use it, though."

"Record your message to your dad," Bob said. "I'll send it for you. Call it payment for the repair."

I hurried to the console and pressed the start icon.

"Why didn't your captain have it repaired when it broke?" Yvonne asked. "That seems like a significant safety violation for a small trader."

"It's my ship." Bob pressed a control, and the back ramp slowly hinged upward. "The *Traveling Salesman* ain't my ship. I'm a contract shuttle. If they found out my radio was busted, they'd kick me out of orbit. It's hard to find work with a ship this old."

"Anything else you need fixed?" Chymm asked. "I'd be happy to help."

"Way more than you have time for, kid." Bob strode the length of the cargo hold. The rear door clanged, and the red light above it flashed to green then turned off. "Buckle up. It's time to launch." He disappeared into the cockpit.

I finally found the record screen on the comm system. I pressed the icon and waited three seconds. "Dad, it's Siti. I've been trying to be more independent and less whiny this summer, but this is important. We're being dropped on Sarvo Six as part of the Prime Survival Week exercise. But our gear has been stolen by other cadets."

I directed the camera at our lonely living mod then back to my face. "At least, we believe it's other cadets. We have no proof. But our shuttle pilot says the other flights' supplies were untouched. If you think this is all normal, then I'm sorry that I bothered you. But it feels like a set-up to me. We'll be grateful for whatever help you can give us. Love you." I slapped the save button.

"Siti, hurry." Aneh waved from her seat. "We're lifting off."

I lunged across the compartment and threw myself into the seat. The ship twitched and surged forward. I slammed sideways into the armrest, bruising my hip. Aneh clutched at me, holding me in place. I struggled to pull the straps around me and finally got them locked.

"I didn't get a chance to send it." I closed my eyes and focused on my breathing, to bring my heart rate back down.

"We'll have to trust Bob to send it for us," Marise said.

"Do you?" Peter asked. "Trust him, I mean?"

"We'll have a few minutes when we land," I said. "While the rest of us take the gear out, Chymm can make sure the message went."

Chymm gave me a thumbs-up.

The drop to the surface was rough. "Sarvo Six is known for its turbulent atmosphere," Marise said, her teeth rattling as she spoke. The rest of us grunted and nodded.

When we landed, we scrambled out of our seats. The cockpit door opened. "Unlatch your stuff and get out. They're timing you. Your exercise starts now."

"Peter, Joss, Marise." I pointed at our pallet. "Move the supplies. Chymm, you know what to do."

Wind whistled as the rear ramp hinged down. The cold bit into my skin. My jacket flapped against my sides, a resinous scent tingling my nose. I pulled my jacket tight and fastened it. Liam pressed against my ribs in a warm lump. The strong uniform material kept in my body heat, but my cheeks and ears tingled. "Are you sure this is where we're supposed to be? It seems awfully cold."

"Are you questioning my navigation skills?" Bob stepped in front of me, his hands on his hips.

Touchy. "No, course not," I said. "I'm questioning the coordinates you were given. Our mission brief said it would be temperate."

Bob nodded. "This is temperate for Sarvo Six. It's the dead of night. It'll warm up in the daytime."

"Great. They dropped us at night again." Yvonne shrugged into her backpack and hefted Chymm's. "Does the Explorer Corps always drop teams at night?"

"I don't think normal parameters are applied to student exercises," I said. "They haven't been yet, anyway."

"True enough."

"Get moving, kids," Bob said. He glanced at Chymm, still standing by the communications console, and lowered his voice. "I'll make sure your message gets sent."

"Thanks," Chymm said. "This ancient system might be easy to fix, but it's tough to operate."

Bob snorted. "I had the exact opposite experience."

"Thank you for helping us," I said. "Come on, Chymm, let's go." We turned and hurried down the ramp.

"I'm not doing you any favors," Bob called loudly. He pointed back over his shoulder in a surreptitious matter. "Your mission has started. You'd best get busy." The door began to rotate closed.

I raised a hand then turned back to my flight.

"This isn't our site." Marise stood with her arms crossed, staring straight ahead. With two crescent moons in the sky, there was enough light to see. We stood on a sandy beach by a small stream. Thick trees filled the opposite bank before it sloped steeply upward. The cliff seemed to run along the stream as far as we could see.

Behind us, the land stretched out in an endless, empty plain. Scrubby bushes dotted the landscape. Contrary to the mission briefing, it looked nothing like our landing site on Earth.

"It's weird how the trees end at the stream," Peter said.

"It's something to do with the biology here," Marise said. "I read about it in one of the case studies. But we don't want to camp here. There are animals. Big ones. They aren't predators, but they could trample us."

"Plus, this is a floodplain." Joss pointed at the beach. "See those marks? The stream rises—probably very quickly. Who knows how often or and what season."

Marise raised her hand. "I know. I read about that too. There are several rainy seasons, and you're right, we don't want to get caught here."

"Well, it's a good thing we don't have much to move," Peter said dryly.

"Where are we going to go?" I asked. "Are we near the coordinates we were given?"

Chymm grunted. "I'm working on it." He fiddled with one of his many devices. "Yeah, we're close. About five hundred meters that way." He pointed across the stream at the steep hill.

"Perfect." I bit my lip. "Anyone have any ideas how we can get up there? We don't have our grav belts."

"What about the grav lifter on the living mod?" Peter suggested. "Without the additional supplies, it might lift Aneh, at least."

Joss looked up the slope. "She can ride up and drop a rope. We should be able to climb up."

"If we had a rope," Yvonne said. "Our climbing cable was in our supplies."

We all groaned.

"I have some in my bag," Chymm said. "It's nano cable, so it's very thin and very strong. But I don't think it's long enough to reach up there."

"I have a grav belt," Aneh said.

I stared at her, my mouth open.

"Where did you get that?" Joss asked.

Aneh's face flushed, and she looked away. "I checked it out to practice for the team. I might have *accidentally* kept it in my bug-out bag. Since I was carrying it everywhere."

I snickered. It wasn't like Aneh to do something against the rules, but she was so desperate to earn a slot on the drill team.

"You're a lifesaver." Joss hugged the tiny girl.

"Which way do we want to try this?" I asked. "We can daisy chain

Aneh's grav belt to the mod's lifter. That should give us enough power to lift the cube and two people. But probably not very high. We'd have to shove it up the hill. Or someone could wear the belt, and Aneh could ride on top of the cube."

"Is the grav lifter permanently attached to the cube?" Chymm asked. He took his backpack from Yvonne and moved toward the box.

I pressed the access panel and swung it open. "As far as I know, it's integrated with the mod." I thought for a moment. "But that doesn't seem very efficient, does it? The Explorer Corps equipment almost always has multiple uses—they try to be flexible. I bet there's a way to detach it."

"Anyone got a light?" Chymm fumbled in his bag.

Five beams of light hit the panel, and laughter echoed off the cliff. "I got this," Yvonne said. "The rest of you, save your powerpacks." The other lights snapped off.

"Joss, why don't you and Aneh see if there's a way to cross the stream without getting soaked? In case we can't go straight up." I turned to Marise. "Do you have any reference material about the potential for flood here? Would it be safe for us to spend the rest of the night and make the move in the morning?"

Marise held up both hands. "I got nothing."

"Siti, I'm going to collect some dry wood," Peter said. "We can start a fire if we need to."

I shook my head. "No. I don't want to attract attention."

"A fire would keep wildlife away," Peter argued. "And the other cadets just landed, too. Even if they see our fire, by the time they get here, we should be gone."

"We know they have power supplies," I said. "Bob said they also have weapons. And we saw what they did in Trial by Fire. Instead of doing the logical thing, which was to set up a base camp, they chose to attack others. Do you think they learned anything?"

"They learned they're untouchable," Yvonne said. "They learned they could take our things and hurt people with no consequences. That's not someone I want to tangle with."

Peter nodded. "Fine. I'm still going to gather some firewood." He held up his hands. "Don't worry, I won't start one unless we need it." He wandered toward the stream.

"Good plan," I said. "How're you doing, Chymm?"

"I got it!" Marise said. "I was looking through my research, and I found the manual for the living mod." She flicked the file hovering over her hand to Chymm. "I'm glad Lawrence told us to reload our saved files."

"You're right, Siti." Chymm stretched the hologram in his hand so we could see the diagram. "Right here, instructions for disconnecting the grav lift. Let's take it apart."

"Wait!" I opened a channel to the whole team. "Blue, assemble." I flicked the comm off and turned back to Chymm. "As soon as Aneh gets back, you put on her grav belt. She can ride the cube up. Then the two of you can disconnect the living mod. She stays up there while you ferry the panel back down."

"Are you sure she'll be safe up there alone?" Chymm asked.

"Anyone bring a stunner?" I looked at the others. They all shook their heads.

"I don't have a stunner, but I have a weapon." Joss strode back into the circle, with Aneh on his heels. He reached for a holster he'd strapped to his leg and pulled out a small gun. "It shoots tranquilizer darts."

"Did everyone but me bring in contraband?" I asked.

"We all did. You did, too." Peter pointed. A little blue-and-white head poked out of my jacket pocket.

I rubbed Liam's soft head. He pushed against my hand, purring. "I wish I'd brought something a little more useful. We should have planned for this. What else have we got?"

Marise started ticking things off on her fingers. "Joss's tranq gun. Aneh's grav belt. Chymm's electronics and cable. Peter's camp stove. I've got some rope."

"Why didn't you say so when we were asking about rope?" Joss asked.

Marise shook her head. "It's not enough to climb that cliff. But it might be helpful. And don't forget the hammocks and the extra meal pacs."

I looked at Yvonne. "What did you bring?"

She shrugged. "I've got chocolate."

"Yes!" Joss pumped his arm.

Aneh pulled the grav belt out of her bag and handed it to Chymm. He held it up. "I dunno—this thing was built for Aneh. I don't have the same girlish figure." He slid the belt around his doughy waist and tried to close it in the front.

"Crap," Joss said. "That thing is never going to fit me."

"Me neither," I said.

"New plan." Chymm handed the belt back to Aneh. "I'll ride on the cube, and you take the belt."

"Will it hold you?" I asked.

"Good point. Not while it's connected to the cube." Chymm looked at each of us. "Peter, you're pretty slender. Can you get that belt on?"

Peter sighed but took the belt from Aneh. Stretched out to its full length, it barely fit around his waist. "What about Marise?"

The girl shook her head. "I understand the theory, but you don't want me near the electronics, remember?"

"You go with Aneh," Chymm told Peter. "I'll show you two how to take it apart."

While the three of them gathered around the cube, I turned to the others. "Is that thing going to lift you?" I asked Joss. "How much do you mass?"

Joss flexed. "Ninety kilograms of pure muscle."

I rolled my eyes.

Marise pulled up the specs. "After they disconnect it from the cube, it'll lift him. Easily."

Once Peter and Aneh were convinced they understood the instructions, she climbed on top of the cube. We used Marise's rope to tie her to the mod. "We don't need you falling off from way up there," I said. "Take Joss's tranq gun—whoever stays up there should keep it."

They nodded. Peter sucked in his stomach and fastened the grav belt. "I can hardly breathe." His voice sounded strangled.

Joss clapped him on the shoulder. "I always knew your tiny body would come in useful someday."

"We can't all be muscle bound hulks like you," Peter said. "Too bad Abdul isn't still here—this would fit him perfectly."

"Let's launch this shuttle," I said. "My ears are freezing."

Peter and the cube, with Aneh tied to the top, rose from the ground. They went straight up and then headed toward the top of the hill.

The wind came up again, cutting into my skin. I shivered, my teeth chattering. Liam crawled out of my pocket and wrapped himself around my neck. His warm body snuggled against my ears and chin like a live scarf.

"Are you guys okay?" I asked. "It's getting chilly. We probably should have suggested they open up the cube."

"We'll all be up there soon." Joss pointed. High above us, a figure streaked out from the top of the hill pulling a large square behind. Within seconds, she had descended enough for us to recognize Aneh. She dropped to the sand, a meter-square platform landing beside her.

"How much will this thing lift? Can I take two or three people back up?" Aneh fiddled with the belt.

"Joss will have to go alone, but the rest of us should be able to go in pairs," Chymm said. "Now that you know how to work that thing, it'll be faster if you keep the belt on. You can take us up and bring the empty platform down. I'm next." He climbed on and patted the material beside him. "There's room for you, too, Marise."

When it was my turn, I sat cross-legged on the platform and gripped the rings built into its base. Yvonne sat next to me. We rose smoothly, Joss's light dwindling quickly into a pinpoint. Overhead, stars sparkled. I'd been so focused on getting us up the hill, I hadn't noticed. I laid back on the platform, letting my legs dangle over the side, and stared up at the night sky. Liam uncurled from my neck and sat on my chest, chittering softly.

"It's beautiful when you aren't worried about surviving." I took a deep breath. "And that scent—I think it's the trees. It smells a lot like Earth."

"It smells like dirt?" Yvonne asked.

"Earth, the planet," I said. "Not earth like dirt. The place we landed had pine trees. They smelled like this."

"Hold on," Aneh said. "Were going horizontal." The platform lurched, and we slid toward the hillside.

The top of the hill was a flat rocky expanse that stretched as far as we could see. It reminded me of the top of the mesa above our base camp on Earth. I hoped there weren't any caves hidden beneath.

A full-sized living module sat about twenty meters from the edge of the hillside. Meter-high pylons stood upright in a large oval around the mod. Peter, Chymm, and Marise worked on unfolding our smaller cube next to the large one. I sat up and pulled my legs onto the platform as we approached.

"Do we need that module?" I jumped off the platform. Liam leaped with me, soaring across the barren ground. He landed on Peter's shoulder.

Aneh waited for Yvonne to hop down then headed away again. "I'll be back with Joss in a sec."

"We figured we have it, we might as well use it," Marise said. "It doesn't do us any good folded up in a cube. Except for extra seating."

"I totally forgot they said living quarters would be here," Yvonne said. "Why did we decide to bring one?"

I wrinkled my nose. "Because they don't always do what they say? Because relying on them could be suicide?"

"Oh, yeah, that." Yvonne wandered to the larger cube. "Is this thing open?"

"It responded to my handprint." Peter stepped back, leaving Chymm and Marise to latch our few empty crates to the top of the cube. "We should probably reprogram it in case it's got the whole class's prints in memory."

"Good thought." I slapped my hand on the cube and the lock clicked. As I pushed the door open, lights came on inside. This mod was smaller than the ones we'd had on Earth but twice the size of our tiny survival module. The front room had a pair of tables and some electronic equipment. Chymm would be thrilled. The rear room sported columns every eight feet with rings embedded in them. "That's for the hammocks," I told Peter.

"I know. I saw your mod on Earth, remember?" He opened a door on the back wall. "Toilet and sink. I wonder if there's water?" He touched the faucet. "Yes, there is. Showers back there?" He nodded at another door.

"Maybe. Showers are a luxury, so that might be storage." I pushed past him and opened the door. The room inside lighted. "Jackpot! Look, supplies!"

Peter rushed in. "Food?"

I handed him a meal pac. "Yeah, but expired. That sucks. Probably still mostly edible, though." I moved deeper into the storage room. "There's more rope. Solar panels. Some electronics—probably spare parts for the lab equipment. Get Chymm in here." I continued taking inventory as Peter hurried away.

Most of the boxes were unlabeled. Dr. Abdul-James, my boss on the *Return in Glory*, would have been appalled. I chuckled. She would have been appalled by this whole mission. I pulled down another box and peeked inside. Behind me, Chymm and Peter pushed through the door, the others close behind.

"Jackpot!" I shouted again. Grinning, I held my treasures aloft. "Stunners!"

"Nice!" Joss took one and checked the charge. "We'll need to charge these packs as soon as the sun comes up. In the meantime, I'll set a guard around the perimeter. At least we have excellent lines of sight."

"There are plugs in here. Chymm, can you see if they're connected to the solar panels?" I handed the second stunner to him. He nodded, his eyes flitting back to the electronic equipment. "Protection first, then you can look in the boxes. Work before play."

He growled. "Some of that stuff might be essential."

I patted his arm. "I know. But so are the stunners."

He nodded and set to work.

I slid past him into the larger room. "Marise, do you have the manual for the force shield? I want to get it operating right away."

"Got it, boss." She swiped open her holo-ring and flipped through the files. "Here you go. But if there's no power, it won't work."

"Each pylon has a battery—they store power for nighttime. Hopefully, these are on standby mode and not dead." I followed her out of the mod. Of course, even if they had power, that didn't mean they'd left them connected. "Let's get this thing running."

CHAPTER EIGHTEEN

THE FORCE SHIELD ACTIVATED EASILY. Blue static fuzzed between the pylons, the faint glow forming a dome over our heads. A two-meter-wide clear zone surrounded the shield, giving animals nowhere to hide. With the team inside, I felt protected.

"It makes sense," Marise said. "They use these sites every year, and they don't want to lose cadets to wild animals. Besides, this is supposed to be a phase 2 camp—up and running."

"There isn't a lock on this system." Yvonne tapped the panel on the cliffside pylon. "Anyone can open it from the inside or out. It's meant to keep wildlife out, not people."

"Crap." I made a gimme gesture, and Marise swiped the file to me. "The system we had on Earth had security features built in. I thought that was standard, but they expected the Gagarians to show up. Going to a planet without sentient life wouldn't require locks, right?"

"But you don't know if there is sentient life until you get there," Marise said. "You'd think they'd all have a built-in security system."

"We'll set a guard. Although, after they stole all our stuff, I'm not sure they'll bother us. There's nothing left to take." I turned to Joss as he strolled across the plateau.

"Already got it." He pulled up a file on his holo-ring and showed it to me. "I've got the first watch. Go get some sleep."

"Who's with you?" I asked. "I'll send them out."

"Already done that, too." Joss grinned widely. "What? You think the Neanderthal can't use a holo-ring? I can be taught."

Yvonne took the second stunner. "Where do you want me?"

"Normally, I'd say we could leave the cliff side unguarded." Joss gestured to the rocky edge. "But Aneh might not be the only one who brought a grav belt."

"We had enough for the team on the pallet." Marise nodded. "Whoever took our stuff has ours in addition to any they brought."

"It sounds like you have it figured out." I raised a hand. "We'll see you in a few hours." Marise and I headed into the module.

Inside, Aneh had hung the hammocks and was helping Chymm go through the electronics in the boxes.

"There's some good stuff in here," Chymm said.

"Any of it useful for our mission?" I asked. "Or just generally good stuff?"

"Depends on the mission." Chymm held up a circuit board. "I can build a video cam with this. I saw some lenses over there. That way, we have our own vid of anything that happens."

"Outstanding," I said. "Our mission is to establish a base and begin surveying the local area. I don't suppose you have any more grav belts in there."

"There's a whole box of parts labeled grav." Aneh hurried to the pile and lifted a crate to show us the label on the bottom.

"That should be our top priority. Or our next top priority." I looked at the time on my holo-ring. "It's two in the morning local time, but seven pm at the Academy. I think we should get some sleep, so we're ready to get started at daybreak, which is around six-thirty."

"What if someone attacks?" Aneh asked.

"Joss and Yvonne are on guard duty." I headed for the inner room. "They'll wake you and Peter in two hours. The rest of us should sleep." I swung up into the hammock.

"I'm not tired." Chymm dragged another box along the floor.

"Chymm," I said in a friendly voice. "You're making too much noise. You will put those boxes down and go to sleep. Now. Everything will still be here in the morning."

"Yes, mother," Chymm said.

WE GATHERED under the roof of our smaller module to eat breakfast. Peter had set it up as a covered porch with three sides and the closed back against the larger module. During the night, Joss had started a small fire in front of the structure, using the wood Peter had gathered by the stream. We used the fire to heat water for our breakfast.

"Go easy on the rations," Marise said. "Remember, we're here for up to two weeks, and this is all we have."

"I'm going to take my grav belt and go down to the stream," Aneh said. "I'll bet something edible lives down there."

"Animal or vegetable?" Chymm asked.

"Either," Aneh said. "Marise brought the specs for the mission, which included lists of safe-to-eat foods."

"If this was a real mission, we wouldn't have any lists," Joss said.

"But this is supposed to be a phase 2 mission." Marise pointed her spoon at him. "That's why the living mod and force shield were here. There should be stores of supplies, too, but I guess they didn't want to pre-load any of that stuff. "

"Which is why they had us pack it." I scowled. "Too bad it didn't get here with us. Aneh, don't go down alone. Use the grav panel and take someone with you."

"I'll go," Peter said. "As long as I don't have to squeeze into that tiny belt again."

"No, Peter, you stay here," I said. "Neither you nor Aneh got much sleep last night. I want someone awake enough to watch her back."

"I'll go." Marise yawned. "I got a solid four hours."

"That's as much as anyone got," I said. "We'll have to catch up tonight."

That decided, we sat in silence for a while. As the sun rose, the trees outside the shield stilled. The wind must have died down. A bird flew overhead, followed by a V-formation of others. A tiny insect crept across the dirt by my shoe.

"What's our real mission?" Marise asked as she gathered the scraps from her meal pac.

I shrugged. "They said we'd get instructions in a day or two. We need to use these two days—or whatever they give us—to get set up. That means getting our sleep patterns worked out. We need to be sharp when the time comes. Plus, hopefully Chymm can create some useful equipment from the bits and pieces in there."

The girls got their bags and loaded them on the grav panel. Each of us had brought wire and lightweight plastic stakes to create snares. Aneh held up a shovel she found in the supply room. "According to the specs, there are some roots that grow near streams like that one that are edible."

"Go get them." I tossed her one of the empty crates. "Anything that's edible. And take a stunner. You might run into one of the larger creatures." Or another cadet. But I didn't say that.

She nodded and pointed to the grav panel. "It's already there. I've also got a solar panel to charge it."

"You won't need that," I said. "Your jacket should have a solar panel built into the shoulders. If you keep the stunner plugged in while you're carrying it, it will charge."

The others all stared at me. "I don't remember reading that anywhere," Marise said.

"That's what we had on…" I winced and didn't finish the sentence.

"On Earth," Yvonne said. "You can say it. Felicity was the only one who cared, and that's because she was jealous."

"I feel like I'm saying it a lot," I said.

"It's our only real-life frame of reference," Peter said. "No one else has been off planet for a mission."

I nodded. "True enough. Okay. On Earth, our uniforms had charging cells built into the shoulders. They looked just like these uniforms, and mine has a magnetic plug in the hem." I turned up the bottom edge of my jacket to show them.

Everyone else started examining their jackets. "This is so cool." Joss slapped the plug onto his stunner. A light started blinking.

"Chymm, can you check?" I asked. "I mean, make sure they actually work."

Chymm already had his jacket off and was doing something with a piece of electronic equipment. "The leads are connected, and the material in the shoulders appears to be photovoltaic." He laid his jacket in the sun and fiddled with the plug end. He nodded. "Yep, I got a current."

Marise picked up the stunner and attached the lead from her jacket. The lights flickered. "Nice."

After the girls left, I pulled Joss aside. "What can we do to strengthen our defenses? I don't think Black will bother us, but if they do, I want more than two stunners and a tranq gun. How many darts do you have for that thing, anyway?"

"I brought two full cartridges, so twenty-four. The best answer would be if Chymm could add some kind of security to the force field." He raised an eyebrow at the pudgy boy.

"I'll see what I can do," Chymm said.

"Security is the first priority," I said. "Then the grav belts." I swung around. "Yvonne?"

"Water?" she asked. "I already tested it, and it's safe to drink. I guess they want us to survive."

I smirked. "It looks bad if you kill too many cadets."

My holo-ring vibrated. I flicked it, and a message popped up. "Gather around, kids," I said.

Cadet Wronglen appeared. "I know you haven't had much time, but I hope you've got your camps set up. This exercise will be a capture the flag competition. There is a transmitter located within a day's flight of your camp. The first team to retrieve the transmitter wins. Go." His face disappeared.

"Is there any additional information?" Chymm asked. "Frequencies?"

I flicked the message. "No, nothing. You can find it though, right?"

Chymm ran into the mod. Marise, Peter, and I followed more slowly.

"There's some comm gear." Chymm pawed through a box on the table. "If I can connect the receiver to my holo-ring, I can search for the signal."

"Does each flight have a tech genius?" Peter asked. "I mean, if we didn't have Chymm, how would we do this?"

I wandered into the storage room. "I don't know. The equipment we need must be here. I wonder if there's—" I pushed a crate aside and searched the closest shelf.

"What are we looking for?" Peter started on the next shelf.

"This." I held up a small tablet. It had been shoved between two crates. "This should have an inventory." I tapped the tablet, and it glowed, but the charge showed red. "Ask Chymm if the chargers are working." While Peter stepped out of the room to ask, I plugged it in anyway.

"He says yes." Peter leaned over my shoulder as the tablet lit. "What's it got?"

I scrolled through a long list. "These designations must refer to location or a scannable identifier." I pulled the cable to full length and held the tablet near one of the crates. It bleeped. "Aha! This box holds grav belt modules." I started waving the tablet at crates. As it scanned each box, it highlighted the items inside. I handed the tablet to Peter. "Try those on the top shelf."

He stretched the charging cord to full length. "Got it! Frequency scanners!" He tossed the tablet back to me and pulled a crate from the top shelf. As it came off, he stumbled. "Heavier than it looks." He carried the crate to the front room.

"Where'd you find this?" Chymm asked. "Never mind. This is exactly what we need." He pulled out a pair of devices and flipped one on. "Crap. No charge."

"We can work in the supply closet." I jerked a thumb toward the back. "There are charging cables—"

Chymm shook his head. He attached the device to his jacket lead, piled the rest back into the crate, and hurried out the front door.

"Solar charger," Peter said. "Brilliant."

Chymm dropped to his haunches and began fiddling with the device.

"Brilliant," I repeated. "Peter, help me move this table." I lifted one end of the smaller table. Peter took the other, and we carried it out front. I set the crate on the table. Chymm continued to work on his device, still crouched on the ground. I grabbed his elbow and pulled him up. He didn't even look but continued to work as I pulled him to the table.

"This is perfect." Chymm patted the device lovingly. "We've got two of them, so we can triangulate."

"Joss!" I hollered.

"Here." His voice came through my audio implant.

I rolled my eyes. Show-off.

"We've got incoming," he said.

CHAPTER NINETEEN

Joss stood on the roof of the mod facing the plateau. I jerked my head at Peter and raced to the force shield on that side. "I can't see anything from here."

"Four people in grav belts, coming this way," Joss said.

I flicked my holo-ring. "Aneh. Yvonne. Return to base immediately." I didn't wait for them to respond but climbed up the ladder built into the back of the module. "How many people will this thing hold?"

"I dunno," Joss said. "You'd have to ask Marise."

I stood next to him, and he pointed. Four specks floated in the distance, flying a couple of meters above the scrubby brush. "How can you tell those are people?"

He shrugged. "They look like people."

I squinted. "I'll take your word for it." I moved to the edge and raised my voice. "Hey, Chymm. Is there any way to figure out who that is?"

"Try this." His fingers swept toward me.

My ring vibrated as the file arrived. I flicked it, and an app opened. A map displayed in my palm, centered on our camp. The force shield glowed blue, a long diamond perched on the north side of the cliff that zig-zagged east to west across the display. On the screen, five darker blue dots appeared. Each one was labeled with a tiny number. "Is this us?"

"Yeah," Chymm said absently as he continued to fiddle with the equipment. "Zoom out, so you can see the others."

I stretched the screen. The plains seemed to stretch for kilometers in every direction, with the cliff a raggedy slash across the middle. Two more blue dots appeared behind us. "That must be Aneh and Yvonne." I stretched some more. "These dots are green. Does that mean anything?"

"It means they're from Alpha Green," Chymm said.

I straightened and showed the boys.

"How did he do that?" Peter stared at the hologram. "We could've used this on the last exercise."

"I think he made it *because* of the last exercise," Joss said. "He told me he was working on something. How big can you make it? Maybe we can see everyone."

"We can test that later." I pointed at the incoming cadets. "First, we need to figure out how to deal with them."

"I say we meet them at the barrier." Joss swung over the side and slid down the ladder.

I scrambled after him. "Peter, stay up there. And take this." I swiped a copy of the app to him. "If anyone else shows up, let us know ASAP."

"Aye, aye, sir."

I caught his thumbs-up as I slid out of view.

Joss stood by the blue bollard at the north-most point of our camp. From here, we couldn't see the incoming cadets. "They're flying very low."

"Makes sense," I said. "Especially if you know Delta Black has weapons."

"That's right." Joss didn't take his eyes off the horizon. "I wonder if they know that? I'm not sure the other shuttle pilots were as helpful."

"Bob said he took Green dirtside, too," I said.

We waited in silence. Chymm wandered up, holding his devices.

"We're back," Aneh said through the implant.

"Stay at the cliff edge, inside the shield," Joss said. "Spread out. There's only four of them coming—the others could be trying to sneak in behind us."

"I don't see anything," Peter said.

"We don't know how reliable that thing is." Joss ignored Chymm's glare.

"Are those your signal scanners?" I pointed at the boxes Chymm held. "If they are, you should hide them in the mod. And lock the door. We don't know what Green wants or what they might do."

Chymm nodded and hurried away.

"Won't they have their own?" Aneh asked.

"Probably, if they bother to look." I bit my lip. "I think the more important question is, how did they find us?"

"I know the answer to that," Peter called from the roof. "I'll bet they have copies of all our mission briefs. Laghari is in Green. He's a hacker. He probably got every flight's info." He smiled sheepishly. "I tried but wasn't successful."

"I wonder if they'd be open to a trade of some kind." I squinted, trying to identify the approaching cadets.

"What do we have to offer?" Joss asked. "Someone—maybe even them—stole all our tradeable stuff."

"Maybe. If Black took our stuff, maybe they took everyone else's too? Or they might need help with the electronics. Just because they've got a hacker doesn't mean they have someone like Chymm."

"Good point." Joss stepped forward as the four cadets flew into view. "I wish he could lock this thing."

"They obviously didn't want us to do that," I said. "Since they gave us a model without security."

"Maybe previous classes haven't had murderous thug legacies in them." He winked at me. "No offense."

I rolled my eyes. "I'm not murderous or a thug, so none taken." I recognized two of the arriving cadets, now. Tovar, Aneh's crush from the drill team, and Laghari, the hacker Peter had mentioned. The two girls looked familiar, but I'd never met them. I moved closer to the gate bollard and activated my inter-flight audio channel. "Hello!"

They touched down a few meters from us. "Hi, Siti," Tovar said. "Can we talk?"

"How did you find us?" I asked.

Laghari smirked. "We might have seen the exercise plans."

"Including the location of the transmitter?" I asked.

"Maybe," Laghari said, but his lips tightened.

"If you knew where it was, you'd already have gone after it." Joss stood with one hand resting on the stunner at his belt.

Tovar's eyes flickered. "Where'd you get that?"

It was Joss's turn to smirk. "We might have brought it. What do you want?"

Tovar turned back to me. "Delta Black took over our camp."

"What? Already?" Acid poured into my stomach, and my breakfast churned.

"They were dropped first." Tovar glanced at Peter on the roof of the module. "They had weapons—stun rifles."

"How do you know?" Joss demanded.

"We were loading our shuttle at the same time as them. One of the crew members gave them a case. Ariana recognized it as a stun rifle case." Tovar jerked his thumb at one of the girls.

"Those cases are pretty distinctive." The tiny girl tapped the marksmanship badge on her chest. "The competition squad uses them in training. That style of case holds four."

"Did they take any of your supplies?" I asked.

"They grabbed a case of meal pacs. They'd already taken all your stuff when we got there." Laghari shrugged as if there was nothing they could do. "Sorry."

"When we get back to the Academy, will you testify?" I asked. "I plan to lodge a formal complaint."

"Hey, I ain't no snitch!" Laghari held up both hands.

"We don't really need you, since we have the vids," I lied with a shrug. "I thought you'd like a chance to get on the right side."

Laghari went pale. Had he helped Black steal our stuff? Or told them to take ours instead of theirs? If Bob came through with the vid, we'd know, but I wasn't holding my breath.

"What do you want?" I turned back to Tovar.

"We want to collaborate with you," he said promptly. "We don't have enough food to get through the week, and I know you have some expert hunters. We have grav belts."

"Yeah, I was going to ask about that," I said. "Am I the only drill team member who didn't steal one?"

"We didn't steal them. They were part of our rightfully requisitioned supplies."

"Not that model." I pointed to the logo on his belt. "That's a drill team, competition-grade belt."

He glared at me. "We were practicing when they recalled us for the mission. We don't all have experience flying around other planets."

"As it happens, we have grav belts, too," Chymm said. I swung around. He floated a meter off the ground, sliding slowly toward us.

"I thought you said you didn't take any belts?" Tovar said.

"Have you looked in your storeroom?" I pointed at the living module. "There's a lot of useful stuff in there."

"Boxes of unlabeled crap," Laghari muttered. Behind him, both girls were whispering. To each other or to their flight-mates?

"I thought you said Black took over your camp," Joss said.

"They did—this morning. We'd already gone through the crap closet. I can't believe we missed grav-belts." Tovar glared at Laghari.

"I wouldn't recognize a disassembled grav belt," Laghari said. "I'm a hacker, not a wirehead."

"Where's the rest of Green?" I asked. "You have seven other members."

"Some of them went looking for Red. The rest stayed behind to watch Black." Tovar's eyes shifted toward Laghari as he spoke.

"Stay sharp, Blue," I whispered into the flight channel. "Something's not right."

"Why don't you let us come in, so we can talk." Tovar gestured toward the force shield.

"Hang on." Chymm strode up to the bollard. "It's been a little hinky since we got here. Let me…" He opened the panel on the side of the bollard and did something.

The blue glow of the force shield intensified, humming loudly. "Oops." He waved wildly at the green team, then turned his back to them. "I turned up the strength of the shield. I also installed an inhibitor I found in the storeroom. It should prevent them from deactivating it." He turned back to the bollard as if he were still working on it.

"If Black took over their camp," Aneh said through our flight channel, "shouldn't we help them?"

Joss bared his teeth in a humorless grin. "I was getting a bad feeling from them. Good work, Chymm."

"We have no proof Black did anything to them," Peter said from the roof. "However, according to Chymm's app, there are two black dots down by the stream. I suppose it's possible they followed Green here, but it's more likely they're working together."

"How are we supposed to accomplish the mission if we're hiding in our base?" I asked. "I wonder if we'd be better off letting them have the camp?"

"No!" The cacophony of voices almost deafened me.

"No," Joss repeated. "We shouldn't rule that out completely, but I'm not ready to give up yet. Unless Chymm's trick doesn't work."

On the other side of the barrier, I could see Tovar's mouth move, but the open channel wasn't receiving anymore. I raised my hands and shrugged then pointed at Chymm.

"We'll find out in a few minutes," Peter said. "I've now got four bogeys coming up the cliff. Two black, two green."

"Aneh, where are you?" I asked. "Do you have the stunner?"

"Yes, sir," she said. "I'm at the south point of the camp."

I looked at Peter.

"That's where they're coming up." Peter nodded as he turned to face south.

"Chymm, pretend you're saying something to them." I glared at him, as if I were angry. "Yvonne and Marise, I want you with Aneh."

"Here they come," Peter said.

My skin crawled, the point between my shoulder blades burning like a target, but I didn't turn to look. Tovar and his friends moved toward the force shield. "They're attacking!" I cried.

"Field at full strength," Chymm said. "The inhibitor says it's working."

Tovar reached toward the bollard then jerked his hand back. He shook it, as if it had been burned, and glared at us, yelling something. Laghari swung a weapon around and aimed at me. He yelled, too.

"This thing will stop a stunner, right?" My voice cracked.

"According to the specs, it should." Chymm remained crouched by the bollard. "You might want to duck—just to be sure."

I crouched beside him. The bollard provided almost no cover, but the blue glow between the uprights gave an illusion of safety. I squinted through the brilliant static. "He's firing."

The shield glowed brighter a few meters off the ground.

"Peter! Get down!" Joss yelled. Peter dropped to the roof, lying flat.

After a few seconds, it became clear the intruders would not get through the shield. Tovar and Ariana made rude gestures, and all four rose on their grav belts. Laghari fired a couple more shots at Peter, but the shield held.

"They're leaving!" Aneh called.

"Good work, team. Stay where you are. Peter, watch the dots. Or better yet, send everyone a copy."

"I got it," Chymm said. "He can't copy it while it's open."

"Chymm, can they get through the shield?" I flicked my ring and opened the app. The four green dots moved west, curving around us. "It looks like they're joining the group down by the stream."

"When the shield is at full strength, they can't get close enough to open it." Chymm tapped the bollard with a finger. "They get shocked, like Tovar. The problem is it can't stay at this level at night. Once it drops to normal levels, they'll be able to get to one of the bollards. If my inhibitor works, it will act as a lock on the system. If it doesn't..."

"Can we test it?" I asked.

Chymm waggled his hand back and forth. "The easiest way to test it would be to send someone outside and have them try to come in. You think it's safe to do that?"

"Thanks to your fancy app, yes." Joss pointed at the screen hovering over my palm. "We know where they are. Can you open just this section?"

"I can open the gate here." Chymm waved at the static. "I'll have to turn the intensity down, though."

"Now is probably the safest time." Joss held up his stunner. "They're busy regrouping. Let me out, and I'll try to get in."

"They can't hear us, can they?" Yvonne asked.

Joss and I exchanged a look. "I hope not." I turned to Chymm. "Can they?"

Chymm waggled his hand again. "With the shield on, they can't. If they're close enough when we open the gate, or if we use the open channel, they can."

"Let's try it then." I checked the app again. "All of them are by the stream. Everyone, keep your voices down. Chymm, open the gate."

Chymm fiddled with the bollard, and the brilliant cyan static faded to a sky blue. Then a space about a meter wide cleared next to the bollard. "Out you go," Chymm said.

"I'm going with him." I hurried through the gap. "You watch my back. I'll test the system."

Joss took up a stance a meter away from the gate, facing outward. I stood with my back to him, facing Chymm, and nodded.

The gate closed. Once the blue settled to a uniform color, I approach the bollard. Tentatively, I reached out. Static crackled over my fingers, but nothing happened. I touch the bollard, placing my hand against the access plate embedded in it.

The gate opened.

"Is it tuned to me?" I asked.

"No, the inhibitor doesn't have a recognition sequence." Chymm reached inside the bollard. "If it's on, it'll keep everyone out. Has to be opened from inside. Try again."

I stepped back and the gate closed. This time, the static charge lifted the tiny hairs on my arm, but I was still able to deactivate the gate.

"Was your inhibitor on?" I asked.

Chymm nodded. "I guess I need to work on it a bit more."

"Come back inside, Joss," I said.

"Hang on." Joss held up a hand. "I hear something." He turned, a grin spreading across his face. "I can hear their comms."

CHAPTER TWENTY

I stared at Joss, my mouth hanging open.

"How is that possible?" Chymm demanded.

I pointed at Joss. "He used to be in Delta Black. He's still connected to their flight channel." I raised my voice, too excited to use the comm system. "Peter! Come down here."

"And they call me the Neanderthal!" Joss flashed a grin over his shoulder. "I know how to use the comm."

"If you can hear them, maybe they can hear you. Maybe you two shouldn't use the comm anymore."

Joss shook his head, not turning. "I was on their all-flight channel. They won't have ours."

"What about Felicity and Terrine?" I asked.

He shrugged, his back still to me. "Only if they bother listening. Maybe we shouldn't use our all-flight channel anymore. There's only seven of us, so we can use a group call instead."

Peter jumped the last few rungs of the ladder and landed beside me. "What's up?"

I explained and told him to step outside. "See if you can hear anything."

He saluted me and jogged through the gate. I rolled my eyes and closed the gate.

We watched Peter's face through the blue static. He spoke to Joss then flicked his holo-ring. His brows drew together in concentration, then he nodded and gave a thumbs-up.

"Open the gate." When the blue cleared, I told the boys to come back inside. "I want to see if you can hear them from in here."

"I'll stay out while Peter tries," Joss said. "That way we'll know for sure if they're actually talking."

With the gate closed, Peter grinned. "They're chattering up a storm, but nothing useful. I only hear a couple of voices, though. Not any of the legacies. Maybe there's a distance component?"

"Now what?" Chymm asked.

I waved that off. "Now that we know, we have someone watch the app twenty-four seven. Or twenty-six eight, or whatever the local diurnal rhythm is. And we have Peter and Joss check Black's comm system on a regular schedule." I triggered the all-flight command. "Charlie Blue, assemble. By the fire."

"Do you need me?" Chymm asked. "I want to keep working on this."

"Don't test anything by yourself." I narrowed my eyes at him. "Call for backup."

"You got it." He settled cross-legged in the dirt next to the bollard and flicked his holo-ring.

"I'll watch the app," Peter said as we moved toward our covered porch.

I ducked under the mod cube roof, even though it was at least half a meter above my head. "If those guys by the stream start to move, let us know right away." I sat, leaning against the porch's back wall. The others gathered around me. Marise poked at the firepit. "Joss, set up the rotation. Two people on duty around the clock. On top of the building is probably the best place."

"I'll use the current rotation." He flicked the file above his palm. "One person watches the app, the other watches the perimeter. Switch off every twenty minutes. I'm going to stroll over to the cliff and see what our friends are up to."

I looked at the faces gathered around me. "Now what? We can stay safe, but we can't complete the mission. We have a limited food supply."

"And it looks like our visitors just emptied one of your snares, Aneh," Joss said as he returned to the porch.

Aneh muttered something under her breath that sounded like cursing. I stared at her in amazement. "You don't say words like that."

"I do when someone steals my food," Aneh said. "And my skills."

"I suggest we leave a small team here to secure the camp," Marise began. "Then, while we know where they are, the rest of us go out and find that transmitter."

Yvonne nodded. "There's no reason we all have to stay here. And I am not going to let them win."

"I agree." Peter stretched the app window in his hand. "They're moving. They're leaving one green and one black by the stream. The others are headed that way." He pointed north.

"Is that the direction the signal is coming from?" I asked.

Chymm shook his head. "I've been too focused on the shield. I have no idea."

"Marise, you're smart." I pointed at her. "Can you help him?"

"You know I'm not good with electronics," she replied. "I don't want to blow anything up. Maybe Yvonne would be better."

Yvonne chuckled and jumped up. "Chymm, what do you want me to do?"

"For now, stay by the gate. I'll show you how to close it."

While they worked, I turned back to Aneh, Marise, and Peter. "We keep someone on watch. We turn up the power if they come too close. Peter and Joss can monitor their conversation. But there's only two of them. They can't do it full time."

Peter glanced up from the app. "I think we follow Yvonne's plan. Two of us stay here to guard the camp, and the other five go after the prize. We don't care what they're saying, unless they're planning an attack on us. And we'll see that coming, thanks to Chymm."

I rubbed the back of my neck. "Sounds reasonable. But we need to be very careful. Laghari fired a stunner at you. They're willing to hurt us over this. That's crazy."

"I have to admit," Aneh said. "I'm rethinking my commitment to the Academy."

"I know what you mean," Peter said. "I'd love to explore new planets, but it's not worth getting killed over. At least not in the training phase."

"That's something we haven't talked about," I said. "This whole thing is way out of bounds. If the leadership is willing to overlook cadets firing weapons at each other, then maybe we should all throw in the towel. Stay here in the camp, ration our food stores, and wait to be picked up. Winning the exercise isn't worth the risk."

"No." Marise's yelp echoed off the wall behind me. "I worked too hard to get into the Academy to give up."

"But if we can prove—"

She cut me off. "You saw how well that worked. Even if we had vid proof, we'd probably have to go to internal affairs or over Zimas's head. Would they believe us? I'm not sure I'm willing to take that leap of faith."

"What are you suggesting?" I asked.

"I'm suggesting we do what Yvonne and Peter said. We leave someone here to protect our camp, and the rest of us complete the mission. We have the skills and, thanks to Chymm, the equipment to do it. We stay out of the others' way and don't engage if they're around. I have no desire to get hurt."

I bit my lip. Somehow, I had become the leader of this flight, and I didn't want anyone to get hurt. But I also didn't want Delta Black to win. No, I didn't want the *legacies* to win. And I didn't want to play their dirty game. I activated the comm channel. "We watch, we sneak out, we stay safe, but we complete the mission. Anyone disagree?"

"I think it's our best shot," Peter said.

"I'm in," Chymm said. "And I've got the scanners up and running. We can head out immediately."

"What about you, Aneh?" I asked. "You can stay here—it's probably the safest place."

She shook her head. "No. I'll stay here if you think it's best for the team. But if you're going to do this, then I'm all in."

"Let's get started." I stood and dusted off the back of my pants. "The faster we win this mission, the sooner we can head home."

CHAPTER TWENTY-ONE

WE LEFT Chymm and Yvonne in the camp. Chymm wanted to keep working on his gadgets, and Yvonne figured the exercise would provide ample future opportunities to succeed, as Lawrence was fond of saying.

"I'm almost done with this last grav belt." Chymm lifted a disassembled belt from the table. He'd repaired three belts from the closet and was now attaching the lifters from the mod cube to some webbing. "You don't want to go too high."

"Why not?" Aneh asked.

"Do you trust me that much?" Chymm asked. "Because I don't. Stay low enough that if it breaks, you won't die on impact."

"Thanks for the warning," I muttered. "We'll make Aneh do anything way up there."

"You'll need to split up." Chymm handed a device to Joss and another to me. "Based on my best guess, I'd say you want to be about a klick apart. That should give you enough distance to triangulate the signal and home in on it." He flicked the screen and demonstrated the device. An arrow appeared on the screen, but it spun in circles. "They won't give you a good direction if you're too close together. Once you get it locked in, you can converge."

"Everyone have their tracking app?" I asked the group. "Peter and

Marise, you'll come with me. Aneh, you're with Joss. When we're close to the target, we'll angle back together. One member of each team watches the app at all times. Boys, you keep listening for Black."

I finished loading my backpack. "Yvonne, we'll check in at the top of the hour. If you don't respond, I'll try again on the quarter hour. If anyone notices the others closing in on us, alert everyone. We'll take supplies for two days—that doesn't leave you two much."

Yvonne shrugged. "I can set some more snares down by the creek if those last two idiots ever leave."

"Don't engage," I reminded her. "We don't know where the weapons are—or even how many there are."

"Got it." Yvonne flashed a thumbs-up. "Good luck."

"You, too." I slung my pack over my shoulders. "Charlie Blue, anyone want to chicken out?"

"Hell, no!" they hollered together.

I swung my arm in a big circle. "Move out."

BY MID-MORNING, the flat plain felt like an oven. Sun glared down and reflected off the ground below, sucking the moisture from everything. A rhythmic crackling stopped and started. Yvonne said it was caused by insects. We flew low above the scrubby brush, our toes breaking off bits of taller bushes. The sharp scent of the broken twigs tickled my nose. Even the breeze caused by our movement failed to cool us.

Liam leapt off my shoulder from time to time, soaring for a few meters before landing again. In the desert air, the brush of his fur felt rough against my parched skin. "How much farther?"

"The Black team is still about two klicks ahead of us." He flicked a finger at the hologram in his palm. "They're still going due north, though."

We'd split with Joss and Aneh right outside the camp. They'd gone northeast while we headed northwest for about two klicks. Now we were heading just east of north, angling toward the signal our devices had triangulated. Joss and Aneh occasionally popped up on our right, but they were too far away to recognize, and like us, they stayed low.

I checked my clock. "Yvonne, status."

"We're good. The idiots down by the creek haven't moved. No one new on the horizon. Chymm thinks he might have solved the inhibitor problem. I'm testing it now." There was silence for a second then a yelp. "That hurt! What did you do? Siti, I'll call you back."

"Check in next hour. I can wait until then to find out what Chymm did." I chuckled as I signed off. Making the bollard painful to touch would be as effective as installing the inhibitor—if the batteries could sustain it all night.

"I wonder if we should try to find Charlie Orange," Marise suggested.

"Why would we do that?" I asked.

"It would give us more personnel," Marise said. "We only have seven people. Delta Black still has twelve, and they've teamed up with Green, who has nine or ten."

"Do you know anyone in Orange well enough to trust them?" Peter asked. "Because I don't. They seem okay in the dorm, but we haven't spent much time together. The only cadets I know outside of Blue are Delta Black, and I wouldn't trust them, ever."

"Duh." Marise grinned, taking the sting out of the word. "A few of them are in my martial arts class, but we don't exactly talk. The most important thing to know is I can take 'em all to the mat. One at a time."

"We're getting close." Peter gestured to the hologram in his palm. "There are three black dots ahead, and they've slowed down."

"Where'd the fourth one go?" I flicked on my audio implant. "Can you hear them? Do you think they know where they're going?"

"This is a different group," Peter said. "Those four went farther west, remember? Maybe they don't know where this thing is?"

"I'd say they have a general idea." Marise changed directions, heading off to our right. "But I'm not sure they triangulated like we did. Maybe even with Green helping, they are spread too thin."

"They aren't stupid." I opened Chymm's app and stretched it as wide as it would go. "Remember, Laghari is a hacker."

"Yes," Peter said. "But Laghari is a Green. LeBlanc and Lee aren't going to trust him. They'll try to keep Green as far away from the prize as possible while still making use of them. They've probably got them distracted. If we count three ahead of us, and the two behind our camp, and at least two more at Green's camp, that's seven. That means there's five more possibly closing in on the target. And not a Green in sight."

I increased the lift on my grav belt.

"Stay low," Peter said. "If you get too high, they can see you."

"I want to see them," I said, but I dropped back. "I wish we knew who each of these dots was."

"Let me listen for a while," Peter said.

We skimmed along over the rough terrain. As we got farther from our cliff edge, the rocky plateau became a series of small ridges, gradually rising to the low hills. The signal we were seeking was in the foothills about five klicks away. The sun beat down. Sweat trickled down my back and sides. I slurped some water and rehung my bottle on my backpack.

"It sounds like Kerensky and Thomas. I can't tell who the third one is." Peter shook his head in frustration. "I'll bet LeBlanc, Lee, and Felicity are already on their way to the prize."

"I could have guessed that," Marise said.

Forty-five minutes later, we reached the foothills. Short, sturdy trees with long needles covered the jagged terrain. A tinkling stream flowed into a small pool that had no obvious outflow. Joss and Aneh waited for us in the shadow of a rocky crag.

"The evil trio passed about ten minutes ago," Joss said when we arrived.

"Why didn't you stop them?" Marise blurted out.

"How should I have done that?" Joss raised an eyebrow. "Besides, do we want to stoop to their level? Our mission is to find the prize."

Marise stomped her foot in frustration. "I know. And you're right. But that doesn't make me want to play nice."

"Yeah, it's hard to play fair when they aren't." Aneh said. "But even if we were cheating, attacking them would have been a bad idea. We only had the one stunner with us, and they have several. If we'd been really lucky, we could've taken out one of the boys. Despite Joss's confidence in my fighting abilities," she rolled her eyes, "I think Felicity would have won."

"Fair enough," Marise said.

"I'm glad you didn't try it," I said. "We need to stay one hundred percent above board on this. I don't want to give them any reason to get rid of us." I looked at Peter and Marise. "Do we need to rest, or are you good?"

Peter shook out his arms and legs. "Those grav belts get tiring after a while but not like walking. I'm fine."

"Keep communications to a minimum," I said. "Sound carries and we don't want them to overhear us. Let's move out. Joss, take point."

We lifted off the ground, following a narrow valley up into the hills. We could have lifted higher and flown direct, but I didn't want to attract the attention of the other teams.

Joss held up a hand. He was about fifty yards ahead of us but still visible near a twist in the canyon. "There's someone there," he whispered through the comm system. "Didn't you see them on the app?"

Peter stretched and contracted the hologram. "There's nothing!"

"What are they doing?" I asked.

"Not moving," Joss said. "Just laying by a large rock. I almost didn't see them."

"They aren't dead, are they?" Aneh asked.

My head jerked around.

"I don't think so," Joss replied. "But I can't tell from here."

I opened a call back to camp. No response. I left a message. "Chymm, why would someone not show up on your app?"

"If there's only one person, it should be safe, right?" Aneh asked.

"No." I jerked my head toward Joss. "If we can't see one of them, and we don't know why, maybe there are more."

"Hang on," Peter said. "I hear something."

We waited.

"*Chokin' blasters!*" Joss said.

"About what you'd expect," Peter said, his eyes narrowed. "It's Terrine."

I glanced toward Joss then back to Peter. "What?"

"That's Terrine up ahead. She's hurt, so they left her behind while they went to the objective. Just now, LeBlanc suggested leaving her, period." He looked at me, his eyes bleak. "He doesn't want to carry her back. Felicity convinced him it wasn't a good plan."

"Are we sure they can't hear us?" Marise asked. "Maybe this is a trap."

Peter and I exchanged a wide-eyed glance. "If they can hear *you*," I said to him, "then they might try something like this."

He shook his head. "No. I can only hear them when I'm on their channel. We obviously got left in their access links when we transferred. We aren't using the all-flight channel anymore, so even if Terrine and Felicity have access, they won't hear anything."

"Why haven't you noticed it before?" I asked.

Peter grimaced. "I never tried that channel until Joss suggested it. Maybe it's always been active? I don't know why Joss even flipped it on."

"I say we risk it," I said. "I can't believe Terrine would be in on one of their dirty plots."

"She might not have had a choice," Marise said. "Those legacies don't give a crap about anyone else. And you heard what she said back on the ship—they do what they're told."

"I trust Terrine." I lifted off the ground and skimmed forward to Joss's position. "You stay here. All of you. I'll go see what she's up to."

I didn't wait for them to respond but headed around the rocky outcropping. About fifty meters ahead, she slumped in the shade of a large boulder. I slid forward, soundless in my grav belt. Her face was gray, and a film of sweat covered her forehead. As I touched down, her eyes opened.

"Siti?" she whispered.

"What happened? Where's your flight?" I stayed out of reach as I looked her over. Dust covered her uniform, and there were several tears in the tough fabric. Her face bore scrapes, and a bruise had started to bloom around her right eye. She didn't have a backpack or a grav belt.

Her lips pressed together—pain? Or maybe anger? Her eyes seemed dazed. I held out my water bottle. "You want a drink?"

"Thank you." The words were barely audible. She took the bottle and sipped from the straw without sitting up.

Liam squirmed out of my pocket and looked around. I stroked his head as Terrine drank, staring at the bruised girl.

"Are you hurt?" I asked.

"My leg." She took another drink. "And I think a rib."

I glanced over my shoulder, but the others stayed out of view as ordered. "Can you sit up?" I stepped closer and stretched out a hand. Liam jumped off my arm and soared around the little clearing.

Terrine didn't even notice. She grunted and took my hand. I braced my feet, half expecting her to pull me down, but her grip was weak. I pulled, but she moaned loudly. I lowered her back to the ground. "Why didn't you call for help? Mission control back at the Academy could send someone."

Her head wobbled from side to side, and she blinked hard, her eyes glassy. "They'd kill me if I call for help. They don't want any marks against them." She huffed out the ghost of a laugh and held up her left hand. "That's why LeBlanc took my ring."

"What?" Leaving a teammate behind because they were injured was horrible but taking away their ability to call for help was nothing short of criminal. "Joss! Marise! Come help me."

Joss and Marise zipped around the hill and flew toward us. Aneh and Peter remained out of sight as I hoped. "Marise, she thinks she has a broken rib, and there's something wrong with her leg. Can you help her?"

"I wish Yvonne were here." She knelt beside Terrine and dug through her backpack. "I have a basic med scan, but Yvonne is our expert."

I glanced at my chronograph. "We can get her on a call in about ten minutes. See what you can do for now."

As Marise worked on Terrine, I turned my back and glanced up at Joss. "What should we do? We can't leave her here, and we don't have the personnel to take her back to camp."

He stared at me. "You think it would be safe to take her back to camp? Once she's inside..."

"We'll know in a minute if she's really hurt. I don't think even the legacies have a way to lie to a med scan." I glanced over my shoulder. Marise worked quietly over the girl lying in the dirt.

"Two cracked ribs," Marise read off the screen on the med scan as it worked. "Hematoma on her leg, sprained ankle, and minor concussion. What the heck happened?"

"Grav belt died," Terrine said. "They said it was fully charged, but I didn't have a chance to check. No reason to disbelieve them."

"Where is it now?" I asked.

"They took it," she answered. "LeBlanc said he was going to take it up higher where the solar panels would catch better sun. He said it's too dark to charge here."

"Really? Too dark?" Terrine was in shade, but the rest of the valley was bright with sun.

"Did you bring your belts from the Academy, or was yours found in camp?" Joss asked.

"They had three when we arrived." Terrine took another sip of water. "Not the Academy's, but personal belts. The rest of us had belts in the supply pallet."

Joss's jaw tightened. "Lee and LeBlanc had top end models. They brought 'em with them. I don't know *how* they got around the no outside equipment rule."

"How high were you?" Marise asked.

"Too high," Terrine said.

"They took her ring," I said to the others. "So she couldn't call for help."

"They'll be back for me," Terrine said, but she didn't sound convinced.

"They took her supplies—if she had any." I jerked my thumb at her. "They didn't even leave her water."

"We should call for medevac," Marise said.

"No!" Terrine tried to sit up but sank back with a groan. "They'll disqualify me—maybe the whole flight. And I have to live with them. For the next three years." Her eyes snapped to mine, pleading.

"We can strap your ribs," Marise said. "And your ankle. And Yvonne might have something for the hematoma. But we can't treat a concussion in the field. They didn't give us that kind of equipment."

"Aren't they supposed to be watching us?" Joss asked. He looked up and waved, as if a camera might be pointing at him. "If mission control was going to send someone, they would've already done it, wouldn't they?"

"Good point. Let's build a stretcher." I pointed at him. "See if you can find anything we can use for poles. Marise, can I speak with you for a minute?"

Marise patted Terrine's arm and stepped away to talk to me. Liam flew up and scampered onto Terrine's chest. She roused enough to exclaim and touch his blue and white fur.

"What do you think?" I darted my eyes toward the injured girl then turned back to Marise.

"I think she's really hurt, and they took her ring. If she's still loyal to them after that, then she's crazy." Marise crossed her arms. "And I don't think Terrine is crazy. Plus, Liam likes her."

I nodded. "I think he's a good judge of character. We can't leave her here. We'll build the stretcher. We should've brought the lift panel instead of cannibalizing it to make a belt."

"We had no way to know that," Marise said. "That thing is unwieldy. We'll have to take turns carrying her."

Joss zipped up, dragging two twisted branches with him. "These are as straight as I can find. The trees here are squirrely."

"What about the hammock?" Marise said.

"Brilliant!" Joss pulled off his backpack and dug through it. He opened a small drawstring bag and shook out the thin, tough material. "Let's get her in this, then we can attach the rings to our belts. With the grav lifters on, she'll be easy to carry."

"Will we be able to lift off?" I asked. "Or will we have to walk?"

"Our belts should be strong enough to lift her, too. It will be slower, but we can still get off the ground," Aneh said through the comm link. "It will probably work best if Marise and I do it. Less total mass for the lifters."

"All right," I said. "Join us."

When Aneh and Peter joined us, the two boys lifted Terrine. With a little grunting and a couple muffled moans, they got her into the hammock. Then Aneh and Marise connected the ends to their grav belts and lifted off the ground.

Aneh grinned. "Good thing I came along."

I nodded. "Good thing you took your position on the drill team seriously."

CHAPTER TWENTY-TWO

"We got bogies," Joss said. "Three Delta Blacks dead ahead."

We'd been carrying Terrine for about twenty minutes, but it felt like hours. The heat pounded into the valleys between the hills, and even in the shade, the temperature never dropped to comfortable. The belts took most of the weight, but we knew Delta Black was nearby, and we were all jumpy.

"Who was with you?" I asked Terrine. When she didn't answer, I banked closer to the hammock and jiggled her arm. Liam blinked up at me, his face reproving. "Who was with you?"

"LeBlanc, Lee, and Riviera."

"Let's get up into the woods." I pointed up the slope. As we continued deeper into the hills, more trees had appeared. They were short and twisted but would provide some cover.

"They're going to know someone was here," Joss said as he followed me up the steep terrain. "There's no way Terrine walked out."

"I don't really want to confront them at this point," I said. "Do you?"

"That hasn't worked out well for us," Peter said. "I like the hide in the woods plan."

We dropped behind a thick stand of trees. Aneh split off and flitted up onto a rocky outcropping. She crept forward until she could see over the edge. Lying flat, her uniform blended into the dusty background.

"That's cool," Joss whispered.

I swallowed a chuckle. "I'd forgotten the smart fabric did that." Our uniforms were made of a material designed to provide automatic camouflage. We hadn't noticed the gradual change in coloring as we moved into the greener hills. The effect was obvious when Aneh landed on the pale stone.

"Hush," Marise whispered.

I pulled up the app and stretched the hologram across my palm, careful to keep behind a tree. In the valley a few meters below us, four black dots moved along the game trail. "Can you hear anything?"

Peter and Joss shook their heads. "They aren't using the flight channel."

A shout of laughter echoed up the hillside.

"I guess they found the transmitter," I said. "They seem pretty happy."

"Let's wait till they get by and keep moving," Peter said. "I'm sure they'll call back to base when they notice Terrine is missing. We'll hear that."

"Roger." I stretched the hologram in my hand larger. Several green and orange dots clustered near the base of the foothills. Yellow dots were scattered across the hills to our west, and a few red dots lay on the edge of the screen. "I don't see Purple anywhere."

"White is missing, too," Marise said.

"Maybe they didn't figure out how to make the scanners work." I closed the app and peered down the hillside. "They're well past us. Let's get moving."

"I'm going to stay here," Aneh said. "I can see down the valley to where Terrine was. And I'll be able to let you know if the others come up. Not that I don't trust Chymm's app, but it's good to have eyes on the competition."

I nodded and gave a thumbs-up.

"What if we need to get up higher?" Peter asked. "You heard what Chymm said about these belts. You've got the only reliable lifter."

"How about this?" I suggested. "Let's take Terrine up there. Then Aneh and Marise can swap belts."

Marise gave me the stink eye. "You know that belt won't fit me."

"Fine," I said. "Aneh and Peter can swap belts."

"I have a better idea." Marise stood and connected the hammock ring to her belt again. "Joss, grab the other end of the hammock. When we get up there, I'll stay with Terrine, and Aneh can go with you."

"Just do it," I snapped when Joss opened his mouth to argue.

Marise and Joss lifted the hammock and skimmed across the ridge to Aneh's perch. A few seconds later, Joss and Aneh returned. The four of us lifted off the ground and hurried up the canyon.

About half a klick farther, the signal on our scanner dropped to a lower tone. A light on the side it turned green, and a message appeared. "Objective achieved. Return to base."

"That seems kind of anticlimactic," Peter said.

"Kinda like the last exercise." Joss tapped the device in his hand.

"You don't think Delta Black did something to the transmitter, do you?" I asked. "I mean, could they have forged the signal somehow?"

Joss shrugged. "We're in the right location. I wouldn't put it past them to try something, but they weren't far enough ahead of us. Unless they had some prebuilt device, and that seems unlikely."

"Is there a way to check the stats?" Peter asked. "Like an exercise scoreboard?"

"I'm sure they have one back in mission control, but no one's mentioned a way to see it from the field." I flicked my holo-ring and scrolled through all the exercise information. "Nothing here. We can suggest it for next time."

"Yes, because I'm sure making things easier for the plebes is their goal," Joss said with a snicker. "We have to assume this is it. The message appeared on the scanners, so..."

"So, we're wasting time." I nodded. "We've let Black get into our heads. Let's go."

CHAPTER TWENTY-THREE

THE RETURN to camp was as anticlimactic as reaching the objective. Thanks to Chymm's app, we were able to avoid the other flights. Heading directly south across the stony plane got us back to camp as darkness fell.

We touched down by the blue shield. I had called ahead, and Chymm was waiting by the bollard when we arrived.

"How do I know it's really you?" Chymm called through the comm.

We stared at him.

"You can see us." I gestured to my chest then at the others. "You can hear us. What do you want, a blood sample?"

Yvonne smacked the back of Chymm's head. "Open the gate, wirehead. Who else would it be? Do you think Delta Black had facial mods while they were out there? Besides, they're showing as blue dots on your precious app."

Chymm grinned and opened the gate. "Can't be too careful."

"Yes, you can," I said. "Yvonne, can you check Terrine?"

Aneh and Marise carried the sleeping Terrine into the living mod, with Yvonne on their heels. Liam jumped out of the hammock before they reached the door and soared into the darkness.

The rest of us gathered near the fire. The temperature had dropped, and the warmth and light were welcome. Peter and I unfolded a second wall of the mod to block the wind.

"Any news from our friends?" I asked Chymm.

"No. The watchers streaked out of here a few hours ago." He poked the fire with a charred stick.

"I wonder if that's why I can't hear anything?" Peter asked. "The Black channel has been silent all afternoon."

Chymm shrugged. "Maybe they are talking privately? The legacies probably don't use the all-flight channel very often. Why d'ya think they left? Did they think the exercise was over?"

"It's supposed to be two weeks," I said.

"The last one was supposed to be a full week, and we were done in one day," he said. "With the special treatment they're getting, they probably figured they'd be done soon."

Yvonne came out of the mod. "I've given her a med boost. It won't fix the concussion, but it should help stabilize her until they can evacuate her. Did she call in to mission control?"

I shook my head, explaining about the missing ring.

"Then we need to call her in." Yvonne flicked her own ring. "This isn't something we should mess around with. She could have permanent damage if we don't get her to a med pod. This is way beyond my skill set."

Joss grabbed her hand, collapsing the call app. "If we call, they'll DQ us."

"She's not even in our flight!" Yvonne said. "They can't disqualify us for her! Even if they could, brain injuries are nothing to mess around with!"

"Have you met these people?" Joss leaned in, looming over her. Then his shoulders dropped, and he released her hand. "But, yeah, you're right. If she's in danger, we need to get help."

We sat in silence while Yvonne initiated the call. "I can't get through. There's no outgoing signal."

"Maybe you need to be outside the camp?" Peter slowly got to his feet. "The force shield could be blocking the signal?"

Chymm shook his head. "No, that's not right. I didn't mess with those frequencies." He rolled upright and lurched around the living mod to the closest bollard.

I followed with Yvonne and the boys.

"Clear." Peter raised his hand, the app open in his palm. "No one around. Anywhere."

Chymm opened a gate, and Joss and Yvonne stepped through.

"What's that?" I pointed at a light moving quickly across the sky. "Satellite? Shuttle?"

"There are a few towns on Sarvo Six," Chymm said. "I've seen some air traffic over that way." He pointed the opposite direction.

"But that's where Green went," I said. "After we talked to Tovar and Laghari. And Black came from that direction."

He shrugged. "I don't have a map. There could be towns all around us."

"Good point. It's a big planet. That's definitely a shuttle, though." I squinted at the bright pinpoint. "It's on a landing pattern."

The light grew brighter then dropped quickly. It disappeared behind the low hills to the west, illuminating the ragged silhouettes. Then it was gone.

"I bet they're recalling Black," Chymm said. "They've completed the mission and are getting picked up."

"You don't know that. Yvonne, did you get a call through? Are they coming to get Terrine?" I asked.

Yvonne shook her head. "I still can't get a signal. My ring won't connect to the satellites."

Joss flicked his palm, and the ring lit up. "Mine, either."

"There's another shuttle." Peter pointed to the eastern sky. "I think Purple was that way. They must have had a different objective from us. Or they got there really late. I never saw them on the app."

A third shuttle soared overhead. The rumble of engines rolled across the plain.

"Maybe they called about Terrine's injury? Is she ready to be moved?" I asked.

Yvonne raised her hands. "I dunno. She's as stable as I can make her. Hopefully they'll send a medic down." We headed back into the camp.

"Did you see any medics on the *Traveling Salesman*?" I asked.

"No, but we were locked inside that stupid compartment the whole time." Yvonne ground her teeth. "They could have had a whole hospital wing on that ship, and we'd never have known. I'll check on her."

'Guys," Joss said, hurrying through the gate. "We got a message from mission control. Here, let me play it." He flicked his ring.

An image of Admiral Zimas flashed into his palm. Wronglen and the other two cadet squadron commanders lurked in the background. Liam climbed up my arm and growled at the hologram. As I stroked him, his volume diminished, but he continued to vibrate under my hand.

"Well done, plebes." Zimas didn't smile. "You've completed the first task. Black and Green flights are awarded extra points for completing first. Additional supplies are being dropped to them."

"If anyone is injured, respond to this message immediately. We put cadets' health first. Individual injuries will not result in flight disqualification." She paused, glancing off screen.

"Due to multiple injuries sustained during a rockslide, Purple flight is being evacuated. They'll forfeit the competition and will have to complete their exercise back at base." A map replaced Zimas's face, with an area in the east marked in red. "Do not enter this restricted zone—it is extremely unstable. Yellow flight is being relocated." The admiral's face replaced the map, and this time she smiled. "I won't show you where they're being moved to, obviously."

"Watch for a shuttle to land and take off." Peter pointed east. "We need to know where they're taking Yellow."

"On it," Marise said.

"Joss, go back out and reply to the message." I pointed through the open gate. "They need to pick up Terrine."

He shook his head. "I tried. I'm not getting a connection. I recorded a message and set it to auto-send. But that won't work inside the force shield."

"Chymm!" His head snapped up at my yell. "Why can't we send messages? We should be able to connect from inside the shield—those things are built with a comm pass-through. On Earth," I winced, "we could contact the ship—when it was close enough. And speak to teams outside the camp."

"Did they have boosters?" he asked.

I bit my lip. "Yeah. But that was because we had no satellites. Or not enough of them. I think."

He nodded. "Standard procedure is to drop a team, deploy the gate beacons, then return to orbit and deploy comm micro-sats. Phase 1 teams use boosters."

"But that doesn't explain why we can't talk to anyone." I pointed upward. "There are comm sats up there. And your app works inside the shield!"

Chymm nodded again, his eyes far away. "Sarvo Six is an older fringe world. Their sats might be the older, less agile.... let me see what..." His voice trailed off, and he wandered away.

"I'm going to stay outside the shield for a while longer," Joss said. "I can stand guard there as well as in here, and that should give my ring a chance to connect. Maybe coverage is limited, and we have to wait for a satellite to fly overhead." He checked the charge on his stunner and hurried into the darkness.

"Marise, keep an eye on the app. We don't want anyone sneaking up on Joss." I pointed at the living mod's roof.

Marise saluted and jogged to the ladder.

"Now what?" Aneh asked.

"Shuttle at three o'clock," Peter called out. "That must be Purple leaving. Or Yellow getting moved."

We all turned to watch the engines flare brightly against the star dusted sky. The shuttle rose smoothly, arcing west. It passed to our north and landed again behind the same ridge in the west.

Peter flicked his holo-ring and pulled up the tracking app. He flicked a couple of controls, and yellow stars appeared.

"What are you doing?" I asked.

He shrugged. "I'm marking their projected location."

"I didn't know you could do that!" I tried my own app. Peter's stars glowed faintly on the edge of the screen.

"I can't make it big enough to see exactly where they are," Peter said. "Those stars are approximate place holders. But you can draw a line around them." He demonstrated on his own hologram, and the line appeared on mine. "Now we'll get a notification if they cross that line."

"I thought Chymm said he wasn't a programmer?" I played with the interface. "Can we set up warnings for Black, too?"

"Sure." Peter made a few more swipes and flicks. "There. Got all of 'em." He glanced at me through the hologram. "Chymm didn't create this app, you know. He borrowed the code from WorldMaps. It's open source. Still, it's a nice bit of repurposing."

"I couldn't do it, so it's magic as far as I'm concerned." I started across the camp. "I'm going to check in with Joss."

CHAPTER TWENTY-FOUR

PETER WOKE me at four the next morning. "Your turn to stand guard. Yvonne is on the south side until five."

I rubbed my eyes and followed him outside. He handed me a warm mug.

"What's this?" I sniffed. "Cocoa? Where'd you get this?"

He grinned. "Yvonne brought chocolate, remember? If you add a bit to the 'beverage, hot' from your meal pac, it's passable cocoa. And it stretches the chocolate."

"I guess I should stop throwing those out," I said. The hot beverage was universally reviled by every CEC explorer I'd ever met. Trust my genius flightmates to fix something no one in the history of CEC had managed.

"You didn't throw them out, did you?" His voice sounded anxious. "We'll need those calories before this is over."

I shook my head. "No, they're in the 'save for later' box in the storeroom." Since we started out short on food, we'd instituted a strict rationing and no waste policy.

He held my cocoa while I connected the stunner to my charging cable. "It's in the yellow." I rechecked the connection and tapped the lights on the side. "When's sunrise?"

"About two hours," he said. "Your jacket should still have a charge. Finish your drink—I'll take the cup back with me."

I slurped down the last and handed him the mug. "Good thing CEC supplied us with dishes," I said sarcastically. "Too bad they didn't provide the food to go in them."

Peter's lip twisted. "They did. It's right over there." He pointed west.

"Yeah. Get some sleep." I bumped my elbow into his side, then took up my place by the north bollard.

The next hour passed uneventfully. I checked the app from time to time, but no one was moving. Black and Green were probably passed out from eating all the extra calories. And who knew what new goodies they'd picked up with the prize drop? We needed to make sure we won the next round. I stretched the map. The ridge the shuttle had landed behind was roughly equidistant from the transmitter we'd located in the first task. I scanned the horizon—nothing moved.

I went back to the app. The forbidden zone was also about the same distance from that goal. The Academy's attempt at equality, perhaps. I plotted an arc on the map that included us, Black, and Yellow. If they were trying to be fair, did that mean the next objective would also be equidistant? If so, it would have to be right on top of the first beacon.

Except with Purple out of the picture and Yellow moved closer to Black, the geometry changed. If only we knew where the others were. Maybe we could backtrack them using the data from the app. I started swiping through interfaces, stopping every few minutes to scan through the shield for visible threats.

Out on the dark plain, nothing moved. Even the wind died, so the scrubby brush stood motionless under the moonlit sky. Taking a break from the app, I opened the gate and stepped through. The sharp, dusty scent of the bushes tickled my nose, and I sneezed. Liam climbed out of my pocket and scrambled up my arm, his nose twitching. I blew out a deep breath, sending a foggy trail into the darkness.

With a flick of my fingers, I brought up the communications screen on my holo-ring. A flashing yellow icon indicated no connection. I switched to the local channels and listened. Nothing.

Liam tweaked my ear. I turned my head to rub my cheek against his silky fur. "What is it?" He yanked, his little claws digging into my skin. "What? Do you want me to go back in?"

He pulled harder.

With a little shrug, I returned to the camp and closed the gate.

A scream of rage pounded through the force shield. Other voices hollered, muffled through the protective dome. Stunners crackled against the shield, lighting it up brilliant against the dark sky. I lunged forward and yanked open the panel on the side of the bollard.

"We're under attack!" I cried. The light from my ring illuminated the tiny panel inside the bollard. I slid the tab on Chymm's makeshift inhibitor. The screen brightened, making my eyes water.

"Where is everyone?" I yelled.

"Your comm is off," Yvonne yelled back. She said something else in a lower voice.

I flicked my holo-ring and pulled the comm screen up again. "Crap." I had turned off my connection to the flight when I was listening outside the gate. I flicked the icon, and a jumble of voices assaulted my ears. Behind me, my flight mates tumbled out of the living mod.

"Stunner fire on the northern gate," I reported. "It looks like at least three bogeys. They are not showing up on the app. I cranked up the shield."

The stunners stopped as quickly as they had started. We couldn't hear anything over the static of the shield on high. Joss grabbed my arm. "Which direction were they firing from?"

I pointed, and he took off that way. "Marise! With me!"

I wanted to go, too, but my assigned position was the north gate. I'd almost let the enemy inside, and I wasn't going to make another stupid mistake.

"Those little blasters!" Joss's voice came through the implant, low and angry. "They're laughing."

"Chymm," I called through the comm. "Why couldn't I see them on the map?"

Chymm hurried to me, his gaze on his palm. "I don't know. We should be able to see everyone. They're here now." He pointed to four black dots along the northwestern edge of our camp. Two blue dots glowed nearby, but inside the perimeter—Joss and Marise.

"We couldn't see Terrine." Aneh joined us, rubbing her eyes.

I scowled. "Terrine didn't have her ring on."

Chymm raised his head, eyes wide. "If they figured out we can see them, they might have taken theirs off."

"How would they know?" I demanded. "We haven't been around them enough for them to guess."

"Maybe they had someone on the inside." Peter's eyes darted toward the living mod.

"Are you suggesting Terrine told them?" I asked. "She wouldn't do that. They abandoned her."

He shrugged. "We don't know that. Maybe it was a set up."

"She was injured. Badly." I crossed my arms. "They wouldn't do that to a teammate." I didn't *think* they would do it on purpose.

"You don't know them," Peter said. "Joss and I lived with them for two weeks. LeBlanc is ruthless."

"You think they beat her up on purpose? Or rigged her grav belt?" I stared, aghast. "Why would she still help them?"

His shoulder twitched. "Maybe she was injured accidentally, and they decided to take advantage of it."

"I still can't believe..." My voice trailed off. Terrine had warned us on the ship. She said the flight had learned to *do what they were told.* "If the legacies told her to do this, would she?"

"I've barely met her," Peter said. "But those guys are good at brainwashing people. You've seen how the rest of their flight behaves around them. And she's been with them for six weeks. Who do you think she's loyal to?"

"If I'd gotten hurt and taken in by Delta Black, you'd bet I'd be reporting back to you guys," Aneh said. "Expecting her to remain loyal to us all these weeks was kind of short-sighted."

I smacked my forehead, imitating Chymm. "I can't believe I was so stupid."

"It wasn't just you," Marise said. "We all bought it. We thought she was our friend."

"How did she communicate with them?" I asked. "She didn't have a ring."

"Maybe she dropped a message for them on the trip back here," Marise said. "We were moving pretty fast and low to the ground. She could have written a note and dropped it over the side of her hammock. They were watching us and swooped in to pick it up."

"Wrote a note? With what?" I scoffed. "I think we would have noticed."

"Let's find out." Joss stomped past us and into the living mod.

"Wait." Marise grabbed his arm. "Maybe we can feed them information."

Aneh cocked her head. "You mean lie to her."

Marise nodded. "Yes. And then she would lie to them."

"What are we going to lie about? What can we tell her that would be beneficial to us?" Aneh asked.

Marise shook her head. "I don't know yet. We'll have to be careful what we say around her. And when we figure out something useful, we'll use it."

Joss ground his teeth. "I'd rather have it out with her right now."

"Have it out with her how?" Peter asked. "You look like you want to punch something, and she's injured, so it better not be her."

Joss rounded on Peter. "How about I punch you instead?"

Aneh jumped between the two boys. "No fighting. Do you want them to win? They would love to see us fight."

I glanced to the east. Purple streaks glowed above the dark hills—the red sunrise through the blue force shield. "It's almost dawn. I imagine we'll get our next objective soon. Go get some food. We can talk more later."

"Why don't you go with them?" Joss said. "I'll stand watch."

"You already did your turn," I said. "You can relieve me later—if you're on the schedule."

He growled. "Not till tonight."

"Maybe you should go hit something," I suggested. "It might make you feel better."

"I'd rather hit some*one*. But some*thing* will have to do." He stomped away.

CHAPTER TWENTY-FIVE

We gathered around the empty fire pit. The sun was well above the horizon now, and visibility was good. Joss stood atop the living mod, scanning the horizon with robot-like efficiency. Yvonne guarded the southern edge, and the rest of us watched the app almost obsessively.

"Is there a way to have the app notify us if someone removes their ring?" Marise asked.

Chymm shook his head. "Yes and no. I've already tweaked it to alert me if anyone within our scanning range suddenly disappears. But they shouldn't be able to disappear by taking their rings off. They don't stop transmitting just because you take them off."

"Maybe they have a faraday cage," Peter suggested.

"A piece of ferian-laced foil in your pocket would do the trick." Chymm scowled. "But we didn't have any of that here. And why would they think to bring it?"

"What about this?" Peter held up a meal pac pouch and pointed to the tiny lettering on the side. "It says ferian-laced packaging for longer shelf life." He pulled off his ring and dropped it inside.

Chymm slapped his forehead. "It can't be that simple." He flicked the app then stared at Peter in consternation. "You're gone."

Peter pulled the ring out.

"And now you're back." Chymm dropped his head into his hands, muttering under his breath.

"You had no way to know." Peter patted the other boy's shoulder. "Why would anyone put their ring into a meal pouch? How did they figure it out?"

"Once they knew we were tracking them," Chymm cast a dark look toward the living mod where Terrine still slept, "they could have—Laghari knew I was working on something like this. If Green and Black are working together…"

"That brings up a really good question," I said. "Why is Green helping Black?"

"Why not?" Marise lifted her hands. "They've been trailing in the rankings all summer."

"Yeah, but everyone knows those guys don't play fair." Aneh pointed her spoon at Marise. "They'll throw Green under the shuttle in a heartbeat as soon as they stop being useful."

"If they hang on long enough, that could see them in second place." Marise glanced toward the living mod. "It's way better than they were doing before."

"Do you think Terrine has a ring on her?" I pointed at Peter's discarded meal packet. "We didn't search her. She could keep it in a pocket then pull it out and talk to them whenever she's alone."

"We need to keep watch on that girl," Peter said grimly.

"Or take her ring." Marise grinned. "When she's asleep, we'll go through her stuff."

"I thought we were going to use her as a triple agent," I said.

"We have time," Marise said. "Now that we know how she's hiding it, maybe Chymm can come up with a cool device that will shield her even when she wants to use it."

Chymm's eyes lit up. "If I can isolate the part of the force shield that interfaces with ring transmissions, I could develop a directional jammer." He pulled out an app and started making notes.

"Let's not forget we have a mission," I said. "Or we should have a mission. If we can't see the sats in here, could we have missed the mission brief? We could be way behind the other flights."

"Calm down," Marise said. "Yvonne's been going outside to check every fifteen minutes."

I should have known that. I was supposedly in charge of this group. "Did you tell me she was doing that?"

Marise shrugged. "Joss set it up. We decided the southern gate, with the cliff and all, was a safer place to check. You don't even have to step outside the shield—just stick your hand through until the comm lights up. Last time I checked, the sats were still not registering. Hey, Yvonne." Her voice dropped as she activated her implant. "What's the status?"

After a second, she shook her head and turned back to us. "Still nothing. She'll let us know."

"That reminds me." I explained my thoughts on the location of the next objective. "If they're trying to be fair, the next mission should be in this area." I zoomed my holo-map out and drew a circle around the area. "We could head that way, in hopes of getting a jump on it."

"But they didn't know they'd have to close the eastern side until the rockslide happened. They might have planned all the missions for this area." Peter pointed to the first transmitter, now identified by a small number one.

"They were pretty quick to move Yellow," Marise said slowly. "Where did they put them? Do they have extra camps set up all around this continent? Maybe the move was already planned, and the rockslide was coincidental."

"Or planned," I said. "Or not real. Maybe Purple is still out there, somewhere. That message was recorded. There's no guarantee the other flights got the same message. Maybe they told Purple that Yellow had been relocated?" I clutched my hair. "This game sucks."

"I say we focus on what we know." Aneh patted my shoulder. "Let's get our gear together for the next mission. Figure out what we're going to need—like food. I don't want to play Black's stupid games. Who cares if they beat us by cheating? Let's do the best we can with the supplies we have and leave the rest up to chance."

We started by setting more snares. Joss stood guard while Aneh and Yvonne laid their wires along the tiny trails by the stream.

"I wish these were inside the perimeter." Peter bounced from foot to foot just outside the southern gate. The narrow strip of land before the drop-off was barely wide enough to stand on.

"Would you stop jumping up and down?" I said. "You'll fall off the edge!"

He grinned. "You know, I used to be scared of heights."

"What changed that?" I asked.

His face darkened. "There's worse things to be afraid of." His eyes met mine, and his expression lifted. "Remember that observation window at the Dome?"

"The one way up the cliff?" I pointed upward.

"Yeah. The first time Katy showed it to me, I was terrified she'd fall through the glass. After I was...after I woke up from deep sleep, we used that observation room to plot our escape from the Dome. It became a symbol of safety, I guess."

"I don't know much about your time in the Dome," I said softly. "You'll have to tell me sometime."

His lips twisted. "Maybe. When we aren't worried about starving or being attacked."

I laughed. "When's that going to happen? I never used to get attacked or kidnapped before I met you."

The others rose on their grav belts, drifting closer to us. Joss gave a thumbs-up. "Snares set."

"I hope those idiots are too lazy to try anything." Aneh's face wrinkled. "They have plenty of food now; they don't need ours."

"I wouldn't put it past them to destroy our snares just to mess with us," Joe said.

"I wonder if Chymm has anything that could help?" Yvonne suggested.

"Like what?" Joss made shooting motions, and we stepped back inside the perimeter. He closed it behind us.

Yvonne shrugged. "Some kind of magic idiot-repelling device."

"We wouldn't want to use it then." Peter smirked. "Joss would be out of commission."

Joss punched Peter's shoulder.

Chymm raced out of the living mod. "Check this out!" He stopped before us and tossed a tiny device into the air.

"Is that the drone you brought?" Peter's eyes darted around, following the thing as it flew.

Chymm scowled. "Yeah, but look at this." He pulled up a vid on his holo-ring. "The feed is screwed up. When I connect the drone—physically—to a monitor, I get great vid. But as soon as I go wireless, it scrambles."

"Do you think the network is bad here?" Joss asked. "It's a pretty poor planet. And I doubt the Academy would put many credits into infrastructure upgrades. The whole point of this area is to mimic remote planets."

"That's the thing." Chymm flicked a few icons, and the view changed. It was still full of static, but as the drone went higher, we could make out a few details of the camp. "These things don't use a network. They're designed to report directly to their base. They usually deploy hundreds in a cloud and set up relays to send the signal back to the camp. That part is working fine—as far as I can tell."

The drone dropped slowly, the view growing increasingly fuzzy. "The vid is corrupted here." He pointed to the ground. "Something in the camp is disrupting the signal before it leaves the drone."

"Maybe that one's defective." Peter reached out, his palm up. "Can I see it?"

"Sure." Chymm landed the drone. "I checked several of them. They all work fine when physically connected. If this one is defective, they all are."

"Have you tried it outside the shield? Maybe something in here is causing the problem." Peter turned toward the southern bollard again. "Could there be a device like the one you put in the playing fields?"

"I haven't tried it outside yet." Chymm hurried after him, and we all followed. "But remember our first mission? Siti said all the vid of us and Delta Black was bad." He glanced at me. "I still wish Wronglen had gotten that vid to me."

I shrugged. "He said he would, but maybe he was just trying to get on my good side. He hasn't been helpful since that day." If anything, he'd been more dismissive toward me since. I'd given up wondering what his game was. We'd have to survive despite him.

Chymm waved that away. "You said the vid was bad when we were alone, but worse when we were near Black. As if someone set it up so that Black could mess with us, specifically, without retribution."

Aneh gasped.

We all looked at her.

"Really?" Chymm muttered. "You hadn't thought of that before?"

Aneh's face went red.

"Sorry." Chymm bumped his elbow against Aneh's arm then turned back to us. "I think these drones are set up the same way. They appear to be working fine, until you actually try to watch the video. And I'll bet if we could access Black's drones, they'd be the same. When you put multiples together, the signal gets worse."

Peter opened the gate and sent the drone through it. We watched as Chymm flew the device straight out from the camp. The farther it got from us, the clearer the vid became.

"You have got to be kidding me," Chymm muttered. "There's something here, in this camp, that's messing with the vid before it leaves the drone."

"Or there's software on the drone that reacts to something in the camp, messing with the recording," Peter suggested.

Chymm pointed at Peter. "Or that."

Joss's eyes narrowed. "What do you want to bet it's not the camp?"

"What do you mean?" Chymm waved wildly at the invisible drone. "Obviously it's the camp."

"Maybe it's us." Joss crossed his arms.

"What?"

"On TbF, the vids were bad any time we were on them." Joss waved his finger, encompassing all of us. "We're inhibiting the drone."

Peter nodded. "Let's test it. Aneh can fly out there with the drone."

"I can't even see the drone," Aneh protested.

"That's okay. Just go out there, and Chymm can fly it near you," he said.

"Why me?" Aneh asked.

"You have the good belt," Joss replied.

"She can't go alone," I said.

"I'll go along for protection." Joss puffed out his chest.

"If you can go with her, it doesn't have to be her," I said. "You don't have the good belt."

"It's worked fine so far."

Aneh held up her hands. "It's fine. I don't mind going." She lifted off the ground and moved toward the gate. Joss went with her.

"Don't stay so high," Chymm reminded them. "There's no reason you have to be way up in the air."

Joss flashed a thumbs-up, and they angled toward the ground, skimming over the tops of the trees on the steep hillside. When they reached the stream, they streaked away, a meter or two above the ground.

We watched the vid in Chymm's palm. It swooped as the drone dropped. As it approached Joss and Aneh, the vid scrambled.

"Crap." Chymm flicked his palm. "You can come back. You were right." Joss and Aneh flew back toward us, and the vid cleared.

"Can you figure out what's doing it?" I asked Chymm.

He grimaced. "I'll try. If it's something connected to our individual identifications, it might be hard to find. If it's a physical device—they'd have to put one on each of us."

"Hang on," Peter said. "Joss, take off your jacket and go back."

"On it." Joss shrugged out of his jacket and handed it to Peter. Then he zipped away again. He grew larger in the vid on Chymm's palm.

"That's it!" Chymm pointed at the vid. He danced around in excitement. "No static!"

Laughing, Peter put a hand on Chymm's arm. "Stand still so we can see it."

Chymm stopped jigging. He was right, the vid was clear.

My lips pressed together. "That can't be accidental. Someone in the Academy is helping Black."

"We already knew that," Aneh said.

"Yeah, but this makes it feel so much more real. Purposeful." My ring vibrated. "Now what?"

"Now we plan the next mission," Joss said as he stepped onto the ledge.

CHAPTER TWENTY-SIX

THIS MESSAGE CAME from Cadet Wronglen. Joss threw it onto the projector in the front room. "Time to step it up, Charlie," Wronglen said. "Each squadron has a different objective this time. The flight that completes the objective fastest wins this round."

The vid changed to a map. A spot near the foothills glowed. It wasn't the same location as before but the next valley over and easier to access. Wronglen's voice continued to narrate. "There's a signal coming from this area. It's simulating an injured explorer, and your job will be to retrieve them and evacuate to the camp. You'll need to take all medically necessary precautions."

"That makes no sense," Yvonne said. "Why would we compete over an injured person? Shouldn't we be working together on this?"

"You know none of this stuff makes sense," Terrine said.

We all whipped around to stare at her.

Yvonne hurried to her side. "You shouldn't be up."

"I'm so bored in there." Terrine rubbed her eyes. "I've slept all I can."

"Why don't you sit out in the sun?" Yvonne suggested, urging the other girl toward the porch.

"I want to help you," Terrine said.

"Right," Joss barked. "You want to help us."

A hurt look crossed Terrine's face. "You don't know me. I do want to help."

"That's why you told them about our app." Joss strode to the two girls, looming over them.

"What do you mean?" Terrine asked. "I haven't told anyone anything. How could I? I don't have a ring." She held out her hands, fingers spread.

"Are you sure you didn't leave it somewhere?" Joss asked. "Like in a shielded pouch in your pocket?"

"Joss!" Hadn't we just decided not to confront her?

"Maybe it wasn't her," Chymm said. "I told you, Laghari knew I was working on this app. Maybe he figured it out. We shared code in the lab sometimes."

I hurried forward. "Terrine, please. You've been with Black a lot longer than you were with us. We would expect you to stay loyal to them. If our situations were reversed, I would stay loyal to Blue."

Terrine blinked, her eyes wet. "I understand. I'll stay away so you don't feel I'm a threat. And feel free to go through my stuff. Oh, yeah, I don't have any." Tears spilled down her face and she turned away. Yvonne glared at us behind Terrine's back and led her away.

"You didn't have to be so mean," Aneh said to Joss.

"I don't trust her. I don't know why you do." He crossed his arms.

"She's our friend." Aneh crossed her arms, mimicking Joss's stance, staring up at the much larger boy.

"Let's not fight about this," Peter said. "Now that she knows where we stand, we'll make sure she's not in the loop. Then she has nothing to report—if she is working with them. And we don't have to accuse her of anything."

"You're so reasonable," Joss growled. He shook his head hard. "Let's plan this mission. We are on the clock."

"We'll leave three people with Terrine." I flipped open a planning app and slid markers onto the screen. "Marise, Chymm, and Aneh, stay here. We'll take Yvonne since she's our medic. Peter and Joss will provide security."

"Maybe you should stay here," Aneh said. "I'll go on the mission. I have the good belt, remember?"

"No. We know we're supposed to bring back an injured person. It's better if we have stronger people."

She pointed at Peter and Joss. "They can do the lifting. Besides, with the hammock and the grav belts, it's easy. I helped carry Terrine."

"Aneh, I want *you* to stay with Terrine." I looked around the group and leaned in conspiratorially. "She needs someone who believes her. Besides, you can check the snares and deal with any game you catch. You're the best with all of that."

"I feel like you're punishing me." Aneh pouted.

"Not at all." I stared into her eyes. "I think the best deployment of personnel means leaving you here. We need food, and you're the best at procuring that. Don't go down there alone. Marise can help you."

Aneh nodded grumpily. "I guess. But don't do anything fun without me."

"I don't think this will be fun." I patted her arm. "And I wouldn't dream of it."

THE MISSION WENT off without a hitch. We reached the coordinates and found two training dummies—one painted blue, the other orange. Yvonne ran a med scan and immobilized our patient. We loaded it onto the stretcher we'd devised from one of the spare hammocks and a piece of shelving.

"Good thing we beat Orange," Joss said. "They might've messed with our patient."

"Do you really think that?" I asked. "Technically, we're on the same team."

"You heard what Wronglen said," Peter said. "We're competing against them. If they learned anything from Black, they would damage *our* patient."

Would they? As far as I knew, they hadn't had much interaction with Black. And Felicity didn't hate them the way she hated us. "I don't want to play that game. Let's go back to base."

Yvonne and I connected the hammock to our belts. As we zoomed across the plain, five members of Orange approached from the west. I raised my hand in greeting. They didn't respond. "Friendly."

"What do you expect?" Peter said. "We've got to be way ahead of them in the standings."

"Did you see which direction they came from?" I asked.

Peter nodded. "Maybe we should do some investigating?"

"I wish we had more people." I glanced over my shoulder. "There are still twelve cadets in Orange. That means seven of them are at their base."

"Or waiting to ambush us," Joss said darkly.

"Where would they do that?" I gestured to the flat plain. "If they were going to jump us, they should have gotten to the foothills before we did."

"Maybe that was their plan," Joss muttered.

"Paranoid much?" Yvonne asked.

"Just because you're paranoid doesn't mean they aren't out to get you," Peter said. "And we know they are."

Joss pointed at his friend. "What he said."

We returned to the camp and touched down by the north bollard. Chymm opened the gate and let us in. "Hurry," he said.

"Why?" Yvonne and I deposited our patient on the ground near the bollard.

Chymm shut the gate and turned the field up.

"We were attacked twice while you were gone." Chymm fiddled with the bollard again. "Both times came out of nowhere. They must be coming all the way from their camp without their rings. They destroyed Aneh's snares and killed the animal she'd caught."

I hurried across the camp and stared down at the stream. The scrubby trees on the hillside hid the hunting ground from sight.

"How'd you know?" I asked as Chymm peered over my shoulder. "I can't see anything."

"I put a drone down there." He pulled up the vid. It skimmed along the tiny game trails, slowing to record the destroyed stakes, tangled wire, and a splash of blood. "The vid went to crap as soon as they showed up, but after they left, I was able to do a recording."

"I hope they didn't torture the poor thing," Aneh said. "And that they took it with them—didn't leave it to waste."

"They're trying to starve us out—they didn't want to leave it for us." I didn't tell her they probably did torture it while the cams were scrambled. She didn't need to know that.

"They're probably hoping we'll forfeit," I said as Joss and Peter came up behind me. "I wonder if they know we can't contact mission control."

"Maybe we should have waited and talked to Orange," Joss said. "See if they're having the same problems."

My eyes went wide. How could I not have thought of that?' "That's a fantastic idea. Let's go!"

"Now?" Joss asked.

"Yes." I grabbed his arm and dragged him across the camp. "If we hurry, we can catch them before they return to base. Come on."

Peter stepped in front of me. "Are you sure that's a good idea?"

"No, but we need to do something." I pushed around him. "Mission control isn't responding. We have no vid coverage. Our food will be gone soon, and we're already eating way less than we should be. We have an injured cadet on our hands who doesn't even belong to our flight. We need to find out if they know anything and ask them to send a message on our behalf if they can. I don't care if we have to forfeit."

"Wait, I do!" Marise said. "I don't want to get washed out over this!"

I stopped. "They aren't going to send us home for forfeiting. Purple had to go back—they have to finish their exercise at the Academy. The admiral isn't going to wash out a whole flight. Do we stay out here, hurt and starving, or do we go home?"

"If we have the chance, I vote for home," Peter said. "But I'd rather send Terrine home and get some more food and continue the exercise. If that's an option."

"Agreed. That's what we'll tell them." I looked at each of the others. They nodded, one by one. "Marise?"

She stared at me for a long moment then sighed. "Yes."

"You agree, Yvonne?" I asked through the comm.

"I agree." Yvonne's voice sounded tired. "Terrine doesn't want to go back, though."

"Is she with you right now?" I asked.

"Yeah."

"Terrine, you have two options." I looked at the others for confirmation. They nodded as I spoke. "You can go home for medical care, or we'll take you back to Black. Your choice. You don't get to make decisions for our flight."

There was silence. Then a sniff. "You're right. I'm sorry. I'll forfeit. I don't want to ruin your exercise."

"You need real medical care," Yvonne said. "Not this."

I disconnected and pushed Joss toward the gate. "Let's go, before we lose them."

"Take this!" Chymm dragged a meter-long device behind him. Two handles, like a bicycle, were welded to the front of a cylinder about a hand-span wide.

"What is that?"

He grinned. "It's my own version of an air bike. It doesn't actually lift—your grav belts have to do that. But it'll get you there much faster. Straddle it, like a bike, then rotate this grip forward to accelerate. Back to decelerate. Have you driven an air bike before?"

I shook my head. "I've ridden on the back of one. But it was dark." I glanced at Joss and lifted a shoulder. "I'm game."

"Let's do it. You're rad, man." Joss held up a hand, palm out.

Chymm stared at Joss's hand then raised his own.

Peter snorted. "It's a high five. Ancient Earth ritual." He leaned forward to slap Joss's hand. "Kind of died out during the pandemics, but Joss's dad started a comeback in the Dome."

I grabbed the handles of Chymm's air bike and lifted. "This is heavy."

He pulled a lead off the cylinder and attached it to my grav belt. "It's not wireless, so you have to connect manually. Once the grav belt is on, the mass is transferred to the belt and you won't feel it. But let Joss get on, first."

Joss stepped up behind me, putting his hands on my hips. I flushed a little. *Get a grip, Kassis. He's a teammate and we're on a mission. Nothing else.* "Now what?" The words came out a little breathless, and I grimaced.

Chymm didn't seem to notice. "Set your grav belt to one meter and turn it on."

The cylinder tilted sideways as I let go with one hand.

"Maybe you should add a second set of handles when you get a chance," Joss suggested. "So I can hold it up while she connects."

Chymm nodded absently, swiping into his note app.

I flicked the belt controls and set us to one meter.

"Oof!" Joss grunted as my feet lifted off the ground. The weight disappeared from my left hand.

Chymm glanced up from his notes. "You should set your belt to the same altitude, Joss."

"Thanks," Joss said in a strangled voice. One of his hands left my hip.

Peter snickered. "Probably should do that first next time."

I leaned forward to grab the other handle and righted the "bike." Joss transferred his grip to my belt.

"Ready?" I asked.

"As I'll ever be," Joss said, his voice still muffled.

"Open the gate, Chymm." I twisted the handle, and we slid forward and out of camp.

CHAPTER TWENTY-SEVEN

Joss leaned forward, his chest touching my shoulders. "I could walk faster than this." His breath tickled my ear.

I gave myself a mental shake. *Focus, Kassis.* "I'm getting a feel for it. I'll kick up the speed." I cocked my wrist, twisting the handle forward.

Nothing happened.

"I thought—"

The bike lunged forward. "Yikes!" I clamped my fingers onto the handles and pulled back on the right one.

Joss yelled, and his fingers slid away from my belt. The bike stopped. I bit my lip to keep from laughing and turned to look over my shoulder.

Joss hung in the air about ten meters behind me. He shook his fingers then tapped his belt, moving toward me. "A little warning would be nice."

"Apparently, there's a delay. At least you didn't end up on your butt." I faced front again as he climbed on behind me. "Maybe you should hold on tighter."

"No kidding." He slid his arms around me, gripping his own wrist and resting his hands against my belly. "Let's try that again. Slowly."

"You think you could do better?" I didn't give him a chance to reply but eased the accelerator forward. The bike hesitated then lurched ahead. "I'm speeding up." I twisted the handle a little more.

"That's more like it." Joss settled back, his arms relaxing a bit. "How fast does she go?"

"Let's find out." I rotated the handle forward. After another long pause, the thing picked up speed, shooting us across the plain fast enough to make our eyes water. I leaned forward to cut down on drag. "Remind me to ask Chymm to make goggles," I yelled.

"What?" Joss yelled.

I debated releasing the handle long enough to initiate a call on my holo-ring, but I wasn't sure what would happen. My audio implant pinged with an incoming call.

"Can you hear me this way?" Joss asked.

"Much better. We probably need to put together a checklist for this thing."

Joss laughed. "That sounds like something Marise would do. Way too organized for me."

"Marise is going to keep us alive," I replied. "And a checklist would have saved you a bit of pain."

"Good point." He wiggled a bit, and the bike slalomed.

"Stop that!" I yanked the handles, trying to straighten our flight. We swerved wider.

"Relax," Joss said. "Loosen your grip and let it even out."

"I'm trying," I muttered. When I stopped trying to correct, the bike settled into a straight course. "The good news is, we know how to turn now." I leaned a little to the right, and the bike curved that way. Then I swung us back.

"Nice," Joss said. "Next time I get to drive."

"Sure, when we have more time, everyone can have a turn." I squinted. "Are we still headed the right direction? Check our coordinates, will you?"

"No sudden movements, okay?" He let go of my waist and sat back. The movement left my back exposed to the air and suddenly cold. "You pointed us toward where they first came onto the map?"

"Yeah. If it takes them about the same amount of time to get their patient as we did, then we should meet them right about where they first showed up."

"Turn us a little to the left—about ten degrees. But wait until I'm holding on again." His fingers wrapped around my belt again. "Okay, go."

We turned smoothly and continued onward toward a spectacular sunset. Pink and orange streaks lit up the western sky. The light faded quickly, the hills to the west turning into silhouettes. We skimmed above the plain, our toes brushing against the scrubby plants. The dusty scent of the brush grew stronger.

"There." Joss reached over my shoulder, pointing.

I followed the line of his arm. Faint points of light moved toward the darkening hills. "We should reach them in a few minutes."

He didn't reply. I leaned forward again, hoping to increase our speed.

The lights grew quickly as we approached. I eased back on the accelerator. After a moment, the bike slowed. By the time we returned to camp, I would be pretty good at anticipating this thing.

"Hey!" Joss called out. "We need to talk to you!"

I slowed the bike to match their speed, grinning to myself at my skill. The bike stopped suddenly, and I slammed against the handlebars, Joss ramming into my back. Charlie Orange slid right by us.

"What are you doing?" Joss demanded.

"Sorry." I twisted the handle a fraction, and we eased forward. I pulled up next to Mel and Cress, the skinny little guy who always seemed to be in charge. "Can we talk?"

Cress held up a hand, and the flight stopped.

We slid on past them until I could get the bike to hover. "How do I turn it around?" I whispered to Joss. I felt him shrug behind me. "Fine. I'm putting us down. Half a meter." I reached for the controls of my grav belt and reset the altitude.

"Crap," Joss muttered.

Charlie Orange laughed. Joss dropped behind me, his knees banging into my back. "Give a guy some warning."

I pushed my toes against the ground, twisting the bike around. Joss slid sideways then grabbed my belt again and pulled himself upright. "You should've expected that," I told him.

"Fancy machine you got there," Cress said. "Too bad you don't know how to drive it."

"It's a little finicky," I said. "But it got us here fast." I squinted in the dim light. "Can you reach mission control?"

Mel and Cress exchanged a glance. "We got the mission brief. Obviously. But there's no uplink," Cress said.

"We can't connect to the sats," Mel said. "We figured it was part of the training. Relying on yourself. On phase 1 mission, there's no one to call."

"Except this was supposed to be a phase 2 mission," I said. "That means the ship that transported us here should still be in orbit. And communications would have been set up when they dropped the jump beacons in phase 1. Phase 2 teams can call home or at least send a message home."

Cress shrugged. "Why do you care? Don't tell me Charlie Blue wants to forfeit?"

"No!" Joss and I said together.

"We have an injured cadet," I continued.

"That's a forfeit," Mel said.

"No, it's not," Cress said. "Who got hurt?"

"She isn't even one of ours," I said. "Delta Black deserted one of their cadets after she got hurt. We brought her back to camp."

Cress laughed. "That was stupid. They tried to take our food, you know. Sending someone to infiltrate your camp seems like an easy way to steal your stuff."

"They don't need to steal our stuff," Joss said. I gave him a warning look, but he shook his head. "They need to know in case they're able to get through to mission control. Delta Black took our supplies before we even left the ship."

I watched the boys carefully as Joss spoke. Did they look guilty? Did they know? "Did you help them?" I asked.

They exchanged a look again and shook their heads.

"Siti," Joss whispered through my implant. "Take us up. About three meters. They're trying to sneak around behind us."

I flicked the controls of my grav belt. I glanced down and hit three meters. The bike rose smoothly.

A hand grabbed my ankle as we lifted off. I kicked, hard. The fingers gripped tighter, and I started to slide sideways off the bike. Joss grabbed my waist, pulling. I kicked harder. The hand fell free, and Joss yanked me up onto the bike.

"What the hell!" I yelled.

"Back off." Joss's voice was hard. He pulled the stunner from his belt. "Make your own bike."

"You can't blame us for trying," Cress said.

"Yes, we can." I glared at him. He probably couldn't see it in the gathering darkness, but I hoped he could hear the anger in my voice. "Did you learn nothing from TbF? Explorers are not military. We don't fight with each other. We work together."

"Tell that to Delta Black," Mel muttered.

"Don't need to," Joss said. "They're working with Green."

"They are?" Cress's voice cracked. "That's just what we need. Those guys in Green are almost as bad as the legacies."

"Exactly." I reached over my shoulder to flick on the light attached to my backpack. Then I remembered I left my pack in the camp. Stupid. "Do you have a light?" I asked Joss softly.

The light flicked on, shining over my shoulder at Cress's face. He flung out a hand. "Hey!"

"Sorry, it's getting dark." Joss did not sound sorry. The beam of light moved around, pinpointing the location of each of the Charlie Orange cadets. "Why don't you all stand over there?" Joss moved the light to the rest of the group. The two who had tried to grab the bike trudged to join their peers.

"What did you want?" Cress asked. "We can't send a message for you."

"Then I guess we can't help each other," I said. "Thanks for your time."

"Wait a minute," Cress said. "Don't leave. Maybe we can work together, too."

"So you can steal our bike?" I scoffed. "That ship's launched. Besides, you can't do the only thing we wanted you to do—send a message."

"Maybe we can." Cress turned his own light on, shining in my eyes.

I squinted. "Which is it? Can you send a message or not?"

"If you can get us one of those bikes," Cress said, "I'll make sure your message gets through next time we get a sat connection."

I snorted. "No deal. If you get a sat connection, so will we."

"You sure about that?" Cress lowered the light so I could see him grin.

"What do you know?" Joss demanded.

Cress shook his head. "I don't know anything. But I've heard rumors that the administration would love to see all of you disappear. Zimas wasn't happy to get the Neanderthals. And she doesn't love your dad."

Joss stiffened on the bike behind me. "You're lucky I'm way up here, you little twerp."

I tapped his knee. "Stay calm," I whispered. I raised my voice. "How about this? If you get through to mission control and they come pick up our injured cadet, then we'll help you build an air bike. I don't know if we have the parts to make a second one, but you probably do. The camps were all supposed to have the same supplies, right?"

"If we get through to mission control and they pick up your cadet, you *give us* your bike," Cress countered. "If we have the materials, we'll give them to you to make a second one."

"Deal," I said. I had no doubt Chymm would come up with some other equally useful device in the meantime, and we might be able to trade it instead. I didn't want to give up my new ride.

"You said they stole your supplies," Cress said. "You must be getting low on food. You got any more tech to trade? We could spare a few meal pacs."

"No, we can't," Mel said. The cadets behind him grumbled in agreement.

"We've got plenty." Cress glared at his flight mates. "If they've got something else as useful as that bike, I'd be willing to give up a few meal pacs for it."

"I'd have to discuss that with the rest of my team," I said.

Joss whispered through the implant, "What about the app?"

"Do we want them to have that?" I whispered back.

"What happened to working together?"

"They tried to steal my bike," I said. "Plus, we know the app is not one hundred percent reliable since Black was able to spoof it. I'm not sure it would help them much."

"That's why it's the perfect bargaining chip."

"Good point." I raised my voice. "How about this." I explained about the app.

Cress, Mel, and the other Charlie Orange cadets gathered together, whispering.

"I guess they forgot they can use their audio implants," I muttered to Joss.

"If they haven't had to use them much... "

"We'll give you four meal pacs for that," Cress said.

"Four," I scoffed. "It's worth at least a case."

"We don't have a case. We have four spares. And that's only because we have a couple good hunters in our flight."

"Deal," I said again. "Give us the meal pacs, and I'll swipe the app to you."

"Nice try," Cress said. "Give us the app, and we'll give you the meal pacs."

We glared at each other for a few seconds.

"Set the food over there." Joss pointed to the east. "Then we'll swipe the app to you, you check it out, we pick up the meal pacs, and everyone's happy."

"Fine." Cress turned his head. "You heard him, Mel. Do it."

Mel glared at Cress then turned and flew off. He stopped about fifty meters away and dropped to the ground. It was too dark to see what he did, but when he lifted off, there was a small pile of rectangles on the ground.

"Go check them out," I said to Joss. He lifted off the bike and flew toward the pile.

"Stop!" Cress yelled. "Not till I got my app."

"Calm down," I said. "He won't touch them. He's just looking."

Joss stopped a few meters from Mel and shone his light on the ground. "I see four packages," Joss said. "They look different from ours."

"Different how?"

"I dunno," he said. "The labels are the same. They're a different shape. Lumpier."

"After they've rattled around in a backpack for a while, they sometimes look lumpy." I squeezed my legs against the bike to hold it in place and let go of the handle. Then I flicked my ring and swiped a copy of the app to Cress.

Cress grunted. "Got it. How do you—oh. This is cool. Nice. Let's go, guys." Mel zoomed back to the group, and they headed off without another word.

I stared after them for a second then eased the bike to Joss. As I approached, he dropped to the ground, and picked up the packages. He shoved them into his backpack and slung it onto his shoulders.

I dropped so he could climb on, and we headed back to camp.

CHAPTER TWENTY-EIGHT

"You guys gotta try this thing in the morning," I said as we landed inside the camp. Chymm closed the gate behind us and turned up the static.

"Aren't you worried about draining our batteries?" Joss asked Chymm.

"He figured out a way to connect the shield to the living mod," Peter said. "The shield gets priority, so we might have trouble turning on the lights in the morning, but it's enough to keep the force shield running on high all night."

"That's amazing!" I grinned at Chymm. "We're so lucky to have you. We were able to trade your app for more food."

A cheer went up. Joss shrugged off his backpack and pulled out the meal pacs. "Hey, this one is open!" He held an open meal pac near the fire so we could all see.

"What did they do?" I muttered. "There'd better be food inside."

Joss's jaw tightened, and he dumped out the contents. Four red stew pacs and a pile of flat rocks fell out. "Those *chokin' blasters*. I can't believe we fell for that. I should've checked—"

"It's not your fault." I gripped Joss's arm. "I gave him the app."

"At least we got the stew," Aneh said. "What about the others?"

Two of the meal pacs were intact. The fourth one held a dozen hot beverage packets and more rocks.

"Ugh. We need more food." Joss threw the packets down.

"Those are calories. Don't waste them!" Aneh scurried forward to scoop them up. "I'll put these with the rest."

"Take the full meal pacs, too." Joss tossed them at Aneh. She dropped the beverage packets as she swiped at the meal pacs then dropped them, too.

"Don't take your anger out on her," Yvonne growled, squatting to help Aneh pick up the dropped food.

"Sorry, Aneh." Joss sounded contrite. "I need to punch someone. Again." He stalked away.

"What's he going to punch?" Aneh asked.

"Don't worry about it." I turned to the rest of the group. "He's right, though. We need more food."

"I set some new snares while you were gone," Aneh said. "Chymm will send the drone down at first light, and if we've caught something, we'll get it."

"Can you leave one down there?" Peter asked. "Set it on a rock. It would act as an early warning device—it wouldn't even need to be pointed at anything in particular. If the vid fritzes, someone from Delta Black is nearby."

Chymm slapped his forehead, making the rest of us wince. "That's brilliant! Why is everyone having brilliant ideas except me?"

"Maybe it's the lack of food," Aneh said.

"Which brings me back to the other point," I said. "We need to get some—probably more than Aneh can trap. What are our options?"

Peter's eyes narrowed. "Are you thinking about stealing it from one of the other flights?"

"I prefer to think of it as liberating our own stores, but yeah." I grinned.

"Do we have the people and equipment to do that?" Yvonne asked.

We all groaned.

My brain spun, ideas rattling around like pebbles in a jar. Nothing concrete or useful.

"This might be a long shot..." Joss said.

"When did you come back?" Peter looked up in surprise.

"I just walked up. Y'all were snoozing." He dusted his hands together and sat. His uniform was covered with little twigs and dirt.

"We weren't sleeping—we were thinking," Peter said. "Ya got something on your sleeve."

"What might be a longshot, Joss?" I broke in.

"Is it possible Purple might have left some food behind? Their camp was evacuated." He slapped the duff from his arm and swept it into the fire. It glowed and burned quickly. "There were some meal pacs here when we arrived. Wouldn't they leave that kind of stuff behind rather than carting it back to the Academy?"

I looked at everyone else, a tiny spark of hope warming in my chest. "Do you think that's possible?"

Marise shrugged. "Meal pacs last for decades. Leaving them is cheaper than taking them back."

"I think it's worth investigating," Joss said. "The bullet bike will get a team there and back super fast. And we'll be hovering, so unstable ground isn't an issue."

"We'd have to set down to get the supplies," Peter pointed out.

"Good point. But if it looks unsafe, we abort the mission," Joss said.

"Oh, that reminds me. I made another—what did you call it?" Chymm looked at Joss. "A bullet bike?"

Joss grinned. "It's not really a bike—no seat, no wheels. And it flies like a bullet."

"We get it," Peter said.

Joss punched his shoulder.

"Did that help?" Aneh asked.

"What?" Joss looked confused.

"Punching his shoulder. You said you wanted to punch something."

Joss cackled. "You call that a punch? I barely tapped him. No, that wouldn't help at all if I was still mad. I ripped out a few of those stupid scrubby bushes instead." He slapped the shoulders of his jacket again, dislodging more bits of brush. "Those things are tough. Good workout. And it's good to have a cleared zone inside the perimeter."

"They burn bright and hot," Chymm observed as Joss flung a palmful at the flames. "Might be handy for signaling—if we need something low tech."

Aneh nodded, but the rest of us ignored him.

"Let's do it." I slapped my hands against my thighs and stood. "At first light, Aneh and Joss will check the snares. Peter and I will head for Purple's camp. If we get a new mission, we'll do that first, obviously. Otherwise, we go."

Yvonne raised a hand. "Marise and I can go with you two on the other bullet bike. Chymm, Joss, and Aneh can hold down the fort. There's nothing more I can do for Terrine, and if you have a problem in the landslide, you'll need me."

"Good call." I raised my eyebrows at the others. "Sound fair?"

"When do I get to go on a mission?" Chymm asked.

"How about you do the next one?" I suggested. "Right now, we need you coming up with new tech stuff. You're crazy good at it and wicked fast." I told them about my agreement to give the bullet bike to Orange when—if Terrine was evacuated.

"Don't you think that deal is null, since they cheated us on the food?" Joss said.

"Good point." I wrinkled my nose. "Although, if they can get Terrine evacuated, I'd be willing to give them something."

"How about a bullet bike full of rocks?" Joss suggested.

"Works for me."

PETER WOKE me at four to stand watch.

"What, no cocoa this time?" I whispered.

"You can have a hot bev, but there's no chocolate left."

I shuddered. "I'd need to be a lot hungrier than I am to go for that offer."

Peter patted his stomach. "I think I'm getting close. G'night."

I stepped out into the darkness and checked in with Yvonne. "Anything going on?"

"Nope." Her voice sounded tired. "Nothing moving over here. Chymm rigged a drone for night ops."

My ring buzzed. I flicked it open, and a vid popped up showing a flat, gray expanse.

"It's down by the stream, looking toward the plain. Rotates constantly. You don't have to watch—it's set to ping us if anything new shows up."

"Does that include animals or only people?" I took up my station near the north bollard.

"Both, if the animal is big enough. A herd of those cattle-like things that chased Mason off the cliff came by a while ago. Weird that they migrate at night."

I grunted agreement. I didn't care about the herbivores that chased Mason. He should have used a grav belt. "Hey, do you have a copy of that vid?" After showing it to us, Lawrence had sent each of us copies.

"I don't, but Marise might. She saved everything related to this exercise. Why?"

"I dunno." I squinted through the blue static of the shield, but I could barely see the empty plain outside. "I just wondered if it was filmed near here. Maybe something in it could help us."

"Charlie Blue must have been stationed at a different camp last year. That lake is nowhere near us."

The lake. I slapped my forehead like Chymm and pulled up a map of Sarvo Six. The lake in that vid looked huge. And there was a low cliff overlooking it. I tried to remember more details as I scanned the local area. "Hah!"

"What?" Yvonne asked.

"That lake. I found it on the map. You aren't going to believe this." I stretched the map larger, so I could see more detail of the area.

"What?"

"That lake—or at least a lake—is east of here." I chuckled.

"Why wouldn't I believe that?" Yvonne asked.

"If I'm correct, Charlie Blue was assigned to Purple's camp last year. That vid was taken in the restricted zone."

CHAPTER TWENTY-NINE

"Nice. We should be able to find it easily," Peter said two hours later when we woke the rest of the crew.

The sun hadn't risen yet, but a faint glow backlit the eastern mountains. I focused my solar lamp on my backpack. "I've got everything I need. You ready to go?"

Peter nodded. "I'm glad I don't have to wear Aneh's belt this time."

"We have to wait until they get back from the snares, though," I reminded him. "Even Joss can't climb that hill in the dark."

"I'll bet he could." Peter's lips twitched. "Don't suggest it though—he'd consider it a challenge."

"Challenge? What kind of challenge?" Joss asked as he and Aneh stepped through the southern gate.

"Pizza eating," I said. "When we get back to the Academy. I'm putting my credits on Yvonne, though."

"No way Yvonne could eat more pizza than me!" Joss puffed out his chest.

Peter made a gimme gesture at the other boy. "Belt, please. Have you seen Yvonne eat pizza? She's incredible."

Joss handed the grav belt to Peter. While he adjusted the length, I lifted the bullet bike. "Did you guys test the new one?"

Chymm nodded. "That is the new one. And it works just like the old one."

"I was hoping you tweaked the accelerator. There's quite a delay between turning," I twisted my fist forward, "and moving."

"Yeah, I need to work on that." Chymm rubbed the back of his neck. "But I was focused on producing another one, not perfecting the design."

I gave him a thumbs-up. "As long as it gets us there. What do these babies run on, anyway?"

"Same thing as grav belts." Chymm tapped my shoulder. "It's all solar charged. It should get you to the restricted area and back with no problems. But you can always plug it in to your jacket charger. These things are incredibly efficient. And I used the universal connector, so you can slap the lead on."

"But we can't run while we're charging, right?" I lifted the cable. "This thing is linked to my grav belt when we're moving. So, I can't—"

He shrugged. "Sorry, failing of the design."

"It's not a failure. This thing is fricking amazing," Joss said. "Any chance you can make another one? We've got five grav belts…"

"I'm out of parts." Chymm frowned.

"Send us a list," I said. "Maybe we can find them at the Purple base. It's worth a shot."

Pink and purple streaks backlit the mountains as we activated our grav belts and climbed onto the bullet bikes. Thick shadows still covered the plane outside the north gate, but no one lurked there. Chymm dropped the force shield, and I shone a light around the entrance. I gave him a thumbs-up, and we headed out.

The new bike worked exactly the same as the old one. Now that I'd grown used to it, I found it easy to compensate for the lag. Peter rode with me while Yvonne piloted the second bullet. Marise sat behind her, arms strangling Yvonne's waist and eyes clamped shut.

We'd gotten smarter and tethered the rear rider's belt to the pilot's so the two would stay together. That meant the passenger didn't have to hold on, but Marise appeared to be taking no chances.

I toggled the audio implant as we pulled away from camp. "You sure you want to be here, Marise? It seemed like Joss was itching to go."

"No, I'm fine. I..." She pried her eyes open. "They look so...rustic...compared to real air bikes."

"Rustic." Peter chuckled. "Good description. They sure can move, though. You'll let me drive on the way home, right?"

"Sure. Maybe."

"Hey, don't hog all the fun."

I grinned, knowing he couldn't see it. "I'll let you drive. Unless we're running away from something."

"What would we be running away from?"

"Those herbivores?" Marise suggested. "According to my research, they roam all over these plains. I'm surprised we haven't seen more of them."

"I wonder if Aneh could rig up a snare for one of them?" Yvonne suggested. "Even a smallish one would provide more food than we'd need for a month."

"Joss could shoot one with his tranq gun," Peter said. "If they're susceptible to that tranquilizer. But more importantly, are they edible?"

"Yeah, the meat is digestible," Marise said. "It's not as nutritious—for humans—as the Earth variant that's been seeded, but if we had to... we'd have to find them first."

"There was a herd by the stream this morning," Yvonne said.

"I wonder why the settlers don't round up those cattle?" Peter asked.

Marise shook her head. "There aren't any settlements around here. The CEC owns all this land. They keep a chunk of each new planet for training."

"And to finance missions," Yvonne added.

"What?" I darted a look at the other bike. "I thought CEC was funded by the government."

"It used to be—back when you were a kid." Yvonne laughed. "That always cracks me up. You're almost as old as my mom. But fifteen years ago, I think—"

"Sixteen," Marise supplied.

"Sixteen years ago," Yvonne nodded, "the government cut funding. They said we had enough planets for now and didn't need to explore anymore. So CEC went private. They're using resources on new planets to fund missions. There's a platinum mine on Lovell that provides a nice income stream."

"Lovell? They hadn't reached there when I left for Earth." I hadn't realized CEC had gone private. I wondered if Dad knew. "Peter, did you know all this?"

Behind me, he moved, and the bike wiggled. "I don't pay much attention to politics. It was probably discussed during the treaty negotiations, but…"

"I thought you were supposed to be a representative of your people?" I asked.

"I was for first contact, but I stepped back after you left. There were a lot of changes after we took care of the Hellions. I don't remember hearing anything about the status of the CEC, though. I assumed it was a government organization. But you know what they say about assuming."

"Yeah." My lips twisted as I stared across the slowly brightening landscape. "I guess it doesn't matter right now. Let's worry about the mission."

"Speaking of missions, isn't it odd they haven't given us a new one?" Marise asked. "Leaving us here doing nothing is kind of a waste of time."

"Maybe that's part of the training—to see how we deal with the boredom." Yvonne snorted. "Not that we've had time to get bored."

Light streaked across the sky followed by the unmistakable rumble of shuttle engines. "Where's that going?" I asked. "Anyone got a signal?"

The girls shook their heads.

"My ring isn't connecting to any satellites," Peter said. "And that shuttle isn't transmitting any communications links. There's nothing."

"They're too high to tell where they're landing." Marise stared into the sky. "Maybe Orange was able to get our message through and they're coming for Terrine?"

"But that shuttle isn't headed anywhere near our camp." I looked over my shoulder, and the bike curved away from Yvonne and Marise as I leaned. I corrected our path.

"No, it's not." Peter paused then continued, "Chymm says they've got nothing, signal-wise."

I grimaced. "I say we stick to the plan. If we get a mission brief, or a recall, then we'll head back. We'll tell them we were surveying the plains. You don't think they're tracking us, do you?"

"Of course they are," Peter said, his voice disbelieving. "How stupid are we? They're going to know we went into the restricted area."

"Unless," Yvonne said.

"Unless what?" I snapped when she broke off.

"We could take off our rings," she said. "We'll stop short of the restricted area. One of us takes all the rings and continues on a path around the edge of the plain—maybe back toward the last two objectives. The others go into the restricted area to do our recon and get our food."

"Are you crazy?" I gaped at her. "We'd have no communication at all. You know the audio implants don't work without your ring, right?"

"Oh, right." Yvonne went silent.

"I've had this holo-ring since I was eight," Marise said. "When we were on TbF and we couldn't connect—that was terrifying. And all my research data—I wouldn't be able to access any of it."

"I'm not worried," Peter said. "I never had a holo-ring until I came to the Academy. I'll go in."

"You can't go alone." I took a deep breath. "Peter and I will go without our rings. You two keep moving. Circle north then back to the spot where we split up. We'll meet you in two hours."

CHAPTER THIRTY

TWENTY MINUTES LATER, we stopped near the eastern foothills. "Let's test this theory before you leave." I took off my ring and handed it to Marise. "Peter, watch the app—I want to know if I seem to be going with them. Yvonne, go about two hundred meters that way." I pointed.

They flew away. Peter and I watch the hologram over his palm. The blue dot labeled number seven continued onward with three and six. We cheered.

"Marise," Peter said. "Put Siti's ring in a meal pac." He waited a second. "Then *open* one and stick the ring in it. You don't have to eat anything." He nodded at me. "They're doing it."

Dot number seven disappeared.

"Take it back out. We don't want anyone watching to notice." I reappeared on the screen, and the three dots sped toward us.

When the girls arrived, Peter handed over his ring. "How are we going to contact you?"

"I wish we had some of those radios you used on Earth," I said.

"We should've asked Chymm," Marise said with a laugh. "He'd probably whip one up out of twigs and worn socks."

"We'll plan on meeting here in about two hours," I reminded them.

Peter crossed his arms. "How are we going to know when it's two hours? We don't have a clock. All of that is on our rings."

"You're some kind of ancient Earth woodsman." I waved my arms. "Don't you know how to tell time by the sun or the smell of the trees or..."

Peter rolled his eyes. "I can guesstimate." He held up his hand, fingers parallel to the horizon. "On Earth, each finger is about fifteen minutes. It's probably less accurate here, since the days are a little longer, but close enough." He stacked his other hand atop the first one. That's about two hours." Then he moved the lower hand on top of the upper hand.

"It's about nine-thirty." Marise flicked her holo-ring and pulled up a clock. "Three hours after sunrise. So, we'll meet you back here about eleven-thirty. That would be five hands above the horizon."

"We don't have five hands." I snickered. "Is that going to give us enough time to get to their camp and back?"

"If you're not here, we'll wait another hour." Marise tucked Peter's ring into the side pocket of her backpack. "If you're still not back, we'll put all the rings in a meal pac and come after you."

"Don't wait," I said. "Fly by—slowly. If we're here, you'll see us. If not, keep going, and circle back. Your bike should have enough power to make two or three circuits if necessary."

"But we're only doing one." Marise gave me a stern look. "If you're not back, we're coming to get you."

I nodded. "Deal."

They headed away, and we angled our bike into the hills.

"ARE you sure were going the right direction?" Peter asked.

"No, I'm not." I gritted my teeth. "I think we are. We were supposed to follow this valley then branch off into that smaller one. But that didn't get us anywhere."

"I didn't think that small valley was right," Peter said.

"You didn't tell me *not* to turn that way," I snapped.

"Sorry, you're right."

I glanced up at the sun. "We'll go a little farther, then it'll be time to turn back."

The first valley ended in a box canyon against a steep mountainside. According to what I remembered of the map, the restricted area started at the end of a dogleg gorge but clearly not that one. We backtracked to the main valley and turned up the second branch which looked more promising, but it was taking much longer to reach the end than I expected.

The bike eased over a rise, and the valley opened up before us. In the center of the valley, a force shield protected a camp by a lake.

"Bingo!" Peter said.

I yanked the bike over hard, sliding us around in a wild turn. Our legs brushed against the scrubby undergrowth, and I pulled the bike upright. Peter yelped, and his fingers dug into my belt. I ignored him and drove us back over the rise.

"What the heck!"

I shut down the bike and flipped my grav belt to zero meters. We dropped to the ground with a thud.

"You could warn a guy."

"There were people down there," I said. I pulled the bike away from our legs and pushed it behind a large shrub.

"I didn't get a good look. I was too busy hanging on for my life."

"Come on." I scrambled up the rise, taking the last few meters on my hands and feet.

We lay on our bellies in the dusty undergrowth, peering down into the valley. The camp stood in the center of a wide bowl, with hills on all sides. A lake filled most of the bowl, and a low cliff overlooked the edge. A small stream wound away from the lake, disappearing between two hills to the south. The faint blue of a force shield glowed around the entire lake. An old living module perched on the nearer shore, and a second one—newer and much larger than the one we brought—stood beyond the first. Half a dozen people moved around the structures, carrying crates and bundles inside.

"They don't look like cadets," I said. They wore black tactical clothing rather than Academy uniforms.

"Who do you think they are?" Peter asked

I shrugged. "This was definitely a flight's camp, though. I recognize the lake from that vid of Mason."

"You're right, but I think they expanded the force shield. It's way bigger than ours." Peter pulled a piece of paper out of his backpack and spread it on the ground before us. It was a rough drawing of the area.

"Where did you get that? And where was it when we were getting lost?"

Peter grimaced. "I don't trust holo-rings. You grew up with them, but they're new for me. When we talked about investigating over here, I drew a sketch of the map. Just in case."

"Again, where was it when we were getting lost?"

"In my backpack, where it wouldn't get blown out of my hands."

I squinted at the lines. "That blind canyon wasn't on here! It's not my fault we got lost."

Peter patted my shoulder condescendingly. "Let's focus, shall we?"

I scooted away from the lip of the rise. A stone dug into my side, and I cursed under my breath.

"Where are you going?" Peter hissed.

"Back to the bike. We aren't going to get any food here. Too many people."

"Those aren't cadets." He turned away and squinted into the valley again. "There are no Academy markings on anything. Maybe we can ask for food. Or to use their comm gear. Or both." As if it had been listening, his stomach growled loudly.

I shimmied back up the hill and looked toward the camp. "I suppose we could ask them. But something doesn't seem right. This is Academy land. If they are from the Academy, we will get disqualified."

"At this point, I don't care." Peter turned to glare at me. "They left us here with no food and no communications. Doesn't that strike you as completely irresponsible? We aren't explorers, we're students. They're supposed to be watching—available to help if someone gets hurt. Terrine's injury should have been enough to bring them down, but they didn't come. In my mind, that means they don't care. And I don't want to belong to an organization that doesn't care."

"You're probably safe anyway," I said. "The treaty protects you."

He shook his head. "The treaty got me a slot here. What I made over that was left up to me. But like I said, I don't feel any allegiance to an organization that deserted me."

"Good point." It had taken me a long time to decide I wanted to be an explorer cadet. I applied twenty years ago because my dad expected it. But I'd agreed to go to Earth because I wasn't sure I wanted to be a cadet. After our adventure there, joining the Corps seemed like the logical answer. But nothing at the Academy had been what I expected. Maybe I was naïve, but the whole legacy thing had caught me by surprise. And the fact that LeBlanc, Lee, and Felicity got away with—well, everything—made me a little ill. Was this how the Corps operated, or was it just the current commandant? When we got on active duty, would they get the same favoritism?

All those questions didn't matter right now. I had a flight that was hungry, and they were depending on me to get them food.

"You're right. We should go ask to send a message."

He nodded. "And for lunch."

I smiled faintly. "And for lunch."

Neither of us moved. The people in the camp continued to put away their gear.

"Who do you think they are?" Peter asked.

I shook my head. "No idea, which is what's bothering me. If they aren't from the Academy, why are they here? This is Academy territory."

"What are those?" Peter pointed across the valley. A stack of large crates stood near the far end of the lake. Light glinted on the logo emblazoned on the side.

"That's a mining company," I said. "Or at least it was twenty years ago. Remember what Marise said about the Academy making money off their land? Maybe they discovered something valuable here and rather than have cadets use it for training, they decided to dig it up."

"It's odd that they would shift those two flights in the middle of an exercise." Peter drummed his fingers in the dirt. "Why not wait until the exercise was over?"

"I dunno. Maybe they aren't supposed to be here?"

"Then moving Purple and Yellow was a very bad idea. It drew attention to this area."

"It drew *our* attention to this area," I said. "Maybe they're using the exercise to cover their tracks? The locals wouldn't notice a couple more shuttles coming in and out. And they don't care what *we* see."

"Besides, they think we'll follow directions." Peter chuckled. "Good cadets don't go snooping around in restricted areas."

"No, but hungry ones do."

Peter rubbed his eyes. "Let's think this through. The Academy dumped us here for an exercise, but they aren't providing support. They kicked the cadets out of this area." He glanced at me. "That was definitely the Academy's work—the message came from Zimas." He rolled over onto his back, and stared up at the brilliant, teal-colored sky.

"And the only time Zimas has been connected to this exercise," I said slowly. "Why did she suddenly get involved?"

"Does it matter?" Peter flipped onto his stomach again, staring into the camp. "Whoever they are, they must have communications. They can help us."

I put a hand on his arm. "The Academy went to a great deal of trouble to keep us away from here. To me, that means they're up to something. I'm not sure we should let them know we know."

"Maybe it's the hunger talking," he said, "but you're crazy. You're seeing conspiracies everywhere."

"How can I not?" I asked. "The legacies are clearly involved in a conspiracy—one to keep them out of trouble."

"That seems pretty minor compared to starvation," Peter said.

"You're not starving. But you are hungry. Eat something already." I reached for his backpack.

He slapped my hand away. "Keep your hands off my food, woman."

"Get up!" barked a deep voice.

CHAPTER THIRTY-ONE

WE ROLLED OVER, staring up at the figure looming over us. It was a tall man with long hair and a blaster aimed at Peter. Behind him, a woman with spiky hair pointed her blaster at me.

I gulped. "Who are you?"

The man jiggled his gun. "I ask the questions. Who are you, and why are you here?"

"We're Academy cadets." I tapped the patch on my shoulder. "We've lost—"

"We've lost track of the rest of our flight," Peter spoke over my words. "We went out foraging and got lost. The rest of the flight is out here somewhere, too. I don't suppose you could spare some food?"

"Didn't you kids get the message?" The woman lowered her weapon and whacked her companion's arm. "Put your gun down. These kids are no threat." She turned back to us. "There's been a landslide here. This area isn't safe. We're here to investigate."

"With weapons?" I asked.

The two stepped back, and the woman gestured for us to stand. "There are wild animals around here. It pays to be safe."

I exchanged a look with Peter. There were no dangerous animals around here, except the herbivores. And as we had seen in the video, the biggest danger from them was being trampled. Or forced into a lake.

"Sven, run down to camp and grab a few meal pacs for these kids." The woman jerked her head toward the rise.

The man stared at her. "You're going to give them food and send them away?"

The woman nodded. "They said they were foraging for food. Let's give them some and get them back to their friends. How many kids did you say are out here?"

Sven gave the woman another stare then turned and headed over the rise. The woman gestured for us to follow.

"There are twelve of us." Peter waited for me to precede him then fell in behind me. "Four back at camp, and six more out here with us. We'd appreciate anything you can give us. Our supplies were pilfered by another flight."

"I hope the Academy will punish them," the woman said. "That doesn't sound like something good cadets should do."

I pinched my lips together, resolved to say as little as possible, so I didn't contradict Peter's story.

"I hope so, too," Peter said. "But in the meantime, we're getting hungry."

"Why don't you call for help?" the woman asked. "Surely they wouldn't leave you here to starve?"

Peter made an uncertain noise. "Probably not. But if we ask for help, we're admitting we can't complete the mission on our own. That won't be good for our scores. Say, you won't tell them you helped us, will you?"

"Of course not," the woman said with a chuckle. "It'll be our little secret."

"Which department do you work for?" Peter asked. "Are you part of the Academy or another branch of the Corps?"

"We are independent contractors," the woman said. We reached the bottom of the hill, and she moved up beside us. "We're from a mining company, but my specialty is geo-structural integrity. That's why they sent my team to investigate the landslide."

"Makes sense," I muttered. While Peter and the woman chatted, I checked out her gear. She wore a soft-armor—the type explorers wore on dangerous planets. She had two spare chargers for her blaster and a projectile weapon strapped to her leg. Her gear was black—no logos or identifying patches. The kind of gear worn on black ops—at least in entertainment vids, that's what they looked like. She didn't strike me as the scientific type, but maybe miners were more outdoorsy than the typical scientist.

She stopped in a low spot where the camp was out of view. "Let's wait here for Sven. The team is pretty busy, and we don't want to disrupt anything." She turned her back to the camp, pinning us with her clear, blue stare. "Which flight are you from?"

"Delta Black," Peter said promptly. "I didn't think anyone outside the Corps knew anything about our flights."

She shrugged. "I had a friend who went to the Academy. Years ago. I think she was in Blue flight. Chalky Blue, or something like that."

"Charlie Blue." The words popped out of my mouth before I could stop them.

"Chalky Blue," Peter said with a smirk. "I like that. We call them—" He broke off. "Sorry, I can't say that in polite company."

The woman snickered. "I can imagine. Say, didn't you get the warning?"

"What warning?" Peter asked.

"There's an automated warning on the perimeter of the restricted area. You should have gotten a 'turn back' announcement when you crossed the border."

Peter held up his hand. "No holo-ring."

The woman's eyes narrowed. "They dropped you without holo-rings?"

"Of course not," Peter said. "But I told you, someone pilfered our food. So, we're going stealthy right now. Left the rings with the cadets back at camp so no one would see us coming."

"You kids weren't planning on breaking into another flight's camp, were you?"

Peter ducked his head. "No, ma'am." He gave a convincing imitation of a cocky Delta Black pretending to be contrite.

The woman laughed. "Good for you! Here's Sven with some meal pacs. Make sure you share those with your team." She winked.

Sven strode up carrying a shrink-wrapped case. "Two dozen. I put down your name, Telia."

The woman's lips pursed, but she didn't say anything.

"Should be enough for a couple of days if you share. Or a couple of weeks if you're careful." He handed the meal pacs to Peter.

"Thank you." Peter pointed to me. "She'll carry that."

I took the heavy package. It was unwieldy, but Peter was playing legacy jerk, so I went along.

"We'll get out of your way," Peter said. "If you give me your contact info, I'll make sure my dad sends you an *appreciation gift*."

Telia's eyes narrowed. "Your dad? Who are you?"

He froze for a fraction of a second. "I'm Derek Lee."

"Admiral Lee's son?" she asked.

Peter nodded.

"Admiral Lee is a woman," she said.

"So?" Peter looked a little sick.

"You said your *dad* would send me a gift."

"Dad does all that stuff. Mom's too busy." He shrugged, as if it were obvious.

Telia looked him over. "Sure. Admirals are busy, aren't they? But don't worry about it. I don't want them to know I gave some of our supplies to a pair of cadets."

He shrugged again. "Suit yourself. Thanks for the food." He turned and headed up the hill.

I gave them an anxious nod and followed. My shoulders itched, and I resisted the urge to look back. When we reached the top of the rise, Peter turned and raised a hand then climbed over. I struggled in his wake, lugging my prize.

When we reached the bush where we'd left the bike, Peter took the case of meal pacs. "Let's strap the crate to the bike. I can tether my belt to the bike and follow behind."

"Turn around." The voice came from below us.

My head jerked up. Four cadets pointed blasters at us.

Peter set the case on the ground and rose slowly, his hands away from his sides. "Where'd you get those weapons, Aris?"

"None of your business," Aris said. "Don't move. Telia, we got intruders."

We waited, keeping our hands visible. Two of the cadets sauntered up to us and started to pat us down. My searcher patted a little too enthusiastically in the wrong place, and I grabbed his index finger in my fist. "Watch it, creep."

He tried to jerk away, but I squeezed his finger and bent it back.

"Let go, you bitch!" he cried.

"You started it." I smiled, my eyes narrow.

"Enough," Aris barked. "Leave her alone, Fendel. Kassis, let go, or I'll hit you with a stunner."

I glared at Fendel, then dropped his finger. He backed away, swinging his blaster around toward me.

"Hold it!" Telia and four others came over the rise. "You were supposed to let them go, Aris."

"They were stealing our stuff." The boy gestured to the crate of meal pacs.

"I gave them those meals. And they weren't yours, they're ours." Telia's eyes narrowed. "But maybe I'll replace them with some of yours."

"LeBlanc won't let you—"

"Little LeBlanc's not in charge. I am." Sven stepped forward. "What do you expect us to do with these kids now? We could have let them go back to their camp, and they'd have been none the wiser. Now they know you're working with us."

Aris flushed. "You told us to watch the trails…"

"Once you warned us about these two, you were done," Sven said.

Telia raised her hand. "Too late now. Let's get them back to camp. You kids go back to work. If you see anyone else, tell us, but *don't* confront them."

Aris ground his teeth then jerked his head at the other cadets and turned away. They slunk down the valley and out of sight.

Sven turned to Telia. "Search them. They said they didn't have their holo-rings. Make sure they don't have any weapons."

Telia handed her blaster to another man and sauntered down the hill.

I raised my hands away from my body. "There's a glider in my jacket pocket."

Telia glared and stuck her hand into the pocket. "Gah!" She yanked her hand away. Liam came with it, teeth sunk into the webbing between Telia's thumb and forefinger. She shook her hand, hard, and Liam spun away.

"Liam!"

Crack! Pain lanced through my cheek.

"Hey!" Peter yelled.

I blinked tears from my eyes as Telia's blurry form spun toward Peter. I launched myself at her, shoving her backward.

"Stop!" Sven roared. His voice was accompanied by the sound of weapons cocking.

We both froze. Modern weapons have no need to cock, but the sound is terrifying. I assume that's why the manufacturers continue to include a cocking mechanism. I don't think it actually does anything except tell the person on the other end that you're serious. They obviously were.

Telia backhanded Peter, sending him sprawling.

"I said stop," Sven said in a cold voice.

"He deserved it." She clamped her left hand over the bite. "Did you see what bit me?"

"Probably her glider," the man said. "You know the CEC is overrun with the things."

"Cadets aren't allowed to have them," one of the other men said.

"Cadets also aren't supposed to steal supplies or raid contractors," Telia said. "Clearly things aren't going as usual at the Academy."

They all laughed.

"Are you connected to the CEC at all?" I asked.

"None of your business." Sven feinted toward me, and I stumbled back. He laughed, his beady eyes disappearing into the sun wrinkles around them.

"Let's go," Telia said. "We're behind schedule already."

Sven grabbed my shoulder and pushed me up the hill. I stumbled and fell, catching myself with a hand. I used the movement to look behind me.

Two bright eyes blinked at me from the shadow of a scrubby bush. Liam dropped his jaw in a grin and scurried away.

"Get up," Sven growled.

Peter took my arm and helped me. We climbed up the rise. As we crested the top, Telia and her team split apart, leaving a wide aisle for us to pass between them.

"Don't try anything stupid," Telia said. "Maybe we'll let you go home."

The others laughed again.

CHAPTER THIRTY-TWO

THE THROBBING in my cheekbone kept time with my heartbeat. I pressed my face against the cool metal shelf support, but it didn't give much relief. They'd dumped us in a supply closet in the large living mod and locked the door.

"Here's a tylo-patch." Peter held out a flat packet.

"Where'd you get that?" I took it, peeled off the outer layer, and pressed it against my neck. Relief flowed through my face.

"It was in my pocket. Telia missed it." He shrugged and slid down to sit opposite me. "We got a bunch of those from your dad after the treaty signing, so I always keep a few on hand. I've got some skin sealers, too."

I smirked, but the movement made my cheek hurt again. "Colonialism at its best."

Peter raised his eyebrows.

"Get the natives hooked on substances they can't make themselves." I pointed to the patch. "Then they're dependent."

"We aren't uneducated." Peter's lips twisted. "Zane included medical equipment and access to manufacturing in the treaty. You have to keep us healthy if you want a base on Earth."

We sat in silence for a while. An emergency light glowed over the door —barely enough for us to see each other. As soon as the door shut, we'd pawed through the shelves above us. They were filled with electrical and mechanical equipment but nothing useful like a screwdriver or an axe.

"What now?" I finally asked.

"If Chymm were here, he'd have built a door dissolver by now." Peter gestured to the shelf above his head.

"Or a portal back to camp. That's more his style."

He nodded. "Or a jump gate to take us to Earth."

"He'd have to build a ship, first." I rubbed my stinging eyes and blinked back tears.

"I have no doubt he could do it." Peter's eyes narrowed. "You aren't crying, are you?"

I sniffed and shook my head. "I'm just so mad!" A couple tears leaked out, and I slapped them away, knocking against my cheek. "Ow!"

Peter pushed up to his knees and swiveled to sit next to me. The metal shelves pressed against the middle of my back, but the box on the bottom gave a little support. Peter put his arm around my shoulders and shook me gently. "I'm mad, too."

"You don't look it," I sniffed.

"I learned to hide that a long time ago." He turned toward me, and a little of the rage leaked through his eyes. He blinked, and the anger was gone.

I leaned my head against his shoulder. My stomach growled. "I wish they would have let us have one of those meal pacs."

"Keep your adversary weak." He gave me another squeeze. "How long do you reckon before Marise and Yvonne stumble into camp?"

"I'm hoping Liam will warn them."

Peter blinked. "You think he's that smart?"

I shrugged. "He was smart enough to lead you guys to me in the caves."

"Exactly. He'll lead them right here. And that idiot Aris and his lecherous friend will grab them."

"He got me inside the camp before Delta Black attacked us." I pulled away from his arm, glaring. "He pulled on my ear until I went back inside. As soon as the gate was closed, he stopped. Then they hit us."

"I admit the little guy is smart. And he undoubtedly has your back. But

I'm not convinced he's smart enough to know they should stay away this time."

"Yeah, I know." I sagged against his shoulder again. "Wishful thinking, I guess. Maybe Yvonne and Marise will be smart enough to watch and wait instead of following him?"

"In the meantime—" Peter pushed me aside gently and got to his feet. "Let's see if there's something we can use in here."

"We already went through all that stuff." I grabbed the closest shelf and pulled myself up.

"Yeah, but we were looking for obvious tools. Maybe there's something that wasn't designed to—" he made a jerky motion "—but could be used for prying. Like the case of this—whatever it is." He hefted a box the size of a rev-ball and pulled on the edge of the case. The plastek snapped off in his hands. "Okay, so now we know that is too brittle for prying."

I smirked. "Is it heavy? We could throw it at Sven next time he opens the door."

Peter set the box back on the shelf with a grin. "I'll make a pile of chuckable stuff here."

I pulled a box from the shelf and sifted through the electronic parts. "There's a tiny screwdriver here." I held up the little tool then pointed at the upper corner of the closet. "I could probably unscrew that air vent."

"Then all we need is a shrink ray and a long twine ladder, and we can escape!" Peter set a few more things aside.

"How long do you think we've been gone?" I asked after a while.

"From Marise and Yvonne? Long enough that they'll start looking for us."

"And it's mid-day out there. Nowhere to hide." I tucked the screwdriver into my pocket and put the box back.

"Did they notice our bike?" He rubbed the back of his neck. "If the girls see that, it should be enough of a warning."

I thought back. "I'm not sure they saw it behind the bush. But that means the girls might not see it either. Unless Liam shows them."

Peter's shoulders twitched, but he didn't comment. We kept searching.

"Hey, this might work to pry the door hinges off."

I straightened up and stretched my back. "Go for it."

While he fiddled with the door, I did some more stretching.

"Crap." He stepped back, hands on hips. "These hinges are—I've never seen anything like them. At home, the door and the frame have rings that fit together, and a pin holds them in place. Then the hinges swivel on the pin. If you pull the pin out, you can pull the door away. I don't see how these work."

"Lemme look." I pushed him aside. The door panel fit tightly into the frame. In the darkness, it was hard to see the outline of the door, and there were no rings or pins anywhere. I thought back to our module on Earth. "When we open these up, the panels unfold, like paper. Then you activate the section through the holo-ring, and it stiffens. The doors open and close like the panels, but they don't stop folding when the panel is activated."

"Tell me something I don't know," Peter grumped. "I set up our little mod, remember?"

"Yeah, but you didn't do any doors." I patted his shoulder. "So, you wouldn't know they aren't like Earth doors."

"Back to the drawing board," he said.

"What?" A chittering sound caught my attention. "Hey, that sounds like Liam!"

"I don't hear anything."

"Sh!" I held up a hand and cocked my head. The noise repeated. "Look! The air vent!" Two bright eyes peered at us through the vent. I pulled the tiny screwdriver from my pocket and held it up. "I'm coming, Liam!"

"Give me that," Peter said. "You aren't tall enough to reach the vent."

"I can climb on these shelves." I put the tool back in my pocket and put my left foot on the lowest shelf. Gripping a shelf on each side of the narrow aisle, I pushed up and put my right foot on a shelf on that side. Alternating sides, I climbed up between the two freestanding racks. "Good thing these aren't part of the cube. I don't think they'd hold me."

"Really?" Peter's voice sounded surprised.

"Yeah, the integrated shelves can't take a lot of mass. Li told me a rover or a large predator could plow right through one of these mods. That's why we have the force shields around the camp."

"How large a predator?" Peter's voice sounded odd. I glanced over my shoulder, and he flexed in imitation of Joss. "How about a human?"

"But these shelves aren't part of the mod." I wiggled a little, rattling the two structures.

"No, but that wall is." He pointed past me, toward the wall with the vent. "Maybe we can—how did you say it? Plow right through."

I looked down at him. "You might. But that would make a lot of noise. They'd just grab us again."

"Maybe. If we knew what they were up to, we could wait until they're all busy. Or maybe we could take it down quietly."

"Let's get the vent cover off and get Liam inside, first." I used my screwdriver to pry the vent cover away from the opening. It was a rectangular hole to the outside, about ten centimeters by twenty. Liam jumped from the opening, landing on my shoulder. He rubbed his silky fur against my bruised cheek. I winced, and he stopped.

Liam chittered again. I stroked his head. "You're such a smart boy!"

"Liam, come down here so Siti can get off the shelves." Peter held out a hand.

Liam nuzzled me one more time, very gently, then leapt to Peter's outstretched arm.

I peered through the vent. Although most of the walls of a mod were literally paper thin, the rear wall was thicker. This was the wall all the others were folded into, and it provided the structure for the building. Another louvered panel—with a corner missing—covered the other end of the rectangular opening. Liam had evidently chewed a hole to gain access.

I jumped down, the landing jarring my sore cheek. "You are such a good boy!" Liam soared to my shoulder.

CHAPTER THIRTY-THREE

WE SPENT the next few hours continuing our inventory of the closet. After we'd dug through all the unused electronics, we tried some kids' guessing games and played with Liam. Then we all took a nap.

The click of the door lock yanked me out of a light doze. Liam scuttled under the closest shelf.

"How sweet," Telia said. "Look at the little cadets, all curled up in a nest."

I rolled to my feet. "You can't keep us here. They'll know we went missing, and they'll come looking."

Telia smirked. "Who's they? The Academy's comm satellites have been down for days. Strange malfunction." She shook her head in mock dismay. "Besides, you left your rings back at your camp. They won't have any idea where to look for you. Sarvo Six is a big planet."

I ground my teeth. "What do you want?"

She tossed a couple of packages on the ground. "Touchy. I brought you dinner."

"I don't suppose you could let us use the bathroom," Peter suggested, bouncing from foot to foot.

Telia's eyes narrowed. "One at a time. Don't try anything."

He held up both hands. "I wouldn't dream of it." He cocked his head at me. "Mind if I go first?"

I waved my arm at the door. "Please, by all means."

As soon as they left, I tried the door. Locked, of course. I picked up the meal pacs and ripped one open. The first packet of Chewy Nuggets disappeared before Peter returned.

"You're up, princess." Telia waved her blaster at me.

Peter stepped into the closet, holding the door open for me.

"Princess?" I followed her out of the room.

"Shut the door and try the lock." She shoved the weapon toward the door.

Peter swung the door to me, and I pulled it shut. Then I tried the handle. It turned more than I expected, but the door didn't budge. "Satisfied?"

Telia's eyes narrowed. "Watch it, princess. You want food or the bathroom, you need to make nice with me."

"Sorry. I'm just hungry." I let my lips twitch in a fake smile. "Thanks for the food. Which way?"

She pointed across the large workroom. Counters ringed the walls, leaving the center clear for two large machines. On the far side, there was a door with a small, frosted window at head-height. I pushed the door open and entered a short hallway. An open door on the left led to a common room. A door at the far end of the hallway was closed. The facilities were on the right.

"In and out, princess. Make it quick. No funny business."

I nodded and went in. This was an internal room, so no window to sneak out. I did my thing and met her in the hall. "Why do you keep calling me princess?" That was a nickname Cadet Wronglen's lovely aunt had bestowed on me during the voyage to Earth. Had Telia learned who my father was?

She shrugged. "All you cadets are princesses. Entitled. Lazy. Too good to work for a living."

I ground my teeth and tamped down my angry reaction. "Were you an explorer?" I moved slowly, trying to get a peek into the common room as we passed.

"I enlisted for a term." She poked me with the weapon. "Security forces, guarding North Grissom field. Saw way too many cadets in my four years. Back to your closet."

The common room seemed to be empty. The smell of food lingered, but the lights were off. "Where is everyone?" I asked.

"None of your business, princess." She poked me again. "They have work to do."

"Searching for our flight-mates?" I suggested. "Or babysitting Delta Black?"

She barked a hard laugh. "That's a good description, but the brats aren't my problem. They're off on another of your little missions."

"Another mission? You have to let us go—we can't miss it!"

She laughed again. "Sorry, your mission is not even on the bottom of my priority list. You'll stay here until we decide what to do with you." She raised an eyebrow. "What were you two doing out here alone? That's right, I know you didn't have any flight-mates out here. The kids didn't find anyone, and we sent the drones as soon as we caught you. No one else around. Did you two sneak away from your flight for a little nookie?"

My shoulders twitched. "No. With Peter? No."

She laughed again, this time sounding more genuine. "Hit a nerve, did I? He's a good-looking kid. But kinda skinny."

"He's my friend." I turned and glared at her. "I'm not going to discuss my relationships with you."

Telia leaned in close. "You'll do whatever I tell you to do, princess." She lifted the blaster. "I hold all the cards."

I crossed my arms. "You aren't going to use that. If we get hurt, the Academy will come looking for you."

She smirked and took a step back. "You don't understand how the land lays, do you? They don't give a crap about you. If they did, they'd be here, checking their comm satellites and bringing you snacks. Get back in your box." She waved her hand at the access panel and the door unlocked.

My breath caught in my chest. She was right. They should have sent someone to check on us as soon as the comms went out. But I wouldn't give her the satisfaction of seeing my fear. I raised my chin and strutted past her. "Thanks for your help," I said over my shoulder.

"It won't happen again," she muttered, and the door snapped shut.

I opened my mouth, but Peter held up his hand. He leaned against the door, listening. "Can't hear a thing," he whispered. "The sound-proofing on these things is amazing, considering how thin they are."

I nodded. "I noticed that, too. Did you find out anything? The common room was empty. That door at the end of the hall—based on what I know of these mods, that's probably another storage room. Maybe they keep the food in there."

"I was thinking the same thing. They were eating in the common room earlier, so…" He dropped to the floor and leaned against the door. "I hate to tell you this, but Liam took off again."

"What?"

He pointed at the air vent. "After you left, he went that way. I don't know if he was trying to follow you, or…"

"Did he think I was deserting him?" I wailed.

"No, of course not. Maybe he's looking for the others."

"They haven't caught Marise and Yvonne. In fact, Telia thinks we were out here alone."

"That's good, right?" He lifted the open meal pac. "You want to share one and hang on to the other, or split 'em up?"

"Maybe they'll figure out how to rescue us." I took the open package. "I took the Chewy Nuggets out of this one, so it's mine. You can have the other one."

"Are they both the same?" He pulled the tab on the second one and dumped the contents into his lap.

"Yeah." I showed him the number on the side of mine. "Standard pac number two. Red stew and rice."

He made a face as he pulled out the green envelope. "At least they gave us the whole pac. They could have eaten the good stuff first."

"Like Joss." I sat against the other set of shelves, remembering our picnic on the way to New Lake.

"Like Joss." Peter held up his packet as if toasting. I tapped my empty one against his and settled in to wait.

THE GRISSOM CONTENTION

Although we couldn't hear anything through the door, the air vent was another story. Occasionally, voices filtered through the opening. Most of them were male, and we heard snatches of conversations as they passed by. These involved many swear words and crude comments.

"I'm getting a real education," Peter said after I pretended I didn't understand another repulsive remark.

"I've gotten so used to your accent, I forget you didn't grow up with the same vocabulary I did."

"Oh, I probably did, but they were different words back then." He laughed. "My mom tried to keep me away from that kind of language, but you know kids. The Mylinchek brothers took care of that." His face darkened at the thought of his old bullies. He'd finally faced them—and won—but the memories must still bother him.

I jumped to my feet. "I'm going to climb up and see what's going on." I scrambled up the shelves. They shook ominously as I neared the top, so I moved more carefully.

I pushed a box aside and slid onto the top shelf. I had to bend over to keep from bumping my head on the ceiling, but I could see through the air vent.

"Can you see anything?" Peter asked.

"The outer vent cover is in the way." I pushed my arm through the opening and shoved the cover. It flexed but didn't fall out. I shoved harder.

It creaked and snapped. The cover fell away. I yanked my hand back and held my breath. No one shouted. "I got the cover off. You want to come up and look? We can move the stuff on that other shelf."

Peter peered at me. "I'm good. You can let me know if you see anything interesting." He leaned his shoulders against the door, arms crossed as he regarded me with a smirk.

I rolled my eyes and turned to the vent. "I can see part of the lake. There are big machines like the ones in the outer room on the edge of the lake. They might be dredging? Or maybe they're using the water to process something."

"How many people are out there?"

"Two that I can see. Probably more out of view. Wait, someone's coming." I leaned forward, my ear against the opening. Two men moved by, arguing about a sports team. "Nope, nothing."

I leaned against the wall, watching through the vent while Peter closed his eyes and snoozed against the door. The sun moved lower, and the hills cast long shadows across the lake. My eyes drifted shut.

I WAS FALLING through space in a never-ending drop. Stars spun around me. I tried to move, but my legs didn't respond. The stars spun faster.

Whomp! I landed with a thud.

"Ouch!"

"Siti, are you okay?" Peter crouched beside me. "You fell off the shelf."

I blinked in the dim light and took stock of my body. My cheek throbbed again. My arms were fine. My legs felt dead. "I can't move my legs!"

"That little fall couldn't have been enough to paralyze you."

Pins and needles stabbed my calves. I rolled up to massage my lower legs. "I think they fell asleep."

He laughed.

"It's not funny." I glared.

"It's a little funny," he replied. "I fell out of the top bunk when I was seven."

I sat up and swatted his leg.

"By the way, Liam's back." He held out his hand, and the furry creature leapt to my shoulder.

"That doesn't mean you can laugh at me." I nuzzled my face against Liam's fur.

"Yeah, but he brought gifts." He held up a small packet.

"What's that?"

"Our holo-rings."

CHAPTER THIRTY-FOUR

"No way!"

"Way," Peter held up the package with the ghost of a grin. "Someone made a little backpack for him. Here's your ring."

I took it and slid it on my finger. It jiggled loosely. "I think this one is yours."

We traded. I flicked my ring and it glowed, the light comforting in the dark closet. I activated the comm system. "Yvonne? Marise? Where are you?"

"We're on the rise near your bike," Yvonne replied through the comm. "I can't believe Liam did that!"

"You need to move," Peter said. "Find a safer place to hide. Take the bike with you."

"On it," Marise said.

I scratched Liam's blue stripes, paying special attention to his ears. "He's really smart."

"He's too smart," Marise said. Her voice sounded wavery, as if she were jiggling up and down. Probably on the bullet bike.

"What do you mean?" I touched my nose to Liam's and whispered, "She doesn't know what she's talking about."

Peter rolled his eyes.

A sigh came through the audio. "He's too smart to be a sair-glider. They are good at protecting explorers, but there's been no documentation to indicate they understand the kinds of things Liam does. How did he know we wanted to get those rings to you?"

"Maybe he didn't. He found you, then he came back to Siti," Peter said. "You made the backpack. He happened to be carrying it when he came back."

"Not really." Yvonne's voice held a tinge of wonder. "He told us to give him the rings."

"He can talk?" Peter crossed his arms, his face a mask of disbelief.

"Don't be silly," Marise said. "But when he found us—maybe we should save this discussion for when you're free."

"Good idea. If the Academy can track our rings, maybe Sven and Telia can, too," I said. "We need to get out, now."

"Who are they?" Marise asked. "Are they from the Academy?"

I told them Telia's explanation. "I don't believe her, though. I mean, if that were the case, why did they lock us up?"

"And why are they working with Delta Black?" Peter asked. "Did you get the new mission?"

"What new mission?" Marise and Yvonne asked together.

Peter and I exchanged a narrow-eyed look. Was the "new mission" a subterfuge? Or had Charlie Blue been left out of the loop?

"I wish Chymm was here," I stared at my ring, then looked at the door. "He could figure out how to open the door."

Peter smirked. "It's not a problem." He stood and pulled the handle. The door opened a fraction then hit his foot.

I opened my mouth, but he held a finger to his lips. We listened.

Nothing.

He pulled the door a little farther open. The outer room was dark. He flung up a hand and peered around the edge of the door. "It looks clear."

"How'd you get the door open?" I whispered.

He pointed to the door jamb. A thin strip of skin-sealer patch covered the lock sensor. "Trick I learned from Zane. Of course, we used duct tape over a physical latch…"

I grinned and flashed a thumbs-up.

We crossed the dark room and eased into the hall. The common room door stood ajar. Voices and the clinking of cutlery on plates reached us. A waft of delicious smells poured through—so much better than the meal pacs. My stomach rumbled. I clamped a hand over my belly and put my eye to the crack. The room was well lit, and a couple of Delta Black cadets sat at a table eating. I eased the door shut. The sounds cut off.

"I guess Black is back from their mission." My nose wrinkled.

"Or there wasn't a mission." Yvonne's voice came through the comm again. "We've moved to a spot about a klick farther south. We're on a hillside where we can see the camp."

"Stay low. They've got drones," Peter said.

"They don't seem to be using them very diligently," I said. "Maybe that's Black's new mission—to guard the camp. Good thing they're crap at that."

The others snickered.

"Let's see what's behind door number two." I pointed at the presumed closet on the far wall.

"Are you sure we want to chance it with them sitting in the next room?" Peter asked.

"Too risky." I contemplated the first door. "There has to be some way we can get more food."

"I'll bet they keep the meal pacs in that closet." Peter pointed. "What if we wait until night then grab some stuff on the way out? Telia said anyone in camp could open *our* door. They probably have the locks set to the default."

"You lived on Earth too long," I said with a smirk. "They aren't going to be hampered by the dark. In fact, I'd expect them to be more vigilant at night. They're operating under the assumption they're safe because of the landslide lie."

"Except they know we disregarded it." Peter took my hand and pulled me toward our cell. "And we told them there are six other cadets wandering around the hills. They've probably sent out a search team—or some drones, or both." He pulled the skin-sealer from the door jamb, revealing the red sensor.

"What are you doing?" I asked.

"Checking the locks." He flicked his holo-ring, and the faint red light on the door jamb turned green.

The handle turned easily under my hand. "Let's try it with the door actually closed." I swung it shut.

Peter locked and unlocked the door. We grinned at each other and did a high-five.

"They sent out drones." I returned to the previous conversation as we went into our cell. "But they gave up because they didn't find anyone. At least that's what Telia said."

"Some of the Delta Black cadets might still be out there, working on their next mission," Peter said, his face sour.

The beginnings of an idea tickled my brain. "We need Chymm. Yvonne, can you and Marise bring him here? Aneh and Joss can hold down the fort."

"What are you going to do?" Peter asked.

"I'm going to wait in my cell like a good girl." I swung the door wide. "Chymm is going to hack into their surveillance and give us a clear shot out of here."

CHAPTER THIRTY-FIVE

THE EVENING DRAGGED ON FOREVER. We played more games, then I climbed on top of the shelves again to watch. The occasional worker wandered by, but I didn't learn anything useful. While I watched, I taught Liam tricks using bits of my meal pac for treats.

"Don't waste too much of that," Peter said. "He can feed himself."

I shuddered. "Insects. He'd much rather have meal pac bits, right Liam?" The glider regarded me with bright eyes.

"I'm going to try the girls again." Peter pulled his holo-ring out of the Chewy Nugget pouch. We'd decided to keep them hidden except when necessary. The ring lit up the dingy little room. "They've been gone for hours. You don't think they got caught, do you?"

"If Telia caught them, they'd be in here with us."

Peter held up a finger. "Where are you?" He listened, and his eyes widened. "What? Is everyone okay? What did they get?"

"What's happening?" I pushed my feet over the side of my perch and felt for a lower shelf.

"*Those blasters!*"

"Peter, what's going on?" I jumped down and grabbed his arm.

His eyes focused on me. "Hang on, let me tell Siti." He rubbed a hand over his face. "Delta Black took over our camp."

"Is anyone hurt?"

Peter shook his head.

"Why? How?"

"The girls think Terrine let them in." He winced as he said it.

"No. She wouldn't." *She warned us*, the little voice in my head insisted. She told us her flight had been brainwashed to do whatever the legacies demanded. "I thought she was too injured to do much."

"Yvonne got her fixed up as well as she could," he said, as if I hadn't been there. "Maybe she was faking the concussion? Waiting for a chance to let them in?"

I flicked my ring and joined their conversation. "Why did they do it? We didn't have anything to take. And they've got a sweet deal here."

"I don't think this was about getting anything," Yvonne said. "This was about taking away our base. They want to destroy us, since we beat them last time. Plus, Felicity really hates you."

"This was all to get back at me for not playing her game?" I stared at Peter. "That can't be it."

"Felicity is a narcissist in the truest sense of the word," Yvonne said. "In her mind, she's the only important thing—the only real person. The rest of us are here to serve her. She can't tolerate anyone who doesn't bow down before her greatness. You didn't play her game, so you must be destroyed. And the rest of us with you."

I rubbed my neck. "I can't—" I shook my head. "It doesn't matter. Everyone got out safely, right? Where are you now?"

"We're on our way to you," Yvonne said. "You wanted Chymm, so we're bringing him. Joss and Aneh stayed by the camp. They're watching Delta Black from the woods below the camp."

"Hi, Siti," Chymm said.

"Hi, Chymm," I replied automatically. "That wooded area isn't very big. How are they hiding? And how are they watching?"

"Don't worry about it," Yvonne said. "Joss and Aneh can handle themselves. They'll report back to us if anything goes down. We'll call you back when we get up there."

The call disconnected, leaving Peter and I staring at each other. "Now what?" I asked.

"What did you want Chymm to do?"

"I figured he could get into their surveillance system and help us escape. We might need his help to get through the force shield, too." I sighed. "I want to know what they're doing out there."

"Why?"

"Because they locked us in a closet, and I want payback," I grumped. "They need to pay for what they did to us. And whatever underhanded business they're up to out there."

"It does seem kind of shady."

"What part clued you in?" I asked. "The part where they locked Academy cadets in a closet? People doing honest work don't kidnap students."

He grinned. "Yeah, there is that. But is vengeance your thing?"

I sighed. "No, but I do want to take them down a peg."

He held a finger to his lips and pointed toward the vent. "Sh! Someone's coming."

Three or four voices talked over each other, with some laughter sprinkled in. The casual profanity curled my ears, sprinkled with slurs and jokes. I shook my head. Nothing useful.

"Do you think it's lights out time?" I whispered.

"I doubt they have an official lights out, but maybe they go to bed early?" Peter held up crossed fingers. "Shall we go now?"

I nodded. "Where do you think they put our bug-out bags? I hate to lose them."

He shrugged. "Not sure we have a choice."

The door rattled. Telia looked in. "Last chance for the crapper, children."

"Why do you have to look after us?" I asked as I pushed past her to the workroom. "I mean, instead of one of the others?"

She snorted. "I don't *have* to. I volunteered. Trust me, you don't want any of those guys near you."

I stopped at the door to the loo. "Really? They're that bad?"

Her eyes twitched. Was that a twinge of guilt? "They're not exactly upstanding citizens. I wouldn't leave a girl—or a pretty boy like your friend—alone with any of them. You should thank me for taking care of you."

Her cold tone sent a shiver through my veins. "Thank you," I said. "I appreciate it."

"Shut up and do your business." She poked the weapon at me.

When we'd both made a trip to the facilities, she tossed two more meal pacs into the closet. "I'll see you in the morning. You might want to see if you can barricade this door because anyone in camp can open it."

The lock snapped shut.

"What was that about?" Peter asked.

"According to Telia, our captors are not above a little raping and pillaging," I said. "She's trying to protect us. Fortunately, we won't be here long enough to need it." I pointed at his chest. "We are getting out of here. I saw our bags in the other room. On the workbench to the left. I'm not sure what's in them."

He nodded. "Yeah, I spotted them, too. Do we wait for full dark or try to get out now?"

"I think we should go soon. The predators come out at night. The two-legged kind. Maybe Marise and the others can create some kind of diversion?"

He pulled the Chewy Nugget pack out of his bag and dumped our rings into his palm. "See what they can cook up. I'll grab our bags."

WHILE WE WAITED FOR CHYMM, Marise, and Yvonne to create their diversion, I stretched out on the top shelf again, lying on my stomach to peer out the vent. As the sun dropped behind the hills, deep shadows filled the valley. The strange equipment in the lake became indistinct hulks. A man wandered by, the glowing tip of a smoke rod casting weird shadows on his face.

"It'll be dark soon." Marise's voice roused me. "You ready?"

"Ready," Peter confirmed in a low voice.

Below, the smoke rod paused, as if the man had stopped to listen. Then he continued on his way.

I slid off the shelf, trying to make as little noise as possible. I grabbed my bug-out bag and shoved my remaining meal pac inside. After making sure Liam was sleeping in my pocket, I swung the bag over my shoulder. Peter grabbed his, and we waited by the door, our holo-rings providing the only light.

"Go," I said.

"Counting down," Marise said. "Ten. Nine…"

Peter flicked his ring, and the door unlocked.

"Four. Three…"

He eased the door open. The outer room was dark. Light shone through the frosted door panel.

"Two. One. Now."

Blam!

The overwhelming electrical crack made the hair on my arms stand up. The light in the other room went out.

CHAPTER THIRTY-SIX

WE DARTED ACROSS THE ROOM. No light shone through the window at the top. I pushed it open a fraction and paused to listen. "No one's there. Come on."

We slipped into the hall and ran toward the closet at the other end. I flicked my holo-ring, but it didn't connect to the mod's app. "Crap. No power, no access."

"These things should default to open." Peter rattled the door handle. "What if someone got stuck in there during a blackout?"

"I think they're smarter than—"

The door swung open. Maybe they had frequent blackouts and decided access to equipment was more important than security. We moved inside. Light flashed wildly across the closet as Peter raised his hand.

"There!" The light stopped on a case of meal pacs.

"And there!" I focused my light on another crate. "Grav belts! Jackpot."

I yanked the box off the shelf. It nearly hit the floor when the weight took me by surprise. After setting it down, I yanked the top off and tossed a pair of belts to Peter. "Wrap each of those around a case and let's go."

While he did that, I pulled out a second pair of belts and clipped one on. Then I grabbed two more and slaved them to mine. They'd trail along behind like an electronic tail. He finished and took the belt I handed him. I slaved the food to his belt. The crates rose off the ground, bobbing like corks in a stream.

"Step one, check," Peter said with a grin. "On to step two."

We tiptoed into the hall, and through the door to the common room. The room was empty, and the outer door open. Outside, bright lights burned.

"If we go out that way, they'll see us," I said.

Peter turned inward. "Out the back it is."

We ran through the short hallway and back into the large workroom. Big double doors took up most of the back wall. They were secured with a latch and seemed to operate on a sliding track.

"That's a custom set up," I said. "At least, none of the mods I've seen or read about have manually-opening cargo doors."

"What do you do if power is out and you need to get big equipment in or out?" Peter asked.

I shook my head. "You're thinking of this like a colonist. Explorer Corps' job is to explore. If we lose power, it's because we didn't prepare properly. They should have a backup for these mods. That way, if local wildlife manage to take down your power system, you can still get in and out. But you aren't going to need to move heavy equipment until after the power is restored. That would take priority."

Peter nodded absently. He unhooked the latch and pulled on the door. It slid easily, barely making any noise. "Well maintained," he muttered. "What does that mean?"

I assumed the question was rhetorical and ignored it. "Let's get out of here." I slid through the opening and skulked along the dark back wall of the mod.

"We need to go that way." Peter pointed directly ahead. A slash of deep shadow led from our hiding place to a bollard at the southern end of the now inoperative force shield. "Now. Before they get the power back."

We darted across the dusty ground, leaping over scrubby bushes and rocks. I stumbled, but Peter grabbed my arm.

"This is stupid." I tapped my grav belt and lifted off. Peter smacked his forehead and followed suit. We streaked across the ground. I glanced back. The crates and spare belts trailed along behind.

"What's that?" a rough voice called out. Lights swung in our direction.

"Get down!" I hit the emergency drop button on my grav belt and thudded to a stop, centimeters above the dirt. I flicked the off icon and dropped to the ground, raising a small puff of dust. It tickled my nose. I slapped a hand over my mouth, smothering a sneeze.

Peter pawed at his belt. He stopped moving but continued to hover.

"Hit the red icon," I hissed, crouching below him.

Lights panned across the landscape, driving toward us. One slid over Peter then reversed and headed back to him.

"It's not working," he whispered in panic.

I lunged toward him and slapped his hand out of the way. I flicked the controls and yanked him flat.

The light glared over our heads. I lay in the dirt, my bruised cheek throbbing against the gravel, my eyes squeezed shut. The spotlight showed pink through my tightly closed eyelids.

Then it moved away. I opened my eyes, but all I could see was the fear in Peter's as he stared into my face. The pain in my cheek pounded in time with my heart rate, too fast to count.

I tipped my chin upward, trying to see where the spotlight had moved.

Peter rolled slowly to his stomach. He put his hands on either side of his chest, ready to jump up. "We should go now. We can follow their light."

I took a deep breath, trying to slow my heart rate. "I think we should stay until they stop looking."

"That won't work." He shook his head, raising a small cloud of dust. "Chymm said they'll be able to turn the shield back on easily. We'll miss our chance."

Liam crawled out of my pocket and up my arm to my cheek. He chittered and yanked on my ear. "Liam agrees." I tapped my grav belt and lifted a few centimeters off the ground then rolled to my stomach. "Let's do this. Stay low."

We slithered around the bushes through the darkness like a pair of wingless dragons. As we neared the force shield, a pale wall of static rose between the bollards.

"Crap. We're too late." I glanced back at Peter.

"No, look." He pointed straight ahead.

I looked again, and the static had disappeared.

"Hurry," I whispered. "Before they get it back up." I increased to top speed. We burst out of the last of the bushes and streaked across the two-meter-wide clear area inside the force shield. As I hit the barrier, the static came up again. I was moving too fast to stop and sailed through, fire singing through my nerves. Blue static raced over my skin, burning fast and cold. I bit down hard to stop the scream that rose to my lips.

I crashed into another scrubby bush, the rough twigs raking against my sensitive skin. Throwing caution to the wind, I rose a little higher and barreled toward a small stand of bent trees. When I reached it, Liam leaped off my shoulder, and I dropped to the ground, flat on my face.

Something thudded next to me. I rolled to my feet, hands in a defensive position.

"Ow." Peter sat up, rubbing his arms. "That stung."

"Did the crates get through?" I scanned the local area, but I couldn't see anything. There was no moon yet, and we had moved far enough into the trees that they blocked the light from the camp.

Peter held one hand over the other and flicked on his holo-ring. Light glowed pink through his fingers. He gestured with both hands. "There."

The two crates lay tumbled in the underbrush.

"That tethering command is amazing," Peter said.

I chuckled. "It was probably created for explorers avoiding stampeding wildlife. You don't want to leave anything behind."

"Like Mason." Peter laughed.

"Exactly." I laughed. It wasn't that funny, but the giggles wouldn't stop. I laughed harder and slammed my hand over my mouth. Tears rolling down my cheeks as I leaned against the stunted tree, silently howling. Peter sat in the dirt, gasping for breath between bouts of laughter.

Shouting from the camp stopped my laughter. We peered through the trees.

Three figures stood by the bollard we had slipped past. Another one crouched beside the upright, undoubtedly trying to repair whatever damage our sabotage had caused.

"Which way did they go?"

"I'm not sure. They could be anywhere."

They spread out along the flickering blue fence, peering into the darkness beyond.

"Someone needs to check the surveillance feeds."

"The power was out."

"That shouldn't matter—those things have batteries."

"Send those damn kids out to look."

Their voices trailed off. The creaking of insects started slowly then filled the night air. Across the bowl, something crashed, and voices swore. The insects stopped then resumed.

I lowered myself to the ground and flicked my holo-ring. "Yvonne? Chymm? Marise?" I whispered. "We're out. But we need to move."

"Roger." Marise's voice came through loud and clear. "We are on the rise beyond the lake."

"I see you," Peter said. He'd opened our tracking app, set to the dimmest level. Three green dots appeared on the east side of the lake. "We'll have to skirt around the camp, but we should be there before daybreak."

"I have a better idea," Yvonne said. "We'll meet you by the stream. Two klicks south of the camp."

"Agreed." I ducked instinctively as a sonic boom rolled across the landscape. The man by the bollard looked up then returned to his work.

"Another incoming shuttle," Yvonne said. "It looks like they're going to land here."

"New plan," I said. "I want to see what they're up to. Peter and I will wait here and watch. We'll meet you downstream as soon as we can get there. And now that we're out, everyone should stash their holo-rings in a meal pac wrapper. Assume Black knows we can see them. Soon, they'll know we escaped. They'll be looking for us."

"Do they have our app?" Chymm asked.

"Don't know, but they could have gotten it." Peter raised his eyebrows at me. "Or something similar."

"Roger. We'll keep rings off," Marise said. "We'll wait at the rendezvous for about two hours then move two more klicks along the stream."

"Be careful," Yvonne said. "We didn't work this hard so you could be recaptured."

"Yes, sir," I said cheekily. "Siti out."

I glanced at Peter. He stared back at me, his arms crossed. "Why do we care? Let's get out of here. They're still watching for us!"

"They are up to something—something bad for the CEC. Or at least bad for the Academy."

"We don't need to risk our lives over this." Peter didn't move.

"Do you really think we're risking our lives? They wouldn't hurt us." I took a step away from him.

"They locked us up." He glared at me. "You said they were up for a bit of raping and pillaging. Do you think murder would stop them? They aren't going to let us go. What's the first thing we would do when we got back to the Academy? We'd turn them in. They can't risk that if they're doing something illegal."

"We don't know who they are. We didn't have our holo-rings, so we couldn't take any pictures or vid. We had no proof of anything." I leaned down to untether the food crates. "We can leave these here for now. Mark these on the map, so the others can get them if we don't get back."

"If we don't get back?" Peter's voice rose a little. He bit his lip and tried again, softer. "If we don't get back—" his eyes narrowed "—it's because we're dead. If we go back in there and get caught, they aren't going to let us go. Or if they do, they'll let us go on the other side of this planet, in a tiger infested jungle with poisonous snakes and no clothes."

I snorted. "I doubt they'd go to that much trouble. It would be much easier to just shoot us."

"Exactly." Peter shook his head. "Is finding out what they're doing worth that risk? We can wait out the exercise then tell your dad. He can decide what to do about it. That way, we stay alive."

"Agreed."

Peter sighed with relief.

"After we find out what they're doing with the shuttle." I rose off the ground. "I want to be able to give him all the facts. You stay here with the food. I'll be back in a flash."

I set my grav belt to full speed and stretched out flat. All the sit-ups we had been doing during PT time paid off as I was able to stay horizontal until I reached full speed which held me there naturally. I flew a handspan above the straggly bushes, paralleling the force shield around the camp. When I reached the northeastern end of the camp, I found a small boulder and stretched out on my stomach to watch the landing pad.

A few minutes later, Peter landed beside me.

"What are you doing here?" I demanded. "Who's watching our stuff?"

Peter stretched out next to me. "I was more worried about who was watching you."

I grinned in the darkness but didn't answer.

The roar of the shuttle preceded its approach. Two men hurried across the camp, stopping at the edge of the landing zone. The shuttle soared over our heads and hovered.

It settled to the tarmac. The engines cut, and the door opened. A man and two women, all wearing CEC utility uniforms, stepped out.

Peter and I exchanged a look. "Academy?" he mouthed to me. I lifted my shoulders in a shrug.

"Welcome," the man said. It sounded like Sven.

"We don't have time for pleasantries." The woman's voice carried easily through the night air.

"That's Admiral Zimas," I whispered in shock, as she continued to speak.

Peter hushed me.

"Surely you didn't fly four days to tell me that," Sven said. "You could've called."

"No, I didn't come all this way to chat." Zimas strutted forward, the other two following her. "I came to see the merchandise."

I squinted, but it was impossible to read name tags at this distance.

"I wonder—" Peter broke off. "Yes." He shifted next to me, thrusting his hand in front of my face. "Look, the Academy directory works here."

In his palm, the hologram displayed the names and pictures of three officers. Admiral Zimas. Admiral Lee. Admiral Myers.

I stared, open-mouthed.

Peter took a screenshot.

"Put your ring away," I hissed.

"If we're here risking our lives, let's get proof," he said.

"Right this way." Sven made a sweeping gesture and led them toward the stack of crates with a mining company logo on the far side of the landing zone.

"Come on," I whispered. "I want to see what they're here for."

"I don't think—"

I didn't wait to hear what Peter didn't think. I launched myself away from the boulder sticking to the shadows close to the ground. Here, the hills rose steeply behind us. This time, I moved slowly. At this speed, I couldn't maintain a horizontal position for long, so I hunched over and floated along like a beach ball in the waves.

A faint rustle caught my attention. I glanced back to see Peter following, as I'd expected.

Suppressing a grin, I activated my audio implant. "There's a perfect boulder to hide behind right there." I pointed toward the far end of the camp, about twenty meters beyond the crates.

We zigzagged through the bushes and finally arrived at the boulder. Once again, we crept to the top, stretching out on our bellies. Liam crawled out of my pocket and scampered away.

"Liam," I hissed.

"He'll come back," Peter whispered. "He always does."

The admirals stood with Sven and the other man beside the two-meter-tall crate. The side was open, like a door, and Sven's partner shone a light on the contents. The three admirals blocked our view of the inside.

"Move," I whispered. "Just a little to the left."

"Me?" Peter asked.

"No. I want Zimas to move so I can see what's inside."

"These are not the crates you're looking for," he said.

I ignored him and continued my subconscious suggestions.

"What do you think, Admiral?" Sven asked. "It's as pure as I've ever seen. And just laying across the bed of that lake for the taking."

Zimas lifted something, as if weighing it in her hand. "I'll take the sample with me. I want to get it tested independently. But if it truly is as pure as you say, we're sitting on a gold mine."

"Better than a gold mine," Myers said.

"A senidium mine." Admiral Lee nodded in satisfaction.

"Technically, it's not a mine," Sven said.

"I don't think they care," the other man muttered.

"Did you take care of the other problem?" Zimas asked as they moved back to the shuttle. Sven's partner shut the crate.

"The kids?" Sven asked.

Zimas's hand snapped onto Sven's arm. "Let's call it the other problem." She emphasized the word "other" in a hard tone and glanced over her shoulder at her companions.

Myers and Lee dropped back, apparently waiting for the other man to finish locking the crate. Zimas urged Sven ahead.

"It's under control," Sven said.

"They can still hear him," I whispered to Peter.

"I guess they think they can pretend they can't," he replied. "What do they call that—plausible deniability?"

"It doesn't look very plausible to me." I pointed, my finger moving between the two groups. "They're right there. We can hear all of them. And why do they want to 'take care' of us? Zimas can kick us out when we get back."

Peter laid a finger against his lips. His voice dropped. "Because she doesn't want us to tell anyone what we saw. Which tells me this isn't an Academy operation. It's a Zimas-Myers-Lee operation."

"What are you saying?"

"I'm saying they're embezzling the senidium from Academy lands." He shrugged. "Now that we know why they're here, and we know they want 'to take care of us,' I suggest we take care of ourselves and get out of here."

"Works for me." I turned to look for Liam. He bounded across the top of a nearby rock and leapt straight into the air. Then he dropped back to the rock. "What's he doing?"

"I think he just caught a snack." Peter grinned. "Lots of bugs around here." He brushed something from his sleeve as he spoke.

"Ew."

Liam leapt across the space between his boulder and ours and landed beside me.

"You're a good little glider, but take your bug breath somewhere else." I pushed his head gently away from my cheek.

He made a few conversational sounds and worked his way into my pocket.

Down in the camp, the admirals returned to their shuttle. The two men stepped back, and the craft rose. It hovered over the bowl for a few moments then made a leisurely circle around the perimeter. With a loud roar, it rocketed away.

"Keep searching," Sven yelled. "We need to find those kids."

"That's our signal to get the heck out of here," Peter said. "I suggest we head up into these hills and work our way around to the meeting point."

"We need to go back and get that food."

I looked out over the bowl. The power had returned, and the shield glowed a steady blue. Portable spotlights were moving into position, their light stabbing into the darkness surrounding the camp.

"They're going to launch drones, if they haven't already. We need to get away." Peter slithered off the boulder, pausing in its shadow.

"We should've brought those meal pacs with us." I joined him in the darkness.

"Why do you think it took me so long to catch up to you?" He grinned and pointed.

The two crates sat side-by-side in the dust.

I bit my lip to keep from squealing and threw my arms around him. "Let's find our flight."

CHAPTER THIRTY-SEVEN

THE TREK WEST into the hills was easy with our new grav belts. We headed straight up the steep gulley behind us, jumping over into another valley when we reached the top.

Peter pulled out his paper map when we stopped. "Instead of trying to work our way through these hills, why don't we go up?"

"Up?" I asked.

"Yeah. These are real grav belts, not something cobbled together by a cadet in the dark using leftover parts. The night the Hellions attacked New Lake, you went up pretty high. It didn't seem to faze you."

"These things are made to go as high as you might need. The real limiting factor is oxygen. I suppose if you put on a spacesuit—"

He waved his hand in front of my face. "Siti, focus. We don't need a spacesuit—we don't need to go that high. I want to get high enough to be invisible in the dark. Then we skirt around the camp—" he drew a circle on the map with his finger "—and drop over here to meet the flight. They won't be looking up, but I don't want to fly right over them."

"Brilliant." I tapped the controls on the front of my belt. "Let's go."

We rose to an altitude of fifty meters over the landscape. The camp came into view to our east. The lights swept through the brush surrounding the force shield. Teams of two or three miners lifted off, taking portable lights with them to scour the hills.

We soared high over their heads as they followed the path back to the plain.

"Maybe we should tell Marise and the others to get a little farther away," I said. "Those teams will reach our rendezvous point pretty fast."

Peter gave a thumbs-up and pulled out his ring to make the call. "I left a message—they must have their rings off, too."

The hills fell away steeply as we went south, and we dropped with them. The camp disappeared behind us. The wind was cold, so I pulled my collar up around my face and tucked my hands in my pockets. Liam curled into my fingers, purring.

Far below, the stream grew wider then disappeared completely.

"Where'd it go?" I asked Peter.

"I think it goes underground." He slid closer to show me his map. "I have one that shows subterranean features—see the underground river? That explains why the plains are all so dry and dusty."

"Why do you have a geological survey on your holo-ring?" I asked.

"I used to live in a cave, remember?" He grinned sheepishly. "I was curious what we'd find here. Did you know there are traces of senidium listed on that survey? I'm surprised no one tried mining before."

"Sven said there are deposits sitting on the floor of the lake, waiting to be picked up." I shrugged. "Maybe the deposits on the map aren't enough to bring in big miners, and they didn't notice the deposits in the lake until recently. Since this property is owned by the Academy, they would want to capitalize on that discovery."

"But why all the crazy? Why did they send Purple and Yellow into this area and then pull them back out with a phony story?" He angled away from me, heading toward the new rendezvous point.

I veered after him. "Maybe they didn't know about the deposits until the cadets got here? Someone probably went swimming—or fell in like Mason."

He chuckled. "Could be. But why not wait until the exercise is over?"

"I dunno. Maybe they were afraid Purple would fill their pockets with senidium and send it home to their parents?"

"I'm sure it makes a lovely Mother's Day gift." He pointed. "There's our meet-up."

We angled into the little valley. The sun was beginning to rise behind the mountains. Without the force shield to tint it purple, yellow, red, and orange streaks splashed across the sky in a glorious display. Distant low mountains stood silhouetted against the fiery light.

"Finally!" Marise jumped up as we landed. "We were beginning to think you'd gotten caught."

"Why would you think that?" Peter asked.

Marise squirmed. "You got caught once—it could happen again."

"What's the plan?" I asked. "Peter, give them some food."

He flicked a salute at me and opened one of the crates.

"We were hoping you'd have one," Marise said as she caught a meal pac. "A plan, that is."

"Have you heard from Joss and Aneh?" Peter asked.

Yvonne nodded. "They're fine. They said most of Delta Black left—they think there are only two cadets holding our camp."

"Then I say it's time to take it back." I nodded at them. "If Chymm can take down the shield of a mining company, he can break into our own camp."

Chymm's face burned, and he smiled. "I might have a few ideas."

WE MET Joss and Aneh in the narrow strip of trees that grew alongside our stream. We were about two klicks east of our camp, so we felt safe. Peter and I handed out more meal pacs, and we sat by the stream while Joss and Aneh ate.

"I fixed a drone." Chymm's voice was garbled as he shoved more food into his mouth. "Did I tell you that?"

"Yes, Chymm, you've mentioned it a couple of times." I tried not to smirk. He'd talked non-stop all the way here. He'd managed to isolate the signal from our jackets that was disrupting the vids. Now we could record any conflicts with Black.

"It can't fly through the force shield, of course." He put the rest of his meal pac into his bug-out bag and dropped it on the ground. "But it can record from outside. And if any Delta Blacks mess with Aneh's snares, the cam I left there will still fritz and warn us."

"We should have left one inside," Joss muttered.

Chymm slapped his forehead. "Why didn't I think of that?"

I held up a hand. "We didn't expect them to break in."

"True." Chymm paced in front of the stream. "They broke in by having a mole inside. *We* should have left someone behind."

We stared at him.

"Who would you leave behind?" Aneh's voice ratcheted up an octave.

"Doesn't matter—it didn't happen." Peter made tamping motions. "Unless Chymm has put together a time machine, we have to go forward."

Chymm's eyes lit up. "Wouldn't that be something…"

"Chymm, no time machines!" I said. The others laughed, but I could see his brain spinning off into fantasy. "Focus on the present. Can you deactivate the field from outside?"

"It depends," he said. "If they haven't messed with my inhibitor, probably not. If they have, they likely broke it, so we can turn it off."

"We'll send someone up to test that theory later," I said. "For now, let's assume they've left it alone. Can you deactivate it?"

"Maybe we can cause some kind of diversion to bring them outside—like Chymm did over there." Marise tipped her head toward the eastern mountains, hidden behind the trees.

"How did you turn off their force shield?" I asked.

Chymm shrugged. "That was pure luck. They installed a more sophisticated version than the Academy puts on cadet camps. But they never bothered to change the passcode. I tried the default and it worked."

I blinked. "They did that with the door locks, too. How could they be so inept?"

"Maybe they did that on purpose?" Peter suggested. "What were you talking about before—plausible deniability?"

"How does leaving the default passcode give them deniability?" I asked.

"I get it," Joss said. "It's Academy equipment. If they mess with it, then obviously they were up to something. If they leave it alone, they can claim they were—what did they say—doing a study?"

"I think they could claim that anyway," Yvonne said. "I'm not sure you understand what plausible deniability means."

"I'm not sure you understand—"

I cut Joss off. "Please, guys, now that we've eaten, we should be able to focus, right?" I turned back to Chymm. "Keep thinking about how to take down our own shield. I think the distraction idea is a good one. Speaking of distractions—has anyone received a mission brief?"

We looked at each other. Every face reflected the same puzzlement.

"No. We haven't gotten any messages since the patient evacuation exercise." Joss used finger quotes to emphasize the words "patient evacuation."

"Shouldn't there have been at least one more mission?" I asked. "Telia said Black got one."

Marise nodded. "I looked at past PSW exercises. A lot of that is classified because they don't want us to know what's going to happen. But the little I could find indicated cadets were given assignments every day. How long have we been here?"

"I dunno. Six, seven days?" Peter suggested. The others nodded.

"We're way behind on direction." Marise folded her arms. "Mason told me they had twelve separate missions on his PSW."

"Mason?" Aneh asked. "When did you talk to Cadet Mason?"

Marise's cheeks flushed. "I asked for his help on an assignment a few weeks ago. We got to talking. He's nice."

Chymm shook his finger at the girl. "Don't get involved with the flight sergeant. That's sure to get one of you in trouble."

"We aren't *involved*." Marise's nostrils flared, and her face went even redder. "He helped me with some research. And I asked him a lot of questions about PSW. He wouldn't tell me much, but I got a little out of him."

"Why didn't you tell us?" Joss demanded. "We could have been milking him for information all this time! You could have used your feminine wiles to get—"

Peter smacked Joss's arm. "Shut up."

"This is why I didn't tell you." Marise shot to her feet. "You insensitive, muscle-bound—"

Yvonne stood and put an arm around Marise. "Ignore him. He's an ape."

Joss puffed out his chest. "I'm a Neanderthal, thank you very much!"

"Stop!" I jumped up. "We aren't getting anywhere. Can we please focus on the mission—or, I guess, the lack of mission? If they—" I pointed upward to indicate the satellites "—aren't talking to us, is it just us, or all the flights? And if it's all of us, what does that mean?"

"I say we go pound on the door of our camp and demand Delta Black let us back inside." Joss patted the tranq gun on his hip. "If we can get them to open the gate, I can take them out."

"They're probably too smart for that, but we could try." I looked at each of them in turn and stopped on Peter. "How do they feel about you?"

"How would I know?" he asked.

""We know they hate me. And they probably don't like Joss." I grinned at the bigger boy. "He's too 'alpha' for them. But maybe whoever's up there would talk to you? And—Aneh?"

"I'll try." Aneh stood. "They must be wondering about the missions, too. We can ask if they've heard anything…"

"Perfect. We'll follow you. Stay out of sight but provide backup." I turned to find Chymm. He was still pacing beside the stream. "I don't suppose you have an invisibility cloak?"

Chymm's eyes went wide. "Do they make those?"

"No."

His face fell, and he turned away.

CHAPTER THIRTY-EIGHT

ANEH AND PETER lifted to the south gate, perching on the narrow ledge outside the force shield. Joss and Yvonne followed them up, hovering behind the few trees that grew on the steep hillside.

Peter activated his comm on the Black channel and called out, "Hello!" He relayed the conversation to the Blue channel, so we could all hear.

Marise, Chymm, and I watched through Chymm's drone. It was small enough that they wouldn't notice it among the other bugs outside the force shield.

"What do you want?" A girl with long blue hair approached the gate.

"Hi, Ranissa," Peter said. "This is Aneh."

"Hi." Aneh waved. Her voice echoed weirdly through her own connection and Peter's repeater.

Ranissa sighed. "What do you want, Russell?"

"We want our camp back," Peter said. "But failing that, we'd settle for a conversation."

"Did the rest of your flight leave you behind?" Aneh asked.

Ranissa's chin went up. "They didn't leave us behind. We're guarding our conquest."

"Why do you need a conquest?" Aneh asked. "Last I heard, CEC is about exploring new worlds, not conquering within the Corps."

Ranissa blinked. "But LeBlanc said we needed to take you out."

"Take us out? Why?" Aneh asked again. "We weren't doing anything to you."

"You were cheating us of our win." The blue-haired girl crossed her arms.

"We weren't cheating. We were following the instructions," Peter said.

Aneh glared at him then turned back to the girl. "You're winning now. There's no way we can beat you. We just want somewhere safe to sleep at night."

Ranissa bit her lip. "But you're cheating. I was told to keep you out."

"Did you know your flight had another mission?" Aneh asked.

Ranissa's eyes narrowed. "What mission?"

Aneh shrugged. "We didn't get the mission brief. But you should have."

"There are no satellite connections here." Ranissa glared.

"There are at your camp?" Peter asked.

I looked at Chymm. "Is that possible? Could they have coverage when we don't?"

"Easy." Chymm gestured overhead. "The links are microsats. Generally, they're set up to provide denser coverage over populated areas, and they can be retasked as more are launched. Whoever controls them could create a hole over a particular location."

"Great. Maybe we can use satellite logs as evidence they've stacked the deck against us. But we weren't getting sat connections in the mining camp, either." I rubbed my eyes and refocused on the conversation coming through my audio implant.

"...so you could go back to your camp and participate in the rest of the mission instead of missing out," Aneh was saying.

Ranissa's nostrils flared. "You're trying to trick me into giving your camp back."

"No, I'm not trying to trick you at all. You know it's the right thing to do." Aneh smiled.

"It's not what LeBlanc and Myers said. I have to do what they tell me."

"Or what?" Aneh asked.

"Did they lower the fuzz?" Joss asked through the comm.

"The fuzz?" Chymm scowled. "What do you mean?"

"The level of static," Joss said. "I don't think the shield is on full power. Yvonne and I are going to fly around to the other side and see if we can get close enough to turn off the shield."

"Go!" I pointed at Chymm. "Tell Peter to keep them distracted. Marise and I will drop in from behind the mods when they get it down."

While Peter and Aneh kept at Ranissa, Marise and I hurried through the woods. When we'd gotten around a bend in the stream, I pointed upward. Marise nodded, and we rose smoothly. Or at least, I rose smoothly. Marise jerked and stopped.

"What are you doing?" I hissed.

"There's something going on with my belt."

"Is that one of the ones Chymm built?" When she nodded, I scowled. "I thought you said he had the manual?"

"He did, but you know Chymm. He probably tweaked something." Her belt hitched again, and her teeth clenched. "This is why we only used Aneh's belt for high-altitude stuff."

"We should have switched you to one of the new ones. Get closer to the hillside." I moved laterally, beckoning her to follow.

She adjusted her belt and let her feet settle on an outcropping of rock. "Now what?" She gazed down the steep hill beneath us.

"Now we'll tether your belt to mine." I alighted next to her and shrugged off my backpack. "I have some cable in here…" I dug through the bag and pulled out a spool of the snare wire. "It's probably not strong enough to take your entire weight, but it might help. We'll loop it several times. And slave your controller to my belt."

She took the cable and slid the end through the metal carabiner loop on her belt. "I'm not sure these belts will tether."

"Let me look at the controls. You keep looping the cable through. Give us about two meters of length." I handed her the spool and bent awkwardly so she could still reach my belt links. I swiped the controls on her belt and poked the interface.

She giggled.

"Stop that." I tapped through a couple of screens and found the command. "We're all set. This should keep the cable taut between us. If your belt starts to fail, I'll feel it, and we'll get to safety. It looks like your battery is low. Plug it into your jacket."

She followed my instructions. I yanked on the cable, and it seemed to hold. "Let's go." I lifted off the rock, and she followed.

"We can see the front gate," Joss whispered in my ear. "If they're watching our rings, they'll know."

"Ranissa hasn't looked at her holo since Aneh and Peter started talking to her," Chymm reported. "And whoever else is in there is probably asleep. I hope."

"I'm moving to the bollard," Yvonne said. "Joss, stay back and cover me with your tranq gun."

"The good news is they can't shoot us without dropping the shield," Joss muttered.

"Someone is moving inside!" Yvonne's tone was sharp.

Marise and I rose above the edge of the hill. The two mods blocked our view of both gates. A small herd of herbivores grazing in the grassy clear zone along the shield scattered as we approached.

"Chymm, can we shut the shield down from one of these other bollards?" I asked. "There are two here that are out of view of the others."

"Negative," Chymm said. "Those are relays. If you had a big enough piece of equipment, you could ram it into the shield and short it out, but it would take a large piece of heavy metal."

"Like those mining machines at Black's camp," I said.

"Sure, let's run back and get one of those." Marise rolled her eyes.

I shrugged. "I guess we hope Yvonne can get the gate down." I dropped to the barren stretch of land beyond the end of the camp. In a real explorer camp, this would have surveillance, and they'd spot us immediately. But without cams and only two defenders holding down the base, we were safe enough.

The shield fizzed brighter then disappeared.

"Go!" I yelled. I slammed my hand on my belt controls and dragged Marise across the line.

CHAPTER THIRTY-NINE

WE BARRELED over the scrubby brush, zipping around the end of the living mod. Or at least, we tried. Just as I reached the corner, the cable went tight and yanked me to a stop. Marise dropped to the ground behind me.

"What happened?" I touched down and scrabbled at the belt. "We don't need this cable anymore!" The carabiner fought me, and my fingers slipped.

Marise batted my hands away and slipped the cables free. "Run!" She took off at a sprint, leaving the cable in a pile on the ground.

I hit my grav belt controls and streaked after, overtaking her as we reached the middle of the camp.

Peter, Aneh, Joss, and Yvonne stood around the edge of the cleared fire circle. Joss held his tranq gun at his side while Yvonne aimed her stunner at a cadet sitting cross-legged on the edge of the patio. Two more cadets lay on their faces in the dirt. A small pile of weapons lay in the dirt beyond Joss.

"Terrine!" I stopped short, staring at the girl. "I thought there were only two cadets here."

"There were only two Delta Black cadets here," Yvonne said. "They didn't take Terrine back to camp with them."

"She let us in," Joss said.

"I thought Yvonne dropped the gate. Which reminds me, someone needs to get that back up," I said. "There are cattle right over there."

Peter nodded and hurried away. "Chymm, get up here," he called as he ran.

"No, it was Terrine," Joss said.

"What did you do to them?" I pointed at the two prone cadets.

"I told them to lay down and shut up," Joss said, waving his tranq gun. "They complied."

"Don't hurt us," Ranissa whimpered.

"Put that away. We aren't going to hurt anyone," I said. "We aren't Delta Black."

"It doesn't hurt anyway," Joss said as he slipped it back into his holster. "Just makes you take a nap."

I shook my head at him then turned back to the two cadets. "Get up. Sit next to Terrine."

The two rolled over. Ranissa scooted on her rear end, perching at the end of the terrace as far as she could get from Terrine. The second cadet, Juarez, rolled to his feet, lunging forward. Joss stepped in, almost lazily, and grabbed his arm. With a quick twist, he got Juarez into a headlock.

"This is much worse than a tranq dart," Joss said. "The headache from a choke out is killer."

I pointed to the terrace. "Ranissa, move over. I want Juarez on the end. Joss, watch him."

Joss manhandled Juarez across the dirt, pushing him to the plastek floor. When the cadet was down, he stepped back and pulled the tranq gun from his holster. "If you move, you'll get a dart in the chest."

Juarez glared. "You stole our victory! Traitors!"

The rest of us exchanged looks. "We haven't stolen anything," I said. "Delta Black is getting—and completing—missions the rest of us haven't heard anything about."

"They're also eating fresh hot meals and getting showers," Peter said. "In their fancy illegal camp over the hills."

"What are you talking about?" Juarez asked.

"I'm sure you'll find out soon enough," I said. "You're going back to them."

"No, you can't send us back," Ranissa said. "They'll—" She broke off under Juarez's stare.

"They'll what?" Joss asked. "Be mad at you?"

"They'll be punished for failing their mission," Terrine said. She leaned against the wall of the mod, her face pale.

"And it's all your fault, you traitor!" Juarez lunged at Terrine. Terrine screamed. Juarez froze then crumpled across Ranissa's lap, a dart sticking out of his shoulder.

Joss waved his tranq gun and grinned. "This stuff is fast acting. We need to get some for home."

Ranissa pushed Juarez, rolling him into the dirt. Then she scuttled backward, crab-style, until she sat with her back against the mod.

"Do we have anything to secure him?" Joss asked.

"I have slip ties." Aneh raised her hand and twisted around to open a side-pocket of her bag. She pulled out two flexible strips and crouched to wrap them around Juarez's wrists and ankles.

"You are terrifyingly capable," Chymm said.

Aneh turned pink. "We use them on cattle back home. And I once won a prize for hog tying."

"What about them?" Joss nodded at Terrine and Ranissa.

"I think Terrine has proven herself," I said. "She didn't let them in. Did you?" I stared at the girl.

She hung her head. "I did."

"What?"

She took a deep breath. "I told you on the ship—we do what we're told. They wanted to win, and they said you were stealing our victory."

I stared at her. "Stealing it? By performing better? How is that stealing?"

She whimpered. "It almost makes sense when LeBlanc or Lee says it. Besides, they threatened to frame my dad. Lee's mom could do it. No one is going to take a sergeant's word against an admiral. Or three admirals."

Ranissa growled at Terrine. "Traitor! You should get expelled. They stole our victory!"

I rounded on Ranissa. "In TbF, you attacked us. You stole our equipment and food. You could have followed the mission rules, but instead, they convinced you to attack other flights. That's on them. And you."

She spat at me.

I rolled my eyes. "You're going to have to improve your distance if you want that to be effective. Your flight leaders have been cheating and stealing since day one. If you think that's okay, then go back to them. Start walking."

"We have grav belts." Ranissa stood.

"Not anymore," I said. "Those are ours now."

"Same goes for any food," Marise said. "I'm sure you'll get plenty of that when you get back to your friends."

Ranissa's face went pale, and she slumped to the patio. "I can't go back. They'll punish me!"

"Punish you? How?" I asked.

Ranissa's lips pressed tight together.

"If you don't follow directions, they make you do all the work—cleaning, getting the rooms ready for inspection, writing study notes. And they don't let you go to chow." Terrine wrapped her arms around her stomach as she spoke.

"How is the administration not noticing this?" I asked of no one in particular.

"What makes you think they aren't?" Peter's lips twisted. "Zimas has made it very clear she's more concerned with what the other admirals think—and whatever is going on over there—" he waved to the east "—than with our training."

"Good point." Behind me, Juarez groaned. I stepped to the side so I could keep him in my line of sight. "What do we do now?"

"We get rid of them." Peter pointed at Juarez and Ranissa. "Then we figure out how to reach your dad."

"What about me?" Terrine asked in a small voice.

"I vote she stays with us," Aneh said.

I nodded. "Me, too."

The others exchanged a series of glances and stares. Finally, Marise nodded. "We agree."

"I'm sick of hiding out here, waiting for a mission that isn't coming,"

Joss said. "I say we head for civilization and see if we can connect to a sat. Get Bob down here to pick us up."

"But the exercise isn't done," Aneh said. "If we go home, they'll expel us."

"I'd rather go home than be treated like this," Joss said.

I held up my hands. "Yes, if we go home, they'll expel us. But what if we can provide prove of what's happening over there?" I pointed toward the camp. "They kidnapped cadets. They're stealing senidium from the Academy. Let's get some evidence and take them down. Then we win."

The other cheered.

Chymm put up his hand. "Uh, one question."

"Yes?" I nodded.

"How do we do that?"

CHAPTER FORTY

WE LOCKED Juarez and Ranissa in the bathroom while everyone caught some sleep. In the morning, Joss and Yvonne gave them some water and pushed them out the north gate. We ate breakfast while we planned our mission.

"Chymm's drones are working now," I said. "We need to record the operation over there and take that vid with us."

Peter glared through the fizzing blue force shield at the two cadets cowering outside. "Get walking, you two!" He pointed east. "Your flight is that way!"

"They aren't going anywhere," Marise muttered. "They're more afraid of LeBlanc than of us."

"What did he do to them?" I mused.

Peter's face darkened. "You don't want to know. LeBlanc is like a cult leader. He's very convincing—for some reason, people are willing to ignore facts and believe anything he says."

"He convinces you that the rest of the galaxy is out to get you," Terrine said. "And that only he can save you. It's textbook cult stuff."

"You didn't buy it," Peter said.

"I wanted to fit in," Terrine replied. "But not badly enough that I was willing to overlook what he was doing. When they took your stuff during TbF, I was concerned, but then we heard you won that one."

She sipped some water. "Back on campus, none of us were willing to take the chance of reporting them. The legacies are untouchable. Julian tried to turn them in—he was expelled a week later for supposedly cheating."

Peter stared. "I wondered where he went. That dude was smart—no way he needed to cheat."

"Exactly. They framed him." Terrine twisted her hands in her lap. "No one would cross them after that. I tried to stay out of the way—under the radar. It was hard. They targeted me when I refused to help. Believe it or not, I think Felicity protected me."

"Felicity? I find that difficult to believe," I said.

"I don't know how else to explain it." Terrine looked up. "I'm still here."

"Doesn't matter," Yvonne said. "What do we do with them? They won't go back."

"I say we leave them to fend for themselves." Joss pointed through the force shield. "They can start walking if they want. By the time they reach the other camp, we'll be long gone."

"I'll give them each a meal pac and some more water," Aneh said.

Joss's face hardened, but then he nodded. "You're right. We won't stoop to their level. I'll even let them have their stunners back."

"They'll use 'em on us," Yvonne muttered darkly.

"That's why we'll leave them in the camp." Joss pointed to the living mod. "If we all go to the mining camp, we won't be able to secure this one. We'll leave their stunners here and fly away. When we're gone, they'll probably come back inside so LeBlanc can't blame them for losing the camp."

"But what if we need to come back?" Marise asked.

"We won't," Joss said firmly. "We're getting the evidence, then we're heading for civilization. Or whatever passes for that here on Sarvo."

"It's probably pretty similar to home." Peter smirked.

"It's probably more technologically advanced than home," I said. "They'll have communications with the rest of the galaxy—they just upgraded their jump beacons, remember? And they'll have sat coverage."

"Flying cars?" Peter asked.

Chymm shrugged. "Maybe. What's a car?"

We packed our bags. With the new grav belts from the mining camp, plus the two we took from Ranissa and Juarez, we had enough real belts to carry all of us. Chymm reconfigured the mod panel with the lifters he'd pulled on the first day. We loaded the panel with the extra meal pacs, some water, and what Chymm termed "essentials"—a crate of electronic equipment and tools.

"What about Terrine?" Marise asked me as we finished packing.

"What about her?"

"Do we take her with us?"

I stared. "Definitely. We can't leave her with Black. She can ride on the mod panel if she doesn't feel good enough to use a real belt."

"Hey, my grav belts are real." Chymm came out of the mod with another small crate.

"They're buggy as heck," Marise said.

"I think that's you, not the belt," Chymm replied.

"What is all this crap, Chymm?" I interrupted their good-natured bickering. "More essentials?"

"These are nice-to-haves." He patted the crate he'd set on the panel. "They'll be useful if there's room."

"If Terrine needs a ride, there won't be," I said.

He nodded. "People before stuff. That's why I prioritized before I packed."

I clapped a hand on his shoulder. "Good work." I looked around the room. "Let's get out of here."

Terrine climbed on, and I set the panel to one meter and slaved it to my belt. We went through our checklist, tethering everyone to the two bullet bikes.

"Will they be slower with this much weight?" Yvonne asked.

Chymm shook his head. "The weight doesn't matter. Your belt is negating the weight. The bullet provides forward propulsion."

Joss chuckled. "But will it be slower?"

"Nah," Chymm said. Then he raised a hand and waggled it back and forth. "Technically—"

Joss cut him off. "Good enough for me. Let's get outta here!" He flicked the switch, and the gate opened.

"Turn off the whole force shield." I jerked my thumb toward the far side of the camp. Juarez and Ranissa had started trudging across the plain but hadn't gotten very far.

"Why?" he asked.

I shrugged. "I want them to notice we're gone so they can come back. I don't want them to starve out there."

"You're nicer than they are," Peter said.

I locked eyes with him. "Yes, we are."

He nodded.

Chymm flicked another switch, and the blue static faded.

"Set belts to two meters. Terrine, hold on." I waved my arm in a big circle and pointed east. "Let's go."

We slid away from the camp, angling over the stream, picking up speed as we went. From the corner of my eye, I caught sight of Juarez and Ranissa running toward the camp. At least they'd be secure. And they wouldn't starve if they rationed the meal pacs we'd left behind. Delta Black probably wouldn't relieve them before the end of the exercise.

"Oops!" Aneh laughed and pointed. The small herd of herbivores Marise and I had surprised still grazed near the eastern end of the camp. With the shield down, they'd crossed the border and moved inside the camp.

"I hope they notice they have company before they bring the shield back up," Terrine said with a giggle.

We followed the path we'd taken last night, angling across the lower plain to the hills south of the mining camp.

In the daylight, the place where the stream went underground was spectacular. The water pooled in a small pond then poured over the lip of a low cliff. The narrow spout tumbled down the rock face and disappeared into a wide crack.

"This is probably a good place to set up camp," Marise suggested.

"Camp?" I asked. "I thought the plan was to go get some vid and head out over the hills."

"That's still the plan." Marise pointed to the panel hovering behind me.

"But do we want to take all this stuff with us? And Terrine would be a liability."

"What do I have to do to convince you I'm on your side?" Terrine asked.

Marise shook her head. "It's not that. But you're still not up to full speed. If we have to run, you'll slow us down."

"Good point," I said. "Besides, we might want to wait for dark."

"Aren't you the one who told me that waiting for dark is pointless?" Peter asked. "You said their technology would offset the advantage of darkness."

Joss laughed. "Offset the advantage? I can't imagine Siti saying anything like that."

"Those weren't my exact words, but he's right." I looked at Chymm. "Right? You haven't invented the cloak of invisibility yet."

Chymm waggled his hand in a way that I was really getting tired of seeing. "Yes and no. If they have people actively looking for us, we should stay hidden. But if they're just protecting the borders of their camp, they'll have night vision cams and infrared sensors. Or at least, I would."

"Nobody does things the way you do," Yvonne said. "Are they watching for our rings on the app?"

Chymm shook his head. "I can't believe they have the app. They would have noticed us back at the Blue camp. They think Peter and Siti don't have rings, and that's who they're looking for."

"I still think we should keep our rings shielded as much as possible." Yvonne squinted into the distance. "How close do we have to get to use the drones? That was the plan."

Peter pulled up the local map. "The camp is in the valley about two klicks that way. If Delta Black is looking for us, we need to be ready for that. We don't want to stay by the water—it's too open. We'll hide Terrine and the supplies." He pointed up the hill. "Then we can send two teams—here and here." He set icons on the map in the hills on the east and west sides of the lake. "Then we fly the drones down to camp, get our vid, and get out of here."

I gave him a thumbs-up. "Let's do it."

Yvonne, Marise, and Terrine hid with the supplies in a narrow valley.

The rest of us split into two teams. Joss, Chymm, and Aneh went to the east side of the lake, while Peter and I went around to the west. Since it was daylight, we stayed low to the ground, zigzagging through the small valleys and over the little hills. The thicker trees here gave us plenty of cover. By mid-day, we reached the spot above the boulders where we'd seen the admirals the previous night. We set down in the trees and launched our drone.

It was hard to believe we'd been here only a few hours ago. It felt like days had passed, but the place looked the same. The small mod that stored the senidium was open. Peter flew the drone up to the force shield and hovered.

"Can you angle around to the right?" I asked. "Maybe you can get a look at what's inside."

He shook his head. "The curve of the force shield makes me go higher, and then I can't get a good angle. Why do you suppose they left it open?"

I shrugged. "Maybe they're moving some of it? Or—" I pointed "—they're adding to it."

As we watched, one of the scruffy-looking miners pushed a floating crate toward the mod.

"See if you can get a look at what's inside," I commanded.

"What do you think I'm doing?" Peter asked. His tongue stuck out of the corner of his mouth as he maneuvered the drone. The meter-high hologram hanging between us swooped and turned. As the man approached, the drone flew higher and the view rotated. "Got it."

The camera pointed straight down into the open crate. A jumble of small, smooth, blue stones filled the box. The color was intense—a vibrant teal blue that reminded me of the crystal-clear water at Ebony Beach on Kaku. Dad had taken me on vacation there for a few days after I graduated from school.

I shook my head. "Those stones are almost hypnotic," I said. "The color is amazing."

Peter nodded and cleared his throat. "It is. What else do we need to get vid of?"

"The shuttle is back." I grabbed the hologram and stretched it larger. "Turn the cam that way."

The view turned, revealing the shuttle on the landing pad. "Do you think the admirals are still here? That would be the last nail in their coffin."

"I dunno." Peter continued rotating the drone. "I'm going to go closer to the lake."

"You'll be too high," I said. "The center of a shield this large is thirty or forty meters high."

"See if Joss's team can get closer." Peter tweaked his controls again.

I flicked my holo-ring and connected to the group channel. "Joss, what can you see?"

"Chymm's playing with the feed right now," Joss replied. "He's trying to zoom in. There are several people arguing behind that large mod. One of them looks like Admiral Zimas to me, but we can't get a good shot."

"Any chance he can take down the shield again?" I asked.

"Negative," Joss said. "First thing we checked when we got here. They got smart and reset the password."

"What about the power?" I asked. "He did something to the power last night."

"That's a negative, too," Joss said. "They've got cadets guarding the power supply. Who was dumb enough to put it outside the shield anyway?"

"They have some supplemental solar panels on the hills behind us," Chymm said. "Their main power is from the panels on the roof of the mod. But they needed extra for that equipment, and the best locations are apparently on the hill. They weren't expecting malicious visitors." He snickered.

"Whatever. We need to see if we can get vid. I'll have Peter send our cam over there, too." I signed off and raised my eyebrows at Peter.

"I'm already working on it, but as you said, the shield is keeping me too far away."

"Get out!" Joss barked through the audio implant. "Get out! We've been spotted." The communications link went dead.

CHAPTER FORTY-ONE

PETER SLAMMED his hand on top of the hologram, smashing it off. He slapped a control to recall the drone then minimized the app and jumped to his feet. "Let's get out of here."

"Wait a minute," I said. "Let's be smart about this. They know we're here—they heard Joss talking to us. But they don't know *where* we are."

"The ring tracking app?" Peter asked.

I nodded and pulled my holo-ring from my finger. "Better safe than sorry. Can you fly the drone without your ring?" I pulled an empty Chewy Nuggets packet from my pocket and slipped my ring inside.

Peter shook his head. He caught the drone as it returned and put both it and his ring into another packet.

"Let's go around the north end of the lake," I said. "There aren't any buildings or people up there. Be quiet and watch for guards." I dropped closer to the ground and moved slowly through the trees.

We worked our way around the end of the lake, keeping the force shield in view. When we reached the end, we found a small outcropping of rock on the hill. We set down in the shadow of the rock, among the tops of the trees. Our Explorer Corps uniforms helped us blend into the background.

"I wish we had binoculars," Peter said.

"What are those?" I asked.

Peter explained, holding his hands to his face to demonstrate. "...lower tech than what you're used to, but for this situation, they'd be perfect."

"Yeah, remind me to add those to my wish list of equipment I need when I'm being unfairly targeted during an exercise."

He rolled his eyes. "They're good if the grid is down or the power is out, too."

"Whatever. Can you see Joss and the others?"

He shook his head. "I'm going to risk a drone." He pulled the ring and drone from his pocket and got to work.

The device flew away, and he stretched the view window. Then he pointed, his arm poking through the hologram. "There's something."

I squinted at the holo then pushed it aside. Something moved on the hillside east of the lake. "There they are. How are we going to get them out?"

"Maybe we don't wait to get them out. Those are Delta Black cadets. I say we take them out before they return to the camp."

"Works for me." I pointed toward the force shield. "There's no one standing guard down here. Let's fly low in the clear zone by the shield. Faster and more direct."

"Won't they have cams watching?"

"They might." I chuckled. "But our jackets should fritz their signals, remember? I don't think that problem was specific to Academy cams."

He stared at me in wonder. "It's worth the risk. Let's go!"

We set our rings to one meter above the ground and dove at the camp. I pulled a tight turn as I approached the force shield, almost sizzling my belly against it. We streaked along the two-meter-wide clear zone, our toes brushing against the new grass.

"Bogies at ten o'clock," I told Peter through the audio link. Joss, Chymm, and Aneh slithered down the hill, moving slowly. Derek Lee and another Delta Black cadet followed them, stunners pointed at our friends. "They're coming down the hill slowly. You take Lee; I'll get the girl."

"What are we going to do with them when we get them?" Peter asked.

"We'll figure that out later," I said.

"Slow down. We'll jump them as they hit the flat." Peter dropped back as he spoke.

"Roger," I said, slowing my forward momentum and dropping to the dirt.

We crouched in the shadow of a twisted tree, watching. About fifty meters away, Chymm stumbled down out of the trees on the hillside and onto the grassy track around the camp. Half a second later, Aneh followed.

"Now," Peter whispered.

We lifted off and rammed our belts to full speed. Joss stepped out of the trees and caught sight of us. He did a double take then jumped out of the way. Lee and the other cadet sauntered out of the woods. Peter plowed into Lee. Half a meter behind, I slammed into the girl.

I cut the power on my belt. She hit the ground with a loud, "Oof!" I landed on top of her. Before she could move, I yanked the stunner from her hands and pressed the length of it against her neck, cutting off her yelp. "Don't even think about moving. Or calling for help."

Behind me, I heard scuffling sounds and a yell. Aneh darted forward and wrapped her fingers around the girl's holo-ring. "I'll take that."

"Got 'em," Joss crowed. "Good job, guys!"

"Who has the slip ties?" I rolled off and stood, yanking the girl—Herria—up with me.

"Let me go!" She twisted in my grip but didn't break free.

"We need to get off this track," Aneh said as she restrained the cadets' hands behind their backs. "It's too open."

"You can't do this!" Lee protested.

"You've been doing it all summer." Joss poked the liberated stunner at Lee.

A grin crossed Lee's face. "Yeah, but we have support."

My eyes narrowed. "We know. And we're going to take care of that. Peter, is your drone still recording?"

Peter smirked and nodded. Lee's face paled.

"We need to move," Aneh said again.

The blue static of the force shield protected us a little, but anyone who looked across the lake would be bound to notice us.

I nodded and slid Herria's stunner into my jacket pocket. "Let's get them off the trail."

I pushed the girl up the hill and behind a large boulder. "We probably shouldn't leave them here," I said as I removed her grav belt. "They'll start yelling as soon as we walk away."

"What do you propose?" Joss asked.

"I propose you let us go, and we'll let you walk away," Lee said.

"Shut up, Lee," Joss replied.

"It would be poetic justice if we could lock them in the supply closet in that mod," Peter said, nodding at the camp.

"We can't get inside the force shield." Joss gave his friend a derisive look.

"No, but they can." Peter pointed at the two cadets.

"Too complicated," I said. "We just want to get our proof and get away, remember?"

"Did we get enough evidence?" Chymm asked.

"I don't know," I said. "We got vid of the senidium. We have Peter's screen shot from last night showing the admirals here. And vid of the guy carrying the crate. I wish we could get vid of the admirals."

"I have vid of the admirals," Chymm said.

"What do you mean?" I asked. Probably some vid he'd taken at the Academy.

"When you and Peter were watching them, over there." He pointed across the lake. "Yesterday. I had a drone on you—that's how we knew you were safe."

"You had a drone on us? Why didn't you say that before?" I swung around to stare at him.

He stomped his foot. "I did, remember? I told you about my drone when we flew back to camp."

"You said you fixed it. You didn't say you'd been using it!" I tried to remember our conversation, but he'd gone on and on about the technical specifications. I turned to the others. "Did he tell us that?"

Every face was blank. Joss shrugged.

Aneh turned pink. "I—uh. Maybe?"

"What are we waiting here for?" I asked. "We've got what we need. Let's get out of here."

"What do we do with them?" Joss stabbed the weapon toward the bound cadets.

"Crap."

"I've got the tranq gun." He patted his holster. "They could take a little nap."

"No. We won't do that. I won't leave them unprotected out here." I folded my arms and stared him down.

"It was just an idea." Joss turned to Lee. "You're lucky she's not like LeBlanc."

"She's weak," Lee spat. "You'll never win following someone like her."

Joss shrugged. "We won the first exercise."

"Anyone got any duct tape?" I asked. "I'm not above putting a gag on him."

"Maybe that's the best answer." Peter pulled some tape from his backpack. "Put this over their mouths and let them go. By the time they get back to camp, we'll be long gone."

"Before we go anywhere," Aneh said, "we might want to review Chymm's footage and make sure it's enough."

"Hey—"

Joss interrupted Chymm. "Having one of those blue rocks might be helpful, too."

Liam squirmed out of my pocket and up my arm. I reached up to grab him, but it was too late.

"You have a sair-glider?" Lee asked. "That's against the rules. You are so out of here."

I kicked the sole of his boot. "Because tying up an admiral's son isn't bad enough to get me expelled? I'm over it."

Liam leapt from my shoulder and flew toward the camp.

"Liam!"

Peter grabbed my arm. "Stop. He's fine. He always lands on his feet. We can't go down there—they'll see us."

"If we leave now, he'll never catch up to us." I leaned down and pulled the cap off Herria's head. Then I stripped the patches from her shoulder. "I'm going down. I'll get Liam and come back. From that far away, they won't recognize me, and their cameras should still be on the fritz. Right, Chymm?"

Chymm did his hand wag thing. "Unless they've made the same repair we have. With all these Delta Black cadets on site, they might have isolated the problem."

Lee snorted behind his tape.

"What's that supposed to mean?" Joss asked.

"Figure it out. I'll be right back." I slapped Herria's patches in place of my own and pulled her cap low on my forehead.

"Someone should go with her," Aneh said. "They travel in pairs."

Joss handed his stunner to Peter. "You watch him. I'll go with Siti." He pulled off Lee's patches and hat.

"You'll never pass for Lee," Chymm said. "You look nothing like him."

"I doubt they've paid much attention to what the cadets look like," Joss said. "Or who's with who." He nudged my shoulder. "Let's get this done."

I nodded and pushed through the underbrush. We slid down the hillside and stopped on the grassy verge. "Do you see him?" I peered through the force shield, squinting against the sun glinting off the water and the partially submerged machinery.

Joss pointed to the lake. "There."

The little glider sat on the edge of the low cliff. It looked like the same spot where Mason had fallen in last year. Liam's jaw dropped in a smile, and he dove into the water.

"Liam!" Fear pierced me. "Do gliders swim?"

"Yeah." Joss pointed again.

Liam surfaced and rolled to his back. He looked around again, then flipped and dove.

"What is he doing?" I asked.

"How did he get through the force shield?" Joss squinted at the lake.

I gaped at Joss then looked at the water, baffled. The blue static field lay between us and the shore.

"Is that a known ability of gliders?" Joss asked.

"He never did it on Earth. At least, not that I know of." Now that I thought about it, the little glider had appeared and disappeared whenever he wanted. "He did it here, though. When he found me and Peter in the storage closet. I can't believe we didn't realize... how would he even do that? The fields are built to keep wildlife out."

"What's he doing?" Joss asked. "He's got something."

Liam had reappeared. He floated on his back, his back legs kicking as he angled toward us. Something blue and shiny glinted in his paws.

"He did not just get us one of those rocks," I said in disbelief.

"I think he did." Joss stared through the force shield. "That darn glider got us a piece of senidium."

CHAPTER FORTY-TWO

Joss took my arm and pulled me away from the force shield. "We've been standing here too long. Let's walk up that way then circle back. Liam will find us."

I nodded absently, watching the glider until he disappeared behind the low cliff. Shaking my head in disbelief, I followed Joss along the grassy path.

He stopped suddenly, and I ran into his broad back, smacking my nose. "Hey, give a girl some warning."

"Siti, remember the herbivores that chased Mason off the cliff?" Joss said over his shoulder.

"Yeah?"

"I think they're here for a repeat performance."

I peeked over his broad shoulder. A huge herbivore stood in the center of the path, chewing and blinking at us. I gulped and took a step back. "This is exactly where he fell in, isn't it?"

Joss shuffled backwards, almost stepping on my toes. "Yeah. That must have been before they put up the force shield over here. We need to—there's nowhere to go."

"We go up." I tapped his grav belt then flicked my own to life.

Joss snorted. "Duh."

We lifted off the ground. The animal watched us rise, its eyes placid. Behind it, a huge herd shuffled and munched.

Aneh's voice came through the audio link. "If you move slowly, they won't stampede."

"You can see us?" I squeaked.

"Yeah, Chymm's got his drone out again. And he got the footage!"

"The admirals? Yes!" I tapped Joss's shoulder. "We got 'em!"

"Let's move into the trees." He pointed toward the hillside. "Slowly. Then we can circle back to the others and head for civilization."

"Hey! What are you kids doing?" a deep voice yelled.

My head snapped around. A man stood beside the machinery in the lake, the water above his knees. He shaded his eyes, staring at us. "You're supposed to be patrolling, not goofing off!"

"Cows!" Joss pointed and yelled.

I smacked his shoulder. "Shut up."

"Get away from there!" The man splashed toward us, waving his arms. "Let them pass. Those things can cause all kinds of damage if you spook 'em."

"Are you thinking what I'm thinking?" Joss grinned over his shoulder at me.

"That we should get out of here?"

"That we can cause all kinds of damage." He dove at the herbivores, skimming over their heads.

"Hey, what are you doing? Stop that!" The man in the lake charged up to the force shield.

"Crap!" I chased after Joss.

Below us, the herbivores moaned and rumbled.

The man opened a gate in the force shield and stormed onto the verge, waving a blaster. "Stop that!"

Joss sped to the end of the herd and spun. He swooped to the ground and hurled some stones at the rear-most cows. The animals groaned and broke into a run, barreling down the grassy verge toward the miner.

"What are you doing?!" I shrieked and grabbed Joss's arm. "You're drawing too much attention!"

"Look!" he crowed, pointing.

I spun around. The man shrieked, diving toward the open force shield. The herbivores veered after him. The first one plowed through the narrow gate, slamming against the control bollard. The open shield was no match for their mass and speed. As the herd pushed through, the glowing blue panel frizzed and died.

The animals thundered across the narrow cliff. With a scream, the fleeing man dove into the water. Just before they reached the edge, the herd turned, racing along the top of the cliff inside the camp.

A shout went up on the far side of the lake.

"That's our cue to leave." I dragged Joss into the woods.

The rest of the team met us in the trees.

"This way," Joss said, angling up the hill. "We need to get away while they're busy with the beef."

"What about Liam?" I cried as he pulled away.

"He's here." Aneh rose beside me, pointing to the damp bundle of blue and white fur nestled on her shoulder.

Liam shook himself, spraying both of us with water. Aneh shrieked then clapped a hand over her mouth. The little glider leaped to my shoulder. I nuzzled his damp fur and followed Aneh and Joss.

"We left Lee and Herria where they were." Peter came up beside me. "If they work together, they'll get their hands untied in a few minutes. Then they'll start yelling."

"If they work together?" I snickered. "We've got hours, then."

He grinned. "I wouldn't say that long. Did Aneh show you what Liam brought to us?"

"A piece of senidium?"

Peter nodded. "That glider is crazy smart. Do you think he can understand us?"

From my shoulder, Liam chirped.

"Maybe?" I replied.

We reached the top of the hill. The others swooped over, but I spun around to look back. I couldn't see anything, so I rose slowly, until my head was even with the treetops.

The herbivores had reached the end of the lake where the land sloped gently. They milled about in the shallow water, drinking and splashing. On the far shore, the miners yelled at the animals and each other. As I watched, Lee and Herria stumbled out of the trees, still bound and gagged.

I giggled and followed my flight into the forest.

CHAPTER FORTY-THREE

AFTER MEETING the girls by their hideout, we flew east for a couple of hours. The hills got higher, and the temperatures dropped. We stopped to pile on more clothing and grab a snack then continued on. Following the maps Peter and Marise had downloaded before the exercise, we angled through a low pass. On the far side, a lush valley stretched out before us.

"I have a satellite connection!" Yvonne yelled. "I'm sending the message to Bob."

"I'll send the vids to my dad," I replied.

Once the messages had gone through, I felt lighter. Even if we were expelled from the academy, we had removed the targets from our backs. The evidence was out there, in hands that could make use of it. We could relax and figure out how to get home.

As the sun set behind another range of mountains, we reached the first settlement. A cluster of cabins sat amid a large expanse of rectangular fields. Lights glowed from the windows, and a dog barked as we dropped.

"Put that thing away," I said as Joss pulled his stunner across his body. "These are civilians, not criminals."

"You don't know that," he muttered, but he swung the weapon over his shoulder.

"I'm pretty sure."

"They could be both," Yvonne said. "Some of the newer planets are practically penal colonies."

"Like Grissom?" Peter asked with a grin.

"I'm from Grissom!" Aneh said.

He shrugged. "I never met anyone scheduled to go to Grissom. We were going to Sally Ride. My dad went to Armstrong. Grissom must have been for the criminals."

Aneh slapped his arm. "Funny man."

We touched down on the fringe of grass surrounding the first house, standing outside a low fence. Two dogs jumped and barked from inside.

The front door opened, and a man stepped out. He called the dogs, and they ran to him, sitting obediently by his feet. "Can I help you?"

"We were on a, uh, camping trip," Yvonne said. "We got lost and didn't have any comm signal. We're trying to find the nearest space port."

"Are you Academy cadets?" The guy stepped off the porch. He wore rugged pants and a lumpy, knitted sweater. The dogs sat on the porch, their eyes never leaving us.

"Why do you think that?" Marise asked.

The man snorted. "The uniforms give it away. There've been a rash of cadets getting lost in the mountains this week. You're the third bunch to come this way."

"We have a shuttle coming." Yvonne stepped forward. "If you have the coordinates of the landing pad, I'll send them to him."

He swiped a file to Yvonne. She nodded and walked a few steps away, speaking quietly into her audio implant.

Joss asked, "Do cadets fly out every year?"

The man nodded. "Since they started camping here three years ago. Not usually this many." He wagged a finger at us. "Mostly two or three. The Academy picks 'em up and sends 'em home. Wash-outs, they call it."

"We aren't the usual wash-outs. Thanks for your assistance. We'll go wait for the shuttle."

"You don't need any food or anything?" he called as we lifted off.

"No, sir," I said. "We're all set."

We flew away in silence. The shuttle landing pad was about half a klick west. Yvonne guided us in, and we waited for Bob to arrive.

THE GRISSOM CONTENTION

THE THUD of the shuttle docking woke me. I rubbed my eyes and yawned. Gravity kicked in, dropping us into our seats. The door to the cockpit popped open, and Bob stuck his head out. "We're here. You kids okay?"

I smiled tiredly. "We will be as soon as we get home. Was the *Traveling Salesman* waiting in orbit all this time?"

Bob shook his head. "They headed for Erianda. I sent your message after I dropped you. Before the *Salesman* left orbit, your dad replied. Asked me to stay here and wait for him. My contract was done, so I took the job. Been waiting for you to call."

"My dad? Is he here?" I fumbled with my seat restraints.

Bob pointed through the opening door. As the rear ramp lowered, three people came into view, standing in front of a wall painted with the words "Welcome to the ECS Magellan." Two wore white med tech uniforms with a blue star on their shoulders and chests. The other was my father in his tactical CEC uniform.

I jumped up, but Dad held up a finger. We froze. He waved the two techs forward. They loaded Terrine onto a med float and pushed her away.

"Dad!" I jumped over the float panel we'd secured to the floor and launched myself into the cargo bay.

He caught me. "Siti! Are you okay?" After a long squeeze, he pushed me to arms' length.

"I'm fine. Did you get our vids?" The words poured out of me as the rest of the flight gathered around. "Admiral Zimas is stealing senidium from the Academy. They deserted us on the planet—we had no supplies and no—"

Dad held up a hand, his face tightening. "Yes. I've called the CEC inspector general. A full investigation has been launched."

"You might want this, then." Peter held out the blue stone Liam had retrieved from the lake. "That's what they're collecting."

Dad picked up the rock, holding it up to the light.

Bob whistled. "Is that senidium? A chunk that big is worth a bundle."

"It is. And I doubt the Academy would have seen any of it." He clapped

301

Peter on the shoulder. "Good work. All of you." He bumped fists with the others.

"Actually, Liam found that," Peter said.

Dad's eyes widened. "Liam? He's with you? That little devil. I should have known he wasn't missing."

Aneh smiled timidly. "Commander Kassis, are we going to get expelled?"

Dad grimaced. "The circumstances of your exercise will be investigated. The Academy will review the vids, and they'll make a decision based on all of the evidence."

Aneh's face fell. "We already know what Admiral Zimas will decide."

"Admiral Zimas has been temporarily relieved of command pending the investigation." Dad smiled. "They've brought in an interim commandant until the review is complete and determinations have been made."

We cheered. Dad smiled wearily. "Let's get you kids settled in. It's a long ride back to Grissom."

EPILOGUE

A FEW WEEKS LATER, we stood at attention in the main auditorium. Charlie Blue sat in the left front section of the room. The other five flights had been escorted to carefully separated locations. They'd kept the flights separate the entire time, cancelling all inter-flight sports and activities. We didn't mind—we'd had enough interactions with the other cadets to last a lifetime.

The school's staff filled the middle section of seats. Lawrence and Mason sat behind us. We hadn't seen them since before the exercise. I wasn't sure if they were implicated in the investigations or if that was Dad's way of keeping gossip to a minimum.

"At ease." Dad took the stage. "Good morning. Take your seats."

He crossed the floor and stood behind a podium bearing the Academy symbol. "I'm Commander Kassis. I have been appointed the new Commandant of Academy by the chief of the Colonial Explorer Corps."

I cheered. Everyone turned to look at me, and I grinned weakly.

"As you know, PSW was cut short this year. We had a record number of cadets walk—or fly—out of the exercise grounds. A full investigation has been conducted."

He stared at the staff members in the middle section. "Due to the vids obtained, several members of the senior staff, including Admiral Zimas—

as well as other CEC officers—have been convicted of conspiracy to remove valuable senidium deposits from Academy land on Sarvo Six for personal use." A hologram of the crate of blue stones appeared behind him.

Dad went on. "The exercise has been declared null. All disciplinary actions taken this summer have been reviewed and anyone who was wrongfully expelled has been reinstated. They will arrive today, if they chose to return."

The whole room cheered this time. Someone booed, but it was impossible to pinpoint.

Dad glared. "Furthermore, you may notice some gaps in your ranks. Several cadets have been expelled for behavior unbecoming an officer. We realize the circumstances surrounding the exercise were unusual, so we have tried to be as lenient as possible. However, there are some actions that can never be condoned."

I did a quick headcount—all seven of us present and accounted for. Then I squinted at Delta Black. Some of them fidgeted in their seats. "Can you see who's missing?" I hissed.

Peter's lip curled. "Looks like LeBlanc might have been cut. And Riviera—he was LeBlanc's enforcer. The rest of them are all there."

"Even Felicity? Lee?" I whispered.

He shrugged and nodded.

"I will give you the facts of the situation. You may relay these facts to your family when you see them next week. You will not speak to any media—they have been briefed. Any cadets breaking that dictate *will* be dismissed."

He flung up a map of the exercise ground. It zoomed in, centering on the mining camp. "Last summer, a senidium deposit was discovered by a cadet in Charlie Blue. He didn't realize what he'd found and returned to the Academy carrying a sample." A holo of a heart-shaped blue stone appeared.

Marise gasped. "That's Mason's. He showed it to me!"

"Mason fell in the lake and discovered a fortune without realizing it." Peter snickered. "You didn't recognize it?"

"Why would I?" Marise countered. "It's a pretty blue rock. Big deal."

I tuned them out, trying to focus on my father as he continued, "Another cadet saw the sample this spring and recognized it. He mentioned it to Admiral Zimas. She used the exercise as cover to sneak in a private scouting team. They began reclamation activities and collected several tons of the deposits. She was aided by Admirals Lee and Myers. Those three flag officers and two lower ranking officers have been court-martialed. Charges are being filed in civilian courts against several enterprises that worked with the admirals."

He cleared his throat. "Most of you know Cadet Felicity Myers and Cadet Derek Lee. They are still cadets in good standing. They have no control over their parents' activities and cannot be held responsible. I expect each and every one of you to treat them with the respect you give every fellow cadet."

"That answers that question," I muttered.

Peter's lips thinned.

"Your flight mates who were unfairly expelled have been invited to return to the Academy. Those who accepted are arriving now. You have the rest of the day to help them settle into your dorms. Tomorrow, we're back to a regular schedule." He nodded at a senior cadet standing at the foot of the stage.

"Attention!" the cadet called.

We all leaped to our feet.

"Carry on." Dad turned and went down the steps.

Bright sunlight greeted us as we emerged from the building. A pair of shuttles stood on the tarmac beyond the quad, and a string of cadets struggled toward us, pulling luggage floats. Three of them turned toward our dorm.

"Franklin!" Aneh called. "Rendi! Abdul!" She raced away, flinging her arms around the boys.

We grabbed their bags and lugged their gear up the stairs, laughing and joking. When we reached our floor, it was quiet, but one door was open. I peeked inside. "Terrine!"

She smiled tremulously. "They moved me back to Charlie Blue."

"You didn't bring Felicity with you, did you?" I peeked under the bunk, as if she could be hiding there.

Aneh's face fell. "You didn't?"

Terrine shook her head. "No. Just me. If you'll have me."

I looked at the rest of the team. "I think this is where you belong." Every head nodded. "Welcome home."

Find out what Siri gets involved in next in *The Saha Declination*. Available fall 2021.

AUTHOR'S NOTE

March 2021
   Hi Reader,
   If you're still here, I guess you enjoyed my story. Thanks for reading! If you liked The Grissom Contention, please consider leaving a review on your retailer, Bookbub, or Goodreads. Reviews help other readers find stories they'll like. They also tell me what you like, so I can write more.
   The next story in this series, *The Saha Declination*, is coming out this fall. If you sign up for my newsletter, I'll let you know when that is ready. You can also download free prequels—including one featuring Joss's dad, Zane Torres, as a teen—and find out about sales. I promise not to SPAM you. If you haven't read the prequel series, Recycled World, it's available now.
   The spring weather is starting to arrive here in the northern hemisphere. More importantly, the vaccine is rolling out—I'm scheduled to get my first dose this week! I can't wait until we can start seeing people face to face without masks again.
   I'm currently working on the next book in my *Tales of a Former Space Janitor* series. It's a crazy romp involving protein shakes, a zero gravity baby, and interstellar espionage. If you enjoy humorous science fiction mysteries, you might like it.

As always, I need to thank a few people. Thanks to my sprint team: A.M. Scott, Hillary Avis, Paula Lester, Kate Pickford, Alison Kervin, and Tony James Slater. They keep me working when I really don't want to.

Thanks to Paula at Polaris Editing for the editing. Any mistakes you find, I probably added after she was done! Thanks to my husband, David, who manages my business, and to Jenny at JL Wilson Designs for the beautiful cover.

And of course, thanks to the Big Guy for making all things possible.

Newsletter sign-up:

Printed in Great Britain
by Amazon